Fide et Fortitude
(Fidelity and Fortitude)

adamant eve

adamant eve

John Braybrooke

PENTLAND PRESS, INC.
ENGLAND • USA • SCOTLAND

PUBLISHED BY PENTLAND PRESS, INC.
5124 Bur Oak Circle, Raleigh, North Carolina 27612
United States of America
919-782-0281

ISBN 1-57197-021-5
Library of Congress Catalog Card Number 96-68132

Copyright © 1996 John Braybrooke

All rights reserved, which includes the right to reproduce this book or portions thereof in any form whatsoever except as provided by the U.S. Copyright Law.

Printed in the United States of America

This novel is dedicated to the victims of terrorism and those who have the wisdom and humanity to dispose of their weapons and settle their differences by peaceful dialogue.

Acknowledgment

My thanks to S.C.L., M.M., D.C., A.K., and W.S. for reading the work and for valuable comments.

author's note

The characters in this novel are purely fictitious and any resemblance to persons either living or dead purely coincidental.

To the author's knowledge there is no connection between the IRA and the Mafioso nor to drug running. This is a work of fiction; the two deviants are purely imaginary and invented to add further spice to an interesting plot.

The historical aspects of the novel, which must involve historical figures, have been carefully checked from several sources; for written history is the opinion of historians and the latter are not always in agreement.

In any society the murder, maiming and suffering of innocent men, women, and children in order to bring about political change can never be justified no matter what the cause. Dialogue is only likely to succeed in an atmosphere of peace and trust where there are no pistols pointing at the heads of participants and where there is no threat of a recurrence of violence should agreement be delayed or not reached.

The answer to the Irish problem is simple: unification can only become a practical reality if the wills exist on both sides of the border. The removal of weapons from the hands of all fanatics and terrorists would enable the people to live in an atmosphere of peace where trust and friendship can gradually be built up. Then, and only then would the will for unification be present. Without the will no solution is possible. It is of interest that in physics Newton's Second Law of Motion states that "for every action there is an equal and opposite reaction." The same applies to terrorism: violence begets violence and just perpetuates hatred from generation to generation. Any decent responsible human beings who care for the future of their children should refrain from perpetuating hatred.

chapter one

On the morning of the bombing, Sean stood on the station platform beneath the glare of fluorescent lights.

"MIND THE GAP!" The voice came out strong and clear through the loudspeaker. Sean smiled as the train came to a halt.

"MIND THE GAP!"

The crisp English voice announced the warning again in the underground station as the doors of the tube train opened and passengers rushed to alight and board. Sean carefully stepped over the gap between the carriage and the platform, and the sliding doors hissed to a halt behind him. He held himself steadier with the handholds as he made his way to a seat, then made himself comfortable as the train accelerated and roared swaying through the tunnel. The clash and clang of racing metal wheels on steel rails echoed from the tunnel walls, its metallic ribs seeming to add spite to the sound.

Sean had not been long in London and the novelty of the situation still dwelt in his mind. He had recently joined an East End medical practice and, being the junior of four partners, was under a year's probation before being accepted as a fully-fledged partner. He knew he had much to learn, for his colleagues had been in the practice for a number of years and were very much his senior in both age and experience.

However, he felt fairly confident; two of the partners hailed from Eire as did he, and their Pakistani colleague was a jovial man with whom it was easy to associate.

Three Irishmen and a Pakistani, reflected Sean. Three Catholics and a Muslim; Christian true believers and an Islamic heathen, or was it Christian infidels and a Moslem true believer? Sean laughed to himself at the thought. Actually he knew that with the increasing numbers of Indian and Pakistani immigrants in the neighborhood, Dr. Bannu Sind had joined the partnership to help cope with the language problem and to encourage the new residents to use the practice. And it was successful, which was the reason he found himself in London.

The clattering motion of the coach eased as the train left the dark tunnel and entered a brightly lit station, interrupting his thoughts. He read "Embankment" on the station sign as the train came to a halt. He leapt to his feet to change for the Bakerloo Line. The doors hissed open and he exited with several other passengers, dodging some waiting boarders who crowded too close to the doors.

Threading his way through hurrying and standing figures, Sean followed the signs to the Bakerloo Line and boarded the train for Piccadilly. He was in good spirits for he had the afternoon and following day off and intended to see something of the great metropolis, treat himself to a good dinner and see a movie. The city always intrigued him. He had several times made short visits en route to stay with an aunt living in the county of Essex.

He had always enjoyed the visits, usually accompanied by his sister, for his aunt's family had always made them welcome and they had a lot of fun with his cousin, although Richard was ten years his senior. It was odd that his half brothers, Morgan and Eamon, had never visited England. His mother remarried after losing his father in a plane crash. She had waited two years and he often wondered if her wanting to get him through medical school and his sister Morag through university had made her agree to marry again. His stepfather was not unkind to either Morag or him, but he showed a marked preference for his own offspring and imbued them with his strong Irish Nationalist ideals.

Sean looked around the carriage and noticed the different ethnic peoples present. Indian or Pakistani, Black, Chinese, some Caucasians—what a cosmopolitan crowd, he thought, as the train came to a halt at Piccadilly, quite a contrast to the faces he had seen when first visiting London many years ago. He alighted and made his way through the link tunnel to the escalator, passing a notice bearing the legend "No street musicians permitted." Beneath the notice was a man in his twenties playing a guitar with a cap at his feet in which several silver coins were on display. He smiled to himself and, mounting the escalator, was rapidly borne to the top where he mingled with the busy crowd in the booking hall. Striding across to the Regent Street exit he bumped into a man and woman running down the stairs. They said "sorry" simultaneously, and he was surprised to hear strong Irish accents, but before he could comment, they hurried across the hallway towards an exit to the street on the other side.

Mounting the stairs he emerged in Piccadilly Circus and stood beside a protective rail to observe the statue of Eros. It must have been recently cleaned, he felt, for it stood gracefully glinting in the sunlight.

He made his way to the statue standing beside the plinth. The mighty heart of London beat around him as he stood there watching the traffic swirling past. He had always been fascinated by the big city. Black roomy taxis, cars, lorries, motorcycles, and the odd bicycle and double-decker buses drove around him while pedestrians thronged the pavements, all moving through their various routes of passage like the blood corpuscles in an artery. This was the lifeblood in a city that had once been the center of the greatest empire the world had ever seen. Now it was but a shadow of its former self; a small island off the coast of Europe; a little democracy with an inherited constitutional monarchy whose main function was to provide a head of state, set an example of family behavior, act as a focus for the Commonwealth Club, attract tourists and provide the sense of security for the indigenous population of the isles that historical continuity alone provides and which is envied by younger countries without it. How things had changed. Yet change was still on its way, for the islands were now an unwilling partner in a so-called Common Market for which the population had been tricked into voting. Instead of it being in a trading partnership of equals, it was now a minor component in a political setup where individual sovereignty was being subordinated to the economic wishes of the two senior members.

Sean stood gazing at the crowds of sightseers and passersby, some standing and staring as he was, and others rushing past, occupied with their busy lives and in too much of a hurry to appreciate their surroundings. He heard the blowing of horns from the direction of Piccadilly Avenue where a traffic jam was making itself manifest. Several police sirens—or was it ambulances?—could be heard in the distance.

A deafening explosion shocked him out of his reverie and made him jump by its unexpectedness. Screams and the crash of falling glass rent the air and a pall of smoke slowly drifted into the square. A bus had halted in front of him and, making his way round it, he ran with others to the corner of the circus and looked down the avenue. A cloud of smoke, the aftermath of the explosion, was being fed by several fires from blazing vehicles.

Sean went running towards the source and the screams and sounds of sobbing became louder. As he ran, he trod on shards and splinters of glass blown from shop windows and vehicles. Carnage met his gaze.

"Oh, my God!" he said out loud and his stomach felt sick with horror. Obviously a car bomb had exploded; several passersby had been blown into shop windows and lay there, some writhing in agony and others inert and unconscious. A crumpled corpse lay at his feet, and nearby a Jewish woman knelt screaming over her rabbi husband whose face was badly lacerated and bloody, with a cheek bone exposed and glistening white.

A child lay bleeding, her right leg severed at the femur by a piece of flying metal. The child's mother lay motionless a few feet away, her chest smashed in. Other crumpled forms lay nearby, many twisted into grotesque shapes. Several bodies nearer the source of the blast had their clothes blown off and they were naked and bleeding, some unconscious, others dead.

"What madmen have done this?" he thought, and then his medical training took over. It was difficult to know where to begin.

Sean knelt beside the little girl, tore a strip from her dress and attempted to stop the flow of blood from the stump of the femur that remained. He tied a knot in the strip of cloth and, placing it over the femoral artery, pulled the strip round the leg, tying it tight. The blood stopped spouting and he knew he could do little else until proper medical equipment was available.

Removing a large sliver of glass from the back of a woman lying nearby he placed a makeshift pad over the wound to diminish the flow of blood.

A Sikh, his turban partly torn by a piece of flying metal sat dazed but silent, showing stoic fortitude. "Let me help you, I am a doctor," Sean said, as he looked at the man's head. "I think your turban saved your life," and he rearranged the remnants of the turban to reduce the bleeding. Looking up, he saw a pretty red-headed girl looking deathly white as the final remnants of blood flowed from her carotid artery. He realized that help was too late. Beside her a man was trying to raise himself but could only use his right arm and leg. The blast had caused complete paralysis of his left side. As Sean worked, ambulance and police sirens screamed around him.

He saw two soldiers pulling passengers and a dazed driver from a fiery cab. Several vehicles which had been blown into others were blazing. Some police and people were attempting to pull out victims and not always succeeding, being driven back by flames and paying for their heroism with badly-burned hands and faces. Out of the corner of his eye, he noticed several bystanders vomiting, nauseated by the carnage.

He moved from one victim to another, doing what he could in first aid, until he came to a man with his intestines exposed by a piece of twisted metal that still lay embedded in his body. The man had caught the full force of the blast which had lifted him off his feet to collide with two passersby, a blonde young woman and an Indian dressed in a sari. Both lay unconscious and spotted with blood. Quick examination showed that none of the blood was theirs and all they appeared to suffer from was bruising and concussion. The Indian woman had a nasty bruise, a facial hyphema which was swelling rapidly; the blonde woman's head must have collided with the Indian's face as she was knocked into her.

Ambulances and police arrived. White-coated doctors and paramedics rapidly worked their way from one victim to another. Sean turned his attention to the blonde woman. As he raised her head she moaned and opened her dazed eyes, the most beautiful lavender-blue eyes he had ever seen.

"Just relax. I am a doctor. The ambulance men will be here shortly to take you to hospital."

She stared blankly at him and then, hearing the groans and crying around her, attempted to rise. "Please lie where you are. We'll get you on a stretcher and to hospital for a checkup."

He felt her relax in his arms, found her handbag and put it under her head, then smiled and said, "You'll be OK."

Sean rose and walked to a white-coated figure who was injecting a victim. Sean announced who he was, and suggested that he come to the casualty department in one of the ambulances and help with the victims. Hearing his brogue, the white-coated figure raised his head and gave Sean a sharp look. "Come if you wish," he replied, his English accent sounding in noticeable contrast to the Irish.

A cab driver lying conscious and in pain adjacent to them said, "I don't want any help from a bloody Irishman."

Sean felt shocked and then realized that the carnage was being attributed to the Irish Republican Army. He felt like saying that Middle East terrorists could have been responsible, but refrained from comment.

Two paramedics were loading their final patient into an ambulance and he took a lift with them to the local hospital. As the ambulance threaded its way out of the debris and stalled vehicles, he noticed fire tenders were present and the flames of the burning vehicles were being got under control, and with the siren wailing they made their way to the hospital as quickly as possible through the traffic. Once there, the victims were rapidly conveyed to the crowded casualty department.

Sean asked to see the registrar and introduced himself. "Pleased to see you, Sean. I'm Hamish Cameron." He pointed to a room. "Scrub up there, grab a gown and return to me." Sean did as requested and then got to work, assisted by a nurse who had delayed going off duty in view of the emergency.

A black casualty with bandages encompassing his head and face was placed before him. Sean undid the bandages and then wished he hadn't. The casualty's face was such a mess that Sean realized he would never see again. He looked at the nurse who had murmured, "The bastards," and remarked, "The surgeons will look after this chap. Put him on a saline drip." He entered a note in the case record and gave it to the nurse.

A policeman walked up to him, escorted by a porter. Sean recognized him as one of the people who had been dragging unconscious casualties from burning vehicles. Both his hands were badly burned and his eyebrows were scorched as was the side of his face. "Lie down here, officer," Sean said, and the nurse helped him onto the casualty table.

"I'm going to give you an analgesic to relieve the pain." The policeman nodded and murmured, "Thanks, it'll help." He was obviously in agony with the burns but courageously kept silent while the needle was inserted. Meantime the nurse busied herself preparing burn packs for his face and hands.

"Was it the IRA?" she asked.

The officer nodded his head. "They phoned a warning two minutes before the bomb went off." The nurse looked at Sean. "The IRA does not represent the Irish people," he said defensively, and continued to attend to the burns.

"Up to the Casualty Ward," he said when finished, and added, "if there is room."

He saw a number of victims and the taxi driver who had previously refused help was brought before him.

"Hello. We meet again."

Recognizing Sean, the cabbie said, "Sorry, Doc, I know you ain't responsible for the bleedin' bastards!"

"Not to worry," Sean replied. "Now let us see what we can do for you," and added, "where is the pain?" The driver pointed and Sean examined him.

"I'm afraid your collarbone is fractured. I'm going to make you more comfortable and then we'll take an x-ray."

Gently lifting the cabbie's left arm, he moved it across his chest.

"Oh, Christ," said the driver. "Is that what you call comfortable?"

"Sorry. Look, we'll give you an injection to relieve the pain." Sean nodded to the nurse who had the syringe ready. "Just a little prick," said Sean.

"That's what the actress said to the bishop," joked the driver, crudely trying to make light of the discomfort while his arm and shoulder were being bandaged. "I am afraid there is quite a queue for the x-ray department, so have a good rest in the meantime." Sean smiled at him as he walked away escorted by a porter. He asked the nurse to get the next casualty wheeled in and then went over to the sink to wash his hands.

Turning back, he found himself looking down at the face of the blonde girl he had attended to on the pavement. She looked at him with her incredibly expressive eyes and he felt his heart miss a beat.

"How do you feel?" he asked.

She smiled wanly. "As if someone hit me on the head with a sledgehammer."

"Not far off!" Sean commented. "Let me take a look."

He moved her lustrous hair gently as he examined her head. There was a marked swelling about the left occipital region. With a medical penlight he shone the light into her eyes and checked her pupillary reflexes which seemed normal. He instructed her to watch the penlight and moved it in the cardinal directions.

"It doesn't look as if the damage is serious, but you had better stay here for an x-ray and observation. Also, we may send you to the optometry department for a visual field examination. You've had a nasty concussion. Incidentally, what is your name?"

"Eve," she replied, "Eve Eden."

"May I have the case folder?" he asked the nurse. She handed it to him and he made his notes which included the possibility of skull fracture, and at the same time noticed her address. It was not far from his practice. "She is the last one," commented the nurse.

Sean felt relieved and looked at his watch. Five hours had elapsed since he had entered the hospital. He smiled and added half to himself, "And this was my afternoon off." Then addressing her, he said, "Eve, we'll get a porter to take you to the ward and for now just relax," then added, "Is the headache bad?" Eve nodded. "Nurse Anne will give you a couple of pills and make you more comfortable. OK, Anne?" he added, turning to the nurse, who smiled in assent.

"I'm off to see Dr. Cameron, and it was nice working with you, Anne."

He turned and patted Eve's shoulder and felt a thrill of excitement as he touched her. "You're in good hands, Eve."

She smiled as he left her and that smile he would never forget.

Dr. Cameron was removing his surgical gloves when Sean found him. "Ah, there you are, Sean. Just in time for a cup of tea—or do you prefer coffee?"

"Anything wet, Hamish. I am as thirsty as the Sahara Desert. Actually, tea will be fine."

"Good, I have fifteen minutes before I have to justify my existence again. Come this way."

Hamish led Sean to the refectory where they grabbed two cups of tea and some biscuits. "Where are you in practice?" asked Hamish.

"I'm a junior partner with Drs. McMurrough, Liam Fitzgerald and Bannu Sind in Docklands. I've been there a month and was enjoying an afternoon off."

Hamish laughed, "Bit of a busman's holiday."

"You can say that again."

"Still, we were very glad of the extra help. A Saturday afternoon is a bit early for a 'rush hour'; that really starts Saturday evening. How do you like working in England?"

"Not bad," replied Sean. "The Family Practitioner Service seems to run well although I am surprised at the paper work. However, we are getting things reorganized to cope with that. We are certainly busier than in Ireland. Incidentally, where did you study?"

"Edinburgh, and you?"

"Dublin, then I spent a year in general practice before coming to England. The pace of life is certainly quicker here in the Metropolis."

"We were certainly busy this afternoon." Hamish paused. "I'm sorry I said that—please don't take it the wrong way."

"Not at all," smiled Sean. "Do you know this will be the second time today that I have said that the IRA does not represent the people of Ireland. If those fanatics really want unification they are certainly going the wrong way about it."

"My apologies," said Hamish and, as if to make amends added, "It's Sunday tomorrow. I'll be doing the rounds at 9:30 with Mr. Lilienthal, but should be free after 10:30. Perhaps you would like to have lunch and take a look at the city, assuming you are not otherwise engaged?"

"Why I'd like that," replied Sean. "Maybe I could see some of the patients I attended . . . just to see if they survived my ministrations?"

Hamish laughed. "Why not? Join me in the casualty ward at 9:30 and we'll go from there."

Sean decided to return to his apartment, feeling too tired to remain in the city. He made himself a makeshift meal, sat down and switched on the television to watch the news. The bombing dominated the reporting. The camera crews had not wasted much time in getting to the scene. He looked at the screen with mixed feelings; then his interest was suddenly aroused when he saw Eve Eden being carried on a stretcher into an ambulance. He felt a quickening of his pulse and determined to see her in the morning. No woman had had such an effect on him before and he found it disquieting. He switched off the television, put a CD in the player, undressed, showered and got into bed. He relaxed and fell asleep to the strains of a Borodin String Quartet. Visions of Eve Eden haunted his dreams.

The following day he arrived at the hospital ward as arranged and was met by Hamish Cameron who was accompanying a tall, gray-haired specialist.

"Mr. Lilienthal, may I introduce you to Dr. Sean O'Neill? He helped us during the 'rush hour' yesterday afternoon."

"How do you do, Sean," said Mr. Lilienthal. "I saw your name on the records. You did a fine job and we all appreciate your help."

"How do you do, sir," replied Sean. "It was a pleasure."

"Sean would like to see some of the patients he attended to," remarked Hamish Cameron.

"By all means. They're mostly in the wards we will be visiting, so please come along."

Sean felt excited at the thought of seeing Eve again and was not disappointed. She was sitting up in bed and gave him a lovely smile of recognition.

"How do you feel, Eve?" asked Mr. Lilienthal.

"Not too bad," she replied.

"You will be pleased to know that there is no sign of a skull fracture. I am going to keep you here probably until some time this afternoon, for I want another two tests carried out and the results of them will not be known until then. I'm afraid you will have a headache for a few days and you should have at least three days off work."

Then he added, "Will you have anyone to fetch you?"

"No," replied Eve, "but I'll manage."

Mr. Lilienthal nodded and Sean smiled at her as they moved on to the next patient.

That afternoon Sean and Hamish lunched in the city, then boarded a river bus at Charing Cross and were conveyed downstream to Greenwich. Sean had never visited it before and was intrigued and impressed with the old observatory, the Maritime Museum and the fine old buildings originally erected for Naval Pensioners. He and Hamish photographed each other astride the Greenwich Date Line of Greenwich Mean Time and the zero of longitude.

"If one stands astride here exactly at midnight," remarked Hamish, "one will have one foot in yesterday and the other in tomorrow."

Sean grinned, and then they went to visit the Painted Hall and afterwards the full-rigged barque, the *Cutty Sark*. They both admired its lines and functional design.

"What a place," remarked Sean. "It just oozes with maritime history. The English certainly knew how to sail."

"Yes, but they needed Scottish engineers to run their machinery."

Sean smiled at this demonstration of chauvinism and, looking over the starboard side of the *Cutty Sark*, asked, "What is that yacht there?"

Hamish followed his gaze. "Oh, that is the *Gypsy Moth*—Frances Chichester's yacht—the one he made a global circumnavigation in. Like to see it?"

"Sure," and as they walked towards it Sean commented that his cousin was a keen sailor. "He's an ophthalmologist in Essex and has a yacht at Burnham-on-Crouch."

"Has he now, lucky devil. Maybe I can scrounge a sail sometime."

"Do what I can," said Sean.

They stood beside the ketch admiring her fine lines and, after reading the legend "Gipsy Moth 111," entered the cockpit. A guide met them and explained the vessel's layout, gave a brief history of Francis Chichester and showed them some charts of the route taken. Hamish recalled that the lone sailor had a very rough passage sailing round Cape Horn. "Yes," the guide agreed. "The Pacific was not so pacific on that occasion."

"That fellow certainly had guts, but no guts no glory," commented Sean.

Leaving Greenwich, they boarded the river bus and proceeded upstream.

"I expect you would like to come back to the ward to see how Eve Eden is getting on," remarked Hamish, grinning.

"Good Lord, did it show?"

"It showed with both of you. But as you are single and unattached then medical ethics are not transgressed. However, she may have been discharged already." The last comment gave Sean an anxious time until they entered the hospital. Eve was preparing to leave the ward when they arrived. The houseman had already seen her and informed her of the results of the test. A nursing sister had given her a letter for her GP. Hamish discreetly withdrew before Sean entered the ward. "Hello, Eve. Ready to go home?" She looked at Sean and smiled, then appeared somewhat crestfallen as a thought crossed her mind. He saw the letter in her hand. "Is that for your doctor?" She nodded in assent. "Who is he?"

"Dr. McMurrough." Sean could have jumped for joy. "Don't laugh," he said, "I work at the same practice."

"I thought you worked here at the hospital."

"That was a temporary thing during the emergency," he replied. "Look, I left my car here this morning. May I give you a lift home?"

Eve looked at him, paled and then blushed. "This morning I heard you say you had no one to fetch you," he added. Eve still looked uncertain. "Come on, I shan't eat you. I've had tea," he added coaxingly at her hesitation.

Then she smiled. "Thanks, you are very kind."

They drove towards the East End through busy traffic as pleasure seekers were wending their way home. Sean attempted to draw Eve into conversation, but her reticence made him realize that she was still probably reacting to her previous day's experience and so did not press conversation on her.

Eve directed him to a street of yellow brick terraced houses where they stopped before a door that could have been improved with a fresh coat of paint. She turned to him and said, "Thank you, Sean, you have been very kind and I do appreciate all you did for me."

"May I see you again?" he asked. Eve shook her head. "Are you spoken for? If so I am not surprised."

"Please," she said and, opening the car door, quickly alighted. "I'm sorry, but thank you and please do not think I am ungrateful."

He watched her, admiring her perfect figure as she went to the door. It was opened by a dark attractive girl who let Eve in. Then the door closed with a finality that made Sean's heart sink. He reflected that he had been wrong to take an emotional interest in a patient, and with such self-critical thoughts drove to his apartment. Yet he continued to feel a deep sense of longing to see her again and could not get her out of his mind.

chapter two

A month before the bombing, Eve was sitting in a British Rail coach looking out of the window as the train made its way from York to London. She felt comfortable, for the gentle swaying had a relaxing effect on her despite misgivings about her move. On the horizon she could see clearly in the morning sunshine the green clad hills slowly drifting past. Nearby, trees, fields, cattle, sheep, gamboling lambs and the odd dwelling sped by with greater rapidity, the closer they were to the line.

The clear sky of this spring day uplifted her spirits which she badly needed. Life had not been easy for her, although she had been well looked after by her grandmother. She had appreciated the love that had been lavished on her since her parents had died so tragically. Before then it had been unsettling enough when her only brother had gone to America. They had not been very close, due mainly to the difference in their ages; eight years was almost a lifetime to a twelve-year-old, and a young sister could not share his male interests. However, he had protected her when necessary, and the boys in the village and school had had a healthy respect for her brother's physical prowess. As a result, they kept clear of her as well, and this continued after he had left home despite her physical attractiveness.

Her maternal grandmother had come to live with her parents and Eve six years after her brother had gone. Ruddy of complexion, she was a fit country woman who was wise enough not to intrude more than she could help into the lives of the other members of the family. Her entry had in part been an economic necessity. The Edens were not well-off, her father being an employee on a farm. They lived in a tied cottage and so never had the opportunity to become property owners. The presence of her grandmother had enabled her mother to supplement the income as a cleaner in a hotel in York, which was but a short distance from the village. Prior to that, a chronic illness had prevented Mrs. Eden from doing more than the household chores demanded. Later, her health had improved enough to enable her to work, especially when the grandmother took over the demands of housekeeping and cooking in the home. The whole arrangement was symbiotic and, as the grandmother received a widow's pension, the added income enabled the family to save a little beyond their daily requirements. And this had been their undoing.

"Why don't you have a holiday?"

Her father had looked at his mother-in-law in surprise at the suggestion for his first thought had been of the cost.

"Your wedding anniversary is coming up soon and you could have a second honeymoon." Her daughter Ruth smiled at the idea. "It would be lovely," she had said, "but Eve's 'A Levels' are coming up soon and she cannot miss them."

Eve was well aware of this, for to pass the "A Level" examination was essential if she was to get a chance to enter university, and her heart had been set on that. She had always worked studiously and, with eight good "O Levels" already achieved, knew that her ambition to teach was a real possibility. But her parents' anniversary fell on a school day and she could not afford to miss any school time.

"Why don't you two go?" she had said. "As it is a second honeymoon, I shouldn't be there, anyway," she added, mischievously.

Her parents and grandmother laughed at that, and their going was settled. They decided to go to Holland and return via Belgium.

The stay in Holland had been a wonderful experience with the beautiful bulb fields, windmills, quaint old-fashioned buildings and friendly people. Her parents knew no Dutch, but her father had learned some German when stationed in Germany on National Service. His attempts to display his knowledge and impress his wife had not been welcomed by the Hollanders, whose memories of the German occupation lingered long. Fortunately, English was spoken by all the people they met and this made their stay an easy one. It was on a ferry in Zeebrugge that their second honeymoon came to an abrupt end. Unfortunately, the bow doors of the vessel were not closed when it left the jetty. On encountering the swell of the sea, water entered. The forward motion served to increase the flood, the lower vehicle deck quickly filled and the vessel turned on its side with a rapidity that hurled passengers and crew across the decks. They were both rendered unconscious when their flying bodies struck the wall of the saloon, and they stood no chance of survival as they drowned together in the cold North Sea.

Eve received the news two days before she sat for her examinations and the shock stunned her, as it had her grandmother. She went ahead with the examinations, but concentration was difficult and the standard she had achieved was not enough to get her a place either at university or teachers' training college. The return of her parents' bodies added to the depression and remorse in the household. Remorse: both Eve and her grandmother bitterly regretted encouraging her parents to take the holiday. Her grandmother was particularly shattered by the tragedy, but as she had experienced the loss of loved ones before, she was the first to recover. And yet it took time.

Eve spent the whole of that summer in a daze. Her teacher had wanted her to resit the examination in the autumn, but Eve was unable to settle down to the discipline of further study.

Her brother came over to attend the funeral and had been most helpful. He had not found life easy when he had first gone to the USA. It was time-consuming getting a work permit, due to administrative delays and errors, and he found New York a city of violence. He had obtained work in Boston, but it took time for him to be accepted in the community where the original, and most of the many recent immigrants, were Irish. However, his willingness to work, his honesty, reliability, good looks and personal charm had enabled him to improve his lot. At last he was beginning to prosper and realize the American dream that had originally drawn him to the States. He became an American citizen, to his father's disappointment, but he did not have the ties to his mother country that his parents had. In any case, he realized that he could participate more in communal life as a naturalized citizen, and this he did. His knowledge of history, so well taught in his English grammar school, enabled him to sympathize with his Irish immigrant friends, so that their initial gut reaction to anyone with an English accent had been replaced by feelings of genuine friendship. This was for the good, for the activities of Noraid collectors were strong in that neck of the woods.

At the funeral, David sat between his grandmother and Eve, and when they stood for part of the service, he put a comforting arm around each of them. Yet the service passed by as if in a dream for Eve. She had been jolted out of it when the apparent droning of the vicar was interrupted by words that strongly registered in her mind. He had mentioned that God called her parents to his bosom because he loved and needed them.

Why did he need them? she thought. Surely her grandmother's and her love and need were greater? A cynical thought had followed in her mind: He must have needed a lot of people in a hurry when the ferry capsized and so many drowned.

But Eve's religious misgivings had earlier roots. The family attended the local Church of England regularly, more out of social habit than piety. Eve enjoyed singing in the choir and had gone through a period of deep religious feeling. This culminated during a beautiful summer when she visited York Minster and prayed there. The elegance and size of that sacred structure, the sense of spirituality in that house of God and the beauty of the countryside around her no doubt played its part. In addition, there had been the added bonus of passing her "O Level" examinations with distinction in most subjects. The world looked very rosy and the following Sunday she sang in the church choir the hymn "All Things Bright and Beautiful."

Sitting in the train, Eve recalled discussing the hymn with her father after the service, remembering the first verse:

All things bright and beautiful, all creatures great and small,
All things wise and wonderful, the Lord God made them all.
The rich man in his castle, the poor man at his gate,
He made the high and lowly and ordered their estate.
All things bright and beautiful, all creatures great and small,
All things wise and wonderful, the Lord God made them all.

Eve and her father had been close friends, and his response to her comments on the words of the hymn were that it had been written to keep the workers in their place and their fingers out of the rich man's pie. It did not help her religious feelings when he quoted Karl Marx in that "religion is the opiate of the people." Although he had hastened to add that most people need some form of moral guidance and something to believe in, from then onwards her faith gradually left her. However, the loss had been slow and hardly noticed. Her real doubts had begun and her faith had been shattered at the shock of losing her parents. From that time she had felt alone and abandoned by the God she had believed in. The demands and worries of daily life too, had kept her mind well occupied.

Her brother returned to America before he had time to arrange all the family's affairs. He had been most helpful with the funeral arrangements, dealing with the official aspects of the state grant towards the undertakers' expenses and church fees. He had approached the landlord regarding Eve and their grandmother remaining at the cottage, and the landlord had been sympathetic. However, this sympathy was confined to giving them a few months' grace for he required the cottage for a new farmhand, and the dwelling went with the job. David had approached the local council for rented council property but had to leave before anything could be finalized. He had written regarding his parents' insurance and broached the subject of compensation related to the capsizing, but the wheels of bureaucracy moved with the slow speed that guaranteed employment, coupled with a little power, engenders in the low-salaried. So the burden fell on Eve and she had learned to grow up fast.

Eventually, Eve and her grandmother moved to a two-bedroomed council apartment which appealed to neither; but there had been no choice and they made the most of the situation. Eve lived on social security benefits until she found a job. Funeral expenses had been far higher than anticipated, for the undertaker had joined a larger group of morticians that had come to England from the USA. They ostensibly offered greater choice and at the same time increased prices so that what had been a fair family type of business came close to an expensive monopoly. In addition, the move drained their finances.

Finding a job had not been easy, for despite Eve's intelligence and good education relative to most job seekers of her age, she was not fitted for commercial life. She could not type, had no knowledge of shorthand or computers, and the economic recession added to her difficulties. She found a job as a shop assistant, but lost it when the owner went bankrupt. After several fruitless efforts she got a job as a dentist's receptionist. It did not pay well for her employer had pointed out that she had to learn the job and times were hard. He was correct as far his staff were concerned, for only the dentist and his accountant knew of the very nice living he was making with private work as well as the National Health Service. The job lasted for several months and Eve was unexpectedly given a raise. She did not realize that this was due to her employer having suddenly become interested in her good looks. He started to take such an interest in her that it was noticed by his wife, and Eve found herself once more unemployed. Several poorly-paid jobs followed, the experience of which taught her how to keep certain types of the opposite sex at a distance.

Her stay at the council apartment came to an end when her grandmother succumbed to viral pneumonia or, as the doctor called it, "the old folks' friend." This unwise yet sincere remark had been of no comfort to Eve. She had loved her grandmother dearly and knew she would miss her cheerful presence and wise counsel. Once again she felt her world tumble down around her. Attempts to contact her brother were unsuccessful; she was unaware that he had gone to Australia for a month. It was not until he returned to Boston that he found the letter she had written after trying to contact him by phone.

Two days after her grandmother's funeral, Eve decided to give up the apartment and seek employment in London. She had never looked on the flat as a home, and with her grandmother gone it was anathema to her. Within two weeks, she was on the train to London having written to a distant cousin she had never met, hoping she could stay with her for a few days while she looked for a place for herself. She had a few hundred pounds in the Royal Bank of

Scotland, and reckoned it would tide her over the next few weeks. She wrote again to her brother and included her cousin's address, hoping to hear from him there.

The movement of the train and the rhythmic clickaty-click, clickaty-click of the wheels induced a monotonous repetitive rhythm in her mind: go to sleep, go to sleep, go to sleep.

"We're at London, luv." A strong Yorkshire voice roused Eve from the slumber she had fallen into due to the gentle rocking motion of the train. She came to with a start and murmured, "Thank you," and proceeded to retrieve her two cases; they were not heavy and contained all her possessions. With her handbag secured by its strap to her shoulder and a suitcase in each hand, Eve made her way off the train and joined the jostling throng of passengers hurrying along the platform to the ticket barrier. Once past, she was at first bewildered by the size of Kings Cross Station and the hustle and bustle of the multitude inside. She spotted a snack bar near the entrance and, after dodging through the scurrying throng, entered and refreshed herself with sandwiches and tea.

Her next problem was to get to her cousin's home in Newham and she stood outside the station looking at an underground map she had just purchased at a newsstand.

"Can I help you, miss?" A policeman had been watching her. He had noticed her worried look, and the sudden drop of her shoulders when she realized that there was no Newham Station on the diagram. Eve looked up, surprised yet pleased that help was at hand.

"I can't find Newham Station on this map."

"I'm afraid you won't, miss, there isn't one," the officer replied. Eve's heart sank and her eyes became moist.

"What address do you want, miss?" he asked gently. Eve produced her cousin's address and he looked at it, frowned for a moment, then said, "I know where this is. Take the Central Line to Mile End and change there onto the District Line. You only have to walk across the platform. The station you want is West Ham." He indicated the stations on the map and she nodded, saying, "Oh, I see. Thank you."

He warmed to her smile and inquired, "Is this your first visit to London?" Eve again nodded, to which he responded, "If I were you, miss, I'd get an A to Z atlas from the stationers over there and then you will have no problem finding your way around. If you would like to get one now, I will show you exactly where the street is relative to the station."

Eve did not hesitate to follow his advice, and gratefully listened to his explanations and directions. "You are very kind," she said, "and thank you again."

"You're welcome, miss, but do take care. London is a big city."

It was mid-afternoon when Eve eventually found her cousin's address. To her surprise, the door was opened by an Indian woman wearing a sari.

"Yes?" said the woman inquiringly. Then she noticed the two suitcases and quickly added, "If you have anything to sell, I don't want it," and promptly closed the door. Eve's jaw dropped in surprise but, recovering, she knocked on the door again. A second knock was necessary before the door was opened.

"I told you I do not want anything!" the Indian woman shouted at her.

"I'm not selling you anything!" responded Eve, pushing against the door before it closed. "I want to see my cousin Marilyn who lives here. I wrote to her saying I was coming a week ago."

The brown-skinned woman stopped closing the door and looked hard at Eve.

"Wait there," she said brusquely and went to a back room. She returned with a letter in her hand and showed it to Eve.

"Is this your letter?"

Eve looked at it. "Yes."

"Then I am sorry. Your cousin does not live here and I do not have the address where she moved to." She saw the look of consternation on Eve's face and added, "I'm sorry but you cannot stay here. You can find a hostel or bed and breakfast place somewhere," and handing Eve the letter, promptly closed the door.

Eve stood on the pavement feeling tearful at the frustration. She had staked everything on finding work in London and at the back of her mind had hoped for the comforting support of a relative. Now she realized that was not to be, and once more she was again on her own and would have to deal with another frustration.

She wandered down the street taking in her new situation and wondering what her next move would be. There were few people about as she walked unknowingly in the direction of Docklands. She had covered quite a distance before she realized she was lost. Stopping, Eve put down her cases and went to open her handbag when her attention was arrested by a sudden scream.

She looked up and saw a pretty dark-haired woman trying to escape from a black man who was holding her by the arm. "Let me go you bastard," she heard the woman shout, but the man responded by grabbing her around the throat with his free hand. Eve reacted quickly and, picking up one suitcase, ran up to the struggling couple. The big man's back was towards her and with sudden new-found strength, she raised the case above her head and brought it down sharply on his back. She heard the thump as it connected and then the sickening crunch as his head struck the edge of a stone wall as he fell.

"Oh, my God," she said, "I've killed him." She knelt down and looked at his face. The skin of his forehead was broken where it had caught the edge of the wall and blood was oozing out. She suddenly felt sick; she paled and put a hand on the ground to support herself. The dark-haired woman who had been rubbing her bruised wrist leaned over and put an arm around Eve's shoulders.

"You awright, luv?" she asked, in a strong Cockney voice. Eve looked up as she was helped to her feet. There was a look of concern on the woman's face.

"Don't worry abaht 'im. That bugger would 'ave killed me if it 'addunt bin fer you. Fanks very much fer yer 'elp."

She looked down at Eve's suitcase and then, seeing the other one, retrieved it for her. "Where yer goin'?" she asked.

"I don't know," replied Eve, and she explained what had happened when she had called at what she thought was her cousin's address.

"'Ere," said the woman, "you've just done me a bleedin' good turn an' I ain't the ungrateful type. Come along wiv me an' I'll put yer up at my place. I'll carry this bag fer yer. Yer look wobbly."

"What about him?" Eve asked.

"I told yer. Don't worry abaht 'im. If 'e ain't dead 'e bleedin' well orta be. Come on; let's get ahta 'ere." And with that she took Eve by the arm and, giving Eve time to pick up the other suitcase, walked along the road at a fast pace.

Eve, keeping up with her, said, " Don't you think we should call an ambulance?"

"Ambulance!" the woman snorted. "I'd raver call an undertaker. I tell yer' that sod would 'ave killed me if it ain't bin fer you." Then, seeing Eve's worried look, she said, "Oh, orlrite, I'll get a bloke ter phone the 'orspital." Eve looked relieved and docilely followed her new found acquaintance.

They made their way to a shabby looking terraced house and the dark-haired woman took out her key and opened the front door. It had obviously been converted into two apartments, for in the hallway two doorways confronted them.

"Wot's yer name, luv?"

"Eve. Eve Eden. What's yours?"

"Caria. Caria Crompetta. Me farver came over 'ere from Rome. Too many bleedin' Mafia abaht that place fer 'im. 'E wos good ter me but, poor sod 'es dead nah; an' me muvver, too."

"Same with me."

"Then we've got sumfink in common ain't we, Eve," said Caria, opening the right-hand door. But as they were entering, the other door opened and a short thin man poked his head out.

"'Allo, 'allo, 'allo. Wot 'ave we 'ere?"

"Mind yer own bleedin' business, mate," retorted Caria, and, turning to Eve announced, "That bloke's name's Runt Parker an'it orter be Nosy Parker."

She turned to Parker and said, "Nah piddle orf you silly twit."

Parker effected a pained look and replied, "Coo Caria, you ain't arf free wiv yer compliments terday," and looking at Eve, asked, "Who's the pretty bird?"

"It ain't none o' your business!" But Caria suddenly paused and, on reflection, continued with, "This gel is Eve an' she jest saved me from bein' murdered. There's a big black bugger dahn the road wiv 'is 'ead cracked open. Nah be a good boy an' phone fer an' ambulance."

"Orlright," said Parker not unwillingly, then added, "I fort you wos turnin' lesbian."

"Git lorst," Caria retorted and led the way upstairs.

In contrast to the outside, the apartment was tastefully decorated, and her gaze fell on furniture far more expensive than Eve had ever thought to own. She looked admiringly at the red and gold striped satin curtains and then at elegant Louis XIV style chairs that each rested on the four sides of a rich rosewood table. The carpeting was of a floral pattern, dominantly burgundy, with a simple yet tasteful, rosewood cocktail cabinet resting on it. Another cabinet of matching design enclosed a television set and opposite that was a comfortable looking settee.

"Like it, Eve?" inquired Caria, noticing her admiration. Eve nodded.

"'Ere, come an 'ave a look at me uvver rooms," and she led Eve to the kitchen.

This was not large, but it again showed good taste in its decoration and contained a dishwasher and microwave as well as a standard electric oven. All cooking utensils, cutlery, crockery and tableware were hidden in richly decorated cupboards and drawers.

To Eve the bathroom was a dream. Gold faucets gleamed in the hand basin and bath. Eve took a closer look at the bath and realized it incorporated a Jacuzzi. The luxury impressed her and she was about to comment when she saw an unfamiliar basin level with and beside the toilet.

"What's that?" she queried.

"A bidet," replied Caria. "Marvelous fer keepin' yer crumpet an' fanny clean." It was all new to Eve, but she got the message. Then her attention was drawn to a print of an idyllic ancient Greek scene depicting naked youths and maidens dancing.

The print was protected by a perspex sheet carefully secured to the wall above the bath. "Wettin' yer appetite luv?" joked Caria, and added, "Nah come an' see the bedrooms."

And leading Eve through the doors, they entered a room that would have done credit to Madame Pompadour. The room was decorated in pink, with expensive curtains draped in graceful arcs around the windows. A queen-sized bed with a large padded pink velvet headboard rested against the wall at right angles to the window. Built into the headboard were bedside cabinets, and on one lay a remote control for the television set that stood against the wall opposite the bed. A pink comfortable-looking chair was placed on each side of the set. On the wall opposite the window stood a dressing table with a large mirror and beside that a built-in clothes cupboard.

"Nice ain't it, Eve," commented Caria. "It's my room. I'm goin'ter put you in me uvver one. Jest foller me." Eve entered the corridor and then went through the newly-opened door. The dominant color in this room was lilac and like the other bedroom it was tastefully decorated with similar fittings.

Caria was amused at Eve's surprise. "Better orf than you fort eh?" she said. "I'll tell yer all abaht it later. Nah you jest unpack yer fings in 'ere an' then 'ave a barf. I expect yer could do wiv one arter orl you've bin froo." Then she added, "When yer've finished come inter me sittin' room and we can 'ave a bite an get acquainted like."

Eve needed no further persuading and was soon wallowing in luxurious warm water. She even tried the Jacuzzi controls and found the gentle massaging of the jets soothing away her aches and weariness. This is almost too good to be true, she thought, as she dried and dressed. Caria must be wealthy to afford all this. I wonder if she knows anyone who can get me a job.

While Eve was bathing, Caria went downstairs and spoke to Parker. "Did you phone the 'orspital?" she asked him. "Yus," he replied, "An wots more I went dahn an 'ad a look at the bloke. Looked as dead as a bleedin doornail."

"Oh, Christ!" said Caria. "That puts Eve on a bloomin' spot."

"I daht it. The bloke wos assaultin' yer and she tried ter stop 'im. Any coroner would fink it wos deaf by misadvencha, an' I daht the coppers would even bring charges."

"It's the coppers I'm worried abaht. D'yer fink they would believe me as they know I'm in the game."

Parker thought for a moment. "Yus, that could make fings difficult. Wos there any one else abaht?"

"Nah," said Caria, shaking her head. "Not a bleedin' sossidge."

"Yer sure o' that?" added Parker, looking at her quizzically.

"Yus, absolutely."

"In that case the best fing you can bofe do is ter keep yer mouves shut," and on receipt of that final advice, Caria returned upstairs.

Eve found Caria busy in the kitchen after dressing. "Can I help you?" she asked. Caria looked up from her task. "Yus, luv. Git two sets o' knives forks an' spoons from that there drawer an' lay the table in the livin' room. There's some table mats beside the cutlery." She indicated the drawer with a nod, and as Eve busied herself, asked, "Feelin' better nah?"

"Yes, thanks, Caria. How about you?"

"I'm orlright. Me wrist jest hurts a bit. That sod nearly broke it. Still let's ferget abaht 'im an' ave some grub. We've got better fings ter talk abaht."

Eve soon discovered that Caria was a good cook and enjoyed the chicken and carefully prepared vegetables placed before her. "Mmm," she said. "This is lovely and the sauce is delicious."

Caria smiled at the compliment. "'Ere, wash it dahn wiv some Chablis," then she added, "I expect yer fort yer wos goin' ter ave bangers an' mash or fish an' chips. Maybe even pasta stuff 'cos me farver wos an Eytie." And, pausing to drink a mouthful of wine, she continued, "Well, that stuff ain't no good fer yer figure an' I 'ave ter watch mine 'cos a lot of blokes watch it as well."

"Are you a dancer?"

"Coo, that's one way of puttin' it. I do a striptease an' then dance wiv blokes in bed." Eve felt uncomfortable at the receipt of this new intelligence.

"You mean you're a . . . " She could not decide what word to use and Caria supplied the answer without hesitation or a blush.

"Yus, luv, I'm a 'ooker, but I'm a 'igh class one. I don't 'ave no riffraff an' I get a very nice livin'. That is, after the guvnor 'as 'is whack."

"The guvnor?"

"Yus. Yer've gotta 'ave a place ter pick up clients wiv money, an' the guvnor owns a swank night club. Wot's more yer gotta 'ave protection, an' 'e 'as some blokes wiv muscle wot looks after yer proper like." Eve stopped eating and looked around the room which contrasted strongly with the poor conditions she had been used to.

"Isn't there a risk of catching a disease?" she asked.

"Nah, not much. I'm very careful. We gals 'ave good medical advice we do."

Eve was trying to take it all in and, thinking of the bedroom she was to occupy asked, "Do you bring . . . er . . . clients here?"

"Nah, not bleedin' likely. There are some lovely rooms at the club—massage rooms we call 'em, an' sometimes we go ter 'otels as masseurs. We even go ter some blokes apartments an' 'omes when their wives are away. Y' know, businessmen, MPs, Arabs an' the like. Blokes wot 'ave got lots of the wherewivall. But we don't go ter them places very often. Most of us work in the Club."

Eve again looked around the room and wondered whether the "Game" was worth the health risk and possible emotional trauma. It was not the sort of life that appealed to her, although obviously it was one way of making a small fortune.

Her reverie was interrupted by Caria. "Nah, tell me sum'ink abaht yerself."

Eve watched Caria's face as she briefly outlined her history. Caria looked sympathetic when Eve mentioned the loss of her parents and grandmother. "'Ad a lahzy deal ain't yer, luv," she sympathized, and added, "Must say it's nice ter 'ave 'ad a good edjerkashun, but it ain't 'elped yer ter make any bangers so far."

Eve was puzzled by this and queried, "Bangers?"

"Yus. Bangers an' mash, cash. Gor blimey, 'aincha ever 'eard of Cockney rhyming slang; y'know, fings like apples an' pears, upstairs; rahnd the 'ouses, trahsis?" and seeing Eve shake her head, added, "Never mind, luv, I'll teach yer some later."

Eve smiled at the remark, but the word "later" sounded ominous.

"It is very nice of you to put me up for a day or two, and I am very grateful, but I must go to the job center and find work tomorrow. Do you know where the local one is?"

"Yus, but I daht you'll get a job so easy. I orta tike yer up ter the Strand ternight an' rahnd Charing Cross Station. It would open yer bleedin' eyes fer yer. It is in the evening that yer see the cardboard camps set up. There are lots o' gals an' blokes like yer 'oo came ter London ter find jobs, an' orl they find is a bloody 'ard bit o' pavement ter lie on. They can only keep warm at night sleepin' in cardbord boxes. Wot a bleedin' life!"

Caria paused and then continued, "Look, luv. I 'ad a nice girl friend like yer stayin' wiv me, but she 'ad an accident, worse luck. Why doncher stay 'ere? It ain't orl that bad in the 'Game,' an I'd show yer the ropes. Some o' the blokes yer meet ain't that bad, an' yer seldom 'ave anyone nasty. I told yer—the blokes are all well oiled an' a lot o' them are real gents. If we fink anyone is gonna be nasty 'e is introduced to Bounce before 'e as 'is little bit o' fun. It don' arf make 'em friendly when they know 'es arahnd. There ain't a tougher bloke since Man Mountain Dean."

Eve hadn't a clue as to who Man Mountain Dean was, but she gathered that he must have been very formidable. The thought of prostituting herself even with rich men in no way appealed, but she felt it unwise to say so just then. She desperately needed a bed for the night and felt it diplomatic to play safe, so she said, "I'm very tired. Do you mind if I think about it and let you know in the morning?"

Caria gave no sign of hesitation in her reply and said, "Course not, luv. You must be knackered arter wot yer've bin fru terday. Nah, yer must jest go ter bed. An' don' worry abaht the dishes. I'll stick 'em all in the dishwasher an' it'll tike care o' the lot."

Caria rose and took Eve to her room. "A good night's rest is wotcher need. An' don' worry abaht a fing. Yer scratched me bleedin' back fer me terday an' I'm goin' ter scratch yours." And with that parting shot, Caria closed the door. Within ten minutes Eve lay between silk sheets on the comfortable bed, and in her exhausted state soon slept the sleep of the innocent. It was one of the last nights of innocence that she would know.

chapter three

During the period when dinosaurs roamed the earth, a mass of limestone was deposited across the western midland region of England. This ridge, part of the Jurassic uplands, now forms the Cotswolds. The landscape has long been molded by human endeavor to form some of the loveliest of English countryside. The rolling green hills commence where the Cotswolds escarpment rises steeply from the vale of the River Severn. From there they gently slope eastward to the clay vale of Oxford. The oolitic limestones are much in evidence above their fertile soil covering, by the fine buildings and dry-stone walls, for which they are used.

The Cotswolds also give rise to the River Thames at Thameshead in the county of Gloucester, although some would dispute this, claiming that the source is at Seven Springs, the origin of a tributary of the River Churn. Be that as it may, the Thames is a river of history as well as beauty. It meanders through lovely villages sheltered from commercial clangor, between copse-crowned hills, through a country of spires and squires, well-stocked barns, handsome houses and magnificent manors. On each side cattle are to be seen grazing in green meadows, flanked on each side by hedgerows or lines of poplars, beech, birch and elm. Ever present is the dominant English oak to whose shelter farm animals retreat in the noonday heat of the summer sun. Here and there, tributaries with their canals and old wooden locks increase the volume of the water.

Through the ancient city of Oxford, whose university has spawned many famous names in all branches of learning and human accomplishment, the river temporarily changes its name to Isis. Here the gently flowing stream becomes bedecked with graceful white swans, mallards, moorhens and punts beloved by both tourists and students attending the many famous colleges. These latter elegant limestone edifices add their own architectural charm to the river banks.

At Henley, the scene of international rowing, the Thames reverts to its original sobriquet. Further downstream on the south bank lies Runnymede, on the site of which King John signed the Magna Carta, one of the great documents of English history which, perhaps unwittingly, began the reforms for human rights. Written in 1215, clause 39 stated that "No freemen shall be . . . imprisoned or dispossessed . . . except by the lawful judgment of his peers or by the law of the land." In this document, the King was warned not to abuse his position as ruler of the country. Unfortunately, too few people read history, let alone apply its lessons and so the world still remains full of tyrants and oppressed.

Continuing its progress through green and pleasant land, the river passes through the ancient borough of Windsor. Here William the Conqueror built a castle a thousand years ago and Henry I converted it into a palace. Now the site is but the legacy of their work. This oldest of royal homes is a mixture of Medieval and Georgian styles; the world's largest inhabited castle; a monument of majesty.

On the opposite bank stands another royal foundation, Eton College. Founded by Henry V in 1440, students entering through its prestigious portals perpetuate privilege combined with educational excellence.

Downstream and situated in the London borough of Richmond, the river is graced on its northern bank by Hampton Court. Built by Cardinal Wolsey it was presented to Henry VIII, one of the strongest of English monarchs, who presided over the commencement of the English Reformation and whose humanistic beginnings did not prevent the inclusion in his reign of many candidates for the axe and block.

And so the Thames enters greater London, the capital of Great Britain and until recently the center of government of the greatest empire and commonwealth the world has yet to see.

Beneath Teddington, the gentle flow of the river abruptly ceases to be replaced by the tidal influence of the North Sea and English Channel. The increased frequency of bridges above and tunnels below, demonstrates the demand for rapid access of the inhabitants between each bank of the river. The Thames twists and turns through the great city: the sinuous main street, once one of the world's busiest waterways, is but now only the haunt of pleasure craft, barges, river buses and police launches; an echo of its former glory.

Just before Westminster Bridge, Big Ben can be seen rising spectacularly from the palace of Westminster, the mother of parliaments, where edicts and decisions from its corridors of power once encircled the globe. The booming voice of the great clock extends furthest in the early hours of the morning, when the roar of its traffic is temporarily curtailed in a somnolent city. But frequently in these hours of darkness, a light can be seen burning in the clock tower indicating that the House of Commons is still engaged in the nation's business.

Beneath Westminster Bridge the river glides "at its own sweet will" with County Hall, another place of power, the seat of greater London's government, on its now east bank. And while flowing north, Victoria Embankment lies to the west, soon to become the north bank again as the river changes its course at Hungerford Bridge and flows in an easterly direction once more. Just after the ridge is situated one of the city's famed entertainment centers which includes the Royal Festival Hall and the National Theatre.

The Victoria Embankment continues round in a gracious curve to end in the small complex of roads at Black Friars Bridge. Moored on the embankment are H.M.S. *Wellington* and H.M.S. *President*, two river gunboats that have experienced checkered histories which justifies their presence beside the embankment. Across the road from H.M.S. *President* is an imposing red brick Victorian building, Sion College, which houses a theological seat of learning and the City Livery Club. Here, freemen of the city and members of ancient and modern livery companies lunch in elegant surroundings. It is they who elect the aldermen and mayor of the city of London and help to maintain traditions of antiquity.

Beyond Blackfriars on the south bank lies the ancient borough of Southwark, one of London's thirty-two boroughs, which dates from when the Romans built a bridge across the Thames and out of which radiated main Roman roads. It was from the Tabard Inn in Borough High Street that the bawdy bard Chaucer's pilgrims set out on their journey to Canterbury. Here on Bankside stood the Globe Theatre where many of Shakespeare's plays were first produced and the area was the setting for many of Dickens' stories.

Popular phrases such as "to be in clink" and "bedlam" were derived from the prison in Clinke Street and the inmates of Bethlehem Royal Hospital respectively.

Even the USA is not untouched by Southwarks' history: In 1636 an emigrant to New England, John Harvard, founded Harvard University, and a memorial to Christopher Jones, Captain of the *Mayflower*, is to be seen on the riverside. Like greater London, Southwark had its share of German bombing, but despite much devastation, many parts of the ancient borough retain their Dickensian character.

Below London Bridge lies the pool of London, once the main docking area of the city for almost a millennium and a half. The cruiser H.M.S. *Belfast*, veteran of Atlantic and Arctic convoys and the sinking of the German battleship *Scharnhorst*, is moored to the south bank. Downstream, the Tower Bridge spans the river, and its equally-famous landmark, the Tower of London, dominates the left bank. This royal fortress has its origins in the reign of William the Conqueror. With limestone from Caen in Normandy, the central keep, the dominant white tower, was begun in 1078 close inside the older Roman city wall and subsequently fortifications were extended, culminating in the outer curtain of defenses with its six towers. Within this historic structure is the underground Jewel House, the repository for the British crown jewels and regalia.

Through Traitors' Gate, the only direct entrance from the river, passed many prisoners of the state who would meet their execution, or murder, either in the Bloody Tower, on Tower Green or outside the castle on Tower Hill. It was at the latter place of dispatch that the public were enabled to watch the victims breathe their last.

Adjacent to the unique Tower Bridge with its double-leaf bascule, is St. Katherine's Dock. As were all the docklands lying below the bridge, the dock was once swarming with river traffic. Now it is a haven for motor cruisers, a motley group of sailing vessels such as ketches, sloops, cutters, yawls and a few dinghies and inflatables. Relics of more opulent years, half a dozen or so sprit-sail barges also rest there when not racing or carrying barge enthusiasts during the sailing season. St. Katherine's also boasts of an historic ship collection.

Docklands, stretching for several miles downstream, was once the scene of congested shipping, barges and lighters. Here, vessels would congregate from all quarters of the globe carrying goods to and from ports of an empire on which the sun never set. The scene changed when the container port opened at Tilbury, situated further down river. This revolution was brought about by economic necessity. It proved more expedient to load goods in containers at their origin, store and remove them straight on and from the ship and deliver them directly to their destination to be unloaded. It was also accelerated by struggles between management and labor through relics of exploitation and restrictive practices. The bickering also served to further damage a country struggling to recover from an economy shattered by a devastating war, an empire dissolved voluntarily and loss of markets. But as the phoenix rose from the ashes, so the new Docklands was developed as a business, residential and pleasure center. However, the course of redevelopment did not run smoothly and the bubble of general prosperity burst in a worldwide recession. This created mass unemployment and lessened the value of properties so much that investors were forced to reduce rents or sell. And it was the latter that brought about the creation of Londinium.

Londinium, or to give its full title, The Londinium Club, was the brainchild of Boss. Capital for investment was difficult to obtain at the time but the problem was simply solved by voluntary aid from the USA. Those who willingly volunteered the aid did so in the belief that it was to be used for the benefit of relatives overseas. If one considers that all members of the human race are related, then to a certain extent, their belief would be correct. However, it is doubtful if their contributions would have continued had they realized what actually happened to the money. Others contributed towards the same fund because their health or businesses would otherwise suffer. These contributors would not have been surprised had the destination of their labors been revealed to them. The major portion went to support shrewd Mafia investors and a small amount to Libya and friends in Sicily, to pay for the training of terrorists and the supply of weapons of terrorism. What little remained genuinely assisted those in need.

"Lyndin" was the original name for London and meant the waterside fortress. The title "Londinium" was the Roman name for the city and its historic connections added an air of historicity and respectability to the club. Situated on the bank of the Thames and occupying a select place in Docklands, it was designed to attract the wealthy—preferably male. The design of the building itself was in keeping with the affluent aspect of the new Docklands. It stood in its own grounds and was well protected from potential burglars by a brick wall surrounding the grounds. On top of this, surveillance and alarm systems added to the defenses.

Externally, the building showed neo-Georgian influence and was constructed of the same limestone as the colleges of Oxford. Any visitor would have been pleased with the combination of traditional and modern in the interior design and decoration. On the ground floor it sported a bar, lounge-cum-reading room, a spacious dining room overlooking the river, and a small swimming pool, gymnasium and sauna for those members who enjoyed keeping fit for other pleasurable activities. Other rooms on the ground floor included those for the staff and the kitchen. The first floor included a gaming room, massage rooms, well-appointed bedrooms with ensuite bathrooms and, of considerable importance, a business room where computers were connected to the world's stock markets. It was thus on this pleasant site beside Old Father Thames that Boss his modern pleasure dome decreed.

The staff played an important part in pandering to the needs of the club members and they were carefully selected for their role. Boss himself ruled at a distance, having appointed a very efficient manager and administrative staff that were kept to a minimum. They included the manager, Mr. Paul de Vere-Smythe, a charming man who ran the establishment with ruthless efficiency. His pedigree was as impeccable as his manners, polished at one of England's leading public schools. He had a part-time assistant, Eoin Slioghan, who acted as a go-between for him and Boss. Paul de Vere-Smythe's secretary had a dual role. She assisted with office work and also kept the remainder of the staff under her thumb. In her early forties and still of excellent appearance of both face and figure, she was of Greco-Italian extraction. Known to the establishment as Ma, her full title was Ma Donna Ke Babe. Ma kept a special eye on the hostesses and masseurs employed in Londinium, ensuring that they gave every satisfaction to the wealthy club members and privileged visitors. She was well supported by a very polite doorman called Fred, a strong-arm man who answered to the name of Bounce, and Runt Parker.

Bounce played an important role in ensuring that all members of the staff kept in line with the official and unofficial rules of the club. It was not that he read and interpreted the rules. Had he been capable of reading them it is doubtful if he would have understood, let alone interpreted them. He left that task to others, obeyed orders and confined his role to that for which he was physically equipped. There was no doubt that he was tough, really tough.

He had been raised in an environment where one had to be tough to survive. In his youth he had taken great pleasure in bullying his peers and attacking his elders. He had grown to be well over six feet tall; broad and barrel-chested, he made a formidable foe. It is a well known fact that chimpanzees share 98% of their genetic code with *Homo sapiens*; Bounce was blessed with 99%. His education had been marred by the fact that to absorb knowledge, one needed many little gray cells and, regrettably, with these he was not richly endowed. It was all the more surprising therefore that he had the self-discipline to carry out orders, but even to the strongest, one is no match for a well-placed lead missile. Bounce had two sources of leisure: one was to punch up and put down any enemy of Boss; the other was to enjoy the antics of Runt Parker.

Parker was a second go-between for de Vere-Smythe and Boss. He was a different kettle of fish altogether from Bounce. Some five feet four inches tall, he looked upon his lack of height as an altitudinal challenge. He was lean, fast-moving and possessed a ready Cockney wit. His face was naturally sad-looking until one noticed the crow's-feet around his eyes. When he thought of something amusing, that is, amusing to himself and probably diabolical to others, his eyes would twinkle and the laughter lines around them become distinctly manifest. Boss knew Parker's value and paid him well. He had also enough information on Parker to put him in jail for an uncomfortably long time. To a certain extent this was reciprocal and so a bond of loyalty existed between them which was mutually protective as well as symbiotic. Being somewhat short he relied on four things to get himself out of trouble: a natural cunning, his weapon of choice, his agility, steel-tipped shoes and a cutthroat razor. Raised near Tooley Street, his father had been a docker and, mingling with the toughest in the East End of London, Parker had rapidly matured in a school of hard knocks. Not only had his natural talents enabled him to survive, but they had been refined and sharpened by the hostile environment. A master of Cockney rhyming slang and back slang, he had often used the skill to advantage.

How Runt Parker had got into Boss's employ was due to the latter having heard Parker and a mutual crook pull a fast one over a local trader. Although not a Londoner, Boss had worked in the East End for a number of years and had acquired a knowledge of the secret communication techniques of Cockaigne. Using the same lingo, he had suggested to Parker that he make a little money on the side by delivering certain small packages. Parker was short of ready cash at the time and so concurred. He collected and delivered the goods and was promptly paid. He guessed what was in the packages but, as they were sealed, was unable to verify his suspicions and Boss did not enlighten him. He had now worked for Boss for several years to their mutual advantage.

"I've fahnd anuvver gal fer yer ter tike the plice of little lost Anna. She's a real good looker," he announced to Boss.

"Is she willing?"

"I ain't sure, but I've got enough on 'er ter make 'er cooperate."

"And what is that now."

"She finks she's done a bloke in and the bluebottles are arter 'er."

"Did she?"

"Nah. Wots more there weren't no witnesses, but she dunno that. I fink I kin put the fear o' Gawd in 'er so she'll cooperate jest nice."

Boss respected Parker's judgment and nodded. "Right now, get on with it."

■ □ ■ □ ■

Eve was awakened in her new surroundings by Caria entering. "Did yer sleep well, luv? I bror cha a cuppa char," and she promptly placed the tea on the bedside cabinet. Initially bewildered, Eve rapidly shook off her torpor, smiled at Caria and sat up.

"What a nice way to be awakened; you are certainly spoiling me." She drank a mouthful and then, looking at Caria, remarked,

"You know I really must look for a job today. Where's the local job center?"

"I kin git yer a comfy job, luv. Yer only 'ave ter say the word."

"Yes, I understand and appreciate it. Please don't think I am ungrateful, but what you suggest does not appeal to me."

Caria thought for a second or two and replied, "Awright, luv, I'll show yer where the job center is and yer shall see 'ow yer git on, but yer will come an' stay wiv me fer a time cos I owe it ter yer." Eve beamed gratefully and while Caria prepared breakfast, rapidly washed and dressed.

The visit to the job center was disappointing; only one job was available and that demanded skills Eve did not possess. She filled in forms and returned back to Caria's apartment feeling depressed, a feeling that had been increased by conversation with other job seekers. One woman had been out of work for a year and others for similar lengthy periods. Eve realized that the economic depression had affected all parts of the country and not just Yorkshire. It served as a shock for her. Like others, she had imagined that work in the great metropolis would have been more plentiful, but now the truth was all too apparent.

She was greeted at her newfound residence by both Caria and Parker and informed them of her disappointment. The two commiserated with her and Parker did not elevate her state of mind when he broached the subject of the man Eve had felled.

"Y'know that geezer yer dotted on the napper yusterdiy?"

Eve reflected on the question and then nodded in understanding. "Well 'e kicked the bucket an' the perlice are lookin' fer yer."

The intelligence shocked Eve. "But how can that be? There were no witnesses."

"I nevver saw no one abaht," added Caria.

"Probubly warnt, but some of 'is relatives sez they saw 'oo dunnit."

Looking at Caria, Eve said, "We had better go to the police and explain what actually happened."

Caria shook her head. "If the relatives fink they are gonna git compensation aht o' the situashun they'll swear blind you killed 'im. The police won't tike any notice of me word, cos they might know me occupashun an' they'll fink I wos solicitin'."

"What are we to do?"

"I fink the best fing is ter 'ope they ain't got a good description of us an' we keep quiet. I don' fancy a long spell in clink anymore than you do, Eve."

Parker reentered the conversation by adding, "Only Caria, yer an' me knows abaht it an' yer can trust me ter keep me mahf shut like a bleedin' clam. It would pay yer ter come ter work at the Londinium Club; no one knows yer there. By 'anging arahnd the job center or wanderin' arahnd the streets someone might recognize yer. Yer'd be much better orf at the Club. An' wots more yer kin git a bleedin' good livin' which is sumfink worf 'avin in these lahsy times."

"I don' suppose yer fancy sleepin' in a cardboard box at night in the Strand like wot a lot o' unemployed blokes an' gals do?" Caria rejoined the conversation. "Look at me, luv. I got a luvly plice 'ere and I'm still 'elfy an a good looker. I want ter make me pile while I still got me looks an' I'm savin' like mad. Ma makes us 'ave regular checkups so there ain't nuffink ter worry abaht. I tell yer, yer carn go wrong."

Eve, thinking about the fact that she would be going wrong whatever choice she made, felt that taking the job would be the lesser of the two evils. "All right," she said, "you win." But she did not add a thought that subsequently entered her mind: "Oh, my God, what have I let myself in for?"

■ □ ■ □ ■

Eve undressed slowly, not because she wanted to titillate her first client, but because she was nervous and reluctant to proceed with an act she had no desire to perform. It had taken a great deal of nerve to get this far and she felt her courage beginning to fail her. She looked at the man on the bed and gulped.

Since she had decided to accept the offer of joining the "oldest profession," she had regretted it, although she had been made to feel welcome at the Londinium Club. When she had first set eyes on the building she had been impressed by its dignity and, on entering, not a little awed by the interior. Had she been asked she would have described it as very high class without ostentation, typically English in appearance. She admired the quality of the light oak paneling that covered all the walls of the ground floor rooms except that of the kitchen and store room. When she first arrived with Caria, Alf, the doorman, had greeted them with a cheerful, "Good morning, Caria. Good morning, Miss. Lovely day."

And the day had been lovely. The grounds had looked delightful in the morning sunshine. They were not extensive, but enough for their park-like appearance with the small lawn surrounded by shrubs and trees, to give them the air of privacy and tranquillity. A small paved path ran down to the river bank and she had noticed a short floating jetty adjacent to the embankment. The wall surrounding the landward sides of the building stopped abruptly at the river bank. Here at each end was a semicircle of metal spikes with barbed wire enmeshed in it. This was adequate to prevent anyone entering the grounds from the corners at the river's edge.

The floating dock, some thirty feet in length, was situated at the center of the river frontage. It was generally obscured by the bank for it rose and fell with the tide. That morning the river looked extensive with the high tide, and two yachts in full sail were making their way downstream in a gentle southerly breeze. How nice it would have been to be on board one of them, she had thought.

The manager's office had impressed Eve with its dignified rosewood Edwardian furniture and Mr. de Vere-Smythe had risen from his seat and extended his right hand in a cordial greeting. "Please sit down, Miss Eden, or perhaps you would not mind my addressing you as Eve." She had felt very nervous on entering, but the presence of Caria and his genuine courtesy made her feel that he respected her as a person no matter what sordid job she was expected to perform. Had she but known it, Mr. de Vere-Smythe extended the same courtesy to the highest and lowest in the land, for his public school training had ingrained that habit in his mind and he had discovered that it brought about the best results, a useful technique for disarming the wary. She was to learn later that his gentlemanly behavior was still present even when performing a task demanding steely ruthlessness. Had he put a knife into someone he would no doubt have done so saying, "So sorry to inconvenience you."

Mr. de Vere-Smythe had welcomed her to the Club and hoped she would be happy working there. He had said that her job would be that of a hostess and that she would be on probation for a while to see how she fitted in. His secretary would deal with the paper work and other aspects of her employment.

Dismissing Caria, he had opened the door leading to his secretary's office and motioned Eve through. "After you, Eve," he said. She entered and he followed. His secretary was busy working at a computer. Eve noticed she was a smartly-dressed woman possibly in her late thirties but actually ten years older. She was well built, about five feet ten inches in height with a few streaks of gray in her brown hair that gave her an air of dignified efficiency.

"Sorry to disturb you, Ma. Eve, allow me to introduce you to Mrs. Donna Ke Babe whom we affectionately call Ma. Ma, this is Eve Eden who has decided to join the Club."

Ma tapped the "save" key, stood up, and smiled at Eve. "Welcome to the Club, Eve. So you have come to join our little team." Looking Eve up and down she added, "I must say you look really lovely and I am sure you will be a very great asset to us."

De Vere-Smythe interrupted with, "Excuse me, ladies," and, turned to Eve saying, "I shall leave you in Ma's capable hands," he abruptly left the room.

"Please sit down." Ma indicated a comfortable-looking chair beside her desk.

"Now Eve, you will be employed as a hostess and I shall need your National Health Insurance Card and your P 45. You have them with you I hope?"

Eve produced the documents and handed them over.

"I would like your medical card, too, for we register all the staff with Dr. McMurrough. He is a very good doctor and we feel it is very important that the staff stay healthy."

Eve rummaged in her handbag again, found the card and handed it to Ma.

"You will be paid on a monthly basis. During working hours meals will be supplied here and there will be a deduction for them. While you are on probation I shall ensure that Caria has extra money for food eaten at her apartment. I am going to get Jenny to instruct you in your duties here; she is very experienced."

Ma pressed a button on the desk and within two minutes there was a knock on the door.

"Come in," called Ma, and a blue-eyed woman with short blonde hair entered.

"This is Jenny Thalia, Eve," and, turning to Jenny, added, "Jenny, this is Eve Eden and I have assigned you to instruct her on her duties as a hostess. You will do this today, show Eve around the premises and see that Eve has the normal supply of suitable clothes. Eve will start work properly tomorrow afternoon."

Turning to Eve she had said, "If you have any problems, Jenny will take care of them for you."

At that point, the interview had ended with Eve feeling that Ma was very much in charge of the activities of the hostesses and should only be approached in case of dire necessity.

■ ❑ ■ ❑ ■

"Come on now!" The voice with its Irish accent suddenly jerked Eve out of her reverie. She looked at her client with a sinking heart as she reluctantly removed the last of her clothing and felt a strong sensation of loathing. He was a stocky man with thick white hair with a well pronounced middle-aged spread. He lay naked on the bed ogling her with an obviously lecherous look in his eyes which added to her discomfiture. What she noticed in particular was the florid complexion of his face and hands which contrasted with the extremely pale appearance of the rest of his body. In addition there was a birthmark on his left temple which looked like a pair of horns. It was an unusual hemangioma, commonly known as a port wine stain.

"Come on!" The voice was more emphatic now.

Eve moved slowly towards him and, in her nervousness, said in a timid voice, "Please don't hurt me, I've not done this before." His response was to grab her by the arm, pull her onto the bed and force her on her back. He lay heavily on top of her, his hands pawing her body searchingly. She tried to move as she felt his oppressive weight on her naked body and, almost crying, said again, "Please don't hurt me."

"Lie still you bitch, I have paid good money for you."

Eve yelled in pain as he entered and deflowered her.

"So you are a virgin after all," he said, then added, laughing at his own joke, "or were."

She was being crushed under his heaving body, felt his panting breath close to her face and each time she opened her eyes she saw the hemangioma almost vibrating above the pulsating arteries as he unfeelingly used her. Eve sobbed as he continued satiating his animal lust and almost fainted before he finished.

After what seemed hours the ordeal was over, and he slowly got off her and, pushing her to one side, lay contentedly on his back. He took no notice of her and fell asleep.

Eve climbed painfully off the bed feeling torn and bleeding. She walked unsteadily to the bathroom murmuring to herself, "Oh God, Oh God," and, closing the door, sat down feeling faint and sick. Recovering, she cleaned herself with loathing and, returning to the bedroom, quickly dressed and left as quietly and as hurriedly as she could for fear of disturbing him, her first client.

Jenny had not prepared Eve for the brutality or callousness of her first encounter as a hostess. When Jenny had taken Eve under her wing, she had given her the garments she was to wear and demonstrated how to remove them in a way which was intended to arouse the libido of the clients. Eve memorized that lesson with ease and knew she could cope, but when Jenny showed her a copy of the *Khama Sutra* and leafed through a book of photographs illustrating various sexual positions, Eve was both amazed and shocked. "That I will NOT do," she vowed to herself.

Fortunately for Eve, her second client, an MP, treated her kindly. Eve did not know it, but she reminded him of his daughter to whom he was very attached and this inhibited his desire. From then on Eve coped for a couple of weeks spending most nights at the Club with perhaps two at the flat with Caria.

It was through an Arab client that Eve found herself in trouble with her employers. He had tried to make her perform some of the obnoxious antics she had seen in the books Jenny had shown her and, when she refused, had struck her, twisted one of her arms behind her back and caused her so much pain that she was forced to comply. Like her first client, he had left her bruised and tearful and when he had finished kicked her viciously. He then complained to Mr. de Vere-Smythe.

Eve had not anticipated such violence, remembering Caria's assurance that Bounce would look after her. However, the Arab was one of the Club's wealthiest members and, as Eve discovered, this counted more than the howlings of a harlot as she felt she had now become.

Her complaint to Jenny had been received with a laugh. Jenny Thalia was a hard-bitten woman of twenty-seven years of age. Shorter than Eve by a couple of inches, she had an excellent figure and kept herself very fit. An expert in sexual gymnastics, she could cope with any man, and a French guest of one of the members had just about enough strength to whisper, *"Phew! Vive le Sport!"* after a session with Jenny.

She had been born in Eidelburgher in Bavaria where she had spent her formative years. Secondary schooling in England and being married to an English businessman, had not removed her German accent. Her husband wanted to have a family and she did not, so eventually they divorced. She had ambitions of becoming an actress and although she happily hopped into bed with several producers, her sheer lack of acting talent and an Actors Union card did not advance her progress in that field. Fortunately for her, one of the producers was a member of the Londinium Club and, having recognized her true talents, recommended her to de Vere-Smythe; so Jenny found herself in a job she could carry out with consummate skill.

As hard as nails and arrogant, Jenny was contemptuous of Eve and despised her for her naiveté and aversion to the performances that were expected of her. Eve had looked tearful when Jenny showed her no sympathy and Parker, on entering the staff room, noticed Eve's discomfiture.

"Wots wrong wiv 'er?"

Jenny mentioned the Arab's treatment of Eve adding, "She wants him for to drop dead!"

Parker grinned. "Coo. Split 'er infinitive did 'e," and chuckled at his own joke.

Jenny ignored that comment and went on, "I tell her, if any man kicks her again she must bite him in ze bollocks."

Bounce, who had entered with Parker, dimly sensed that his strong arm might be required and joined in the conversation: "Some geezer want a punch up the frote?" Parker's wits were always alert and, recognizing a potentially dangerous situation, cooled the atmosphere and simultaneously placated Eve, by saying, "Ma will sort this out fer yer, Eve." And that is precisely what Ma did.

Reports on Eve's lack of skill had reached Ma's ears but she noted they were only from the voyeurs whose hardened appetites required the extra stimulation skilled practitioners of the art like Jenny could provide. Ma also noticed that a number of Club members asked for Eve. In future she would ensure that Eve was kept away from the voyeurs. Ma did not concern herself with the reasons why Eve was popular with some Club members, but had she thought about it, she might have realized that it was Eve's obvious innocence as well as beauty that attracted them. This innocence made them feel protective and so it flattered their male ego. Some also found Eve attentive when they talked to her. Eve was a good listener but also had a good motive for encouraging her clients to talk. They often grew tired during the conversation and this meant less sexual activity for Eve, for which she was grateful.

It was during one night a week later that a tired businessman had talked himself into slumber with Eve's willing assistance and the additional aid of a bottle of scotch. However, his snores had the opposite effect on Eve. It was a clear night, with a full moon that lit the bedroom and also helped to keep Eve awake. She slipped out of bed, walked onto the balcony and looked out across the garden towards the river. The serene scene had a calming effect on her and she felt more relaxed than she had since starting work at the Club. The moonlight dimly recalled a poem she had once read when at school, but she could not recall the exact words.

"Silver houses with silver eaves, silver trees with silver leaves, silver dogs with silver claws, silver cats with silver paws." No, that could not be right. Perhaps it was . . . then her thoughts were arrested by a cabin cruiser that had been making its way upriver in the flooding tide. Directly opposite the end of the garden it had swung round and was edging sideways towards the dock. Three figures emerged onto the deck and, as the vessel came closer, Runt Parker and Bounce suddenly appeared from out of the shadow of some trees. Two lines were thrown which were deftly caught by Parker and Bounce. They pulled them round two bollards and handed them straight back. Two of the figures on deck then handed Parker and Bounce two large bags each and then stepped ashore. The lines were cast off, hauled on board and the cruiser left, performing a neat, swift maneuver and headed upstream. Eve instinctively moved out of the moonlight and into the shadow when she saw the two passengers walk rapidly towards the house. She noted from their walk and faces which she could see clearly, that it was a man and a woman. They were followed by Parker and Bounce carrying the bags. Parker looked up in her direction before they entered the house and she froze, wondering if he had seen her. She sensed danger and, shivering slightly, slipped back into the room and the warmth of the bed. The snoring had not abated, but Eve was kept awake more by being worried about what she had witnessed. Finally, concluding that they may have been two Club members, she fell into a troubled sleep. Eve was in more danger than she realized.

chapter four

It was five days before the bombing in Piccadilly Street and Dr. Sean O'Neill was busy. One of his colleagues, Dr. Bannu Sind, was on holiday in Pakistan and the bulk of his work fell on Sean. Between seeing patients, his secretary had brought him a cup of tea and a message requesting him to phone the local police station and speak to Inspector Rodney Blanchard. Sean guessed it was in connection with a patient he had been called out to see two days before. The patient was dead on his arrival and Sean had noticed that the deceased's pupils were fully dilated and that there were signs of damage to the nasal lining. He suspected that death was due to cardiac arrest brought about by drug abuse, probably cocaine.

He had called the police and they searched the premises, much to the annoyance of the occupants, and had arranged for an autopsy with the police forensic department. He phoned and the inspector introduced himself and informed Sean that his diagnosis was correct and added, "We have suspicions that crack and other drugs are being distributed in this 'Manor,' but so far we have not been able to find the source. Anyway, many thanks for your help. I understand you are fairly new to this area?"

"Yes, I have been here about a month."

"I would like to meet with you sometime when you are free. Just give me a ring and we might have a drink. I'll buy you a Guinness, of course, to make you feel at home," he added with a chuckle. Sean smiled, saying, "OK. I'll hold you to that," and with good-byes they rang off and Sean called in the next patient.

Waiting in the surgery was Eve Eden. It was her second visit to see Dr. McMurrough. The first had been when she became employed at the Club. Ma had informed her that all the girls received a monthly physical in order to ensure that they were free from infection. During her first visit she had received a thorough examination and been pronounced fit. Although Jenny had instructed her on precautionary hygiene, she did have some qualms about catching syphilis, gonorrhea or, worse still, AIDS. She thought of the two so-called "masseurs" she had seen in the staff room, reflecting that she had not seen one of them for two weeks. The other still attempted to provide services for the odd Club member who had an abnormal sexual orientation. The masseur was a pleasant enough young man of Spanish extraction who answered to the name of Tornilla Popa. With his usual odd sense of humor, Parker nicknamed him Tornit. Parker frequently poked fun at Tornilla. On one occasion when there had been a discussion on films, indicating Tornilla he had remarked, "'Is favorite film is *Fanny by Gaslight.*"

Eve had felt sorry for Tornilla; although she found homosexuality revolting, she understood that genetic or environmental differences were responsible for the sexual orientation. She also knew that not all homosexuals were effeminate and many were creative. She recalled her father mentioning that some famous people had that sexual orientation such as Tchaikovsky, Benjamin Britten and possibly even Shakespeare. He had also informed her that the anti-homosexual attitude of many people was due to ignorance and the primitive psychological reflex of feeling uneasy in the presence of someone different from themselves.

She had shown kindness to Tornilla and he had reciprocated her friendship. The day before she had asked him what had happened to the other "masseur."

"I haven't seen him for three days; is he unwell?"

"In a way," replied Tornilla.

"When will he be back?"

"He won't."

"Why?"

"He helped himself to crack." Then added quickly, "You had better forget I said that," and he walked away abruptly, terminating the conversation.

"Eve Eden, please," Eve heard the receptionist call her name. "Dr. McMurrough is ready to see you."

Eve entered Dr. McMurrough's room and he nodded to her in greeting. "Hallo, Miss Eden, come in. I want to give you a thorough examination and will also need a blood sample. Nurse June will assist." At that the nurse entered and the examination proceeded. When Eve eventually dressed, Dr. McMurrough told her, "Everything seems all right so far. We will get in touch regarding the blood test only if necessary, otherwise I'll see you in a month," and with that, Eve left the surgery, relieved that it was all over.

As she walked towards Caria's apartment she wondered if she was safe from disease despite all the precautions she normally took, but brightened at the thought of receiving her salary on Friday. As she was also due to have the weekend off, a monthly arrangement, she felt more uplifted in her spirits, and walked briskly towards the flat. A black man and woman walking arm in arm approached her, going in the opposite direction, and, as she passed them, she looked first at the woman and then at the man. She noticed he had a scar on his forehead and his face looked familiar. She had walked only a few yards when she stopped dead in her tracks, suddenly realizing who the man was. She quickly looked back and there was no doubt: He was the man she was supposed to have killed.

Eve walked the rest of the way with mixed feelings. She was relieved that she was not a murderer, but felt furious with Parker and Caria for having deceived her. On entering the flat she found Caria making tea. "Ullo, Eve, yer jest in time fer the brew." Then, noticing Eve's look, added, "Wots up, luv?"

Eve could hardly speak she felt so furious; running through her mind was the fact that she need not have gone through all the humiliation and risk involved in her "job," as she contemptuously now regarded it.

"That man," she sputtered, hardly able to contain herself, " . . . the man I was supposed to have killed—I have just seen him and he is very much alive."

Caria looked at Eve and her jaw dropped. "Yer sure?"

"Of course I'm sure. Damn you, Caria, you deceived me just to make me a whore!"

Caria shook her head. "I never dun nuffink of the sort, Eve. It's that sod Parker. 'E bleedin' well pulled a fast one over me as well. I'll skin 'im alive fer that."

Eve regarded Caria with suspicion and then realized that she was telling the truth. "I'm not staying now," she said. "I've had enough of this rotten job."

"I know jest 'ow yer feel, Eve, an' I'd feel the bleedin' sime in yer shoes, but it ain't as easy as that ter git away from the Club."

"What do you mean?"

"The girl wot wos 'ere afore yer came, Anna. She tried ter run fer it an' she 'ad a haccident. She's no longer wiv us; got run over I wos told, but I 'ad a 'int Bounce 'elped 'er."

Eve sat down, taking in this news. She realized that it was dangerous to talk of leaving, even to Caria. If she were to escape it would be better to slip away without informing anyone of her intentions. "I'd like that cup of tea, please, Caria. I'll stay and don't say anything to Parker."

Caria looked relieved. "Yer right, luv. If 'e knows we fahnd aht abaht the black bein' alive 'e might turn nasty. We'd bofe better keep ah maufs shut."

They drank their tea quietly, each busy with her own thoughts.

Caria broke the silence. "Listen, luv. Yer orf this weekend, ain-cha?"

"Yes."

"Well, yer gettin' paid on Friday. Why doncha go ter the West End, 'ave a change from 'ere, see a show or sumfink, or buy yerself some nice togs."

"Yes, I think I will," Eve replied, thinking that it would be a good opportunity to get away from the Club and all it stood for.

When she left the flat that Saturday morning she had her money, bank and checkbooks secured round her waist under her dress. She realized that it would be wise to leave all her other possessions behind for fear of arousing suspicion. She had not seen Parker for two days. It was odd how he would disappear for a day or two and then suddenly turn up unexpectedly. She had told Caria that she was going to the National Gallery and then to an evening show. In order not to arouse suspicion in case she was being followed, she walked to the Docklands Light Railway and boarded the first of two coaches. Changing at the bank, she entered a west-bound train on the central line. Hardly had she sat down when the person seated beside her spoke.

"'Avin a day orf are we?"

She looked up and saw Parker. How he had managed to trail her without being seen perplexed and frightened her. Surely he could have no inkling that she was trying to get away from the Club. She decided to play it cool by asking, "Where are you heading for?"

"Orf ter the West End like you, luv. Got a friend aht there wots named Arfer."

"You mean Arthur?"

"That's wot I sed. 'Is surname is Crahn."

"Very funny," said Eve, wondering how she could get rid of him. Despite the noise of the train traveling through the tunnels, Parker continued to make unwelcome conversation.

"You know that bloke wot wos sick larst week?"

Eve recalled one Club member who had eaten and drunk too much and experienced a violent bilious attack in the corridor. She nodded, intending to humor Parker while she sought an opportunity to give him the slip. "Well, 'is name is Sir Fuller Vitelle." Eve looked at Parker sideways; no hostess or masseur was to ask or discuss the names of the members and Parker might be trying to test her. Apart from that, the name did not ring true.

"He is a knight you say?" asked Eve.

"Yus," replied Parker, "'Es got the 'Order of Barf.'"

Eve laughed just to humor him and at that point a big black man sat down on the other side of her. When he smiled he reminded her of a well-known British boxer whose gentlemanly nature had endeared him to fans worldwide. Beside him was a white man about the same size. They were discussing art, and from their accents were apparently two Americans on holiday. They had reached Tottenham Court Road Station and Eve turned to the black man and said, "Excuse me, but will you please help me? This man keeps following me. I am getting out at the next station. Please stop him from following me." Eve gave him an imploring look with her expressive eyes.

The black man looked at Parker, who could not hear the conversation due to the roar of the train through the tunnel, smiled and said, "Sure, no problem, ma'am."

When the train stopped at Oxford Circus, Eve got up and walked hurriedly to the door, passing in front of the two Americans. Parker rose to follow and suddenly his progress was arrested by the Americans standing up in front of him. The colored man held Parker by the arm in an iron grip. "Excuse me, sir, do we change here for the Northern Line?"

Parker tried to free his arm as the doors closed with a hiss. "Leggo me arm!" he shouted. The man released it, saying, "Sorry, sir, I did not realize the doors would close so soon. Do pardon me."

As Eve walked quickly along the platform she realized her ruse had succeeded and there was a real chance of saying good-bye to an existence she would be only too happy to leave in the past. She found comfort seeing Parker's face glaring furiously at her through the window as he was borne like a prisoner in the train accelerating out of the station.

On exiting Green Park Station, Eve caught a bus to Piccadilly, and sat near the exit door. She sighed with relief when it moved off and there was no sign of Parker, although she knew he must be on the train. Now she could feel free from pursuit. She looked at the shops and buildings as the bus proceeded and, on passing the Burlington Arcade and Royal Academy, decided to alight as the bus was going very slowly. Ahead near traffic lights she noticed a man and a woman leave a large black car. They seemed to be in a hurry as they made their way through the pedestrians in the crowded street. The lights changed to green but the car did not move, traffic in front going away from it. Drivers in cars behind started to blow their horns. A man walked past her cutting out her view of the stalled car when suddenly the world seemed to explode. The man cannoned into her and she felt herself collide with an Indian woman on her left. Eve felt a terrible blow on her head and lost consciousness.

■ ❑ ■ ❑ ■

At the next station, Parker left the train and made for a telephone booth. In the train he had felt frustrated and furious. It was the first time anyone he was trailing had given him the slip and the technique she had used was so simple. In his rage he mentally called her all the swear words he knew, and that being plenty, it gave him time to cool off and think of his next move. He felt Eve would make for her home town, or at least that area. He had learned from Caria that Eve had no relatives in the UK. She had some money but would obviously want to eke it out and the cheapest way to get to York would be by coach, so he would look for her at Victoria Coach Station. Alternatively, she might be in such a hurry that she would take a train from Kings Cross. If he covered the Victoria exit there was a slim chance that someone from the Club might get to Kings Cross before a train departed for York.

At the Club, Ma answered the phone. Her first reaction was to show her annoyance with Parker, but she kept her cool and told him to get to Victoria as soon as possible. When he rang off, she phoned Kings Cross and learned that trains were leaving for York at fairly frequent intervals. From this information she realized that anyone sent there would be going on a wild-goose chase. In any case, de Vere-Smythe was away for the weekend, Slioghan was busy and that left Bounce, who could easily bungle any commission he was given unless assisted by Parker or one of the other staff. There was, of course, the fact that she and Parker could be mistaken. Parker had reported seeing someone standing on the balcony the night the two landed from the cruiser.

"One o' the girls saw Bernadette an' Rory land larst night," he had said.

"Who was it?"

"It wos eiver Eve or Tyeeka," he replied, referring to the Russian hostess Taika. "'Oo wos in room number free?"

Ma consulted her worksheet and saw that it had been Eve. The question was, how much had she seen? It was then that she had told Parker to keep Eve under surveillance when she had her first weekend off. The fact that Eve had given him the slip did not prove that she was running away. She had seemed to have settled down and carried on the job. Jobs were scarce and Eve was not well qualified for alternative work. If she returned, then she was probably harmless. Ma decided to give Eve until Monday morning before putting a search and elimination man into action.

It was towards midnight when Parker returned from his wasted vigil at the Victoria Bus Station. Feeling in a bad mood, he had banged on Caria's door, to her annoyance, and, as it was opened said, "'As that bleedin' cow Eve come back yet?"

Caria, who had seen the report of the bombing on television, was feeling worried and belligerent.

"'Oo the bleedin' 'ell d'yer fink yer are gittin' me aht o' bed at this time o' night?" She paused to get her breath. "Wot 'as it got ter do wiv yer, yer twit. She's got the weekend orf ain't she?"

Parker ignored the question. "Is she 'ere or ain't she? Answer me bleedin' question!"

"She ain't."

"So, she 'as tried ter scarper."

"Wadda 'yer mean 'scarper?'"

It did not help Parker's temper recalling how Eve had tricked him. "She gave me the slip on the undergrahnd, the bleedin' bitch."

Caria now fully understood Parker's chagrin and reveled in it, but she knew it was unwise to push him too far. Eve must be brighter than she thought if she had been able to throw off Parker. No wonder he was annoyed.

"Eve ain't scarpered, she's in 'orspital."

Parker looked surprised. "'Ow come?"

"Cos she wos in Piccadilly when the IRA bomb went orf."

Parker had heard the detonation and read about the bomb in the late editions of the evening paper. "'Ow the 'ell d'yer know?"

"I sor 'er on a stretcher an phoned the emergency line given aht on the telly. She's shook up an' 'as ter stay fer tests."

"I'll go an 'ave a gander at 'er termorrer."

"That's right an' mike 'er worse than ever. Leave 'er alone you 'orrible sod, she'll be back doncha worry. She knows on wot side 'er bread is buttered." Then added, "I'm goin back ter bed ter git some beauty sleep."

Parker responded by saying, "The only fing beau'iful abaht yer is . . . ," but Caria slammed the door in his face before the sentence was finished.

As it was, Parker had no opportunity to go to the hospital. He received a phone call in the early hours of Sunday and did not get back to his flat until the following Thursday morning.

■ ◻ ■ ◻ ■

The woman kept on screaming and other screams, shouts, sobs and the sound of crying mingled with hers. The acrid smoke seemed to engulf her nostrils, choking her; people were flying around her. That child with her leg torn off; blood everywhere and that terrible bang—and someone was chasing her. She kept running but there was always someone or something at her heels like a pursuing hound. She tried to shout to drive it away but could only make feeble noises. And her head ached; oh, how her head ached.

Eve awoke suddenly from her nightmare to see a figure standing over her. A voice spoke as if from a distance and brought her to consciousness.

"'Ullo, luv, I brorcha a nice cuppa char."

Eve pulled herself together and brought Caria into focus. She was standing beside the bed with a tray on which was placed a cup and saucer and a small plate of biscuits. Caria put the tray on the bedside cabinet and studied Eve with an air of concern. She noticed Eve was perspiring and breathing rapidly.

"Yer wos makin' funny noise when I came in. Yer must 'ave 'ad a nightmare, luv."

Eve sat up slowly and nodded. She winced as she felt a pain shoot through her neck and head. Then she made the effort to pull herself together. "Thanks for the tea, Caria," she said gratefully, and, helping herself to the cup, sipped slowly.

"Yer gotta see the doctor this mornin'. I'll go an phone fer an appointment fer yer." Eve smiled gratefully. "Thanks, Caria. You are good to me."

"That's orrite, luv. Yer went froo sum 'ink 'orrible wiv that bleedin' bomb. Sod the IRA, they're a bunch o' bleedin' nut cases!" And Caria left the room.

Eve sat drinking her tea and tried to think clearly. It was not easy with her aching head and she felt tired. When walking in Piccadilly she had felt free and now she was back at square one, a prisoner of her vile occupation again. Everything seemed to have gone wrong. She had slept fitfully, alternating between feelings of frustration and helplessness when awake and experiencing that horrible nightmare when asleep. It was an odd set of coincidences that she had arrived back at the apartment, she mused. Her medical card had arrived in the post that very morning when she had gone to the city. It was the first and only mail she had received during her stay at Caria's and she had placed the envelope containing the card in her handbag.

She knew she had passed out in the ambulance on the way to the hospital and had woken not long before she had seen the doctor. It was during that time that one of the staff had found the envelope and noted her address and the name of her general practitioner. When Sean had offered to take her home she had at first refused, but she felt so weak with the post-traumatic shock and headache that she realized she was hardly fit to cope with the stress of seeking the unknown. She needed time to recover and then she would try again and this time succeed.

One compensating factor was the letter from the hospital to her doctor. At least he would give her time off from the Club to regain her strength. Doctor . . . that was another complication. The vision of Sean had intruded into her thoughts intermittently since she had seen him. She felt attracted to him and he had seemed so friendly. And she badly needed a friend. Caria was friendly enough but Eve could not trust her through her connection with the Club. Eve felt there was no one to turn to. She had written to her brother in America but had heard nothing. It was not like him to delay reply and she rightly guessed that he was away on holiday.

Her thoughts were interrupted by Caria. "I've fixed an appointment fer ten o'clock fer yer. Dr. McMurrough ain't there terday so yer will be seein' Dr. O'Neill."

Eve smiled gratefully at Caria. "Thanks, Caria. You're a brick."

"Listen, luv. You git dressed an' I'll I fix breakfast. I gotta go ter the Club this mornin' ter see Ma an' then I'll come back an' go wiv yer ter the quack's."

As it transpired, Taika accompanied Eve to the doctor. Caria had seen Ma, who had a job for her, and Ma, learning that Eve had returned assumed she had done so voluntarily. At least Eve did not pose an immediate threat to the Club, but it would be wise to keep an eye on her. As Caria was needed, Taika could escort Eve instead.

Eve had liked Taika when she had first been introduced to her. Taika Vozrekin had been born in the Ukraine. Her parents had taken the family to Moscow where they had both worked. Her mother was a road sweeper and her father an employee in the post office. The communist regime had inadvertently collapsed, thanks to the liberal attitude of Gorbachev and the stupidity of the old guard, and so the Vozrakins had experienced the new feeling of freedom, coupled with the trauma of the birth pangs of alien democracy in a totalitarian state. Taika, being very attractive, had found it easy to make money from some of the members of the different foreign diplomatic departments and foreign businessmen in Moscow. She also had the impression that all countries west of the Iron Curtain were heaven on earth. With the fall of the Berlin Wall and the easing of travel, she had accumulated enough money to pay her fare to England. One of the clients in the British Diplomatic Corps was a member of the Londinium Club. She had a gift for languages and so learned English quickly, although she still had a strong Russian accent.

When Eve had first met Taika, Parker had been entertaining Bounce in the staff room. He was singing his version of the nursery rhyme, "Old King Cole." Bounce had heard it before and was always delighted to sing the last word.

Eve was intrigued, then felt disgusted when she heard Parker render:

"Ol' King Cole was a merry ol' soul
an' a merry ol' soul wos 'e.
E' called fer a light in the middle o' the night ter go ter the WC.
The wind blew froo the winder an' give the candle a fit,
An' Ol' King Cole fell dahn the 'ole an' came up covered wiv . . ."

"Shit!" yelled Bounce, guffawing, and slapped his leg, amazed at his own brilliance.

"Coo," said Parker. "Gettin' a bleedin' genius, aincha Bahnce?" and Bounce had smirked, accepting the sarcasm as a real compliment.

Eve and Taika ignored the display, much to the annoyance of Parker; they carried on their conversation without looking at him.

"You were saying that it was very hard living in Moscow during the winter?" Eve had asked.

"Yes, life was not easy. We had a two-roomed apartment and five of us lived there: my two brothers, my parents and myself. It was difficult to keep warm, for often the central heating would break down and the cold was severe."

Eve was fascinated by Taika's accent. "I like the way you roll your Rs."

"It's 'er 'igh 'eels wot mikes 'er bum wobble," interjected Parker, riled at his singing not being appreciated. They had both looked at Parker and then luckily Ma had interrupted, requiring his services. He had left, pleased to have had the last word.

"Eve Eden, Dr. O'Neill will see you now."

Eve left Taika, and for the first time walked to the door with "Dr. Sean O'Neill" displayed on the notice.

"Come in," she heard him call. He had risen on her entry and motioned her to a chair. "Please sit down, Eve. How are you feeling today?"

He looked at her, regarding her from a professional standpoint, and noted her bruised face. The way she moved suggested she was still suffering from post-traumatic shock. When he looked into her eyes he felt a quickening of his pulse and the emotions of a deeper feeling than professional interest came uppermost to his mind. He found suppressing those feelings difficult, but forced himself to speak again as Eve had not replied.

"How are you feeling, Eve?"

Eve had been trying to summon up the courage to tell him of her plight which had made her delay in answering his first inquiry.

"I still feel wobbly and my head and neck ache, but Mr. Lilienthal told me to expect it. No doubt I shall be better in a few days." Eve paused. "Dr. O'Neill, I . . . "

"Please call me Sean," he interrupted.

"Thank you, Sean. That makes what I have to say much easier."

Hesitatingly at first, Eve told Sean of her coming to London to find work and how she had been tricked into prostitution. She told him how she had been followed when she had tried to escape. She mentioned seeing the two people land from the cabin cruiser and Tornilla's reference to drugs. "I have no one to turn to for help but you, and I am not going back to that horrible life."

Sean had expected nothing like this and the information left him surprised, disappointed, confused and worried. He needed time to think and gained it by taking action.

"Let me examine your neck and head," he said, rising and approaching Eve. He noticed that the bump on her head had subsided slightly. He held her head and gently moved it from side to side. Eve winced a little. "Sorry, Eve. There is still a considerable amount of bruising that has to come out." He walked back to his chair and sat down, thinking hard about his next action.

Suddenly he had an inspiration. On his private phone, he dialed the local police station. "Inspector Rodney Blanchard, please," he requested when the phone was answered. "I'll get you through, sir," the operator had replied when he had identified himself.

"Hello Inspector Blanchard, Dr. Sean O'Neill here. I would like to see you personally on a matter of some urgency, but do not wish to discuss it on the phone."

Rodney Blanchard replied in a friendly manner. "How urgent is it?"

Sean thought for a moment. The matter was urgent, but was Eve in any real danger? Her story sounded a little far-fetched and, although he wanted to believe her, she could be fantasizing. In any case, there had been plenty of opportunity to get rid of her since she saw the two people that night. His head was trying to suppress what his heart was telling him. She was probably safe for a few days anyway. "Any chance tonight or tomorrow evening?"

"What about tomorrow evening, say, at the 'Riverside Retreat,' the pub at the end of Stevedore Street. Say 7:30. I'll buy you the Guinness I promised you."

"That will be fine," replied Sean. "But how will I recognize you?"

"Don't worry, I'll recognize you. You will be coming by car I presume?"

"Yes."

"Good. What is the type and plate number?" Sean told him and so the meeting was arranged.

Sean looked at Eve who had been listening to a one-sided conversation and was eager to hear the outcome. "I am giving you a certificate to be off work for a week. Tell your apartment mate that you are to rest every afternoon and do so. I am also giving you a sedative, but do not take more than one at night and none during the day. Come back Wednesday morning at nine o'clock. Arrange the appointment on the way out."

Sean wrote a certificate and prescription form and handed them to Eve. "Don't worry, Eve. I'll help you." Accompanied by Taika, Eve left the surgery in a much happier frame of mind than when she had entered.

■ ❑ ■ ❑ ■

The "Riverside Retreat" was a modern English pub built in traditional lines. Overlooking the Thames, it boasted a large patio on which were placed the chairs and circular tables of patio furniture. A sunshade stood in the center of each table giving a continental atmosphere to the Riverside approach. Artificial bollards lined the riverside itself and these were used as seats by patrons enjoying the vista with its magnificent sweep of the river. Inside, the walls were adorned with prints of sailing vessels, river barges, tugboats and steamers of earlier eras. Glass-covered charts of the Thames were used as table tops and the rest of the decor had a nautical flavor. A ship's bell was situated at the back of the bar out of the customers' reach—this was used for announcing closing time.

Sean had passed a bobby on the beat as he drove up to the car park. Alighting from his vehicle, he walked towards the pub entrance and was approached by a burly man some six feet two inches in height and wearing a tweed jacket; he must have weighed 200 pounds. His tanned face with its ruddy complexion gave him the appearance of a farmer.

"Dr. Sean O'Neill, I presume. I'm Inspector Rodney Blanchard. How do you do?" The burly man held out his hand in greeting. Sean smiled and, shaking the proffered hand, acknowledged the greeting.

"By the way," said the inspector, "please call me Rodney."

"And me, Sean," replied Sean. "Incidentally, how did you identify me? The car park is not overlooked from the pub entrance."

"I have my spies," chuckled Rodney.

They walked in and Rodney ordered Sean a pint of Guinness and a pint of bitter for himself at the bar. "Let's take it outside," said Rodney as they both picked up their respective pints.

At the riverside, away from other customers, they seated themselves comfortably on a bollard each, and with the customary "Cheers," drank a mouthful of their respective drinks. As they looked up and down the river Sean remarked, "A very nice setting for a pub: a gently flowing river with a long history to match."

"Yes. And if it could speak it would have some pretty grim tales to tell," answered Rodney. "But I trust the tale you have to tell me is not grim," he added, smiling.

"That's one way of introducing the subject," said Sean, smiling in return.

Inspector Blanchard listened attentively as Sean outlined the story Eve had told him, regarding Sean without expression. When Sean finished, Blanchard looked down the river in the direction of the Londinium Club and then back to Sean. He looked as if he were about to speak, then changed his mind. After a moment's reflection, he said to Sean, "I advise you to get her away as soon as possible; she is in real danger. When will you see her again?"

"Tomorrow morning."

"Good."

"But why is she in danger?"

"I cannot tell you at this stage. There are some very big fish to catch and they swim in this river sometimes. I ask you not to reveal this conversation to anyone—not even to your colleagues, you understand."

"Not really, but I give you my word I shall discuss none of this with anyone."

Blanchard nodded, satisfied.

"Has she any place to go?"

"No."

"Then we shall have to arrange something. I can fix things for a few days but long term is a different matter."

While Rodney was speaking, an inspiration crossed Sean's mind. He spoke his thoughts to Rodney, who nodded in agreement. They must have been talking for over an hour when Rodney announced it was time for him to go. They parted with a friendly handshake.

The following morning, Eve duly attended Sean's surgery. "Do you think you can leave the house at 2:30 this afternoon without being seen?"

Eve nodded. "Then do so. Just take essentials." He outlined the plan Rodney and he had formulated. Appreciating that Eve fully understood what to do, he finally said, "Take care, Eve, and God bless." She smiled at him and tears of gratitude came to her eyes.

When Caria looked in Eve's bedroom that afternoon at two o'clock, Eve appeared to be in deep slumber. Satisfied, Caria returned to her bedroom, and lying on her bed, switched on the television. She enjoyed an occasional flutter on horses and intended to spend the next hour watching the racing at Kempton Park. Eve had heard the door close quietly as Caria checked on her and she waited five full minutes before getting out of bed. She dressed rapidly and, holding her shoes in her hand, quietly left her room. In stockinged feet she silently slipped past Caria's bedroom door and heard the noise of the TV racing program.

Standing at the entrance door of the flat at the foot of the stairs, she listened with an ear against the wall. There was no sound from Parker's side. She accomplished the tricky part of opening the flat door very slowly in order not to create suction which might have rattled Caria's door and alerted her. Quietly closing the door behind her, she slipped on her shoes and, carefully opening the front door, stepped out into the street. She looked up and down and, on seeing no one, rapidly walked in the direction Sean had instructed her. On turning the corner, she continued at a hurried pace. A car passed her going down the road and she kept on walking. She heard the sound of another car behind her and suddenly it stopped. The door nearest her opened and a man jumped out and took her by the arm.

"Get inside! Quick!" he ordered, and with a pounding heart, Eve found herself sitting between a man and a woman on the back seat of the vehicle.

chapter five

A magnificent May morning dawned upon the great city. Dew dripped from the Tower bridge, with its blue-painted metal bright and glistening in the soft sunlight and smokeless air. The city lay slowly emerging from its slumbers as the odd vehicle, newspaper van and milk delivery trucks moved about, adding the occasional echo to the almost-empty silent streets.

Soon the stillness would be overwhelmed by a gradually increasing crescendo with the influx of the city workers in trains of crowded commuter coaches, chock-full double-decker buses, crammed cars and the assertive black taxis. They would all enter the metropolis, filling the roadways, railways, and tubes like cells in an arterial network; a vascular system undergoing a diurnal blood transfusion, putting new, pulsating life into the capital.

The dignified aspect of Tower Bridge dominated the walkway to St. Katherine's Yacht Haven, situated nearby on the northern bank of the Thames. The nautical flavor of this esplanade leading from the Tower of London is hinted at by a magnificent bronze sundial some ten or so feet in diameter illustrating the mariners' dependence on the motion of a heavenly body. Further down is another bronze which suggests the sea itself, with a beautifully-sculpted dolphin and a fine female figure, sublimely stark, diving down towards it from above.

But before the city's arteries throbbed to the stirrings of life, movement started in the Yacht Haven as several crews prepared their vessels for the opening of the lock gates; two hours before high water they would open and one and a half hours after the peak of the tide they would close. During this limited period, vessels could leave or enter the harbor, otherwise resting inside or excluded. They were prisoners of the tide even as the tide, in its turn, is a prisoner of the sun and moon—all governed by the laws of gravity.

As were the other vessels, the cabin cruiser, *Erinyes* was alive with activity. A crewman was swabbing down the deck still damp with the morning dew; the skipper was testing the engines and electronic equipment, assisted by one of the passengers; and the other passenger was preparing food in the galley, the resultant meal to be eaten as they cruised downstream.

Promptly at six o'clock the lock gates opened, the two bridges spanning the lock rose and a small flotilla of vessels gradually emerged. The bow of the *Erinyes* was caught in the grip of the swingeing current and a sudden surge of power sent her slowly downstream as she and the other vessel temporarily stemmed the strong flow, to later take full advantage of the ebb which would carry them beyond the mouth of the river.

Passing Limehouse Basin, the cruiser left the flotilla to slowly stop at the quayside of the Londinium Club; there, Parker and Bounce awaited. The crewman threw the bow rope to Parker who deftly caught it, and, whisking it round a bollard, handed it back to the crewman, who quickly secured it with two turns round the forward cleat.

The skipper, skillfully keeping the engines running, maintained the vessel close to the pontoon and Bounce stepped aboard carrying two heavy bags. Freed from his previous task, Parker handed Bounce two other similar bags, but one at a time, and then nimbly stepped aboard. With the shout of, "Let go, Eoin!" from the skipper, the crewman detached the mooring rope from the cleat and, hauling it aboard, neatly coiled it and secured it to the deck.

As the cruiser surged forward, splashing spray onto the foredeck from the wake of a passing vessel, Bounce carried the bags to the stern and placed them in the cockpit lazaret; Parker made his way back to the wheelhouse and stepped inside. The skipper looked at him and noted his tired appearance, the cause of which he had already been informed. "Well?" he said.

"Bags on board, bawse."

The skipper nodded. "Go below and get a couple of hours' sleep and tell Bounce to as well," and with "Fanks, bawse," Parker descended the companionway. He found Bounce sitting at the saloon table tucking into a plate of eggs and bacon that Bernadette had cooked for him. "When yer've finished that lot, greedy-guts, bawse says 'ave some shut-eye. We're goin' ta be up late ternite." And with that parting shot, Parker entered a forward cabin and climbed on to a bunk; raising the leeboard, he made himself comfortable and fell into a sound slumber.

On the starboard side across the sweep of a green lawn, the Queen's House and the colonnaded Royal Naval College gleamed white in the clear air. Dominating the stately buildings, the Old Royal Observatory now known as Flamsteed House after the first Astronomer Royal, could be seen on the hilltop behind. Viewed from the river, this superbly-sited baroque group presented a finely-balanced architectural composition to all who cruised past.

The *Erinyes* soon caught up with the other vessel in whose company she had left the Yacht Haven, and, on passing the lower lock of the India and Millwall dock just below Greenwich, the skipper handed Eoin the wheel. He went to the VHF unit and, as the cruiser rounded Blackwall Point, lifted the mouthpiece, checked that it was transmitting on the calling channel, and spoke: "Woolwich Radio, Woolwich Radio, this is yacht *Erinyes*, yacht *Erinyes*. Over."

A few moments elapsed and then came the reply, "Yacht *Erinyes*, yacht *Erinyes*, this is Woolwich Radio. Channel fourteen, please. Over." The skipper switched to channel fourteen and, first checking that he was heard and getting a reply, confirmed an earlier radio message requesting permission to proceed through the Thames Barrier. The response was in the affirmative and added that span B on the south side would be open. Leaving the River Lee to port, *Erinyes* entered Bugsby Reach and, on passing the entrance to the Royal Albert and King George Docks, overtook the lead vessel of the flotilla and made straight for the open span of the barrier. Slioghan took notice of the green arrows and dropped the speed as they passed through.

Downstream they continued, slowing down as they passed the Woolwich ferry loaded with passengers and vehicles, as it crossed from the southern to the northern side of the river. Eoin Slioghan temporarily reduced speed as the cabin cruiser hit the wake of the ferry and called out "wake" to warn those below. The boss came up and stood beside Slioghan as they passed the ugly buildings of Thamesmead, a modern model town built on the site of the old Royal Arsenal at Woolwich.

After passing Margaret Ness to starboard, Eoin commented, "Barking Creek to port." Boss nodded. "Odd thing," he said. "A lot of these Essex rivers have two names."

"Like the Thames being called Isis at Oxford?"

Boss nodded. "About four miles from its mouth, Barking Creek is called the River Roding. Bow Creek becomes the River Lee and Rainham Creek becomes the Ingrebourne. Come to think of it, the lower down the Thames was called the London River, after which it becomes the Thames and then the Isis. It was the Romans who originally called it the Tamesis according to Julius Caesar."

"I read somewhere there was a big abbey just over there at Barking."

"Yes," replied Boss. "Saint Erkonwald built a fine Catholic abbey, but the Danes came upriver, took the younger nuns captive and left the elder women in the building and set it on fire. They later conquered this country, and their descendants have treated Catholics badly ever since."

Eoin, whose hatred of anything British was almost as deep as Boss's, nodded in agreement, although he recalled that England had remained a Catholic country until the time of Henry VIII. However, it did not do to correct Boss.

The vessel cruised past the old town of Erith, now part of Bexley, and where a busy royal dockyard once stood alongside the river. Boss stood holding onto the guardrail as the cruiser was caught in the wake of a large motorized gravel barge belonging to the Prior Company as it made its way upstream. He looked beyond it to Purfleet where he knew a rifle range had been in much use by the Home Guard and army units during the Second World War. He mentally compared their bolt-action rifles with the rapid automatic rifles with which his followers had been trained in Libya; what with those and bombs he still treasured the illusion that the IRA could drive the British out of Northern Ireland. That the Protestant majority in the North resolutely refused to join Eire, despite plebiscites, did not matter.

Fellow members were carrying out a terrorist campaign in the North and they all hoped the Protestants would give in and not want to remain independent. With the so-called Ulster Defense Force and the annual celebration of the Orangemen of the historical defeat of the Catholics, the Ulstermen were not showing any signs of giving in and sometimes he wondered if they ever would. Then he looked towards the Essex side of the river bank and memory of historical events stiffened his resolve.

They had entered Long Reach, and he saw the new Dartford suspension bridge crossing the river above the twin Dartford Tunnels—that elegant structure with its subterranean counterparts which served to bypass London from the east and relieve the metropolis of much congestion. The thought of blowing it up or even one of the tunnels crossed his mind, but he knew it was well-guarded and at that stage it was not among the planned terrorist activities. He looked astern to note that of the vessels that had left Saint Katherine's Dock that morning, only one motor cruiser was in sight. They had quickly left the sailing vessels behind and *Erinyes* had unusually powerful engines. He knew he could show a clean stern to most pleasure craft. He doubted he was being shadowed, but he would be more certain of that once they motored into the North Sea. He did not know the cruiser in the harbor—it had been there only a few days and may have been a casual visitor—but it was rather early in the season for casual visitors, so he decided to take no chances and later could carry out elusive maneuvers if necessary.

They were now passing Tilbury Docks and moved closer to their starboard side to keep well clear of a large container vessel that was entering the dock; she was heavily laden with containers above her decks and she towered above them.

"Increase speed to twenty knots, Eoin," the boss ordered, and the helmsman obeyed. The noise of the engines increased and the bows of *Erinyes* rose in response. Boss looked astern at the cruiser following to see if she was also increasing speed, but she did not appear to do so. Once past the docks, he ordered Slioghan to drop the speed to fifteen knots. He again looked astern and the distance of the other cruiser had increased; it did not appear to be trying to keep up with them, but he intended to keep it under observation.

He glanced back at Tilbury; it was there that Queen Elizabeth I had addressed the English troops in a stirring speech a week after the real danger of invasion from the Spanish Armada was over. Queen Elizabeth, Boss reflected. She and those damned earls of Essex had been the cause of so much sorrow in his country.

It was the First Earl of Essex, Walter Devereux, who had tried unsuccessfully to colonize the Irish province of Ulster from 1573 to 1575. That portion of Ulster had not submitted to English overlordship and, at his own expense, Walter Devereux had taken out an expeditionary force to subdue the region dominated by the rebellious O'Neills. Supported by Scots under Sorley Boy MacDonnel, they were led by Sir Brian MacPhelim and Tirlogh Luineach. As a soldier, the earl had used clever tactics, strategy and treachery and carried out many brutal raids on the inhabitants. Elizabeth had commanded Devereux to abandon the enterprise, but, before complying with her orders, he defeated Tirlogh Luineach and massacred several hundred of Sorley Boy's followers. His contribution to the poisonous relationship between the Protestants and Catholics could hardly be equaled. And then there was Walter Devereux's son, Robert, a favorite of the Queen.

Appointed Lord Lieutenant of Ireland, the Second Earl of Essex had gone out to put down a growing rebellion. However, his campaign was unsuccessful and he arranged a truce with the rebels, then suddenly deserted his post and returned to England to vindicate himself privately to the Queen. The Boss chuckled to himself when he recalled what he had read of the end of the Second Earl. On his return, the Queen had stripped him of his powers and he had then tried to raise the population of London in an unsuccessful rebellion against her; he had been executed for treason. What a pity his father had not had the same ending, Boss reflected; then his thoughts were interrupted by the need to attend to the course.

Erinyes was now twenty-eight miles downstream with Gravesend on her starboard beam. "Two large vessels coming upriver, Boss," announced Eoin, and, as if to confirm his statement, they heard a long blast of the first vessel's siren as it approached the bend in the river opposite Cliffe Creek.

"Keep well to starboard," ordered Boss, and Slioghan complied. "OK, that's enough," Boss said, and the helmsman then reverted to the original course. Boss again called down to the crew below, "Wake!" as they rode the bow wave, and repeated the shout when the second vessel passed them. Both vessels dwarfed the motor cruiser and Boss kept her well clear, for he knew that at speed, too close an approach and their small vessel would get sucked against the side of the larger vessel and that would be the end of the voyage.

The pretty coast of Kent lay to the right beyond Blyth Sands; green fields and woodlands, with the occasional farmhouse and cluster of cottages constituted a picturesque rural setting in the morning sunlight. The banks of the river appeared to slide past more quickly for the tide had changed and the flow was with them. Passing Holehaven with its storage tanks containing enough fuel and liquefied gas to equal a small atomic bomb in explosive force, Boss reflected that it would make an interesting target if properly organized. That the loss of life, devastation and disaster to many would be colossal did not influence the workings of his mind adversely. On the contrary, his fanaticism was such that any means would justify the end he sought.

"You see the black yellow buoy, north cardinal?" he asked. Eoin nodded. "Good, that is Mid Blyth buoy. Steer for it and keep it to the starboard side as we pass." Again the helmsman nodded.

"It is time you were relieved," said Boss as they passed the buoy. "I'll take over now. Go below and send Bernadette up; she can do with some steering practice."

"Course 095," said Eoin automatically as he handed over the steering wheel to Boss. "095," repeated Boss, who was a stickler for accuracy and had trained his crew well. He switched the steering onto autohelm and picked up a pair of binoculars. Training them on a yellow spherical buoy three miles ahead, he kept it in view as he carefully adjusted the automatic pilot to ensure that the cruiser was making directly for it. Satisfied, he then looked astern at the motor cruiser following. There was no doubt it was closer than it had been. As it had to follow the same course downstream it was probably not following them and, although he would know when they left the Thames Estuary, he wanted no company during the mid and latter stage of the voyage, no matter how innocent.

Eoin Slioghan left the wheelhouse and went below and found Bernadette in the galley making coffee. "Boss wants you to steer,

Bernadette." She looked at him and smiled. She had an attractive face and a winning smile, but her eyes showed a cold ruthlessness that spelled danger for anyone who crossed her.

"Your breakfast is keeping warm. Like a cup of coffee?" she asked.

"Sure thing." Bernadette poured him a cup and added milk and sugar. He took it gratefully. "This tastes like nectar," he said, and sipped the hot liquid slowly.

"I'll take one up for Boss," Bernadette remarked as she filled another mug. Then she made her way up the short companionway to the wheelhouse.

Boss was looking at a chart of the Thames Estuary when she came towards him. "I've brought you some coffee," she said.

"Thanks, Bernadette. Time for you to steer, I think. The course is 095, and you see that red and white pillar buoy about a quarter of a mile ahead?" She nodded. "Well, I want you to steer for that and leave it on your port side." He paused, then added, "Before you start steering take a look at this chart."

Bernadette looked down at the chart noting the number 1183 on the corner. The Boss pointed a finger to a point on the chart. "We are here and entering the Yantlet Channel. You can see there are spherical and pillar buoys all the way down for the next ten miles. When we reach Sea Reach number one buoy we will steer along the Oaze Deep and then make for the Princes Channel. I'll check the course and let you know when to alter it, but as long as you follow the channel buoys you will be comfortably on course."

Bernadette took the wheel, repeating the compass course given earlier, and Boss switched off the automatic pilot. At this point, Rory O'Higgins entered the wheelhouse, yawning slightly.

"Had a good rest?"

"Yes, Boss, but it was a bit bouncy at times down there."

Boss smiled, then handing a pair of binoculars to Rory said, "You see that cruiser astern? Well, she may be keeping track on us. Do you know when she came into the dock?" Rory adjusted the binoculars and scrutinized the vessel following.

"She was there when Bernadette and I came aboard just after the bombing."

Boss reflected for a moment. "Then she came into the dock the day before. Once through Princes Channel we'll head for Dunkirk. We will alter course for Ostend later."

Rory swept the portside coast with the binoculars and suddenly said, "That looks like a ruined castle." Boss noted the direction in which he was gazing and remarked, "You're right. That is Hadleigh

Castle, built by Hubert de Burgh, Grand Justiciar of England and Earl of Kent." Then he added, "That's a joke—as if you ever get justice in England."

Both Bernadette and Rory laughed at the comment; their hatred of everything English was such that they ignored the fact that some alleged Irish bombers had recently been released and compensated after winning an appeal.

"How far does the Thames extend?" asked Rory.

Boss thought for a moment before replying. "There is a stone called London Stone, at the east side of the Yantlet Creek in Kent from which one draws an imaginary line to a similar stone, called Crow Stone, halfway between Leigh and Southend on the Essex shore."

He pointed to Leigh and Southend, commenting that the pier was a mile and a quarter long, and then instructed Rory to look south to the Kent coast and pointed out Yantlet Creek. Rory took all that in and then expressed surprise at the length of the Southend Pier.

"I must tell you a story about that pier," said Boss. "A few years ago, a small coaster was apparently on automatic steering and sailed right through the pier in broad daylight. It cut the railway as well. I doubt the fishermen at the end of the pier were pleased. It was alleged that the crew were playing cards at the time. Whether that is true or not I don't know, but it doesn't say much for keeping a lookout—rule number five in the rules of the road."

Rory moved to the starboard side and looked at the coast of Kent. "That is a very good landmark," he said, pointing to a tall chimney which towered above the coastline. Boss looked at it then stated that it was two hundred and forty feet high. He then drew Rory's attention to four cardinal buoys two miles from the harbor mouth of the Medway.

"Focus your binoculars on those buoys. You can see the masts of a wreck in the middle." Rory followed his directions and the masts of the wreck came into view.

"What about it?" he asked.

"That is the wreck of the *Richard Montgomery* and it is loaded with ammunition and explosives. It was sunk during the World War II and is too dangerous to move. I read that there is enough explosive in her to wreck all the coastline in sight—on both sides of the river."

"What are we waitin' for?" Rory remarked, grinning.

"Too late," Boss replied. "I understand the explosive is now rotten thanks to the action of the sea water. Apart from that, the risk would be too great even if some is still lethal. No use thinking on those lines. We stick to our campaign."

"Sea Reach buoy ahead," announced Bernadette from the wheel.

"Good," said Boss. "Keep it to port. When we reach it steer 110. You see that pillar east cardinal buoy about fifteen degrees off the starboard bow?"

Bernadette scanned in the direction indicated and suddenly spotted the buoy. "Is that the one?" she asked, pointing in the direction.

"Yes," replied Boss. "Keep that to port. It is the entrance to the Oaze Deep. Beyond the buoy you can see the Shivering Sand Tower. Steer for that and keep it close to starboard."

The tide was now in full spate and its effect on the buoys was noticeable. They were tilted at an angle and there was a buildup of rushing water on the upstream sides.

The sun continued to shine warmly and the sky remained a deep blue, but there was a noticeable line of small fluffy clouds slowly building up above each coastline a mile or so inland. Boss noticed them and reflected that there would be a strong onshore breeze within an hour or so; it would make the water choppy as the wind would be against the tide. He told Rory to look at the chart and again showed him the course, telling him to keep a good look out for the buoys and also watch the following cruiser. Announcing he was going to the head, he left the wheelhouse and descended below, instructing Rory to call him should he be in doubt about anything or if any other vessels appeared. Once through the Oaze the passage would be down Knob Channel for a short distance before leaving the channel and turning into Princes Channel. He had intended to continue through Knob into North Edinburgh Channel but the cruiser following worried him and he felt it might show its intentions when he turned off the original course.

At the wheel, Bernadette was enjoying herself. She had always enjoyed physical action of any kind and as a child had been a tomboy. She had often fought with her brothers and sisters and also with other children in the village in which she had been raised. She came from a fighting family and bruises were commonplace with the children whether administered by her father, mother or the children themselves.

Her grandfather had joined the Irish Republican Brotherhood and Sinn Fein, and taken part in the rising of 1916. Although the third Home Rule Bill for the whole of Ireland had been successfully passed by the British Parliament, it had been temporarily suspended until the war with Germany was over. Britain badly needed the naval bases in Ireland to help protect the vital sea routes across the

Atlantic and without which the people of the British Isles including Ireland would have starved. However, Bernadette's grandfather, like Sir Roger Casement, was not prepared to wait. Casement had helped form the Irish National Volunteers and had gone to Germany to seek German military assistance and aid.

Unfortunately, the Germans did not think it practicable to provide troops and even balked at the idea of sending officers to lead the Irish volunteers; also, to his disappointment, the Irish prisoners of war in Germany refused to support him. When Casement returned to Ireland in a German submarine in an attempt to stop the uprising he was arrested on landing. The rising took place three days later on Easter Monday. With the proclamation of a provisional Republican government, her grandfather had helped seize the general post office.

As had De Valera, he had managed to escape after a week of bloody fighting when Patrick Pearce and other Republican leaders were forced to surrender. He subsequently joined the newly-formed Irish Republican Army which was organized to undermine British administration. He took part in ambushes and attacks on barracks, and when the majority of the Irish Police resigned, carried out clandestine attacks against their successors, the newly-recruited "Black and Tans," so called because of their temporary uniforms.

Ironically enough, Bernadette's grandfather had lost his life not by the hands of the British or Protestant Unionists, but by the hands of the Irish Free State government under William Congreve in 1923. The Sinn Fein Party did not accept the new Home Rule Bill that had brought about the Irish Free State. Despite efforts by British Prime Minister Lloyd George, who had organized a two-year conference of all Irish parties to form a home rule constitution, the continual bickering, polarization of views and lack of consensus of opinion had resulted in a compromise that split Ireland in two; this enabled the Unionists to have their separate state consisting of six counties and government based in Belfast, and the Nationalists their twenty-six counties and own government based in Dublin.

The compromise suited no one ideally, and it was only accepted when Lloyd George threatened to use force. The newly-formed Irish Free State government had accepted the terms as being the best in the circumstances. British attempts to bring about home rule for the whole of Ireland since 1886 had been frustrated mainly by the Protestant minority. The various risings and suppressive measures in the interim had only served to sour relations between the pro-British Protestants and Irish Catholic peoples.

Unfortunately, the compromise solution included the Irish Free State having membership of the British Commonwealth and an oath of allegiance to the British Crown. What was more obnoxious was the provision allowing Northern Ireland to remain outside the new state if it so wished. De Valera resigned as president of the new state and Michael Collins, who headed the provisional government, put the acceptance to a general election in which the anti-treaty voters, including De Valera's Party, lost. This was not acceptable to the Republicans who immediately started a civil war against their first newly-elected Free Irish Government.

Bernadette's grandfather participated in the ambushing and murder of the head of the Free Irish Government, Michael Collins. The Republican insurrection was put down with strong measures including a new law to execute any Irishmen carrying arms. Unfortunately, Bernadette's grandfather was one of the seventy-seven caught and so ended his life by the hands of his own countrymen.

Bernadette's father was four years of age when his father was executed and his mother never forgave the then-Irish government nor any Irish government since. She had carefully indoctrinated all her children to rebel against any government that did not push for the unification of all Ireland. In 1937, as Prime Minister of Ireland, De Valera had repudiated allegiance to the British Crown and declared independence from the British Commonwealth, making Eire a republic. He replaced the office of governor general with that of an Irish president. A year later, he worked out an agreement with the British government ending British occupation of naval bases at Cork and Berehaven in southwest Ireland and Lough Swilly in the north and settled other factors such as land purchase annuities.

None of these actions appealed to Bernadette's grandmother or her family and government relations with the radical Republicans deteriorated. Again the IRA took to arms, this time against the De Valera government. The latter arrested those members suspected of complicity in the shootings and executed some of them, including two of Bernadette's uncles. Her father continued the legacy of hate and bitterness and imbued this spirit in all his children and so when of age they joined the IRA.

"Time for you to have a break, Bernadette." Boss's voice spoke beside her as the cruiser passed the Shivering Sand Tower. She looked at him and smiled, "Do I have to? I am enjoying myself!"

"I've got something else for you to do with Parker's help."

"And what is that now?"

"By general vote, the crew think you're the best cook on board, so the galley is there for you to create something good. You realize it has gone eleven-thirty and we're all gettin' hungry again."

Bernadette grimaced and said, "OK, but you'll be lucky if I don't poison you all."

"I wouldn't put it past you," he chuckled, and she pulled a face as she descended to the galley. Once below she went to the forward cabin and roused Parker. "Wots up?" he asked, rubbing his eyelids.

"Boss wants you to help in the galley."

"Gor Blimey. Stone the crows. I ain't a bleedin' Cinderella," Parker voiced, following Bernadette out of the cabin.

"No, yere roight—yere more loike one of the ugly sisters!" retorted Bernadette.

"Coo, 'ark oose torkin. You ain't no bleedin' oil painting."

"Watch it," said Bernadette, grinning and holding a carving knife in front of Parker's nose. "Do ye want to become part of dinner?"

"Cor, that confirms it," he said, entering into the spirit of the game. "I always fort you wos a bleedin' cannibal."

She laughed and, putting down the knife, handed him a potato peeler. Parker rolled his eyes upwards on taking it. "I might 'ave known. Orl you Murphys can fink of is spuds."

"You can talk now. What do you English live on? Why, nuttin' but fish and chips!"

Parker thought of a suitable reply but deemed it wiser to keep it to himself as it involved discomfort in part of Bernadette's anatomy. He had discovered that Bernadette could change from the playful to the terrifying if one teased her too much, so he settled down to his task and kept the conversation on an even keel.

Up on deck, Boss had ordered Rory to steer towards Princes Channel. "You see the yellow-black-yellow buoy with the cones pointing to each other on top?" Rory nodded, having spotted the buoy a mile ahead. "Well now, steer towards that and keep it on the port side, which makes the course about a hundred and fifteen degrees." Rory looked down at the compass and adjusted the steering. "A hundred and fifteen degrees it is."

When *Erinyes* reached the West Girdler buoy, Boss looked back and saw that the other cruiser had also rounded the Shivering Sand tower and was on the same course as theirs. It was apparent that they too were going to use the Princes Channel—and this they reached after traveling three miles.

By now, with the wind against the tide, the waves were getting steeper. Boss had considered increasing speed to draw away from the other craft, but with the increased wave height the going would be unpleasant and he did not want to risk seasickness with the crew. He went to the chart table and looked at the chart and noted that they had five miles to go to be out of the Channel and into the North Sea. At the present speed it would be in about twenty-five minutes. He decided that once clear he would head towards the Margate buoy and then towards the North Foreland. This would give the other vessel's skipper the impression that *Erinyes* was making for Ramsgate. When just past the North Foreland he would make an abrupt turn towards the elbow buoy, and as this would be at ninety degrees to his course it would enable him to determine if the other yacht was following him.

He turned and spoke his thoughts and decision to Rory who considered the action the best to achieve results, but added, "What if she is following us, what then?"

Boss smiled at this. "I have an innocent device that will make her slow down for a while. What we will do will be to decrease speed and let her get close. There is a little gadget on board which consists of a rope which floats just below the surface. It has steel wire inside which cannot be easily broken with a wire cutter. Wrapped round their propeller it will put them out of action for a while."

Rory laughed. "You think of everything don't ye, Boss."

"Ye have to survive . . . you should know that."

Rory snorted cynically and nodded. Boss was right; if one was to survive then one always had to be one leap ahead, or better two. He thought back over the years and reflected on how very lucky he had been to survive this far.

At the age of seven he remembered seeing his first British soldier. The young man had smiled at him when his mother had given some soldiers cups of tea. Like many of the Catholics in Belfast they had been thankful that the soldiers had been sent over from England to keep the Protestants off their backs. Prior to their coming he had watched the militant Protestant leader Ian Paisley, at the head of a march to demand the dismissal of the Protestant Prime Minister Terence O'Neill: this because O'Neill wanted to introduce legislation to give Catholics and non-property owners fairer allocation of housing and universal suffrage. The British government under Harold Wilson had long pressed for reforms, but the Protestant militants were frightened of losing their majority in the Northern Ireland Parliament. They knew that if the Catholics gained a majority then a plebiscite could bring about a united Ireland. They knew too well that the British had promised that only with a free vote would Northern Ireland lose its autonomy and this they wanted to prevent at all costs.

He recalled Bernadette Devlin, the Catholic Independent Unity Member for Mid Ulster, megaphone in hand, urging the Catholics to put up barricades and defend themselves against militant Protestants. Paisley had even declared that the British Home Secretary was siding with the Pope against the Protestants.

The antics of the Protestant rabble-rousers had been a godsend to the IRA, which had quietly sent members across the border to capitalize on the unrest.

Rory had been in an adjacent room in his home in Bogside when two strangers had called to see his father.

"Ye've got to help us," they had insisted. "This is the chance we've been waitin' for to unite the old country and throw the Brits out of Oireland forever."

At that time Rory had found it difficult to believe, for the troops had come at the request of Bernadette Devlin to protect the Catholics from the Protestant belligerents. That was why his mother had given them cups of tea and home-made scones. But now things were changing.

He had been imbued with the idea that the Brits were the cause of all the Irish problems. He had even been taught that they were responsible for the potato famine. His mother and neighbors giving refreshments to the soldiers had seemed strange to all that had been instilled in his mind mainly by his father, but also by the history-teaching nun at school; his teacher could not be wrong.

A sudden rapid knocking at the door had resulted in both visitors quickly leaving the room by the door of the room in which Rory had been eavesdropping, and going out the back door. "Tell your father we'll be back," one of them had whispered as they disappeared and closed the door. But the men had panicked unnecessarily.

When Rory's mother had opened the door, a red-faced, panting woman had blurted out: "Your Kevin's been knocked down by the British soldiers and is in hospital." From then onwards, Rory had decided he would fight the British for hurting his brother.

When his mother arrived at the hospital she learned that Kevin had run into the road after a ball when an army patrol car was passing by. Luckily, the driver had seen the group of children playing, slowed beforehand and braked rapidly. His foresight had saved Kevin's life, for the only injuries he received had been grazed knees, a bruised shoulder and slight concussion. She had failed to impart this information to Rory who continued to harbor the idea that his brother had been run over deliberately.

A few days later the two men had returned and again Rory eavesdropped on the conversation. "I tell ye, now is the time to get rid of the Brits. We can shoot the Protestant leaders and make the Orangemen second class citizens for a change."

"How do ye propose to do it? Some of the Catholic women are welcoming the Brits."

"Don't yez worry, we're takin' care o' that situation. Maureen O'Flanagan has already had her head shaved, and the others will soon stop when they know what's in store for them if they don't."

"Ye've been a member for some time now, Diarmuid and we're now givin' ye yere orders to help." He looked hard at Rory's father and said, "Ye've got kids here now, haven't ye, Darmuid?"

Suddenly Rory's mother joined in the conversation. "Ye'll not be involvin' the kiddies now!"

"Calm down now, Mary. The Brits won't be hurtin' them and if they do it will help the cause. Remember what happened to your cousin in 1938?"

Mary did remember. Her cousin Fintan had been a member of the IRA and the De Valera government of Eire had suddenly turned on the organization, it being suspected of complicity in shootings. Some were imprisoned and some were executed—her cousin had been one of the latter.

"He died for the cause and all good Catholics should be prepared to support the cause, no matter what sacrifices they have ta make."

At that point, Rory entered the room to the surprise of all. "Oi'll fight the Brits fer yez," he announced bravely. The gunman looked at him and smiled, "Spoken loike a true Oirishman and Catholic. We can foind a nice little job fer yez. Are ye good at throwing stones?"

"Yes."

"Well, now, that's foine."

"Stones won't hurt the Brits. I can throw petrol bombs jest as well."

Even then his imagination was at work in devising methods to do the greatest amount of damage as possible to his hated enemies.

The real turning point in Rory's life which made his fanatical adherence to violence the only solution for the Irish dilemma, had occurred in Londonderry on 20 January 1972 when he was ten years old.

Two days before that Sunday, on his way home from school in Bogside, Rory had been approached by a soft-spoken member of the IRA.

"I hear ye are a brave lad and helped the cause." Rory had felt pleased and squared his shoulders.

"How would you loike a real man's job and fire a pistol?"

Rory's eyes opened wide in excitement. He and his friends had often played with toy guns. There were several games they had devised and they consisted of Irish freedom fighters against either the police, the Protestants or, preferably, against the British soldiers. They preferred the latter because they frequently heard members of the IRA or the Provisional IRA, known as the Provos, sniping at the Brits. The news of bombings and the blowing up of the soldiers' patrol cars was also part of their daily diet of news.

"Fire a real gun?" he had queried.

"Yes, me lad. No problem fer a bright young man loike yez."

As the importance of holding a real gun dawned on him, Rory felt really excited. "By all the saints that's holy, can I really shoot a gun?"

"Of course, me lucky lad. Now ye made the grade with throwing stones at the Brits and Oi even heard ye threw a petrol bomb. Now we're so proud of yez, we've chosen ye tae use a pistol as well. But . . . " He put his face closer to Rory's and twisting it slightly sideways, partly closed his eyes. His expression included a slight smile disguising a partly concealed threat, "Ye'll be tellin' no one about this at all, not even yere mother, father, brothers, sisters or friends. And . . . " he added, "not even Father O'Malley at confession. It is a secret between us, ye understand."

Rory nodded, "Yes, I understand."

"Good bhoy. Of course, ye know what happens tae anyone who betrays the cause?"

This was spoken as a concealed threat more than as a question. Rory had heard that traitors had their knee caps shot off and were crippled for life. He nodded in affirmation.

"Good. And if yez do the job well there'll be a foive pund note fer ye afterwards. Now I'll tell yez what te do, Rory." And he outlined the action Rory was to take.

The previous year, with so many terrorist shootings and bombings, one hundred and fourteen civilians, forty-eight soldiers and eleven police had been killed; many other innocent bystanders had been wounded by the mindless and indiscriminate bombings. In order to diminish provocative encounters, marches had been declared illegal. Despite the temporary law, two days later, on Sunday the 30th of January, an illegal march took place.

Normally the soldiers kept a low profile and avoided confrontation. On this occasion some were dispersed in platoons along the expected route to come to the assistance of the police if called upon. As the marchers came along the road, a small group of children had looked for an isolated group and found a platoon of paratroopers standing just out of sight of the marchers awaiting orders. The soldiers had adopted all-round defense and Rory had noted their position and reported it to the IRA leaders. He was then sent back with a dozen other children and, as the procession approached, they started throwing stones. The soldiers took little notice and when one of the troopers picked up a stone to throw it back he was restrained by his officer.

At that point, from the protection of the side of a building, Rory took aim at a soldier and fired the pistol. He missed and fired again, hitting the soldier in the leg. Two of the soldiers saw him and raised their guns to fire, but Rory and the other children followed their orders and they ran towards him, forming a screen as he slipped away from the corner and, out of direct sight, ran down the street towards a tenement building. As the soldiers entered the street, some women who had been hiding under cover started banging dustbin lids, the Catholic method of warning. On this signal, a group of gunmen opened fire, sniping at the troops from the building.

Elsewhere, soldiers and police were being shot at by marksmen in the crowd and some started returning the fire. When a gunman was hit, his weapon was quickly taken from him by accomplices nearby; so it was not possible later to establish that those killed or wounded by returned fire had been handling weapons.

Rory was thrilled and excited by the experience, and his hatred of the Brits was increased when he got home later to discover that his sister had been wounded. "See how wicked the Brits are shootin' at ye're sister now, Rory," his mentor had said to him later when pressing the five-pound note into his hand.

As a known member of the IRA, his father had been interned by the Ulster government and this had increased the bitterness towards the Protestants in the household. Later he was to be released when the British government suspended the Northern Ireland constitution, but this move served to increase the number of members available to continue what they considered a legitimate struggle. Shortly after his release, his father had gone to Eire for instruction on bomb-making and he took a more active part in harassing the forces trying to keep peace in the province.

By 1976, the population of Northern Ireland was tiring of the senseless killings. Public revolt came to a head when three small children were killed. They had been playing in a street when an IRA gunman, racing away from a murder he had just committed, ran them down and killed them. To the credit of a Protestant, Mrs. Betty Williams, and a Catholic, Mairead Corrigan, a peace movement was started and a series of marches protesting publicly against the slaughter organized. At one of these, Rory stood watching the demonstration as 30,000 Catholic and Protestant women marched by. He noticed a placard carried between two of the women which read: "In remembrance of all the men, women and children murdered by the gunmen and bombers since 1969. We who have been spared from death and injury remember them today."

The message had left Rory unmoved. At thirteen years of age the excitement of taking part in annoying and "bugging" the police and soldiers was more exciting.

As a Ukranian proverb says: "When the banner is unfurled, all reason is in the trumpet." That the following year the two women founders of the Northern Ireland Peace Movement received a Nobel Peace Prize made no difference to the members of the IRA and the more militant Provisional IRA.

The newly appointed ambassador to Dublin, Christopher Ewart Biggs, was assassinated when a land mine blew up his car near his Dublin residence on 21 July that year. Mrs. Marie Dunn, a leader of the Provisional IRA was shot dead by Protestant gunmen in a Belfast hospital. That year, the death toll was two hundred and ninety-six.

Rory's fanaticism was increased the following year when his father blew himself up when engaged in bomb-making in a house several streets away. In his mind the British were responsible and he was determined to spend the rest of his life taking revenge. By then he was seventeen years of age. He went to southern Ireland to learn bomb-making, pistol- and rifle-shooting and took part in sniping at British soldiers from across the border between northern Ireland and Eire. The Garda did little to stop the killers. Later he participated in the blowing up of patrol vehicles and other hit-and-run operations.

When the IRA decided to start a campaign of terrorism in Germany and the English mainland, Rory was included in the teams. He came close to getting caught in Germany but managed to get away to Belgium and had been picked up by the Boss's cabin cruiser at Ostend.

He had made some mistakes, killing some holiday-makers from Australia in error, but he had no conscience over that. He was convinced that the ends justified the means and anyway, his priest always gave him dispensation during confession. Whether he would have received dispensation had he mentioned his activities was another matter, for murder was a mortal sin. However, he justified his silence on the grounds that he was under oath not to reveal his activities to anyone, and also because he considered that those killed and injured were enemies in battle. The IRA waged total war and did not subscribe to the Geneva Convention.

In 1983 he took part in an attack on a Pentecostal church in which three church elders were killed and after that, his main area of activity was the English mainland. Now he was en route to Sicily to learn more advanced techniques and refine his skills in terrorism. With Bernadette, he was to be absent for three months and then return the way he had left with modern and more powerful explosive devices and weaponry to continue the campaign. In the bright sunshine, at the wheel of the powerful cabin cruiser and another successful bombing achieved, Rory was enjoying life.

"What's your speed, Rory? Fifteen knots?"

"Yes, Boss."

"OK. Drop to five and steer to port. Steer 095."

"095 it is, Boss."

"Hang on below," yelled Boss. Spray shot over the bow as *Erinyes* bounced on a wave, heeling sharply as she turned.

"Not too sharp, Rory. You'll make yourself unpopular below. Ease her round—that's better."

Boss picked up the binoculars and Rory straightened the vessel onto the course. They were now heading directly towards the Elbow buoy. He increased the speed to fifteen knots and the spray rose to hit the windshield. Looking towards the stern quarter he kept careful watch on the other cruiser, but it did not alter course. He watched it as it passed behind—it was still on the southern course and he now felt sure it was heading for Ramsgate and was definitely not following.

"Maybe we worried for nothing," he commented to Rory as he dropped the speed to ten knots. "This sea is a little too bouncy at the moment. It will be easier in an hour when the tide changes."

Slioghan came up the companionway into the wheelhouse and Boss showed him the chart. Telling him he was going to get some rest, he instructed Slioghan to keep the course towards the West Hinder Lightship. They were to rendezvous with a freighter at latitude 51 degrees 25 north and longitude 2 degrees 45 east. Slioghan looked at the chart, noting that Boss had already worked out the course to steer allowing for the speed and tidal changes. He confirmed that he understood and Boss went to his cabin for a rest he felt was well-earned.

It was half an hour before sunset that Boss returned to the wheelhouse. He found Bernadette at the wheel. "Getting some more practice in before you change ships, eh?" he commented. Bernadette smiled at him in agreement as the cruiser sped smoothly over the calm sea. "What's your course?"

"Oh, eight-five."

Boss glanced at the chart and checked the position before replying. "Good. There are about eighty-odd feet of water under us—time for a burial at sea."

He went to the intercom. "Parker and Bounce. Get the bags out of the stern locker; it's time to say good-bye to the cadaver."

Parker and Bounce appeared in the aft cockpit and opened the locker. Bounce lifted out the bags and laid them on the deck. Two of the bags each contained a human leg, one a torso and the other a head. A very neat job had been made of the dissection which showed considerable skill. All teeth had been drawn from the head, a precaution to prevent dental identification should the head be retrieved by a trawler; a very remote chance, but Boss left nothing to chance.

Bounce lifted the first bag to the guard rail and held it there while Parker made several slits in the plastic cover. These were to enable the denizens of the deep easy access for an unexpected but no doubt welcome meal. It also ensured that there was no risk of gases released during decay to add buoyancy to the contents of the packages had they been completely sealed. The slits made, Bounce dropped the bag overboard and it splashed once and disappeared from sight. Within fifteen minutes, all four bags were on their way to the bottom of the North Sea.

Boss, Rory and Slioghan had watched the burial in silence, but as the last bag disappeared overboard, Rory and Slioghan crossed themselves, more out of habit than religious respect. Boss smiled and said aloud, "A fitting end for a fool."

Boss put the binoculars to his eyes and looked ahead then to two points off the port beam. He could see the masts of a container vessel just above the horizon. He watched as the superstructure appeared and took a bearing. Two minutes later he took another bearing and noted with satisfaction that they were on a collision course. In another five minutes the hull had appeared and the distance had decreased to five miles. It was clear to Boss that the larger ship was slowing down but holding her course. To an outside observer this would have been expected, for the vessel was on the point of entering the northeastern end of the channel traffic zone.

Boss looked all round the horizon, noting that no other ships were in sight save a fishing vessel, and that was on the western horizon. He picked up a signaling lamp and signaled the code S-I-F-E. Immediately after he had sent it, an answering series of dots and dashes spelled out N-N-I-N. He then signaled the name of the cruiser to receive the name of the tanker "EL ARABAYANA" in reply. As the distance decreased between the two vessels, Boss was able to clearly see a large green flag draped over the ship's stern.

The big ship was now making less than two knots and was leaving very little wake. Boss took over the wheel and both Rory and Bernadette stood in the roomy aft cockpit while Parker handed them their two handgrips; both believed in traveling light. Boss skillfully brought the cruiser to within thirty feet of the tanker's port side, out of sight of the distant fishing boat, and kept it there as the giant vessel maintained the same course. A derrick swung out from the deck of the towering vessel and a landing net was slowly lowered towards *Erinyes*. Boss eased the speed of the cruiser to bring her stern in line with the lowered netting. As the net reached the level of the deck, Slioghan signaled to the container crew and the net was caught with a boat hook by Parker, who hauled it aboard. Both Bernadette and Rory grabbed the net and pulled it to the middle of the cockpit while Bounce unhooked two small packages from the net. Once retrieved, Bernadette and Rory put their handgrips inside the netting and climbed onto it. Ensuring they were secure, Parker nodded to Slioghan who signaled to the crew of the container vessel and the human cargo was quickly hoisted on board. As the two ascended, Boss gave them a wave to which they responded in kind. *Erinyes* then sped away from the *El Arabayana* at fifteen knots while the larger vessel increased speed to enter the traffic zone.

As soon as they were clear of the big ship, Parker picked up the packages and put them in two waterproof plastic weighted bottles and secured the lids tightly. He then attached a large bag containing salt to each and tied a long line to each, the end of which was secured to a buoy. That job finished, he went up into the wheelhouse and reported to Boss.

"Packages ready, Boss."

"Good. Stand by until I tell you to drop them overboard." Then, turning towards Slioghan, he said, "I want you to steer while I set a course for the drop spot. The present course is one hundred." Repeating the course, Slioghan took over the wheel.

Boss looked at the radar screen; there was a blip to port about a mile away. He frowned, for he had not seen another vessel in that direction earlier. Picking up the binoculars he was relieved to see a can buoy with a cross on top. He looked at the chart and noted that it was a wave recorder. "That's useful," he thought to himself, for with the reading from the Satnav it helped to confirm his position. He reached for the tide tables and worked out a course to bring

Erinyes to the Middelkerike Bank buoy. Nearby was a submarine cable which would be avoided by trawlers.

"Steer two hundred and increase speed to twenty-five knots." Slioghan repeated the order and spray flew each side as *Erinyes* leapt through the water. The cruiser was capable of another fifteen at least but then fuel consumption would be greater and there were other things to do before this voyage was over.

In twenty-four minutes they passed the buoy and he gradually slowed speed until *Erinyes* was one and a quarter cables beyond the buoy. Meantime, Parker had rechecked the packages' attachments and stood waiting in the cockpit for the order to drop them overboard.

"Ready Parker?" queried Boss. Parker signaled an affirmation and Boss called out "drop," at which Parker threw one and then the other package overboard.

Both packages with their attached bags of salt and floats sank rapidly to the sea bed. Boss had calculated well. The salt was timed to dissolve at such a rate that the floats would surface at four A.M. just before sunrise the next day but one, and that would give them time to relax in Ostend for a whole day.

As the packages disappeared, Boss noted the position on the Satnav and also took a bearing on the Middelkerke Bank buoy. "OK, Slioghan. As near to 126 as you can make it." He was feeling elated. In about half an hour they would be in Ostend and would enjoy a good dinner at a quayside restaurant he knew well. So far everything had gone swimmingly on the trip. He chuckled as he thought of just how frustrated the police would be looking for Rory and Bernadette who were now comfortably on their way to Sicily.

Before entering the harbor, *Erinyes* had to wait for clearance as a ferry was leaving. Once clear of the harbor, the three red lights changed to green and with Boss at the helm *Erinyes* motored through the entrance and then turned to port to enter Montgomery Dock. There were not many vessels there and with the yellow "Q" flag and the Belgian courtesy flag flying, they found a berth beside the dock.

While they were tidying up the ship, a light-blue uniformed customs officer came aboard to examine their papers and was quickly satisfied with the documents. He departed without any delay, wishing them an enjoyable stay in Ostend.

■ ❏ ■ ❏ ■

It was twilight when *Erinyes* slipped out of Ostend. The day spent there had been relaxing for all and between them they had acquired several boxes of good wines and a strong handgrip. The latter was strongly made for the contents included gold and some precious stones that had been smuggled into Belgium on a jet plane from India.

They reached the Middelkerke Bank buoy two minutes before the floats surfaced. No time was lost in retrieving them, but no sooner were they on deck when they detached the packages and connected them to another line and salt bags; this was for another dumping prior to entering harbor in the United Kingdom or, alternatively, to ensure rapid disposal should the vessel be stopped for inspection by a customs patrol craft.

It was two hours before sunset when Boss sighted the Naze Tower. *Erinyes* had crossed the North Sea without incident. Once clear of the traffic zone, only two other craft had been sighted, one a fishing vessel and the other a sloop which appeared to be on course for Holland. The cruiser had been on automatic steering most of the time and Boss and the crew had taken turns keeping a look-out. Although their destination was in the River Orwell just beyond Harwich, Boss had not taken the direct route; he wanted to collect the contraband without causing suspicion and made for the Naze Tower. As the cruiser had to pass that prominence the following day en route to the Thames, its presence in the vicinity would not give rise to suspicion.

With the Medusa Buoy and Tower in line of sight, and half a mile from the buoy, Boss carefully scanned the sea all round. On the port bow he could see Walton and on locating the pier, moved the binoculars to the right to place the Coast Guard building in sight. He knew *Erinyes* was being watched, but that applied to every vessel that passed within observing distance and it was part of their job. He chuckled to himself thinking that had they realized what he had on board they would have shown more than routine interest.

He scanned the sea in an anticlockwise direction and apart from three yachts close to the coast, noted that no craft were behind them. To starboard there were several large vessels in the Harwich Channel about five miles away and a few small yachts at least two miles away making for the direction of Landguard Point.

Still on automatic steering, the cruiser was a quarter of a mile from the buoy when Boss ordered Parker to drop the packages overboard; at the same time, keeping the buoy and Tower in line, he took a careful bearing on the end of Walton Pier while Slioghan noted the position on the Satnav.

Once the exact position of drop had been recorded, Boss swung the cruiser in the direction of Landguard Point and slowly increased speed. He ordered Bounce to place the Yellow "Q" flag on the signal mast and within twenty minutes passed Landguard Point and Felixtowe. Proceeding up the River Orwell, a customs launch hailed them and drew alongside, and *Erinyes* slowed.

"Where are you from?" a young-looking officer queried.

"Ostend," replied Boss.

"Anything to declare?"

"Yes."

"OK. I'll come aboard." And with fendoffs in position, the vessels closed and the officer jumped aboard. Slioghan took the wheel as the two vessels slowly made their way upstream and Boss took the officer to the saloon. Once there, he examined the passports and customs declaration form and inspected the boxes of wines and spirits. Boss duly paid the duty and was given clearance.

"Where are you making for?" the young officer asked in a friendly manner.

"We stay here overnight and will make for St. Katherine's Yacht Haven London Bridge tomorrow."

"Well, I hope you have a nice trip. The weather should hold for two more days, then a low is expected." They went up on deck, and as the vessels closed, the officer boarded his own craft and gave a friendly wave as the vessels drew apart.

Erinyes dropped anchor upriver just off the fairway and the crew prepared for an early start in the morning. After a meal and some conversation over a drink, they retired at dusk. The night was spent with only an occasional rocking of the boat as a large craft passed in the fairway, their mooring light bobbing up and down erratically until the effects of the wake had passed.

At four A.M., light began to steal along the eastern rim. The decks were wet with dew when all four had breakfasted, ready to leave just before sunrise. By the time they had reached the pickup point there was a slight mist on the sea and this suited Boss admirably. *Erinyes* could not be seen from the coast guard building on shore and, as visibility was half a mile, sighting the ascended floats was easy. She continued the voyage via the East Swin and Middle Deep to motor up the Thames in good time.

That Wednesday evening, *Erinyes* moored in St. Katherine's Yacht Haven, having deposited the packages and left Parker at the Londinium Club jetty en route. Boss was feeling pleased—everything had run smoothly—but he was not to remain pleased for long.

■ ❑ ■ ❑ ■

It was the following morning when Parker learned that Eve had disappeared and the source of the intelligence was Jenny. Parker had immediately confronted Caria. "Wot the bloody 'ell's bin goin' on. Wot's this abaht Eve scarpering?"

"She's gorn."

"'Ow the 'ell did it 'appen? I told yer ter keep an eye on 'er. Yer must 'ave bleedin' well bin asleep."

"Cool it yer 'orrible sod. She slipped aht wivaht a sahnd. If yer look in 'er room yer will find all 'er fings there. Maybe she's bin snatched."

Parker did look in Eve's room and noticed that all her clothes and toiletries were present. That's odd, he thought. Had she wanted to go surely she would have taken some possessions.

He saw Mr. de Vere-Smythe and explained the appearance of Eve's room. De Vere-Smythe was already aware of Eve's absence and it was he who informed Boss. Although Parker or Eoin normally acted as go-betweens with Boss, Eve's absence was important enough for him to contact Boss directly. He filled in all the details regarding her departure, leaving out nothing. He also informed Boss that he had alerted the organization, including members in the USA of Eve's absence and included a description of her. Boss's face had hardened at the receipt of the news but he commended de Vere-Smythe on his action.

"Good. You showed initiative." Then he suddenly stopped speaking as a thought crossed his mind. "Does Eve have any relatives?"

"Not to my knowledge."

"Then find out and let me know straight away. One other thing is necessary. Tell the organization that Eve is to be disposed of as soon as she is found. There must be no delay in silencing her. Is that understood?"

De Vere-Smythe nodded and wasted no time in passing on the information.

chapter six

"Are you feeling some discomfort?"

Richard looked at the patient, having noticed an increase in the breathing rate. He glanced up at the heart monitor and saw that the pulse rate had increased. The patient murmured, "Yes," beneath the facial mask.

"Mona, hand me the Benoxinate, please." Mona Green, the very efficient theatre nurse had anticipated the order and was passing the small open tube of topical anesthetic before surgeon Richard Rutherford, had finished speaking. Expressing thanks, Richard took the small tube and squeezed three drops onto the patient's cornea. She gasped a little and then relaxed saying, "That's better."

"Fine," said Richard. "Now just relax; I am taking the cataract out now."

The slit in the cornea had already been made, the pupil dilated and the lens capsule opened. He pressed slightly on the eyeball and the cataractous lens slid out of the corneal opening. Sister Mona had the small bowl ready and he lifted the cataract with tweezers and placed it in the bowl. She then handed him the basin with the lens implant.

The theatre nurse had placed the implant, the artificial lens, in the basin ready for insertion. He picked it up with tweezers and slid it through the slit in the cornea, then deftly manipulated it into the capsule. Looking through the biomicroscope, he gently adjusted the implant with a fine probe and ensured that it was properly aligned. He took the needle with fine suture attached and sewed up the slit in the cornea, but before the final stitch, the theatre nurse handed him the syringe and he inserted a bubble of air into the anterior chamber of the eye to prevent the risk of corneal and iridic adhesion. The iris was already fully dilated and the risk of adhesion from that quarter was virtually nil. Carefully tying the end of the last suture, he snipped it and handed the needle and surgical scissors to Mona who, on placing them on the instrument tray, unsealed a tube of physiological saline and passed it to Richard. She held a kidney basin against the patient's face and rinsed the eye as Mona swabbed away the overspill that had missed the basin.

Richard carefully examined the eye and, feeling satisfied said, "All over now. The theater porter will take you back to the ward." He signaled to the porter who, with an assistant, brought the stretcher trolley beside the operating table and between them they slid a stretcher under the patient and lifted her onto the trolley. As she was wheeled out she murmured, "Thank you," to Mona and Richard, who acknowledged her courtesy.

"That's the lot for this morning, Mona. I could do with some lunch. I'll see you in the theatre at eight tomorrow morning. Thanks for your help; it is very nice to work with someone so efficient and on the ball." Nurse Mona smiled in appreciation of the compliment and said she enjoyed being part of the team.

Richard went to the changing room, discarded his green theatre garb, changed clothes and went to his office. It was a small room containing two desks and two large filing cabinets. One desk was occupied by his secretary, a slim tall silver-haired woman who kept the office and records in order with meticulous efficiency.

"Anything new, Pat?" he asked as he entered the room.

Pat looked up, smiled and handed him a file. "This patient has been sent in by Mr. McKenzie with a retinal detachment. He phoned an hour ago."

Richard nodded. The optometrist, Michael McKenzie, only referred patients as emergencies when absolutely necessary and Richard knew that the patient would need an emergency operation that day.

Pat interrupted his thoughts on handing him another file. He opened it and saw that a patient with an acute attack of closed-angle glaucoma had been attended by his registrar earlier in the day and would need his attention. "There was another telephone message from Dr. Sean O'Neill who would appreciate you calling him as soon as possible. Here is his number."

Richard raised his eyebrows and wondered why the urgency. He had seen his cousin once since he had come over to England to practice in London, and Sean was pretty laid-back over most things. Something important must have cropped up for such a request.

He lifted his phone and tapped the number on the keys and was surprised to hear the phone at the other end lifted after the first ring.

"Hello, Sean, Richard here. What's the problem?"

"Sorry to bother you, Richard," said Sean, his Irish brogue being emphasized by the apparatus. "I would appreciate your help on an important matter which I cannot discuss on the phone. Is there any chance of seeing you tonight?"

"Sorry, that will be difficult. I have some emergencies to attend to and doubt I shall finish until very late. How about tomorrow?"

Sean paused before replying but concealed his disappointment and said it would be OK. "Where can we meet?"

"I suggest at the 'Camelot' in Lambourne End. We can have dinner there at say eight o'clock. Is that alright with you?" Sean had been there once before; it was about half way between Richard's home and his apartment, and the rush hour would be over leaving the roads reasonably clear. "That will be fine. I hope Dawn and the family are well?"

"Yes, thanks," Richard replied. "Must dash. Cheerio for now. See you tomorrow."

■ ❑ ■ ❑ ■

"Put your head down and put this over your head." The woman beside her said, in a commanding yet not unkindly tone. Eve leaned forward so that she could not be seen from outside the car and took the wig from the woman. She pulled it over head and the woman helped her to tuck her hair in at the back where it had escaped the encirclement of the wig. She sat up and was now transformed into a brunette in appearance. "I doubt you will be recognized now, Miss Eden," the woman beside her commented.

She looked at her companions, noting that the woman must be in her mid-twenties, wearing a two-piece and, although she smiled and looked friendly, she had an air of being very self-assured. Eve turned towards the man sitting on her left. He, too, was in his mid-twenties, dark, very solidly built and about six feet tall. He was dressed in an open-necked shirt and slacks. He smiled as she regarded him and said, "It is about time we introduced ourselves. I am detective constable Gerald Gautier and this is Woman Police Constable Betty Watchett."

"Call me Betty," the WPC said, "and driving us to your safe house is constable Peter Pladfuss." The driver gave a wave of his hand to indicate he had heard his introduction.

"We're taking you to a house in Barnett which is in the north of London. You will be well guarded there." He turned his head, looked behind the vehicle and then addressed the driver: "That Jaguar is still behind us, Peter."

"Don't worry. I'm watching it. As it did not appear until we were out of Newham, I think it is just going in the same direction. I'll turn off this road shortly and take another route."

Betty noticed that Eve looked a little anxious and almost tearful and patted her on the arm. "There is no need to worry Eve. I don't think we are being followed, but if we are we can easily shake them off or call a patrol car which would stop them. Just relax now; we'll be there in just under an hour."

Eve let the tension slip from her muscles and sat back comfortably. The wig felt rather warm but she felt it was little to endure, now that she was released from the hateful position in which she had felt so insecure and trapped. The thought of Sean entered her mind and she felt a wave of gratitude towards him sweep over her. It was his idea of approaching the police and getting her out of her problem. However, it puzzled her that the police had taken no action against the Londinium Club. Was it because they had no evidence of the activities that went on there, or was it because people in high places used it and any action was prevented by higher authority? If so, did that mean there was police corruption? That idea did not seem very savory and she put it out of her mind by reflecting that at least it was the police who were taking care of her, thanks to Sean's intervention.

Her thoughts were interrupted by Gerald speaking: "The Jaguar is no longer on our tail, Peter. It looks as if we don't have company after all."

"Shame—I'd have liked something exciting for a change."

"I wouldn't," remarked Eve, and at that the others laughed and the journey continued without further incident.

On reaching their destination, the car halted outside a pair of iron gates which opened on Peter the driver, identifying the car's occupants. Proceeding along a short driveway, they reached a large house and Betty, Eve and Gerald left the car. As the three of them walked towards the door, Eve noticed that they were under observation from an open window situated nearby. The door was opened by a uniformed officer from inside just as they reached it.

"Welcome to the Dorchester," said the officer, keeping a straight face. "I am the maitre d'hotel and hope that your stay in this salubrious establishment will be a happy one. I am delighted to be at your service. Call me Dave."

Eve found herself gazing at a powerful-looking man over six feet three inches tall of ruddy complexion, with a high-domed head and sparkling blue eyes.

"Don't take any notice of Dave, Eve," interjected Betty. "He only joined the force because his wife could not stand him at home."

"True. It's the wife you know. She drove me to it."

"OK, you two," Gerald joined in the conversation. "I expect Eve is tired and we'll need to register her and then Betty will show her to her room."

"Spoilsport," said Dave, and conducted Eve to a desk where he had a form of entry prepared and a register. He indicated the place for her and said, "Sign here, please. That is to indicate that you are now one of our honored guests. And may I call you Eve?"

As she wrote her signature Eve nodded at the request. "Of course you may call me Eve. I am not used to formality—thanks for making me feel at home."

Betty took Eve up a flight of stairs to a small bedroom which overlooked a lawn; beyond was a tall brick wall which had barbed wire placed in strands along the top. She felt that the place would be as difficult to leave as to enter.

On looking round the room she saw a single bed, a built-in wardrobe and a small dressing table. She was also surprised to see a small television set opposite the bed. A small washbasin mounted by a mirror stood beside the window. On the wall above the bed was a print of a the well-known Constable painting, *The Haywain*. Eve reflected on the lack of luxury, but it was better to live in Spartan surroundings rather than put up with the humiliating experiences she had endured at the Londinium Club.

"I am afraid I won't have anything to put in the wardrobe," she remarked to Betty.

"We have sleeping apparel and washing gear all ready for you, Eve," and she opened a drawer containing towels, a flannel and a nightdress. "I guess you won't look glamorous in the nightie, but it will keep you warm at night. There is also a toothbrush, toothpaste, shampoo and soap." She indicated a small cellophane packet. "If you will come this way I will show you the shower room and bathroom and toilet units; these are shared between two bedrooms."

Betty took Eve out into the corridor and indicated the respective rooms. "Perhaps you would like to tidy up and then come downstairs to the lounge which is the large room at to the right of the stairs. I'll see you down there. Oh, by the way, you will find a dressing gown in the wardrobe in your room." And with that parting shot, Betty left Eve and descended the stairs to the entrance hall.

On entering her room, Eve took off the wig and threw it on the bed. She then washed and used a few of the cosmetics she had managed to bring in her handbag. Luckily it was large, and contained some of the prized possessions that she knew would not be missed when her bedroom at Caria's was searched. As she applied lipstick, she wondered how long she would have to stay at the safe house and whether a new abode would be equally free from the fear of being caught by de Vere-Smythe, Parker or Bounce. She decided to ask Betty and went down to the lounge.

Betty was sitting in a comfortable armchair with a folder on her lap when Eve entered. She looked up and smiled. "You look smart, Eve. Come and sit here," and she indicated another armchair beside her. Eve sat down and relaxed, surveying her surroundings. The room was about thirty-five feet long by twenty- five feet wide. There were several armchairs with small occasional tables in between each. In one corner was a larger table with some magazines and newspapers on it. The room was light and airy and two pictures depicting English hunting scenes with foxhounds, red-coated riders and typical country landscape adorned a wall.

"How long will I be here, Betty?" asked Eve.

"Just a few days, I believe. This is a transit house and I think Dr. O'Neill is arranging for you to go somewhere else but I do not know where it is at the moment. However, while you are here I have to take a statement from you regarding your involvement with the Londinium Club. We would like you to give all the information you can about the activities there."

Eve looked at Betty and was silent for a moment. She thought about the kindness shown her by Caria and then of Tornilla. Then, recalling the brutality shown her by the man who had deflowered her and the Arab who had kicked her, stiffened her resolve. She launched into the story of how she had met Caria and how she had been tricked into working at the Club. Having a good memory, she omitted little detail and, after an hour, Betty, who had been taking notes, suggested a break.

"Time for tea, Eve. I expect your throat is parched after all that. We'll continue later. Come with me to the kitchen," and she led Eve out of the lounge along a corridor and entered the kitchen at the back of the building. As she made tea, Betty told Eve that Dr. O'Neill would probably visit her that evening. Eve was thrilled at the news and Betty noticed the brightening of Eve's expression, but made no comment.

"Do you take sugar and milk, Eve?" Eve shook her head and murmured, "No thank you, Betty." She thought of the tea Caria had given her, always strong and laced with sugar and milk, but she had always accepted it for fear of offending Caria.

Betty had put two cups, saucers, the teapot and a plate of biscuits on a tray when Sergeant Findlay entered the kitchen. "Only two cups?" he queried, looking at the tray. "Don't I get any elevenses?" Eve looked at him, initially taken in by his tone of voice, and then saw the twinkle in his eyes. She did not know what to make of him but as she got to know him better realized that behind his jocular approach lay a very shrewd and sharp mind. He also impressed her with the detailed knowledge he had of the area in which she was reared and of the small part of London that she knew.

They had left the kitchen and were sitting on the patio facing the lawn at the back of the house. Some sparrows had landed as soon as they sat down and Dave had immediately flicked them small pieces of biscuit. "Friendly little fellows, aren't they?" he commented as they hopped around chasing the tidbits, and as one hopped on to the table, he added, "This one is cheeky too; but it is all cupboard love." He flicked a crumb to the sparrow which grabbed it and then flew off with the trophy in its beak to consume it at what it must have regarded as a safer distance.

He started to talk to Eve, remarking that her accent indicated that she came from Yorkshire and suggested the area. At first Eve thought he had seen Betty's notes and then realized that Dave had had no opportunity to do so. It was then that she began to understand that his presence there was no coincidence. He spoke about having two daughters older than her and was obviously proud of them and of his wife. His jokes about being henpecked were obviously a facade. But with these revelations, he subtly extracted information from her about her life and family. All this was cleverly woven into his comments about places she knew. He was even knowledgeable about the areas in America where her brother lived and another hour had passed before Eve realized it.

Later that afternoon, Eve sat with Betty who spent two hours with her filling in details about her experiences at the Club and of the bombing in London, but this time they were in a small office on the ground floor where Betty sat at a word processor and typed out the information given her by Eve. At the end of the session, Betty went to the beginning of the notes and realized that Dave had entered all the relevant information about her he had gleaned during the morning break in the interim. He had not missed anything.

"You must read this carefully, Eve, and let me know if it is accurate. We are going to use some of this in a short statement about the Club and it may be used as evidence later. Dave will do that, and meantime, read carefully through and tell me if what we have is correct. We have another day or two, so if you think of anything you have missed, please let Dave know. I have to get back to my manor tomorrow although I shall stay here tonight, but he will be around to help you and will also prepare the statement."

Eve nodded, continued to read and could not think of anything to correct. Her experiences were all there in detail and she shuddered as she read of what she had gone through. Perhaps it was good therapy to see it all written down and, she reflected, maybe it would help her to get it out of her system.

"I can't think of anything more at the moment," she said to Betty who looked at her sympathetically. She replied, "It has not been the nicest of experiences for you, but it is now behind you, Eve. I think you have had enough for today so Dave will see you later tomorrow morning and you can read the final statement. Now it is time for a tea break and a walk round the grounds. Incidentally, there are other people here in transit but for security reasons mixing is not allowed. You understand?" Eve nodded.

Betty continued. "I'll be looking after you today and another woman PC will be with you tomorrow." Eve now realized why there was a television in her room for as the "guests" were to be kept apart, a communal television room would not be suitable. She also realized that with the facilities shared between two bedrooms, a police officer would be occupying the other room. The idea made her feel a prisoner once again, but she shook it off and perked up at the thought of seeing Sean. And see him that evening she did. It was approaching eight o'clock in the evening when Sean arrived at Haven House, as it was referred to by Inspector Rodney Blanchard who had issued him with a permit to be admitted. On his admittance, the officer on duty had phoned the inspector who asked to speak to Sean. He explained that he had requested the staff to take a statement from Eve for future use regarding the Londinium Club, and that he looked forward to Richard letting him know as soon as possible if his cousin would take Eve. He requested that Sean hand the phone to the duty officer when their conversation terminated. And to this request Sean complied.

"OK, Constable Healey, he is Dr. Sean O'Neill all right, he's genuine. You can take him to see Eve Eden," and with that rang off.

"If you would be good enough to come this way, sir, you will find Miss Eden in the visitors' room," and he led Sean through a corridor to a small room in which were placed several armchairs. Eve stood up when he entered and blushed a little when the officer announced that Dr. O'Neill had come to see her. "Will you please report to the office before you depart, sir," the officer said as he left the room.

Eve felt a thrill of pleasure as Sean took both of her hands in his. She looked tired but very beautiful, he thought, and he, too, felt a quickening of his pulse as their fingers touched.

"I hope they are looking after you here?" he queried, feeling a little foolish at the question. He had several things to say to Eve but he found her presence somewhat disquieting. The doctor-patient relationship was uppermost in his thoughts but he felt it slipping away as he looked into her beautiful, expressive lavender-blue eyes. Her blonde hair fell down to her shoulders in luxuriant folds and her very movements had the grace of a gazelle. The realization that she had slept with other men disturbed him. To him with his strict Catholic upbringing, that made her seem unclean although he realized that she had not been directly responsible for that mistake in her life. As a Christian he knew that he should forgive her for what amounted to a sin in Catholic eyes. Had not Christ washed the feet of a prostitute? If his savior could forgive so could he, but he still felt a pang of jealousy that other men had used Eve.

That feeling was silly, he tried to reason; he had no claim on Eve. The idea of falling in love with a prostitute no matter how reluctant she had been, appalled him. Yet she was no longer one and he felt he was being drawn to her by an irresistible power over which he had no control. He forced himself to think more clearly when Eve spoke to him in her gentle voice.

"Everyone here has been very kind. I really feel safe, thanks to you. I shall never be able to thank you enough. You have no idea just how wonderful it is to feel free and away from that . . . " She paused at the recollection. "I . . . I just cannot thank you enough, Sean."

"Eve, I was unable to meet my cousin tonight, but will do so tomorrow evening. I am hoping you will be able to stay at his home for a while. He lives in the country and the chances of you being found there are very remote; you should be safe and will have a chance to recover from your ordeal."

Sean had managed to get his main message over to her and, as he spoke, looking at her lovely face, a thought entered his mind that made his heart beat faster than normal. As it surfaced to consciousness it drowned out what he had intended to say, and he stopped speaking.

Eve sensed that something was on his mind and also felt unable to talk. She knew she was filled with gratitude for what he had done and intended to do for her, but at the same time she felt a little frightened. The men who used her had made her mistrustful of men generally, although she knew that was silly. She had been used and abused by men, and deep down was frightened of experiencing such humiliation again. And she felt unclean.

Eve sincerely wished she had never allowed herself to be persuaded to be a "hostess." Hostess! What a corruption of the word. "Hooker," or, more accurately, "whore" was more appropriate. It was a vile occupation and negated all the values her parents and grandmother had taught her. They valued family life and it had worked well for them all. They had been poor but had found great happiness as a family. If only she could marry someone who really cared for her and experience family happiness again it would be wonderful. But what decent man would want to marry an ex-harlot—a woman who had prostituted her body for financial gain?

With her experience, the idea of a sexual relationship sickened her and the memory of prying, unwanted hands made her shudder. She was grateful to Sean for her salvation from her unpleasant situation and also felt stirrings of an emotion deeper than sheer animal desire, but the idea of her emotions taking hold of her frightened her. And, in any case, if she should give way to them, would he reciprocate? Was it not possible that the intimations of deeper feeling towards him were only the start of infatuation and not love? Eve decided to keep these stirrings within her in check, but she could not hide her genuine feeling of gratitude.

Then the implications of what Sean had said suddenly entered her mind. "Did you say I would be staying with a cousin of yours?"

"Yes."

"Has he a family?"

"Why, yes. There are three children in the family. Jean is the eldest daughter. I think she is ten years old. John is two years younger and Jennifer is two years younger than John. They are lovely people and the children are very well behaved." Then he added as an afterthought, "Perhaps that is not surprising for Dawn, Richard's wife, is a schoolteacher. I think you will like them all, especially Jennifer. She is a little pickle."

Eve felt her spirits rise at the thought of being with a family again, albeit not her own. She had felt loneliness since her brother had to return to the USA, despite the enforced company she'd had to keep.

"Do you think they will mind me staying with them for a while?"

"That is what I have to find out tomorrow night."

Eve suddenly looked crestfallen as a thought struck her.

"I only have a few hundred pounds saved. As they live in a village, the chances of finding a job would not be very good. I experienced that in Yorkshire. I could not impose on them and want to pay my way. I did think of going to America but I understand they have a lot of unemployment there, and my brother told me that it takes about a year to become a resident alien and get a work permit."

"Yes, I have read that in the big cities there is a great deal of poverty and also danger."

Sean reflected on what he had said. He realized that he did not want Eve to leave the country. The more he thought about the idea the more he wanted her to stay and see more of her. He knew his cousin would help shelter her, at least for a little while and that was his immediate concern. The other thought he experienced intruded and it made his pulse quicken, but the idea needed thinking through, for Eve might not agree. He dismissed it for the moment.

"We must see about work of course, but at least for the time you will be with them, you can get some social security benefits to go toward your keep."

Sean glanced at his watch. "I had better be going now. I have a very busy day tomorrow. You relax here and leave the worrying to me. I am sure I can get something arranged for you, even if it is on a short-term basis."

They stood up simultaneously and Sean took both Eve's hands in his. He felt an urge to kiss her but resisted it.

"Take care, Eve. God bless and I feel I'll have some good news for you tomorrow night."

"I'll keep my fingers crossed. And thank you again, Sean."

He walked to the door and suddenly turned as an afterthought struck him. "Come to think of it, you won't know until the following morning. I am not allowed to have the telephone number here. Inspector Blanchard will let you know, so I guess you will have to be patient again. Still, patience is a virtue." And at that, with a wave of a hand, he left the room.

Eve stood and watched him go with feelings of gratitude. She, too, had felt an urge to kiss him, but also held herself in check. However, she had thrilled at the touch of his hands and she realized that his interest in her was more than a patient-doctor relationship. She was excited at the thought of staying with his cousin's family, but at the same time somewhat apprehensive; she would relax and be patient as he had advised. He had mentioned that patience was a virtue and she could certainly be patient when necessary. Then the thought struck her: virtue! At first she felt like laughing. She had certainly lost her virtue. And then the implications of that changed her mood into one of bitterness and sadness and she went to her room feeling depressed.

■ ◻ ■ ◻ ■

Richard drove home the following evening; he had enjoyed the meal with Sean. It was good to see him again and he always liked his company. He recalled how he had encouraged him to go to medical school and had attended the celebration in Ireland when Sean had graduated. He was fond of Sean's mother and sister Morag, but his two stepbrothers, Morgan and Eamon, were not so pleasant. They were like Sean's stepfather—bigoted Catholics and very anti-British. They were also very critical of their own government for their cooperating with the British to find a solution to the Northern Irish problem.

He thought over Sean's request for temporary asylum for his patient, Eve Eden. He felt that Sean's interest in her was not just professional and on those grounds had decided to help. However, his wife Dawn and the children were to be considered. With Dawn teaching they needed an au pair, for a friend was collecting the children from school and it was not always convenient. Both Dawn and he were very busy with their respective professions, having someone living in to help with the housework and look after the children would be ideal.

When he arrived home, Richard explained Sean's request to Dawn. "It sounds as if he is in love with her," had been Dawn's first reaction to the proposal.

They had discussed the implications while both were undressing for bed and continued when lying down, while Richard had an arm around Dawn and she rested her head on his shoulder.

"As criminals are looking for her, is there not considerable risk for the children, let alone us?"

"I gather very little. Apparently the police are keeping an eye on the activities of the people who run the Club and they are still collecting evidence to take action and eventually arrest them. It would appear that Eve has only to lie low for a month or two and the police will be in a position to put them out of circulation."

The idea of an ex-prostitute lying low in her home did not appeal to Dawn and she said so to Richard. He chuckled at the unintended pun.

"Full marks for that one. But joking aside, I understand she was coerced into that occupation and was trying to escape from it when she was injured in the recent IRA bomb blast in the city. She was desperate to get away."

Dawn lay quiet for a few minutes. Having another woman in the house and an ex-prostitute at that was not a happy situation. And the knowledge that criminals were after her added another more dangerous element to the whole thing. On the other hand, she, too, liked Sean and, as did Richard, wanted to help him. If the girl turned out to be nice it would suit them to have her help in the home.

Richard took her left hand in his and pulled her closer with his right arm on which she was lying. She snuggled up closer and gave his hand a squeeze and made up her mind.

"I feel we must show compassion to this girl. Certainly she does not appear to have anyone else to turn to in this country. Let us take her on for a month or so and see how we all get on."

Richard paused before replying. "Are you sure?"

"Yes. Just imagine being in her position. I think we should help."

"I suppose you are right. I'll phone Sean first thing in the morning and put him in the picture. It is possible the girl will arrive tomorrow or the following day. I wonder how the children will react," he added as an afterthought. Dawn did not reply, for her doubts had returned, but having uttered her decision to Richard, felt she could not revoke it. Had she known the eventual outcome of her decision she would never have made it. It was the one decision in their lives that they would both live to regret.

chapter seven

Eve struggled . . . her heart pounded, her frantic breathing making strangled noises in her throat with each exhalation as she tried to scream. She felt herself being forced down as she fought against the weight of the man on top of her holding her. She smelled the obnoxious odor of the sweat from his jerking body. His leering red face hovered above hers and the horn-shaped hemangioma on his forehead seemed to be growing until it extended to a single horn on each side of his head. Then she felt pain inside her as his devil's forked tail penetrated her and twisted around and around, carving up her very entrails.

Eve emitted moaning sounds and, flailing her arms, tried to beat the devil off. She felt a blow on her body which jerked her out of her nightmare and she realized that she had struck herself in her sleep. It was that dreadful dream again and she wished it would go away, but she knew, or rather perhaps hoped, that in time it would recede in her memory never to return.

Eve sat up, her nightgown damp with perspiration. She ran her fingers through her hair and, feeling wide-awake, rose, slid her feet into her slippers, walked towards the open casement window and gulped in the fresh air. The night was warm and she looked down into the garden which was clearly visible in every detail in the moonlight.

It was a large garden. The patio, paved with York stone, extended between the two wings of the house and a low stone wall separated it from the lawn. There were three exits from the patio and columns at the end of the walls flanked each one of them. On the top of the columns were stone flower pots from which fuchsias overflowed to form graceful patterns. From the central gap in the wall a paved path led to a circular swimming pool around which grew periwinkle. Beyond that, the lawn stretched some three hundred feet to a bank of shrubs behind which the copse could be clearly seen. On the right of the copse was a large weeping willow, and to the right side of this a small group of shrubs concealed another patio.

Eve looked along the left side of the garden in line with the swimming pool. Along the edge of the lawn in front of a tall hedge of lawsoniana was a row of statues, each on a stone pedestal and which looked almost alive in the moonlight. Eve recalled the names of the statues about which the children had informed her. The first was Pandora, and there was a box at her feet to comply with the legend that from Pandora's box all the evils of the world have sprung. She wondered if people like Parker and de Vere-Smythe had originated from that box.

Next in line was Hebe, the cupbearer of the gods. She smiled to herself as the thought that Bacchus must have made good use of her services and no doubt many of the members of the Londinium Club as well. Next was a statue of Botticelli's *Venus Rising From the Waves* with the large seashell just behind her. Jennifer had giggled saying that the statue should be called "botty chilly" only to receive a stern look from Jean and a giggle from John. The last in line was a statue of Eve with an apple held in her right hand. Jennifer had commented on the statue having Eve's name and she and John had giggled again, only to be chastised by Jean who had told her not to be rude.

It was fun living at the home of the Rutherfords. The children made her feel young for they were so full of life. Eve could hardly believe that she had been there for five weeks. She recalled the day when the police had brought her. They had been dressed in casual clothes and they drove a small BMC City car. They had taken great care to ensure that they were not followed and had driven through many country roads to foil any possible pursuers. Eve had found the journey most confusing but the driver obviously knew the terrain well. Dawn Rutherford had been at the home ready to greet her. She had shown great hospitality to the officers and given them tea before they left.

Dawn was a tall chestnut-haired woman, almost six feet in height and her lissome figure moved with grace. She had a high forehead and Junoesque features. Her beautiful brown eyes were kindly and yet she had an air of authority which made Eve feel somewhat nervous at first meeting. Although she had made Eve and the officers welcome it was not until the latter had departed that Eve felt more at ease. Dawn had taken both Eve's hands in hers and, looking her straight in the eyes said, "I want you to feel at home here, Eve. I understand you are a special friend of Sean's and he is very special to Richard and me. We also respect his judgment and I feel his, in your case, is correct. You will be safe here and we hope your stay will be a happy one. I believe you know we need an au pair, so you will be earning your keep and will be able to feel independent. Although an au pair is an employee, we want you to feel one of the family."

Eve looked at the last statue and recalled the words: "Feel one of the family." The Rutherfords had certainly made her feel a welcome member. They could not have been more kind and considerate. At the same time, her independence was respected and this meant a great deal to her. And she could drive. She had started driving lessons the second week she was there and had passed her driving test only three days ago. This was both pleasing for her and an essential part of her job, for Jean was attending a private school situated some half-hour from the home and, as part of Eve's duties was to take the children to and from school, the use of a car was essential. At the moment, a friend took the children to school but she was moving from the village and Eve had arrived at a timely moment.

During the five weeks at Bracken, Eve and the family got to know each other better and they found that they all got on well. Eve was impressed with the good manners of the children and yet they were in no way cowed into obedience. As Sean had told her, Jennifer was a little pickle. She was quite a tomboy and her eyes would twinkle roguishly as she dreamed up one of her mischievous ideas. She spoke with a slight lisp and this added to her attractiveness.

Eve got an insight into Jennifer's wit when Jennifer was showing Eve her white mice. There were two which were kept in a small cage in the garage. Jennifer had picked up one mouse and, on handing it to Eve, said its name was Castor. Then she had picked up the other saying its name was Pollux and stood stroking it. Eve, being country-born had no fear of mice and petted the pretty creatures quite happily. Jennifer had hoped that Eve would be scared of them and was disappointed. However, she thought of something to say: "Do they smell, Eve?"

"No," said Eve, quite honestly, for the cage was kept scrupulously clean.

"If they don't smell, then what are their noses for?"

"Caught me there didn't you, Jennifer!" at which Jennifer giggled.

"Is it true that black cats are lucky, Eve?" Jennifer asked innocently. Eve decided to humor Jennifer and so replied, "Yes, I think so," at which Jennifer asked, "How does one explain that to a mouse?"

One evening the family was in the music room. Each of the children was learning to play the piano and another instrument. Jean played the violin, John the cello and Jennifer the recorder. On this occasion, Eve was again acquainted with Jennifer's wit. Jean had earlier chastised Jennifer who decided to get her own back. When Jean had played a passage rather poorly, Jennifer said, "You play like the Emperor Nero."

"What do you mean by that?" asked Jean.

"It was because he played so badly that the citizens burned Rome."

"Very funny," said Jean, temporarily caught off guard. Eve looked at Dawn who was sitting at the piano, wondering how she would react. Dawn acknowledged her look with a twinkle in her eyes and said, "Come on, Jean, I think I played the accompaniment too fast. Let's try again and I'll play a little slower this time." To Eve's surprise the ploy worked, and Jean gave Jennifer a "so there" look when they had finished.

The way Dawn handled the children interested Eve who felt that if she ever had children of her own she would bring them up the same way. Most Saturday evenings were spent as a family in the music room. Richard was usually home and took part, playing the viola. When he had Saturday free during the summer they would go sailing, but for Eve that pleasure was yet to come.

During the first weekend at Bracken, Sean arrived on the Saturday afternoon and stayed until the Sunday evening. He participated in the musical evenings by singing Irish songs accompanied by Dawn or Richard on the piano. He had a beautiful tenor voice and it reminded Eve of some old recordings her parents had of an Irish singer named John McCormac. He sang with such feeling that when he, accompanied by Richard, sang "Killarney," it brought tears to her eyes and she had to turn her head and look out on to the garden to attempt to dab her eyes without being seen. It was then that she realized that Sean was a man of deep feeling and she was falling in love with him. She went to bed that night thinking that her world was turning upside down and that emotionally she had been knocked sideways.

The following day, it being Sunday, the family went to the local Anglican church. She was later to learn that Richard was agnostic and Dawn too had serious doubts about religion. However, both the parents felt it right to have their children exposed to the religious experience as part of their education, and church attendance with its fellowship was good for their social development. It also made them think beyond themselves and feel part of the village community. The children were not unaware of their parents' views but only Jean fully understood them. Eve did not have to attend, but decided to go with them as she felt she was participating more in the family life. Apart from that, she enjoyed the singing which recalled the pleasanter memories of her childhood. It was on hearing Eve sing in church that Dawn encouraged her to participate in the musical evenings; first, joining in choruses and later in harmony, duos and solo singing when she had more confidence. She had a sweet soprano voice and she found herself so happy at the house that she would often sing while carrying out her household chores.

Sean did not accompany them to church. Being a Catholic, he attended mass at the local Catholic church situated in the nearest town two miles away. He was very sincere in his beliefs but he respected his cousin for his own views, believing in Christian tolerance and the right for everyone to find his or her own approach to God. He was very fond of the children and would romp and play with them whenever the opportunity occurred. He was waiting for the family that Sunday when they returned from the church service. Jennifer ran up to him and jumped into his arms. He caught her under the armpits with both hands and swung her round and round.

"My word, Jennifer. I won't be able to do this for very long; you are getting too big and heavy!"

"Yes, she is getting as heavy as a suet pudding," said John, at which Jennifer pulled a face at him.

"What did you learn in church today, Jennifer?" Sean interjected, diplomatically changing the subject. Jennifer paused for a second and then retorted, "We had a sermon on Moses."

"Did you now. And what did you learn from that?"

"The Lord said unto Moses, 'Come forth'—but he came fifth and got a rubber duck."

"I don't believe a word of it," said Sean and he swung Jennifer off her feet and made her squeal with delight.

Eve watched them and found her feeling for Sean deepening uncontrollably. But it was not until his second visit to the Rutherford home that she discovered whether or not he would reciprocate her ripening love for him.

That afternoon following Sunday lunch, John asked Sean to see his train set. Sean did not need a second bidding and he, Richard and John were soon engrossed in making the most of the opportunity. It was a large layout, set on a table in the children's playroom. Richard, aided by John, had constructed a double-track gauge "OO" which had sidings, stations, tunnels and bridges. The set was most realistic and Dawn, Jean and Jennifer had painted a small backdrop with mountains and sky to add to the realism.

While the three were engaged with the set, Eve and Dawn walked in and Dawn remarked to Eve, "Men never grow up."

At this remark, Richard looked up with a twinkle in his eyes and said, "Yes, Eve, men never grow up. But I would add that a man is mature when he knows it, and a woman is mature not only when she knows it but when she makes allowances for it."

Dawn laughed and, walking over to him, gave him a kiss and said, "Quite right. Here's a kiss for my big boy." Richard kissed her back, remarking, "And here's one for my big girl."

Both Eve and Sean had watched the incident and he looked at her and smiled. Eve suddenly felt herself feeling self-conscious and blushed. Richard, noticing her embarrassment, was about to say something, but thinking the better of it, drew his attention back to the train set and spoke to John. They decided to take one of the engines into a siding and couple it to some goods wagons, and were soon engaged in pressing switches on the control box.

Dawn had noticed Eve's discomfiture and, letting go Richard's hand, walked over to Eve. "We won't interrupt their fun any longer, Eve. Let us go and prepare tea; we'll have it on the patio."

"Can I help?" said Jean. "Me, too!" Jennifer added, not wanting to be left out, and the four of them walked outside to the patio and started to arrange the patio furniture for tea. Jean had said, "I have a joke to tell you, Eve" and Jennifer had interrupted by saying, "Let me tell it, Jean?"

"No," Jean retorted. "It's my joke, not yours."

"I'm listening, Jean," said Eve, hoping it was not to be as corny as some of the jokes Jennifer had told her.

"Did you know that Donald Duck has been hanged and is now in a state of suspended animation?"

"Oh, no," Eve replied, and then quickly suggested they get the table laid before any more leaves from the children's bumper fun book were repeated to her. But secretly she was very glad that the children accepted her so readily.

Standing at the bedroom, Eve recalled how her heart had pounded when she waved good-bye to Sean. She knew he was coming for another visit the following Saturday afternoon and Sunday. The week had passed by very slowly although she had been kept very busy. She could hardly wait for Sean to arrive, but when he did had found it difficult to speak to him. He had arrived in the early evening and Eve and Jean had helped Dawn with preparing the meal and laying the table on the patio. Richard was busy barbecuing salmon. Sean had greeted Eve by holding one of her hands and said, "How is everything going, Eve?" She had answered his question calmly enough, saying that she was very happy to be at the house and added, "Thanks to you."

"Eve, there is something I want to say to you," but at that point they were interrupted by Jennifer who ran up to Sean, not having seen him enter earlier. "Hallo, Uncle Sean," she lisped, and flung her arms round him. He gave her a hug and replied, "And how is my little mischief?"

Jennifer held a hand each of Eve's and Sean's and swung between them as they lifted her playfully. "Have you heard this poem?" she asked, but before they could reply launched into: "Humpty Dumpty sat on the wall, Humpty Dumpty had a great fall, all the king's horses and all the king's men had scrambled eggs for the next four weeks." She then burst into peals of laughter while Sean and Eve smiled to each other, realizing that the message would have to wait until dinner was over.

It was pleasant on the patio, sitting in comfortable chairs and looking down into the beautiful garden. Eve enjoyed the dinner but her mind kept straying to Sean's previous remarks and she wondered somewhat apprehensively, what he had to say. He, too, seemed a little preoccupied and both Richard and Dawn guessed that Sean and Eve wanted some time alone. With the meal over and the dishes cleared away, they took the children into the music room suggesting they play a quintette.

Eve and Sean strolled down the garden, stopping at the pond situated halfway down to admire some dragonflies that were busy hunting gnats. He took Eve's hand while they stood and watched the goldfish dart under cover as their shadows fell on the water. Their tails could just be seen beneath the water lilies and Sean remarked, "I guess they are wise to the herons. Maybe we should stop frightening them and go a little further." They walked hand-in-hand beyond the graceful weeping willow beside the pond, and then crossed the lawn passing the gazebo and red stone patio on which it was placed. The gazebo was facing the house and, wanting complete privacy, Sean led Eve to the patio that lay hidden near the end of the garden.

It was a lovely May evening, calm and clear and the reddening sky to the west presaged a picturesque sunset. They sat on a stone bench with their backs to an ornamental stone wall which abutted the side of the garden. The patio was a raised area paved with flagstones. It was about twenty feet square and the other three sides were made of a low stone columnar wall with the entrance being formed by a gap in the wall facing them. There were two other benches on each side adjacent to the side walls and in the center was a solid stone urn on a pedestal that put Eve in mind of a church font. Adjacent to each side wall, shrubs grew to a height of seven feet and these gave complete privacy to each side. To the front was the second weeping willow at the edge of the copse, consisting of silver birches, laburnum, lilac, copper maples, beech and other deciduous trees.

"It is very beautiful here," said Eve, breaking the silence.

"Yes. And you add to the beauty, Eve," said Sean, squeezing Eve's hand. Then he looked at her and, taking both of her hands in his, said, "Eve, I love you and want you to marry me. But before you reply, please listen to what I have to say."

Eve had been about to speak but he put two fingers to her lips and she remained silent but felt he could hear her pounding heart.

"You know I am a Catholic, Eve, and if you agree to become my wife, I would like you to become a Catholic too. That is not as easy as it sounds, for I feel you should have instruction in the faith so that you really understand what it is all about. When you understand it, then you would become a member of the true faith through your own volition. That means you would accept the faith because you sincerely believe in it and not just because you were to marry me."

They both sat silent for many minutes while Eve thought over what Sean had said. His proposal had made her feel happier beyond her wildest dreams but there were two things she wanted to clarify in her mind before replying. Firstly, she was uncertain about adopting his faith and, secondly, she wondered if her recent occupation would bring doubts about his love for her later, assuming they married. Eve released her hand from his, stood up and walked to the font-like urn. He thought how beautiful she looked and could observe that she needed silence to think upon his proposal. Perhaps he was asking too much, he felt, but his faith made sense out of life for him and he had never questioned it.

She stood with her hands on the urn, wondering how to tell him of her doubts. The patio walls became bathed in a crimson glow from the splendor of the sunset. The silence was broken by a blackbird singing nearby and a cuckoo could be heard in the distance. Two house martins darted overhead busily engaged in catching their evening meal. Sean watched them until they disappeared and then looked back at Eve who, sensing his eyes on her, turned toward him with tears in her eyes.

He stood up and walked the few steps towards her and held her in his arms.

"What is it, darling?" he asked.

Eve responded to his embrace and held him close. "I love you and I want nothing in the world more than to be your wife, but I am frightened that what I foolishly agreed to do might later come between us and spoil everything. I am more than willing to learn about your faith and for me it is no problem, but the other thing makes me feel afraid, for the thought of what I had to go through makes me feel unclean."

Sean released his arms around her, stepped back and putting a hand on each of her shoulders looked her straight in the eyes. Her beautiful, appealing eyes made his pulse quicken and convinced him that her past would not affect his deep feeling for her.

"Eve, there is such a thing as Christian forgiveness, and if you embrace the faith I am sure you will get dispensation, and then you will be able to feel whole and pure again. We are all guilty of sin at times, if not in our actions then often in our thoughts. If you are really willing then you will make me happier than I shall ever be able to express. Whatever your reply, Eve, I love you and always shall."

He felt her moving closer to him and he put his arms around her once more. Eve again held him tight, kissed him and said in a trembling voice, "Oh Sean, the answer is yes."

The sun slowly sank in glorious golden splendor as they unhurriedly walked back to the house, feeling as if they were already united as one person and living in paradise.

It was three days later on the following Tuesday that the Catholic priest came to visit Eve. She had returned from taking the children to school when the telephone rang. Eve did not answer it, for Richard had suggested she first let all calls be recorded on the answerphone. If she knew the caller then she could answer back and there would be no risk of a chance caller recognizing her voice and tracing her to the house. Richard had pointed out that no one knew she was there and the chances of her being traced to that address by telephone was very remote, however, it was wise to remove all chances of detection.

The priest who had telephoned on the Monday responded to the recorded message. Sean had spoken to him after mass on Sunday and he had enthusiastically agreed to arrange for Eve to receive instruction in Roman Catholicism. Eve had not known what sort of person to expect and was pleasantly surprised to open the door to a fatherly looking man in his fifties who looked surprisingly young for his age. Father Brendan had an engaging smile and a good sense of humor and had put Eve at ease from the moment he introduced himself at the door.

"Hello. Eve Eden, I presume? I am Father Patrick Brendan." They had shaken hands and he entered the house at her bidding.

Eve realized that he was a sincere man who had an air about him which she could only describe as spiritual. They sat in the lounge drinking tea while he explained the course of instruction that he had prepared for her; as it was to last three months, Eve could not help immediately thinking that she and Sean could then be married on September or October at the latest. With effort, she forced her mind back to the arrangements for the instruction. She would go to the local town and attend at the Catholic church hall. There she would meet other people who were receiving instruction in the faith; this would be once a week and would take place on a Thursday for two hours in the morning. She would also receive a written course of lessons which she was to read at home and any questions arising from the course would be dealt with during her weekly visits. He also expected her to attend mass to observe.

Eve was willing to do all this and the prospect of attending mass with Sean filled her with joy. He would be able to come to Bracken three Sundays out of four. During the fourth Sunday, he was on standby duty at the practice. As if reading her thoughts, Father Brendan studied Eve's face and said, "You know, Eve, acceptance of the Roman Catholic faith all hinges upon your sincere belief in God. You understand that?"

Eve nodded and realized that it was a serious matter that would require much thought- and soul-searching. From that moment, she resolved to do all she could to achieve her goal.

Eve listened carefully to all he said and entered the dates in her diary. She was pleased that there would be no interference with her household duties and there would be no clash of times with her taking the children to and from school. Of course, they would be on holiday from the third week in July until the end of August, but Dawn would also be at home and so there should be no problem of the children being left alone. Eve had put the matter to Dawn who had expressed full agreement with Eve's arrangements.

"You have a beautiful place here," Father Brendan said at the end of the meeting, looking down the garden.

"Yes," said Eve. "Only it is not mine. I only wish it were. It belongs to Richard Rutherford, the ophthalmic surgeon and his wife, Dawn. She is teaching."

Father Brendan thought for a moment and remarked, "Oh yes. Mr. Rutherford is a consultant at Westcliff Hospital, Chelmsbridge and Colnford."

He watched two wood pigeons land on the lawn and then a jay with its brown body and blue and white wing feathers brilliant in the morning sunlight. "Such lovely creatures and such a lovely place. There is an air of happiness as well as beauty here—that is a rare combination."

He paused and remained silent for a moment and then smiled at Eve. She both saw and felt his gaze upon her and the impression of an aura of spirituality again made itself manifest to her. Is that what is called being blessed with the grace of God, she wondered?

"Well, time to go I am afraid. I shall see you on Thursday, Eve." She showed him to the door and they shook hands on parting. What an extraordinary man, she thought, as she watched him enter his car, wave good-bye and exit the driveway. She had felt quite happy with the idea of studying Roman Catholicism under his guidance. And the course on which she had started was easy to follow. The term Catholic had come from the Greek word "Katholikos" meaning universal, and she understood that it could be traced to the early period of Christianity when there was only one Christian church.

This unity was not to last long, however, for from the fourth century onwards, various ecclesiastical schisms developed which split the original unity into different factions, the Eastern Orthodox Church being one of them. The largest church retained the identification of the term "Catholic," adding Roman as it acknowledged the supremacy of the Pope, the Bishop of Rome.

She knew from her own religious experience and knowledge that Christianity was the largest of the world religions with more than a billion adherents. Father Brendan had mentioned that her acceptance of, and admittance to, the faith depended upon her belief in God. She also realized that with it came belief in Jesus Christ being the resurrected Son of God and Messiah. This would require commitment on her part but she realized that she could not honestly commit herself unless she had unswerving faith in the teachings of the church.

Eve must have been standing at the bedroom window for some time, for she suddenly noticed that the shadows from the statues had lengthened. While reflecting on the crowded events of the last five weeks she had been staring at one of the statues. She felt a little cold and shivered, for the night air was getting cooler. She diverted her gaze from the statue and looked onto the pathway leading from the end of the garden and jumped in surprise. A figure was standing there, looking ghostly in the moonlight.

chapter eight

"Come in, please," de Vere-Smythe had called out in response to the knock on his door. As Caria entered, he rose to his feet. "Ah, Caria, good of you to come," he said in his cultured voice, indicating a chair in front of his desk. "Please sit down." Caria sat and surveyed the room with its rich oak paneling and comfortable yet business-like furnishings. Then she glanced out of the window at the garden and river before looking at de Vere-Smythe's face. He had been scrutinizing her intently since she first entered the room, but his discrete mode of observation would not have been detected by an onlooker.

"I expect you know why I have requested your company, Caria?" It was more of a statement than a question the way he put it.

"Yus, Mr. de Vere-Smyve," Caria replied. "It's abaht Eve bein' gorn ain't it."

If de Vere-Smythe inwardly winced at the mispronunciation of his name he did not show it. "I would like you to put me in the picture on everything you know about our missing hostess, Eve. I am aware that Mr. Parker has already discussed her disappearance with you, but I would appreciate firsthand information from you yourself."

Caria had expected this and had prepared her story with care. She knew that Eve would meet with an "accident" once her whereabouts were discovered. Caria had a soft spot for Eve and did not want her killed. Oddly, she felt a motherly attitude towards her, not because of Eve's age, for Caria was only a few years older than her, but because of Eve's obvious inexperience of the world. At the same time she did not want to risk her own life and knew that if she concealed anything and was found out later, then her savings would not even be used for her funeral expenses. She had carefully thought over the information Eve had given her during their odd conversations. There was only one fact that she felt it necessary to conceal and that was the existence of Eve's brother. The chances that Eve had confided in anyone else at the Londinium Club were nil. Eve had not liked the work she did and although she had been kind to Tornilla, she had never confided in him. She had disliked the other prostitutes, so Caria was sure that only she knew that Eve had a brother in the USA.

He had written once to her as Caria had seen the USA address on the envelope when she handed the letter to Eve. She had wondered if Eve was on her way to stay with him and, if she kept that piece of intelligence from her interrogator, then Eve would have a chance of staying alive. She only hoped that Eve would somehow contact him and ensure that he did not send another letter to her address. She would have to keep an eye open for the mail in case Parker discovered any correspondence. However, she felt Eve would be smart enough to take action and prevent her brother writing there again.

"I understand Eve lived in Yorkshire before she came here?"

"Yus. She grew up on a farm. 'Er farver woz a farm 'and. 'E and Eve's mum got drahned in the Zeebrugge Ferry disaster. Bleedin' shime fer the poor kid that woz. She lived wiv 'er granny 'arter that. Then 'er gran' kicked the bucket an' Eve came up ter London ter find work."

De Vere-Smythe listened patiently. He was fully aware of all the information Caria had just imparted to him. He was waiting for an opportunity to ascertain any leads as to Eve's whereabouts.

"What about her brothers and sisters?"

Caria was fully prepared for that question and answered, "I didn't know she 'ad any; if she did she never told me." She paused, "But she did tell me she 'as a cuzzin."

"A cousin! Now that is most interesting; and where does the cousin live?"

"I ain't gotta clue. She did live in New'am an' Eve wrote to 'er there, but when Eve fahnd 'er 'ahse some Injuns or Pakistanis woz livin' there. They 'ad no idea where the cuzzin 'ad gorn and tol' Eve ter 'oppit. That's 'ow we met arter."

De Vere-Smythe was aware of the circumstances of the meeting and had no wish to pursue that aspect of Eve's history. Attempting to find the cousin would be a fruitless effort as no forwarding address had been left in her Newham—or had it?

"Did you know her cousin's address in Newham?"

Caria shook her head. "Nah, I do know that she 'ad wrote to 'er and woz given the letter back by the woman wot took over the cuzzin's 'ahse. Maybe she left the letter in the flat."

De Vere-Smythe knew that Parker had carefully searched Eve's room and had found no correspondence of any kind. Eve had certainly covered her tracks well.

"Did you know her address in Yorkshire?"

"Nah. I know she 'ad a cahncil flat in a village near York. But that's abaht all I kin tell yer."

De Vere-Smythe was afraid it was and concluded that Caria was telling the truth. He would contact Boss again and suggest the inquiries be made in Yorkshire. No doubt her previous address could be traced by contacting the local Department of Health and

Social Security, employment offices, or a look at church records, but it would take time. For the moment, there appeared to be no alternative and he politely terminated the interview and courteously escorted Caria to the door.

It was later in the day that he spoke to Boss and informed him of the situation. Boss had listened carefully to all de Vere-Smythe had to tell him and he, too, concluded that the best way of tracing her was to start in Yorkshire. There was also the possibility that she had returned there as it was territory she was familiar with, but this was unlikely. He decided to send Parker to carry out the inquiries in Yorkshire. Parker knew as much about Eve as anyone else and he could be relied on to take any initiative that was necessary. He knew that the small town or village was not far from the city of York itself and this would narrow the field of inquiry.

At the same time he would send Ma Donna Ke Babe to Somerset House, the government records office, to find the village in which Eve had lived. While she was there it might be possible to ascertain if she had any relatives. He arranged for Parker to phone Ma the evening he arrived in York; that should give her enough time for her part in the investigation. The following day, while Ma went to Somerset House, Parker was on his way to York with instructions to get any information that would provide a lead as to the possible whereabouts of Eve.

■ ◻ ■ ◻ ■

Parker hummed to himself as he drove along the country road. He had left the motorway and was glad to get out of the high speed traffic. He enjoyed sleuthing or "sloofin" as he termed it. He had always found pleasure in looking into other people's business and at school had been nicknamed "Nosey Parker," not without some justification. In his fantasies he had considered himself another Sherlock Holmes. He read Conan Doyle's works avidly and had applied the lessons of observation to his many nefarious activities to his profit. One of the reasons why Boss retained his services was because he recognized Parker's skills in ferreting out information and, on this occasion, Parker was the best man for the job.

Parker chuckled to himself at the jokes he had told Caria and Taika at the Londinium Club the day before. The humor was not always in the best of taste but that appealed to both Caria and Taika.

"Did yer 'ear abaht the girl in a' orffice who woz tellin 'er friend abaht 'er Guvnor?"

Both hostesses had shaken their heads in anticipation.

"Well, this girl said ter 'er mate, 'My boss knows a lot o dirty songs.'"

"'Coo,' sez 'er mate. 'Don't sing 'm in the orffice does 'e?'"

"'Nah, course not. 'E whistles 'em.'"

The appreciative laughter of the two girls was matched by the puzzled look on Bounce's face as he struggled with the subtlety of the humor. "An' I gotta anuvver one," added Parker, pleased that the audience was in a responsive mood. "There woz an old girl wot went ter 'er quack an' . . . "

At this point, Bounce interrupted. "Wot's a quack?"

"A doctor, yer silly twit. It ain't a bleedin' duck."

"I think perhaps Bounce is quackers," giggled Taika.

"'Ere watch it," said Bounce. "I fink yer takin' the mickey."

"Nah she ain't," quickly interjected Parker, cooling the situation. "Jest listen ter the rest o' the story, it's a bleedin' good 'un."

And he continued. "Well, this old girl went ter 'er quack an says, 'Doc, I suffer from lots o' flatulence an' . . . '"

"Wot's flatulence?" asked Bounce.

"Fartin'!" retorted Parker sharply, annoyed that his story was being interrupted.

"'The fing is,' she sed, 'I don't make a noise an' don' smell. In fact, I've blown orf free times since I bin in 'ere an' we ain't even 'eard it.'"

"'Well,'" sez the quack, "'The first fing I'd better do is fix yer 'earin' aid.'"

Another tinkle of laughter came from the girls while Bounce looked as puzzled as ever. From that display of verbal witticism Parker had performed a dance, singing, "Knocking Down the Old Kent Road," much to the amusement of his audience, except Bounce, who still looked puzzled.

After the girls had applauded there was a moment's silence and then a guffaw was heard from Bounce. "Coo," he suddenly announced. "The Doc must 'ave 'eard the old girl fart arter all."

"'Oo bleedin' ray. Yer got there, mate. We'll 'ave yer solvin' Sherlock Holmes' mysteries afore yer know where yer are."

Bounce hadn't the faintest idea who Sherlock Holmes was, but would have taken the praise as a great compliment on his deductive skills, had he known the meaning of deductive.

Parker chuckled to himself as he reminisced on the stories. He was now entering the city of York and threading his way through the streets to the hotel where he intended to stay while carrying out his inquiries. He drove round the Minster twice before finding the street he had been looking for. Although he had followed his map it was an old one and the one-way system had been changed since it was printed. It was an old hotel but comfortable and Parker wasted no time in starting his investigations.

The first action he took was to purchase an up-to-date map of the city and a guide to Yorkshire. He already possessed a large scale recent map of Britain which he had used to find his route to York. He sat comfortably at the dining table enjoying his lunch and perusing the maps and guide. Prior to his departure, he had already ascertained the addresses of the local social security and job centers, but was not too sure that he would get much help in those quarters. And he was right.

Having left London very early in the morning to miss any rush hour traffic, he had arrived at York with almost two hours to spare before luncheon. He had wasted no time and his visits to both the job center and social security office had met with the blank wall of officialdom. "We do not divulge the information you request; you must write in for it," he had been icily informed.

Back at the Londinium Club, Ma had tried phoning the DHSS central office but had been told to send in her inquiry by post. They had Eve's social security and employment numbers and expected to get her previous address from that source. Again that would take time and Boss knew that the longer the hunt for Eve was delayed so the chances of catching her would diminish.

Parker's perusing of the map and guide book was interrupted by the waitress.

"Would you like coffee here, or in the lounge, sir?"

He looked up at her, taking his mind off the task in hand.

"Corffee?—er, nah fanks, but yer can git me a cuppa char."

"Char, sir?" she said, looking puzzled.

Parker grinned to himself; either the girl was ignorant of the Cockney use of the Chinese word for tea or the slang he used dated him.

"A cuppa tea, luv, an' I'll 'ave it in the lahnge."

A middle-aged good-looking woman sitting at the adjacent table had heard the conversation and smiled at Parker. He looked at her and his pupils dilated slightly as the wrinkles round his eyes became more manifest as he smiled back.

He rose from his table, collected the reading material and took it into the lounge, seating himself on a settee beside a small table. He looked at the map again and noted the towns and villages in the vicinity; there were plenty to choose from. Unless he got a good lead from Ma in the evening it would be like looking for a needle in a haystack. He reckoned she would find the village in which Eve was born, but her last residence was not in the village, so that would not be of much help. He was still thinking about how to tackle the problem when the lady who had been sitting near him approached the settee on which he sat.

"Pardon me. Do you mind if I sit here?" she asked, indicating the vacant seat beside him. He was about to remark that there were plenty of free chairs in the lounge when her accent and the look in her eyes made him change his mind. He had not looked at her properly in the dining room but this time he used his excellent powers of observation to the full.

The woman looked the motherly type, some five and a half feet tall and had a Rubens type figure. There was a hint of faded blonde in her slightly graying hair and he noticed her blue-gray kindly looking eyes. She wore an expensive looking two-piece, a dark blue top and a matching skirt which made her look slimmer than she was. What attracted him most was the jewelry she wore. Her left hand displayed a turquoise and diamond engagement ring and a similar wedding ring. A diamond-studded eternity ring was present on the third finger of her right hand. A brooch made of gold with golden beryl and aquamarine was secured to her two-piece above her left breast. Her fingers were obviously well-manicured.

Parker took all this in rapidly and stood up, motioning the stranger to sit down beside him. He recalled the display of good manners one was accustomed to from Mr. de Vere-Smythe and had decided to emulate him as closely as necessary in action if not speech. He also quickly decided to drop the adjective "bleedin" in her company. "She might fink me uncouf," he thought to himself. The idea also ran through his mind that, "Blimey, she's a nice lookin' bint an' 'as got plenty o' rocks."

"You from America?" he asked. She nodded in affirmation and said, "Perhaps I'd better introduce myself: I'm Eleanor Fletcher."

"Me name's Albert Parker an' me frien's call me Bert." Actually he had no friends except Bounce and possibly Caria and his nickname of "Runt" was often used by acquaintances, but he saw no reason to appraise her with that intelligence.

"I could not help seeing you studying the maps and guide book and thought you must be a tourist here like myself. Are you from Australia, Bert?"

"Nah. I ain't bin ter Orstrilia, although I 'ad some ancestors go there at the end of the eighteenf cenchury. They went on the convict transports. Captin' Bligh woz gov'nor of Orstrilia then."

Eleanor looked impressed. "The Captain of the *Bounty*. Can you really trace your ancestor back that far?"

"Yus. Me family always lived in Wapping, y'know, dahn by the docks."

"Docks?"

"Yus, London docks. I'm a proper Cockney I am, an' prahd of it. Born wivin the sahnd o' Bow Bells."

"How exciting being born a Londoner."

"I dunno abaht that, but it must 'ave bin fer me muvver an' dad. They woz in the Blitz. At least me muvver woz most o' the time. They tol' me I yelled the bl—," he checked himself just in time. "The place dahn where I woz born."

Eleanor laughed. She liked the little man's sense of humor.

Parker was curious to know why she had sought his company. And he was flattered. Women usually took no notice of him, not that he needed their company. He believed in the maxim, "He travels fastest who travels alone," and he was not the type to get lonely, always finding something of interest to occupy his mind.

At that point the waitress brought in a tray with cups and saucers, a small silver jug of milk and bowl of sugar. She deposited it on the small adjacent table and smiled, indicating which cup held the tea and which the coffee.

"Dyer tike milk an' sugar in yer corfee?" said Parker, remembering how de Vere-Smythe behaved.

"Yes, please. How kind of you. You English have always had a reputation for good manners and it is so nice to be treated like a lady."

Parker inwardly chuckled; if she only knew his normal behavior she would have a shock. This was going to be entertaining and he wondered how long he could keep up the facade.

"You come 'ere on 'oliday?"

"Yes. I've always wanted to visit Yorkshire. My ancestors came from Yorkshire on my father's side. I read *Wuthering Heights* and *Jane Eyre* at school and saw the movies, too. I want to visit Thornton and Haworth where Charlotte and Emily Bronte were born and lived." She paused and then added, "You know, you have a very famous author living here today."

"'Ave we nah. 'Ose that?"

"Why James Herriot, of course, the veterinary doctor. He writes about caring for animals in this countryside."

Parker evinced interest in his expression, saying that he liked animals. He did not add that the only animals he liked were racing horses and greyhounds. He enjoyed a "flutter" and had become quite a good judge of form. Unlike most punters he usually did better than the tote and bookkeepers.

"Oh, I know. Ain't 'e 'ad a program on the telly?"

"Why, yes. The series is based on the book, *All Creatures Great and Small*. I want to get his autograph while I am here."

"Good luck ter yer mate. I 'ope yer do," then added, "Did yer say yer ancestors came from Yorkshire?"

"Yes, on my father's side. The family went to America at the middle of the nineteenth century and crossed the continent on the Oregon Trail. They must have been very tough. They settled in Oregon on the Willamette River near Salem."

"Salem. Wot a funny name; is it Injun?"

"Oh no. It was taken from the Bible and is really 'Shalom,' the Jewish word for peace. The Indian name for Salem was Chemekata meaning 'Place of Rest.' Salem was founded by Methodist missionaries."

"I bet they needed a place of rest arter crossing the USA in a wagon train."

Eleanor smiled at this remark. She felt quite comfortable in his company and it was nice to have someone to talk to who listened so politely. She had read somewhere that the English were very reserved and in him she found the opposite. What was more, he seemed very intelligent despite his funny accent which was interesting to listen to, even if she did not always immediately understand what he said.

"Did yer people always live in Oregon?"

"Pardon me?" Eleanor said, being brought back from her temporary reverie.

"Yer folks, y'know. Did they always live in Oregon?"

"I did until I got married, then I went to live with my husband in California. That is the state south of Oregon. We lived in Los Angeles until two years ago. My husband was beaten up in a race riot and very badly injured. He was unable to work after that so we moved back to live in Ashland."

"That's in Oregon?"

"Sure."

"Ain't it dangerous there? Don't people 'ave ter carry guns and ain't there cattle rahnd-ups an' shoot-ahts?"

"Oh no, not in Ashland. It is a very safe city. The only crime I know of there is of people getting tickets for speeding and illegal parking. It is a cultural center. Do you know we have an Elizabethan theater there and Shakespeare plays are performed every year?"

Parker did not know and couldn't care less, but he carried on showing an interest just to humor Eleanor. "Didn't yer 'usband come wiv yer?"

"Unfortunately he passed over six months after we moved. His injuries had seriously affected his health."

"Oh, I'm sorry," he said in as sincere a voice as he could muster.

"Don't you 'ave any family?"

"I have two stepchildren, both grown up. One lives in Vancouver and the other in San Diego. They are nice but I don't see them very often."

His interest in her had increased: a rich American widow and a lonely one at that! His mind began to formulate plans, then he realized what he had come to Yorkshire for.

"Would yer mind excusin' me fer a minute. I gotta make an important phone call."

"Not at all."

He rose to his feet. "Be back in a minute," and departed for his room. There he got through to the Londinium Club. De Vere-Smythe answered the call and Parker appraised him of his lack of success. He wanted to know if Ma had returned. "No," de Vere-Smythe had informed him. "You had better phone back at seven o'clock; she is bound to have returned by then. If she gets back earlier I'll get her to phone you with the information."

That suited Parker fine; it would give him time to chat up Eleanor and one never knew what might come out of the new acquaintance to his advantage. He returned to the lounge to find her seated in the same place and apologized for his temporary absence.

"'Ave yer 'ad a chance ter see the city?"

"No, not really."

"Well, 'ow abaht yer an me explorin' it tergevver?"

"Oh, that would be nice."

"I gotta be back 'ere by seven fer a business call but am free until then." Which was of course true. "'Ere look. I got a map wiv a walk froo the city an we kin foller that."

He showed a planned route in the guidebook which covered the main features of interest. Eleanor looked at him and smiled happily.

"Oh my," she said. "Gee, that will be super. I'll just go and get on my walking shoes and powder my nose," and she happily went upstairs, returning after ten minutes.

"Let's make a start at the Multiangular Tower. I read it was first built by the Romans in free 'undred."

Eleanor happily agreed to Parker's suggestion; they left the hotel and walked two short blocks to the tower. As they walked, he filled her in with details he had read in the guidebook and noted she was impressed by his knowledge.

"Y'know the Romans built a fort 'ere in '71 an' called it Ebacorum. They used it ter cornker the rest of norf England. Never cornkered the Scots though; they warn't arf savidge fighters; that's why a Roman bloke named 'Adrian 'ad ter build a wall evenchually ter keep 'em aht."

"Mean lot them Scots," he added reflectively. "D'yer know 'ow the Romans used ter tell the difference between the Picts an' the Scots?"

Eleanor shook her head.

"Well, the Romans would frow a few coins on the grahnd an' the Picts never got any."

Eleanor laughed and felt the afternoon was going to be an entertaining as well as an interesting with Bert Parker as a guide. And she was right.

Starting at the Multiangular Tower, they walked into the delightful Museum Gardens, then along St. Leonard's Place with the Theatre Royal and magnificent Regency Houses. From there their route took them to Bootham Bar and the long walk along the top of the Medieval City Wall. To their right the majestic Minster, with its flying buttresses looking graceful in the sunlight, dominated the view even when the wall turned abruptly at a tower.

"Funny fing," said Parker. "The street on our left is called Lord Mayor's Walk. Lots of places 'ere remind me o' London. There's Parleymint Street, Piccadilly, Museum Street, Tower Street an' the Shambles. An a bloke named Guy Fawkes woz born 'ere in Stonegate in 1570."

"What has the Shambles and Guy Fawkes to do with London? I mean, what is the connection?" queried Eleanor.

"Well, Guy Fawkes tried ter blow up the 'ahses o' Parlimint 'cos 'e didn't fink much o' politishuns in them days, an' they ain't any different nah. Every governmint we get makes a proper shambles o' runnin' the country. Proper useless lot they are. Let the country go ter the dawgs. I fink we need annuver Guy Fawkes."

"You should see the politicians in the USA . . . " Eleanor stopped in mid-sentence realizing that it was wiser to steer clear of making political comparisons between the two countries.

They passed through Monk Bar and then walked along Ogleforth Street to the Minster. As the great cathedral loomed above them, Eleanor asked, "Why is it called a Minster?"

Parker had read the answer to the question while waiting for Eleanor and replied, "Minster is the Anglo-Saxon name meaning a large church run as a mission center."

Eleanor was duly impressed. "I think you are very clever, Bert."

Wish I did, thought Parker to himself. Wish I could work aht 'ow ter get me 'ands on them rocks like 'er brooch, wivaht arahsin' 'er suspishuns.

They entered the building, being dwarfed by the massive doorway, and, slowly walking along one of the aisles were silenced by the atmosphere and the sheer grace of the Gothic structure. Eleanor would let out a gasp of delight when she saw something that caught her attention. She admired the stained glass windows, especially the 13th century *Five Sisters*, each of whose lancets is over fifty feet tall by five feet wide. Parker came up with further information when they entered the undercroft which had been dug out so that experts could examine the foundations.

"This plice took two 'undred an' fifty years ter build an' woz finished in fourteen 'undred an' seventy five. Wot dyer fink o' that?"

"Gee, that's amazing."

However, Parker hardly noticed her reply. His attention was arrested by the sight of the vaults in the cavern which contained an exhibition of precious plate. He stood there gazing enraptured at the thought of all the money the plate could fetch if it could only be heisted from the Cathedral.

"The silver and gold is beautiful," commented Eleanor, incorrectly interpreting his interest. "Yerse ain' it? " he replied, his expression being mistaken for one of reverential awe by Eleanor.

They left the Minster, somewhat reluctantly in the case of Eleanor, and walked along Deangate and Goodramgate to the Shambles, or Butcher's Street. Eleanor gave enthusiastic gasps of delight at the street, with its authentic medieval buildings with the overhanging gables and the butchers' slabs on which meat was displayed.

"A bit o' Merry England," commented Parker, to which she wholeheartedly agreed.

They turned left at the end of the Shambles and Parker pointed out the shortest street in York, yet the one with the longest name. "Funny name this street; it's called Whip-Ma-Whop-Ma-Gate. Used ter flog petty criminals 'ere. That's 'ow it got it's nime."

Entering Fossgate, they visited the Merchant Adventurers Hall. Again Eleanor was impressed with Parker's knowledge when he informed her that it had been built in the fourteenth century. His occasional surreptitious look at his pocket guidebook had not been noticed by her.

"Where was the building that housed the city government offices?" she asked.

Parker suddenly stopped in his tracks. Of course; what he should do is inquire about Eve's council house at the Council Offices. The time had just gone four-thirty and he guessed that the office might be open until five P.M. He informed Eleanor of his intentions to find the building and they quickly found directions and made their way there.

When he entered he wondered if he was going to get a brush-off similar to his earlier experiences, but this time he was in luck. A pleasant young man directed him to a room, suggesting he hurry as the office was about to close.

A cheerful, plump middle-aged woman looked up at him from a computer as he and Eleanor entered the room. "Can I help you, luv?" she said in a strong Yorkshire dialect.

"Yus, please young lidy." He slipped in the adjective "young" keeping a straight face, hoping it would have the desired effect. He showed her a visiting card with the name of a well-known London firm of lawyers franked on it, which had been given to him earlier by Boss.

"I work fer this firm o' solicitors an' am tryin' ter trace a girl named Eve Eden for a client wot's left 'er a legacy."

"Oo! Looky her," replied the clerk.

"We fink she lived in a cahncil ahse near York."

"Eve Eden, did you say? Just a minute, that name rings a bell. I think she left her apartment one or two months ago. We'll soon find oot."

She tapped a few keys on the computer while at the same time Parker retrieved the visiting card; he did not want to leave that lying around.

"You're in luck, luv," she said. "Here we are. Eve lived in a council house in Knaresborough." She glanced at Parker who was retrieving a pen and notebook from his pocket.

"No need for that, luv. I'll give you a printout." And on tapping a few keys, the printer beside the computer jerked into life and ejected full details of the address he required.

"Coo," said Parker. "Jest the kippers knickers. Wot's yer nime, luv?"

"Shirley Valentine," the clerk replied with a smile.

"Cor, I fort yer looked like a film star."

She laughed at the banter and retorted, "If you can't find Eve Eden, joost send the legacy to me."

Parker and Eleanor left the room and the doorman locked the door as they departed. "I hope you do not mind but I could not help hearing your conversation."

Parker shook his head. "Not a bit, Eleanor." Which was true. He had visions of telling her that he was a private detective and the important firm of solicitors was one of his clients.

"It's a funny thing," she went on. "A solicitor in the USA is a prostitute and I could not imagine a nice man like you working for a hookers' organization."

He laughed out loudly thinking that she had unwittingly hit the target. "Very funny. In England, solicitors are lawyers. They are attorneys in the USA, I understand. We also 'ave barristers over 'ere," and he went on to explain the difference between barristers and solicitors which involved mentioning the Inns of Court and law degrees.

They were walking back towards the hotel and, while talking, Parker was wondering if Knaresborough was close enough for him to get to in order to make inquiries that evening. He looked at the map as soon as he retrieved it from his room, and discovered that it would take him about half an hour or so to get there. Reasoning that the present tenants in the apartment once occupied by Eve would be more likely to be home if they worked for a living, he decided to go. What was more, he would have that line of inquiry sorted out one way or the other and have something to report back to Ma.

Eleanor asked if he would mind her accompanying him and, seeing no harm, decided to humor her. He had yet to work out a way of relieving her of some of her jewelry and her presence would provide greater opportunity.

They drove thought the picturesque countryside and Eleanor remarked on how green it was. She was excited to see newborn lambs gamboling in the fields and was enraptured by the quaint country cottages. The approach to the town where the River Nidd has a deep gorge in the limestone, brought remarks of admiration from her and they entered the ancient market town in good spirits.

"I read in my guidebook that there was a famous seeress name Mother Shipton who lived in a cave near here," Eleanor remarked.

"Oh, that's interesting," replied Parker, not in the least interested in that piece of information which he considered useless in the circumstances. "'Ave ter visit it sometime," he added, not having the slightest intention of doing so. "Must find me client's address nah though."

Eleanor acquiesced to this and after a few inquiries to passersby for directions, found the apartment which had been occupied by Eve. He was unlucky. The present tenants had no knowledge of her, nor of relatives or a forwarding address. He knocked at the adjacent apartments and one neighbor remembered her but knew nothing of value to his inquiries. He felt somewhat frustrated but at least that line of inquiry was closed.

"Well, that trail was cold," he remarked to Eleanor as they drove back to York. "Not like your Oregon Trail, which must 'a bin a 'ot one most o' the time."

Eleanor smiled. "Yes, it probably was. That reminds me, it's a funny coincidence, but the country the western settlers were looking for was called Eden."

"Coo! Well, fancy that," responded Parker showing an interest, but he was not prepared for what was to follow.

"And there is another funny thing. I told you I wanted to trace my ancestors who came from Yorkshire." He nodded. "Well, I wonder if the girl you are looking for is a relative. I forgot to tell you that my maiden name is Eden."

chapter nine

Sean sat down at the table in the small dining room of the practice. Dr. McMurrough, whom he had found seated there, noticed the frown on Sean's face and gave him a questioning look. Sean was feeling exasperated. An Indian patient had complained that her mother was deliberately being discriminated against in having to wait for a hip replacement. There was a backlog for those operations at the hospital and the surgeons had the final word on who was to be seen. Patients were operated on in order of referral, but sometimes a patient who had to work and had dependents was given priority. He had tried to explain this to the woman and that as soon as a patient was placed on the hospital waiting list he had no more say in the matter. She would not listen and had stormed out of the office, accusing him of racial prejudice. His reason told him that there were always selfish people in all walks of life, but that unfair accusation really upset him. He got on well with the immigrant population and racial prejudice was something he was never guilty of.

"What's eating you, Sean?" asked Dr. McMurrough. As Sean explained, Dr. Bannu Sind entered the room and overheard the conversation. He and Dr. McMurrough both burst out laughing.

"She tried that tactic on me, Sean," Dr. McMurrough said, and Dr. Sind nodded.

"She tried it on me first, for she and her mother are both patients of mine. Do you know the mother has only been in this country five weeks and her daughter emigrated here four months ago. Neither has paid a penny towards National Health Insurance and her husband is on social security. He lost his job at the beginning of the depression."

"I wouldn't let it upset you, Sean; it takes all sorts to make a world," added Dr. McMurrough.

"I doubt it will be the last time you will be accused of racial or social prejudice for that matter," Dr. Sind said. "Believe me, there is more racial and social prejudice in the Hindu caste system than anywhere else in the world."

Sean had been shocked to hear that but realized that Bannu Sind was a Muslim and Hindus and Muslims did not get on well together. With his upbringing, he had always practiced Christianity as he understood it and his choice of a medical career had been largely influenced by this. As had his cousin Richard, he had been guided by an instinct of compassion for humanity as a whole and a desire to relieve suffering in a practical way.

He knew it was ridiculous, but the accusation of racial prejudice kept rising in his mind and made him feel angry. Unlike his cousin, he looked upon all human beings as children of God no matter what their creed—all part of the Catholic family, the seed of Adam. To him, the human race was to be helped and relieved from its suffering which was due to the original sin of the first man and woman. He felt he was an instrument of the heavenly father and race presented no barriers to him.

Racial prejudice! It irked him and he knew he would have to include mentioning his feelings of anger to his father confessor.

The woman had been the last person he had seen that morning and he had advised her to inquire about the waiting list at the hospital. Apparently she had already done that and she had come to him wanting him to write a letter giving her mother priority; this he had refused and that had brought on the accusation. She had stormed out of the surgery muttering in Hindustani and he had told his receptionist to transfer her to his colleague Bannu Sind. Now he learned that she was Bannu's patient anyway and that made him feel more annoyed.

He was still seething when the other partner, Dr. Liam Fitzgerald, entered the dining room. He sat at the table and gave a sigh of relief.

"Phew. It's been a busy morning, surely it has now."

"Anything of particular interest?" asked Sean, who was always seeking to take advantage of his seniors' greater experience. It was the practice of the group to lunch together twice a week to update on cases and any pertinent information. Sean found this particularly useful.

"That patient with schizophrenia I have been treating with Perphenazine, is showing early signs of tardive dyskinesia. I am giving her a small reduction in dosage."

"Have you considered Fluphenazine or Chlorpromazine?" asked McMurrough.

"She has had the latter, and I'll certainly look into the change to Fluphenazine. But I think I'll get her to see Leonard Schwann the neurologist again before changing to another drug."

Dr. Sind spoke: "I had Sam Edetti back; the one who had his leg severed in the recent bomb blast. He's having adaptation problems. I think I shall refer him for counseling."

"We had another patient who was caught in the blast, Eve Eden," McMurrough interjected. "I understand she did not return. You saw her last, Sean. What sort of state was she in?"

"Just shock and slight bruising. She appeared to be coping."

"I understand from another patient, Miss Crompetta, that she has moved. Did she say where she was going?"

"No. I was expecting her to return."

Sean had lied on this, recalling that he had been told by Inspector Blanchard not to reveal Eve's whereabouts to anyone. The fact that he had to lie was also another cause for annoyance to him; he hated to have been forced into that position and made a mental resolve to include that in his confession later. At the same time he said out loud, "That bombing was a wicked thing. I don't know how the IRA expects to change things in the Old Country that way."

"How else can the Brits be got out?" asked Fitzgerald.

"For sure everything else has been tried," added McMurrough.

Sean looked at both of them in surprise; he had not expected that reaction to his comment. They were fellow Irishmen and wanted to see Ireland united as one country. He knew the British had tabled three bills giving Ireland complete independence but they had been defeated by Protestant opposition in Parliament; the fourth one had been forced through because his countrymen would not agree among themselves. In any case, the Protestants had their own parliament in Ulster, and this had been suspended by the British Government only because they were tardy in bringing about reforms to give equal rights and treatment to the Catholic minority in Northern Ireland. When he voiced these facts to his colleagues he realized that they were unreceptive and the past history and the injustices to their ancestors dominated their reason—a gut reaction was what he encountered.

"The Brits can only be shifted by force," McMurrough had said, and Bannu Sind had nodded his head in agreement.

"That's how we got them out of India."

Sean decided not to correct him by mentioning that the reason why British rule ended in India was due to many of the leaders being educated in England and taking back the ideas of democracy. Indian Nationalism did not really start until the country had been united by the British. The departure was largely influenced by Mahatma Ghandi's campaign of passive resistance. He had been educated as a barrister in London but it was his experience of apartheid in South Africa that decided his political course; he actually approved of the Empire until he went to South Africa.

In order to cool the situation, Sean said, "Well, whatever, at least we are all getting a good living out of them now," and with that comment the tension had lightened and the subject changed to matters associated with the practice.

■ ◻ ■ ◻ ■

It was later at Bracken that Sean had related the conversation to Richard and Dawn. He was particularly interested in obtaining Dawn's opinion, for she had majored in history at university and taken her Masters degree with a detailed study of events giving rise to the causes of emigration, conquest, wars and all factors bringing about the changes in population shifts.

They were sitting in the family room on Sunday after breakfast, when Sean introduced the subject to Dawn and Richard. The children were also present and Eve was trying to keep her mind on the conversation between surges of the strong feelings of love for Sean that so dominated her mind.

They all listened to what he had to say about apparently educated intelligent people holding racial prejudices. Dawn opened her comments by asking him if he knew when the trouble between Ireland and the British mainland had started. He presumed it was during the reign of Queen Elizabeth I. Dawn shook her head at this.

"The troubles between Ireland and Britain were first recorded by the Romans. You know the Romans finally conquered England and Wales in 79 A.D. They had successfully invaded the country in 43 A.D. and they governed the country well. Around that time Ireland was not united as a kingdom. Politically, it was divided into little kingdoms or Tuatha. Each was ruled by a petty chieftain who was really a tribal leader. Later they had an overall chief who was only accepted as he was the most powerful chieftain at the time, but it was never fully united until between 1780 to 1800 under British rule. In practice, the chieftains ruled their own territories. They were a warlike lot and were always fighting among themselves and if they wanted to opt out of supporting the overall chief they did so without losing honor. They were continuously also carrying out raids on the British mainland. The Romans recorded many such raids from the third century onwards.

"In the Latin writings or records, the Irish were given the new name Scotti, rather than the old one, Hiberni. In confirmation of the Latin records, native Irish traditions suggest that such raids took place. It was during the second half of the fourth century when Roman power was beginning to wane that the raids became incessant. Roman troops were being withdrawn from Britain to assist in other parts of the Roman Empire which were under attack. The Irish took full advantage of their crumbling power and raids became continuous. That was not all. The Irish started to set up colonies in

Cornwall, Wales and Scotland. It was from the early part of the fifth century that the rulers of Dalraida in Northern Ireland extended their power over areas already settled by Irish in Scottish Islands and Scotland itself. The Island of Arran, Islay and Jura as well as Argyll had Irish settlers.

"In time, the Kingdom of Dalraida became separated from the Irish; and when, in the ninth century, the original inhabitants of Scotland, the Picts, were finally overcome, the Dalraida or Scotti gave the name Scotland to the whole area. After about six hundred years of raids, conquest and settlements originating from Ireland, that is how Scotland came about. While the Romans occupied Britain they were constantly resisting raids on the coast from the Irish and from Scotland."

"Is that why the Roman Emperor built the wall between England and Scotland?" asked Jennifer.

"Of course it was, silly," interrupted John before Dawn could reply.

"Don't be rude John," Richard remonstrated and John murmured "sorry" almost inaudibly.

"Actually, there were two walls built; one ordered by the Roman Emperor Antoninus Pius in 142 A.D. and the other by Emperor Hadrian which was one hundred miles further south and completed in the year 136."

"Didn't Saint Patrick make the Irish Christians stop the raids?" asked Jean. Dawn shook her head.

"St. Patrick was born during the early part of the fifth century A.D. and the Irish raids on the British mainland had been going on for about two hundred years."

Sean smiled at hearing the patron saint of Ireland being mentioned; he knew the history of the saint well and had discussed it with Dawn before. He knew that St. Patrick, or Patricius, to use his correct name, was born in Britain of a British Romanized family. His father, Calpurnius, was a deacon in the church and a minor local official. During one of the Irish raids on the British mainland, Patrick was captured and taken as a slave to Ireland. There he was forced to become a herdsman and comforted himself by prayer. After about six years of almost intolerable slavery, he had a dream that a ship was ready for him to escape and he fled his Irish master and escaped to Britain.

"Mummy, did he get back to his family?" asked Jean.

"Yes. He endured hardship and suffered another period of captivity, but eventually was reunited with his family."

Sean continued the story. "When back in safety in Britain, he experienced another dream in which he was given a letter by someone named Victorious which was headed 'The Voice of the Irish.' As he read the letter in the dream, he seemed to hear Irish voices beseeching him to walk once more among them. He was so deeply moved by the appeal in the dream that he could read no more. This he recorded in a document called the 'Confessio.' Actually, he took a long time before starting on his call for he had many doubts about his fitness for the task. Due to his captivity he had been uneducated, and was determined to rectify that. He was ordained and eventually went to Ireland and converted many Irish to Christianity. He did not convert all and was often in danger. On one occasion, he was even put in chains by an Irish chieftain. He was very diplomatic, giving gifts but accepting none."

"One historical parallel strikes me as being amusing," said Richard. "There are many Christians who hate Jews and forget that Christ was a Jew. There are Irish who hate the British, but forget that their Apostle Saint Patrick was a Brit."

Dawn gave him a sharp look. "You would think of that." She was worried about the way the conversation could go in front of Sean and Eve. She did not want anything to affect Eve's studies in Catholicism, although she herself was agnostic. She decided to get back to certain facts in Irish history and keep away from religious aspects that might make Richard's logical scientific approach cause doubts to Eve and simultaneously upset Sean.

"For the first time in history the Irish tribes were virtually united under one king named Brian Boru. This was about 1000 A.D. and was made possible by a lull in the activity of the Danes who had been invading the country for some time. His reign lasted about fifteen years, but the jealousies, hatred, cupidity and vanity of the tribal chieftains meant a constant struggle to keep power; unfortunately, he was killed in the battle of Clontarf and Ireland was again broken into tribal factions. It is interesting that Christianity still largely prevailed in Ireland; the bishops of Ireland went to Canterbury in Kent to be ordained.

"At the time of Henry I of England, the brother of a British rebel, Arnulph de Montgomery, went over to Ireland and from the Irish king, Murtouch O'Brien, obtained supplies for revolution against the English king Henry I. The king took no action but a later English king did, and that was Henry the second. He invaded Ireland because an Anglo-Norman adventurer, Richard de Clare of Pembroke, also known as 'Strongbow,' had been invited by Dermot McMurrough, the Irish King of Leinster, to fight against the high king, Rory O'Connor. That high king had expelled McMurrough for rebelling against him. Strongbow had conquered a substantial part of eastern Ireland and Henry did not want Ireland to become a rival Norman state. Popes Adrian IV and Alexander III had tried to reform Ireland for Christianity had deteriorated; Irish moral behavior, as well as the way the church was organized on a tribal basis, shocked them. They both encouraged Henry II's invasion of Ireland believing it would further church reform in the country. All the Irish kings accepted his supremacy except some in the northwest. By the Treaty of Windsor, the High King O'Connor accepted Henry as his overlord. The church reforms included the introduction of the parochial system. Later King John of England, who visited Ireland in 1210, established a civil government independent of the feudal lords. English law and a parliament were introduced. The area of English control was known as the Pale."

"Is that where the expression 'Beyond the Pale' came from, Mummy?"

"Yes, Jean, but to continue: The English government tried to curtail feudal privileges which resulted in a revival of Irish political power.

"It was Henry VIII who alienated many Irish with his quarrel with the Pope and dissolution of the monasteries. This was the time of the Reformation and his declaration of King of all Ireland and attempt to make Ireland Protestant upset many of the Anglo-Irish, driving them into the arms of the Gaelic Irish. When his daughter, Mary, restored Catholicism, the extent of resentment against Protestantism was revealed. Her sister, Queen Elizabeth I of England re-introduced Protestantism, and although she did not try hard to enforce it, there were three rebellions. One started by an O'Neill sought to expel the MacDonnell migrants from Antrim. Loyal O'Donnells defeated O'Neill and the MacDonnells murdered him. At the end of Elizabeth's reign, Ireland was reduced to obedience for the first time since Henry II, but the cost was the straining of relations over religion and the Queen's financial resources were badly depleted.

"It was in James I's reign that the seeds of the modern troubles were sown. He introduced religious tolerance, and from 1618, a Catholic hierarchy was in residence in Ireland. At the same time, large numbers of Scots were encouraged to return to Ulster. James united Scotland and England; he was King James VI of Scotland and a Catholic. The newcomers were from the Scottish lowlands and, with a few English settlers, flourished. Trouble again occurred during the Parliamentary rule of the Commonwealth, when Cromwell put down opposition with ruthless efficiency. He was a Protestant and alienated the Catholics. The union of the three kingdoms of Scotland, England and Ireland was effected in 1653 and representatives from Ireland attended Parliaments held in London.

"King James II was eventually dethroned and after his flight to France, he went to Ireland and repealed the Acts of Settlement of the previous government. When William III landed in Ireland to oppose James, the country divided between Protestant and Catholic. But the main issue was not religion but the division of the land. At the battle of the Boyne, James was defeated and that was the start of the Protestant ascendancy."

Dawn paused and added, "And I think that is about enough of the history lesson for the moment."

"There is a lot more to it than that then?" asked Eve.

"Yes, but the real problem is, should the Ulster Protestants have the right to decide whether they want to be part of the Eire government or remain independent. The British government has offered them the choice, but I think they fear that if ever Ireland is united, they will be subject to the same discrimination that they imposed on Northern Catholics from 1922 to the 1960s. The British government has tried to get them to carry out the reforms and that is why they suspended the Stormont Parliament to get justice for the Catholics in Ulster. I only wish the American supporters of the IRA and IRA Provisionals would understand that their funds go to terrorists to commit murder. For some odd reason many Americans think that British soldiers are in military occupation of the whole of Ireland. They are so badly informed and, no doubt deliberately misinformed, that they don't appreciate that the British soldiers were sent to Northern Ireland at the request of the Catholics, to protect the Catholics in Northern Ireland from the injustices of the Irish Protestants. There are no British soldiers in Eire."

"It is an interesting thing that you should say that," interrupted Sean. "Recent world events and the lessons of Vietnam, have made the Americans reluctant to have their troops abroad as peace enforcers as opposed to peace keepers. They don't want their young men and women to be killed keeping aggressive parties apart. Unfortunately, the British soldiers in Northern Ireland are doing just that; young lives are being lost and innocent people are being killed because of funds being sent from America."

At that point they heard a car pull up in the driveway. John looked up and said excitedly, "Here's Vindy and the family." They all rose and Richard and Dawn accompanied by the three children went into the hall to greet the new arrivals.

Sean and Eve watched from the family room window as Dr. Pankash Patel, his wife Charlotte, and their two children, Mira and Vindy emerged from their car. They saw Dawn and Richard walk onto the driveway to greet them and it was heart-warming to see their smiles of genuine affection and friendship. Sean thought to himself, Why can't so many people of different races and beliefs get together in the same way as these two families?

As the newcomers entered the room, Richard introduced them to Eve; they had already met Sean. "Allow me to introduce you to Eve Eden, Sean's fiancee."

"I see Sean has very good taste," said Pankash, making Eve blush.

"Really, Pankash," Charlotte interjected. "You must not embarrass Eve."

They all laughed and were interrupted by the children who came in the room talking excitedly. "Mummy, Vindy and Mira say they have brought their costumes; can we all go swimming?"

"Of course, Jean, but be careful and remember, no diving." And at that remark, the children rushed to their respective bedrooms to change into their swimming costumes, Vindy accompanying John, and Mira, Jean.

Eve quickly learned that Pankash Patel was a general practitioner, for he and Sean started talking shop. Richard suggested they all go out to the patio and have some drinks before lunch. "Who's for a preprandial before we eat?" he asked, then looked at Charlotte.

"Yes, please. Something long and cool."

"And you, Eve?"

"The same please. I think there is some guava juice in the fridge. Can I help?"

"Not for the moment, thank you. You sit and get acquainted with Charlotte and Pankash."

At that Charlotte smiled. "Come and sit beside me, Eve. I was listening to your accent and I guess you have lived in the north, perhaps Yorkshire."

Eve smiled. "That was a very good guess, but," with a twinkle in her eye added, "perhaps I detect an Indian accent somewhere."

Both Charlotte and Pankash laughed at this and he said, "Full marks."

"I hope you do not mind my asking, but how is it that you have the name of Charlotte?"

"Well, Eve, my parents in India were Anglophiles and they read a great deal of English literature. One of the authors was Charlotte Bronte and they named me after her. When I first came to England I visited Haworth in Yorkshire, where the Bronte family lived and that is why I recognized your accent."

"You say your parents were Anglophiles. That is interesting. One gets conflicting stories about the British in India and some of them do not make one feel proud of being British."

"Well, I am not surprised. Some of the British officers made some bad decisions."

"Like the massacre at Amritsar," commented Pankash.

"Yes. The colonel who ordered his troops to open fire on a political gathering which had been forbidden, exceeded his orders and caused a great deal of harm. Of course, the British government had him court-martialed and he was cashiered."

"Did not the arrogance of class distinction play a part in estranging the British and Indian population?"

"Yes, to quite a large extent, but not all the British acted that way, and one should realize that the caste system was far more divisive among the Indians themselves than the British class system, which was analogous. Although the caste system is not officially recognized it is still very strong, and that is part of Hinduism, which was introduced by the Aryans when they invaded India two thousand years ago. The indigenous people were all declared untouchables and designated as the lowest caste. My father was a Bannergee and mother was a Chattergee, and they, being Brahmins, are the highest caste."

"Did the British introduce any benefits?" asked Eve.

"Yes, a great many; there was a civil law code introduced by Lord Cornwallis which was a charter for civil as distinct from political liberty, and an incorruptible civil service whose staff were properly and adequately paid, thus eliminating corruption. Lord Elphinstone encouraged Western learning and science running parallel with an Indian culture and foresaw the ultimate end of British rule. Lord Bentink got rid of *sati*, the burning of wives at their husbands' funerals and also the practice of child sacrifice. He also stopped the practice of *thuggee* in which travelers were ritually murdered by gangs in central India in the name of the Goddess Kali. The English language was an important legacy for it is the most flexible of all languages; modern communications including telephone, telegraph, air and rail transport were introduced and developed. One real benefit was Western education."

Eve asked, "How so?"

"Many Indians came to England for university education. One of the greatest mathematicians of all time was Srinivasa Ramanujan. He came to England in 1914 and was privately educated by British mathematician, Godfrey Hardy, and got a grant from Trinity College, Cambridge. In 1918 he was the first Indian to be elected to the Royal Society of London—one of the world's most prestigious and learned societies.

"One other very important thing was the action of a retired British civil servant, Alan Octavian Hume. He was aware of the rising tide of Indian nationalism and, in the best English liberal tradition, determined to found an organization to give it expression. He wrote to Calcutta University suggesting a founding membership of fifty people and the result was the foundation of the Indian National Congress which eventually became the Indian Parliament.

"Perhaps the most important things were the ideas of a working democracy and liberal humanitarianism which were introduced by Viceroy Lord Ripon."

Sudden shrieks of laughter from the children brought Charlotte's attention to them and interrupted the conversation. "Vindy!" she called out. "Vindy, you are getting too excited. Make less noise."

Vindy, who had been threatening to jump on Jean, looked in Charlotte's direction. "Be careful, Vindy," said his father. "You could hurt someone jumping on them."

"All right, Daddy, I'll be careful."

Jennifer came up behind him to push him in the water but he jumped aside at the last moment and she fell straight in. This time the adults joined in the children's laughter at Jennifer's discomfiture.

Sean looked at the children playing happily together. He thought to himself: "They are not bothering about ethnic differences, perhaps because their parents are mature and widely read enough to recognize that all human beings are the children of God. What a pity that racism plays such a dominant part in preventing people living harmoniously together."

He turned to Eve and smiled and she responded by squeezing his hand. Then she addressed Charlotte. "I saw a film called *Ghandi* and got the impression that almost alone he got the British to quit India by peaceful demonstrations."

"It was a good film and gave a fairly accurate account of his personal efforts to bring an end to British rule, but his two campaigns of non-violence and boycott of the British were not adequately supported. Sadly, he was assassinated by a Hindu dissident," Charlotte said. "Also, the Muslims not only did not cooperate but massacred many Hindus. A number of Hindus wanted a longer period of transition, hoping that the Muslims would remain within India."

Pankash entered the conversation, "Other problems were the fact that many princes ruled their own territories, although British law was enforced, and the British wanted to leave a working democracy where the rights of the minorities would be protected."

"Another impression I got from some left-wing literature I once read was that India was a peaceful country until the Europeans came," remarked Eve.

Here Charlotte replied. "Far from it. The Indian princes were always quarrelling and the reason why the foreign traders obtained power was because they were hired by the princes and maharajahs to assist in fighting their battles. In this way, they got trading concessions and considerable influence. The British under Clive beat the French who were trying to establish a trade monopoly in India."

"I find it interesting that there are certain parallels in Irish history," said Sean, who had been listening attentively. "One has the similar scenario with petty kings, who were really tribal chiefs on the one hand and princes and sultans on the other, quarrelling. The country is taken over and united under British rule. Before leaving, the British try to keep the country as one but religious differences force a compromise. In the Indian continent, India is formed with Pakistan and Bangladesh, and in Ireland the Irish Free State, or Eire, becomes one state and Protestant Northern Ireland another. So Hindu and Muslim want to live apart and Catholic Christian and Protestant Christian want to live apart."

"And neither religious group sees eye-to-eye in either country," said Richard suddenly appearing with a tray of drinks. "Sorry to interrupt, but I could not help overhearing your remarks, Sean. Anyway, these will help to whet your throttles."

"Thanks," said Sean, when a glass was offered him. "*Slangivar!* Unfortunately, too many people are not content with letting others live in peace; they become intolerant and want to dominate. This is not because they are logically right but because of emotional reasons."

"Hmm," Richard commented. "You can say that again. I remember hearing a recording of a lecture by the philosopher and mathematician, Bertrand Russell, talking on decision-making. He pointed out that one may collate all the facts, carefully consider and assess them, and then most people will make their decision on an emotional and not a logical basis. The important question is, why do people do this?"

"Well, before anyone answers that, if there is an answer, from what you are saying, Richard, democracy is not the best form of government because the population will vote emotionally and not consider relevant facts logically."

"I think in the short run you are right, Pankash, for the politicians play on people's emotions in order to get power. Where there is a benevolent and enlightened autocrat, the most rapid progress has often been made. Sadly, unless constrained by strongly enforced fair civil laws, people in power too long either become corrupt or megalomaniacs. It has been said that democracy is the worst form of government but better than the rest, and in the long run this is true."

"You are right about the megalomaniacs, Richard. It was through a megalomaniac that I came to England." Listening to that remark, Eve looked puzzled, and Pankash noticed her expression.

"You did not know that I was born in Uganda, Eve?"

She shook her head.

"My parents emigrated to Uganda from India, as did many Indians. Uganda was a protectorate of the British Empire and one could travel pretty safely in those days. They prospered, owning several shops and sent me to a boarding school in England. Unfortunately, the democracy the British had left the country with was destroyed by President Obote and it became a police state. He was overthrown by Idi Amin who became a tyrant and forced all the Asian population out of the country, confiscating their property. Believe me, any alleged racism in Britain approaches the imaginative when compared with the racism practiced by Amin in Uganda."

"How did your people manage?" asked Sean.

"They had nothing when they arrived here and were given shelter and financial assistant on the British social security scheme. I was given grants by the British government and was able to finish at medical school. What amuses me is that in about 1987 the Ugandans asked the Asians to return as their economy needed their expertise. Frankly I will never go back, I value the freedom and culture in this country too much."

"Uganda rings a bell in my knowledge of Roman Catholicism in Africa. In 1885, the ruler or kabaka of Uganda, Mwanga, launched a campaign against Christians, although they were tolerated by the previous kabaka, Mtesa. Mwanga massacred the Anglican missionary, Bishop James Hannington, and his colleagues. The kabaka was reproached by St. Joseph Musaka, who was an important member of the kabaka's household, for this and also for his homosexual debauchery. He had Joseph beheaded and the Christian pages were burned alive for refusing to satisfy his abnormal sexual demands. Three other Africans and soldiers were martyred also."

"Man's inhumanity to man is written on every page of history," Dawn observed. Sean was about to comment on original sin when Jennifer came running up to him.

"Uncle Sean, can I sit on your lap?"

"Not with that wet swimming costume on, you young monkey."

Jennifer giggled and, accepting a dry towel from Dawn, folded it around her waist and jumped onto Sean's lap.

"My word, you are getting as heavy as an elephant, Jennifer."

"I thought you said I was a monkey."

"All right, a monkey as heavy as an elephant."

"That could not be a monkey, it would be a gorilla. That reminds me, what is the highest form of animal life?"

"Man, I suppose."

"No."

"All right, what is it then?"

"A giraffe."

"Ouch," said Sean, as everyone winced. Jennifer suddenly noticed a butterfly and watched its wavering flight. "Is that a Red Admiral, Uncle Sean?"

"Yes, Jennifer, and it is a beautiful insect."

"Can you tell me, why couldn't the butterfly go to the dance?"

"I don't know."

"Because it was a moth ball."

"Spare us," said Dawn, who had heard them all before from her pupils at school. Jennifer assumed a dejected look.

"Just one more, Uncle Sean?"

"OK, I'll buy it."

"What did the horse say when he got to the end of his nose bag?" she lisped.

Sean shrugged his shoulders, signaling he did not know.

"That's the last straw."

"And if you have any more jokes like that, Jennifer, it will be the last one you tell!" At that, Dawn rose and suggested to Eve that they start preparing for lunch. Richard walked to the barbecue and lit the gas.

It was late in the evening by the time all the guests left and, after assisting in clearing dishes and preparing for the following day, Eve went to bed feeling tired. The children had been in bed for about two hours and she passed by John's open door and entered her room. For the last two nights, Dawn had left John's door open at his request, for he had watched a video of Lawrence Olivier's *Hamlet* and had been scared during the ghost scene.

Eve had just closed her door and was half undressed when she heard John call out, "Daddy—there's a ghost in my room!" On hearing Richard reply and go to John's room, she continued to undress, thinking to herself that the manifestation she had seen in the garden must have been real and not just a product of her imagination. My God, she reflected, there is a spirit world after all.

chapter ten

Parker sat in Boss's office and glanced around the room. Just like Boss, he thought, everything functional, cold and clinical. He returned his gaze to Boss who was looking at him steadily. "So you did not find Eve Eden and you have no idea of her whereabouts?"

"No, Boss, but I do 'ave a lead which is well worf followin'."

"And what is that?"

"She's got a bruvver."

"Has she now. Good, well done. And where does he live?"

"I ain't got 'is address but I understand 'e lives in Boston, Massachusetts. Yer got a lot o' pals there so yer should be able ter trace 'im."

Boss nodded in agreement and did not immediately reply. He doubted Eve would be with her brother, for, to his knowledge, she had no passport. On the remote possibility of her getting to him, it would be an easy matter to have one of his "pals," as Parker called them, to eliminate her. There was one thing he could rely on in America; there was no shortage of guns or people willing to use them for a small fee. But he doubted she was in the USA. It was more likely that she had gone to ground somewhere in the British Isles. The question was, where? It was possible that she had written to her brother and he might know of her whereabouts. On the other hand, if she had any sense she would not risk letting him know where she was. Parker had found nothing when he searched her room.

"Did she ever receive mail?"

"Nah. Not a fing as far as I know. If yer like I'll ave a word wiv Caria." Boss pursed his lips reflectively on receipt of that answer. It was possible that de Vere-Smythe had questioned her on that point, but assuming he had not it would do no harm for Parker to do so.

"Do that. And tell Mr. de Vere-Smythe to send a fax to Dermot O'Rourke in Boston with a full description of Eve Eden. I want her brother found. He is to tread softly and not arouse her brother's suspicions; there is a chance he may not know where she is now, but she may inform him later. Got it?"

"Yus, Boss, an' I'll 'ave a word wiv Caria abaht letters, too."

"Good. Get on with it." And with that curt dismissal, Parker left Boss's presence and made his way to the Londinium Club.

■ ❏ ■ ❏ ■

At the Club, Parker knocked on Mr. de Vere-Smythe's office door and was admitted with the usual amount of courtesy. "Please sit down, Mr. Parker. It is nice to see you back. Now what can I do for you?"

"I jest reported ter Boss an' e' wants yer ter send a fax ter Dermot O'Rourke in Boston." Parker gave full details of Boss's instructions and de Vere-Smythe noted them.

"Right," he replied, "that little matter shall be attended to. Was there anything else?"

"Yerse. Did you ask Caria if Eve received any mail?" De Vere-Smythe recalled his conversation with Caria.

"No, not specifically. It is a good point and I presume you are going to follow it up?"

"Yerse, I'll do that."

"Good. Now before you go, I have some news for you. During your absence we have another gentleman masseur on the staff to replace our late employee. His name is Scott and no doubt you will see him tomorrow. He is of somewhat tender years but you know certain very important Middle Eastern members have unusual tastes. You will meet him tomorrow."

Parker nodded, acknowledging that he understood, then excused himself and Mr. de Vere-Smythe showed him to the door.

Parker walked to the staff room where he found Bounce and Caria seated at the bar. He looked at Bounce and declared, "Allo yer bleedin' great git," slapping him on the back. "Yer look as if yer bin enjoying yerself while I bin away."

"Yeah," Bounce replied. "Bin a bit quiet, though. Ain't 'as much ter do."

"Never mind, I'll fink o' sumfink for yer termorrer." Then, turning to Caria, he smiled. "An' 'ows me luvverly Caria terday? Yer lookin' as beautiful as ever."

Caria gave him a look of contempt.

"Your Caria, that's a laugh. Yer flatter yerself dontcha mate? Anyway, fings woz orlrite 'ere until jest nah."

"Very funny."

Then he changed the subject. "Nah, Boss wants ter know if Eve 'ad any mail?"

Caria paused before replying, knowing immediately why she had been asked that question.

"Come ter fink of it yus, she did. She 'ad a letter from the Social Security Orffice wiv 'er medical card arter she 'ad sent it orf ter 'ave the new doctor's name put on it."

"An' that's all."

"Nuffink else mate, wot I knows of."

As Parker took that in, a small nervous-looking young man entered the room. Parker looked up and immediately surmised who it was. "Yer the noo masseur named Scott I fink." The young man smiled and said, "Yes," in a somewhat effeminate voice.

To Caria's surprise, Parker smiled and held out his hand. "Me name's Parker. Welcome ter the Club, mate." Scott looked relieved in turn and shook Parker's hand. Caria frowned. This was not like the Parker she knew and she wondered if he was up to some devilment. Before she could comment, the intercom buzzed and Ma's voice came through ordering Scott to report to her office. As soon as the door had closed on his departure, Parker turned to Bounce and said, "So nah we got Scott o' the arsantics workin' fer the Club. We'll be 'avin Eskimos next."

Caria laughed while Bounce looked puzzled.

"I'm orf 'ome, Caria. Yer can explain it ter Bounce while I've gorn."

■ ❏ ■ ❏ ■

Arriving back at his apartment, Parker recalled the way Caria had addressed him and contrasted it with the way Eleanor treated him. He thought about Eleanor with very mixed feelings. Why the hell had he given the brooch back to her? Of course, without her being interested in her genealogy he might never have discovered that Eve had a brother. It was odd how it had occurred.

"Yer could 'ave knocked me dahn wiv a fevver," he said to himself out loud, when he recalled Eleanor saying her maiden name was Eden. That night when they had gone to their respective rooms, he had realized that by joining forces he was more likely to trace Eve's relatives than working alone. During dinner that evening Eleanor had shown him some of her family tree which interested him deeply. By using that information it would save him a lot of time, and it had. What is more, he realized that it would give him a better chance to collect some of her jewelry.

They had spent the whole day visiting four churches to inspect records of marriage registers and, although tracing distant relatives, he had not got much further. He might have covered more ground had not Eleanor spent less time admiring the moors and various buildings en route. They had started the search at Pickering, and while Parker was speaking to the verger about examining the marriage register, Eleanor had stood admiring a brightly colored mural painted on one wall. Noticing her interest, an elderly man stopped beside her and remarked, "Quite beautiful, isn't it?" She turned to him and nodded, "What does it depict? It looks like a court scene to me."

"Well, part of it is." He pointed to the lower part. "That is King Herod and there is Salome dancing for the king. Over there is Saint George, the patron saint of England slaying the dragon and there," he pointed to another scene, "one can see Thomas Becket being murdered."

"Wow. How old are the murals?"

"These wall painting are five hundred years old but the church was built in the twelfth century."

Eleanor "wowed" again and the elderly man added, "This town is much older. It was founded by the Keltic King Peredurus about two hundred and seventy B.C. It was the gateway to the moors and is one of the oldest market towns in England."

Eleanor shook her head almost incredulously and said, "Over two hundred and fifty years old. Wow! And to think that where I come from, Jacksonville is considered old."

"Jacksonville?" queried the stranger.

"Yes. It is the oldest town in Oregon and was founded in 1855."

"You're from America then?" Eleanor smiled, nodding her head in agreement, and at that point, Parker, who had overheard the conversation, interrupted, saying, "Sorry ter butt in on yer conversashun but I've fahnd some Edens in the register." And at that, Eleanor thanked the stranger and accompanied Parker to the small vestry where the verger awaited them and showed them the register.

Earlier they had driven past the Hole of Horcum, a huge natural basin in the North York Moors National Park. Eleanor had read about it and had filled in details to Parker. "Did you know that there is a legend that the hole was created by a giant named Wade, who scooped up an enormous handful of earth to throw at his wife. She dodged, and the fistful of soil landed two miles away forming that hill there called Blakey Topping."

"Well, I never. I wonder 'ow she provoked 'im?"

Eleanor had noticed the steam engines on the North Yorkshire Moors Railway. "Gee," she had said, "what cute little locomotives you have here."

Parker had looked across from the road and noticed the train. "Those are nought-six-two tank engines. The water tanks are on each side."

"Oh, I see. We have very big steam locomotives on a private line at Yreka near where I live."

"Oh, do yer?"

"Yes. They pull old-fashioned coaches for tourists and there is an open coach at the back. At the last stop there is a mock hold-up. Cowboys come on board pretending to be bandits and run through the coaches yelling, 'Where's the gold!' Everybody laughs of course."

"Cor, if I wos there I'd keep me mahf shut."

"Why?"

"I got a couple o' gold crahns in me teef."

From Pickering another lead took them to Whitby and driving along the desolate moors they passed the three gigantic spherical domes of the Fylingdales Radar Early Warning Station. "'Ow d'yer like the golf balls?" remarked Parker, as they came into view.

"What are they there for?"

"Well, you know that giant bloke Wade, wot you menshuned, they are 'is golf balls."

Eleanor gave him an old-fashioned look. "Pull the other one."

"It's as good a yarn as the one you told me," he bantered. "Ackshully, that lot is part of the NATO missile defense system built ter let yer know if the Russians are coming only—they ain't, fank Gawd."

At Whitby, Eleanor had gone into raptures over the parish church of St. Mary. When they had walked inside she had again expressed her amazement by exclaiming, "Wow—it's just like being inside a wooden sailing ship."

Parker, too, was impressed, not only by the uniqueness of the building, but he found Eleanor's enthusiasm was infectious and he was enjoying her company. The fact that she treated him with respect and enjoyed his banter no doubt affected his mood, and this encouraged him to share her pleasure.

"Ever 'eard o' Captin' Cook?"

"Yes, of course. He was one of the greatest sea explorers and navigators, and also a cartographer and nutritionist. I've seen a monument to him in Kauai in the Hawaiian Islands."

"'Ave yer? Well, fancy that. This village is where 'e used ter live an' started 'is career as a sailor. I fink 'e ran away ter sea from 'is 'ome in the village o' Marton-in-Cleveland."

"This North Sea must have been a good training ground for Captain Cook, for it has quite a reputation for stormy weather."

"Yer can say that agin, Eleanor. I bin aht on a friend's cruiser orften enuff an' the wevver 'as bin pretty 'orrible at times. Still, it's nice ter git aht an when it's rough it's orl the more excitin'."

Eleanor gave him a look of admiration as he continued, "I sailed on Thames barges when I woz a kid but there ain't many o' them left nah."

So the day passed happily for them both, and although Eleanor had succeeded in obtaining more information on her relatives, Parker had got no further.

It was on the morning of the third day that he found a second cousin of Eve's who had supplied him with the information that he required. He smiled at the recollection of the success. They had traced the relative to a remote farm in Yorkshire and had been made most welcome by the farmer. He and his wife had invited them in to have tea and Parker could still recall the taste of the delicious home-made scones he had eaten there. During the course of the conversation they discovered the farmer, Everard Eden, was more closely related to Eleanor than Eve. Parker was delighted when Everard announced that he had known Eve's parents who had visited his family on occasions. It was he who informed Parker that Eve had a brother living in Boston. He had doubted he would get much further in his search and was debating whether to go back to London when he had what to him was an inspiration.

It was about eleven o'clock in the morning, and he and Eleanor were walking back to the car when he said, "I got orl the information I need, 'ow abaht you, Eleanor?"

"Well, I've certainly gotten plenty to work on. What have you in mind?"

"'Ow would yer like ter see a 'orse race? There's a racecourse near Malton. We kin git there in abaht 'arf an hour or so, an' 'ave a bite o' lunch at a pub on the way."

"What a lovely idea—that would be exciting." And without more ado, Parker drove towards Malton. They stopped at a picturesque old pub en route and enjoyed a quick snack, before continuing on to the race course. And it was there that Parker was in his element.

"Nah the first fing we do is ter go ter the paddock an' 'ave a look at the 'orses."

"Do you know much about form?"

"Wait an' see, mate."

"Don't you have to see what the odds are first?"

"Jest leave it ter me." And at that, Eleanor resigned herself to Parker's display of experience. They watched the horses being led round the paddock and Eleanor noticed Parker's look of intense concentration on each horse and rider. "Make a note o' that one, Eleanor." She looked at the card seeing the name was "Nibbler" and the odds were ten to one. She frowned and said, "Why the odds are high and this one is not even near being a favorite."

"I'm not worried abaht that. I'm gonna put twenty nicker on it, an' if I woz you I'd do the same."

"Twenty what? It sounds obscene."

"Twenty nicker; that's Cockney fer pahnds. An' nah yer know wot it means, can yer tell me why is it that a lady wiv a wooden leg can't change a five pahnd note?" Eleanor shook her head.

"'Cos she's only got 'alf a nicker."

"Oh, Bert, that's terrible," she said, but it put her in a good humor and she handed over twenty pounds, although not without misgivings. However, she need not have worried; within fifteen minutes they were each one hundred and ninety pounds better off. They stopped for two more races before Parker's luck ran out and, at Eleanor's suggestion, they drove to see Sledmere House before returning to York. Parker readily agreed; one of his strong points with gambling was to know when to stop.

At Sledmere, Eleanor was not disappointed. She had read that two hundred or so years ago the Yorkshire Folds had been virtual wasteland. Then a man of vision and energy had built a fine home there. The man, Sir Christopher Sykes and his successors, had transformed the countryside into the fertile attractive farmland they drove through to the property itself.

Inside the building, Eleanor was almost breathless with admiration for the richness of the decorations. The great library, one hundred feet long with its richly decorated arched ceilings, splendid furniture, relics of bygone wars and superb inlaid wooden floors rendered her favorite exclamation of "wow" almost inaudible. The exotic decorations of the Turkish Room which had been copied from one of the sultan's apartments in Istanbul, had a similar effect on her.

That evening at dinner they decided to celebrate their winnings with a bottle of champagne which Parker seldom drank. He found himself so enjoying Eleanor's company that he felt it a special occasion, especially as he thought it would be the last evening spent together and he had been more successful than she realized. Eleanor had reminisced on the past three days enthusing on all they had seen and the things they had done. "Those beautiful homes and churches, so old and so impressive," she had enthused. "I must go to some of the services to experience the real atmosphere sometime while I am here. I am a Unitarian myself but I don't think that it matters what denomination one is. If your faith makes you a good citizen and enables you to live harmoniously with your fellows and makes sense of this life, that is what matters."

"Blimey, you sahnd like a preacher. Anyway, wot's a Unitarian?"

"Oh, Unitarian churches accept people of any faith or belief. It doesn't matter whether you are a Jew, a Muslim, Catholic, Buddhist, Hindu, atheist or agnostic. One can go to the church for worship, prayer, meditation or just fellowship. One is just committed to open honest inquiry to advancing scientific truth. I think it is a nice idea, don't you?"

"Yus, I suppose so. Ain't given it much fort ackshully."

"Don't you go to church, Bert?"

"Nah. I don' go 'cos it's where people frow fings."

"Throw things?"

"Yerse. The priest frows 'oly water at babies, people frow confetti an' rice at weddin's an' the priest frows earf at funerals."

Eleanor burst out laughing at this unexpected reply and added, "Oh, Bert, you are a clown."

She then told him that she had been very impressed by his skill at picking winners at the race course and the confidence he had shown in finding his way around. It was while he was reveling in her praise that she told Parker how much she had appreciated his company. "I have had such a super time and you have been so kind and helpful to me. This will be a memory of a lifetime. I do want so much to keep in touch. We must exchange addresses and telephone numbers," and at that she rummaged in her handbag and produced a visiting card.

Although reluctant at first, caught in the mood of the moment and no doubt the effects of the champagne, Parker had responded likewise; almost immediately afterwards he mentally kicked himself for being a fool. During the course of the day he had deftly managed to relieve Eleanor of a brooch when they had been hemmed in close together by the crowd at the racecourse. So far Eleanor had not missed it, due probably to their having arrived late for dinner and her not having had time to change.

He had been shaken out of his thoughts by Eleanor telling him that she was going to Scotland and then to Scandinavia for a few weeks. "I am coming back to England after that and will be in London for a week or so before flying back home." Then she had added, "I would love to see you again, Bert."

Parker had experienced a strange feeling when he heard what she said, and he had seen the look of genuine sincerity in her eyes. No woman had spoken to him or looked at him like that before. It prompted him to delve into his pocket and produce the brooch he had earlier helped himself to.

"'Ere, I almost fergot. I picked this up earlier terday. Yer know yer will 'ave ter be more careful. I picked it up when I went ter the tote and fergot abaht it in the excitement o' the race."

Eleanor opened her mouth in surprise and instinctively touched her breast on the left side and then looked too, as if she could not believe that the brooch was missing.

"Oh, Bert, what would I have done without you? You really are so honest, kind and good to me. This brooch was given to me by my late husband and means such a lot to me. I just cannot thank you enough."

"Oh, fink nuffink of it, Eleanor. It wos just a bit o' luck."

They went for a walk after dinner and looked in the shop windows lining the quaint narrow streets. It was a warm pleasant evening and it had been Eleanor's suggestion that they walk for she was still wound up with the excitement of the day. They passed two tall helmeted policemen on foot patrol who responded to Eleanor's "Goodnight."

"I think your policemen are wonderful, don't you, Bert?"

Parker had other thoughts about them but managed to say, "Yerse, ain't they just."

"I do like the helmets they wear and it is so nice that they do not carry guns."

Parker was able to say, "Yus, yer quite right there," with some degree of sincerity, thinking of the narrow escapes he had had from brushes with the law.

"Are citizens allowed to carry guns, Bert?"

He shook his head. "Nah. Yer can only use guns like pistols or rifles at a gun club, or shotguns fer game, an' even then the coppers interview yer an' make it difficult ter git a license."

"I wish it were like that in my country. Anybody can get handguns and there were fifty thousand killings last year, not all with handguns of course, but they played a very big part."

Parker remarked, "Good Gawd," and thought to himself, Yer don't need guns ter kill people. He was inwardly glad that he had never been asked to participate in the removal of those who had got in the way of Boss. Boss had others who did that sort of dirty work very efficiently.

Back at the hotel after the walk, they stopped at Eleanor's bedroom door before he went to his room. Eleanor took both his hands in hers and said, "Thank you, Bert, for the wonderful time you have given me. I shall always treasure this memory," and she leaned forward and impulsively kissed him. He was taken by surprise at this and suddenly felt the urge to respond, but something held him in check—some advice given to him by his father many years ago. He replied, "Bin very nice fer me too yer know," and went to pull away his hands but she squeezed them slightly, and the imploring look she gave him signaled that she wanted him to spend the night with her. The thought frightened him, for he had kept away from feminine ties since he was a young man. He simply squeezed her hands in turn then released them suddenly and said, "See yer in the mornin', Eleanor, g'night and sleep tight." And at that, he had turned on his heels and gone to his room.

Parker sat down on a comfortable armchair in his flat still thinking about the events of the last few days. The morning he had left York he and Eleanor had breakfasted together and again she said she would contact him when in London in a month or so's time. She had kissed him good-bye and he thought over that with very mixed feelings. He remembered his father's advice about women and sex and smiled to himself at the recollection. "I tell yer me lad, be careful abaht women, they can be the ruin of yer," his father had said.

"Wos Muvver the ruin o' you, Dad?"

"Nah. I woz lucky. Yer muvver's a good un, she stood by me froo fick an' fin."

Parker knew that was true. During World War II, his father had to work in London as a docker during the worst of the blitz. He himself had been born with German bombers flying overhead and devastating the city. His mother had never left his father's side although she could have been evacuated to the countryside along with many other wives. When ships had been mainly diverted to Liverpool he had been ordered there and she had accompanied him. And she stayed on despite the frequent bombing of that port.

"But I tell yer me lad, your muvver's one in a million. She's me real ol' Dutch she is. Orl the blokes wot I know ave trouble wiv their ol' women. Their eiver like bleedin' dragons or they'll drop their knickers to anuvver bloke as soon as their 'usbands back is turned."

Only once had he been deeply smitten by a young woman, and when she had turned him down because his rival owned a motorcar, he had decided not to take an amorous interest in the opposite sex again. It had not been difficult. His small stature was not an asset and with the way he obtained a living, he was better off without the obligations demanded by female company.

"I tell yer, me lad," his father had said, "sex is an overrated pastime. It can get yer inter orl sorts o' trouble. A bloke named Lord Chesterfield summed it very nice, I fink. 'E said: 'The price is exorbitant, the pleasure is transitory, an' the position ridiculous.'"

Later he had added, "An American bloke named Benjamin Franklin, gave a good bit o' advice ter a young man, an' it's worf finkin' abaht: 'In your amours yer should prefer old women ter young ones. They are so grateful.'" And that piece of advice came back to his mind as he recalled Eleanor. Of course, she was not really old, but she was experienced and to his dismay he found her attractive.

Simultaneously he was annoyed with himself for giving back the brooch when he could have kept it, and she would have been none the wiser—or would she? Like a twit, he had given her his address, and had she suspected him of stealing it the local police would have no doubt been delighted to pin the theft on him. "Them rocks must 'a bin worf a few fahsand nicker. Blimey, I must be losin' me grip," he decided.

The fact that he felt attracted to her made him feel more uncomfortable when he realized that Eleanor was distantly related to Eve Eden and her brother. He knew what was going to happen to Eve when the Boss or his henchmen caught up with her and when he reflected on how Eleanor trusted him, he suddenly discovered that life was more complicated than he wanted. "Oh sod it," he said out loud. "Wot the bloody 'ell do I do nah?"

chapter eleven

The sea voyage had been quite pleasant and Bernadette and Rory had enjoyed themselves, relaxing after the stress and excitement of the bombing. While the container vessel plowed its way across the Bay of Biscay the going had been rough, for there were cross-seas and she rolled heavily. The weather also had deteriorated and gray skies and rain were encountered every day. Both of them felt a little seasick, but the use of scopolamine patches behind the ears for a few days kept nausea away, and they were fully adjusted to the motion of the vessel and sea as they sailed south down the coast of Portugal.

Their first port of call was Lisbon where a number of containers were unloaded and others taken on board. By the time they passed Cape St. Vincent, scene of a great British naval victory during the Napoleonic wars, the weather started to clear, and they enjoyed strolling along the tanker's vast deck in brilliant sunshine after the *El Arabayana* changed course to east, making a swift passage to Lisbon in Spain. Here, more containers were unloaded and others embarked. The first officer, who spoke good English, was standing by Rory when the container vessel drew in beside the jetty. Rory had been impressed by his command of the English language and English diction.

"Where did you learn to speak English so well?" Rory had asked out of curiosity.

"In England. I went to a school of navigation and sat for my mate's ticket there."

"Do you like the English?" said Bernadette who had overheard the conversation.

"I was treated very well while I was there. They are a great seafaring nation and one of their most famous sailors came here to Cadiz."

"Oh," said Rory, somewhat unenthusiastically. The first officer did not notice the inflection in Rory's Irish voice and carried on.

"When England was at war with Spain during the Elizabethan period, Sir Francis Drake came with a small fleet of ships and put out of action a lot of Spanish vessels delaying the Spanish invasion plans by a year. He called that act, 'Singeing the King of Spain's Beard.' He had quite a sense of humor. The Spaniards called him 'El Draco,' the Dragon. He was a brilliant seaman. He was the first captain of a vessel to sail round the world."

"I thought it was Magellan," interjected Bernadette.

"No, Magellan died in the Pacific and never completed the journey."

"You seem to like the English," commented Rory.

"I have no cause not to. I received a fine education in navigation and seamanship when I was there and, what is more, they freed my country from the Italian colonialists, then withdrew and left us in peace. We now have a good leader in President Qaddafi and our country is prosperous."

"The British had more colonies than anyone else."

"True, but they did something probably no other colonial power did."

"And what was that?"

"They dismantled the British Empire voluntarily and did their best to leave democracies in their wake. That the democracies have not all succeeded cannot be blamed on the British."

At that point the officer had to attend to his duties much to the relief of both Bernadette and Rory who did not like the trend of the conversation.

From Cadiz they headed for the Strait of Gibraltar. The coast of Spain was clearly visible as they passed the Cabo Trafalgar, near where Lord Nelson had won his famous victory that put an end to French and Spanish sea power, and spelled the end of Napoleon's ambitions to become dictator of Europe. Continuing now in an easterly direction through the entrance to the Mediterranean, the strait of itself, they stood on the bridge of the tanker and viewed the low mountains of Morocco to the south and the Rock of Gibraltar to the north. Rory recalled to Bernadette that the British had shot some IRA bombers in that very rock several years ago. He would like to go there and plant a few bombs himself to avenge the dead terrorists. They discussed that possibility and concluded that it would be worthwhile especially as it might damage the British tourist industry.

They spent a pleasant few days passing along the coast of Algeria and could see the Atlas Mountains in the distance, shimmering in the heat as each day progressed. Their next port of call was El Diazir, previously known as Algiers. There, more containers were unloaded and others taken on board and from there the *El Arabayana* sailed directly to Sicily.

It was a calm sunny day when the freighter arrived at the port of Palermo. They had spent some time on deck, sheltered on the port side out of the direct rays of the sun and taking advantage of the cooling breeze generated by the speed of the vessel. Later they were invited up on the bridge to obtain a better view, and escape the very fine dust that, with a change of wind direction, was being carried across the sea from the Sahara Desert. Rory and Bernadette had seen from afar the tops of the mountains which rose some 5,000 feet. They passed Isola Igadi and then noticed some smaller islands to the south, before the vessel motored some fifty miles along the Sicilian coast and then turned to starboard to enter the Godolfi di Palermo.

The vessel slowed in its way to the harbor and they noticed that the city nestled in the shadow of a great rock which, with its steep cliffs, dominated Palermo and its large harbor. As they progressed, extensive shipping facilities came into view and there were many vessels to be seen varying from small fishing boats to the odd large oil tanker.

It was a new experience for Rory to go for training in Sicily; previously terrorists were trained in Libya. But for some time the members of the Irish terrorist organizations had been forbidden in that country. When the *El Arabayana* tied up at the container depot, both Rory and Bernadette had their baggage ready. They were met on board by a customs officer accompanied by two swarthy men with black hair and dark brown eyes. One was a big powerful-looking man but the shorter appeared to be in charge.

In a strong Sicilian accent, he announced that they were immigration officials and requested to see their documents. After scrutinizing them carefully and looking hard at both Rory and Bernadette, he returned them and then, formalities completed, smiled and held out his hand.

"I am Mario Gambetti and this is my colleague, Sextus Corripere. Signore O'Higgins, Signora Malone, benvenuto a la Sicilia."

His companion gave a smile of welcome and also extended his hand. Rory felt the powerful grip of Sextus, but Bernadette was surprised when he bowed and kissed her hand instead. With the introductions completed, Mario then requested the two Irish terrorists to follow him, and he led the way while his companion took up the rear and ogled Bernadette as they left the freighter and disembarked. The officer on the bridge gave them a wave as they walked along the quayside to a waiting car.

It was an old but roomy Fiat that was parked at the end of the quay. The leading official unlocked the trunk and Bernadette and Rory put their cases inside, and then the official told Rory to sit in the passenger's seat at the front and Bernadette in the back. He then seated himself in the driver's seat while his companion made a great display of opening the door for Bernadette, and then entered and sat beside her. He gave her a sideways smile and looked down at her exposed knees, but then she gave him a look which was a warning to him not to get wrong ideas.

There were many vehicles on the busy city streets and the honking of horns as well as the stink of exhausts filled the air. As the Fiat drove through Palermo, the driver relaxed a little and commented on various buildings and places of interest that they passed. "In Roman times thees city was a called a Panormus, and there," indicating a magnificent building, "that ees the grande cathedral. Eet is magnifico, yes?" On Rory and Bernadette murmuring their assent he added, "You musta go there for mass one day."

He pointed out other magnificent buildings on either side of the Via Vittorio Emanuele and Bernadette commented on numerous buildings showing scars of bomb damage. "Yes, that happened in 1943 when the Americanos anda the Inglese soldieri took the city froma the Germans."

On Rory asking where they were going Mario replied, "We go to see Signore Luigi Furari. He ees the big boss, whata you call the Godfather. Everyone ees very polite to him." As an afterthought he added that the journey would take them just over an hour.

An unpleasant smell of sulfurous chemicals, garlic and other odors filled the hot humid air as they progressed through the industrial end of the suburbs. Both Bernadette and Rory observed these urbanized areas and the countryside as they progressed, and were struck by the poverty. Many buildings looked shabby and all could have done with a fresh coat of paint. Most of the women they saw were dressed in black and the children had well-worn clothing. They passed several groups of youths hanging around in the streets; unemployment seemed the norm as elsewhere. The unemployment reminded them of southern Ireland but there it ended. The countryside beyond the plain of the Conca d'Oro with its mountains and heat stood out in sharp contrast. There was dust in the air and Mario informed him that it had blown over from the Sahara Desert.

As they progressed along a mountain road, they could see the lower slopes cultivated with almond and olive trees and vineyards. Laurel abounded everywhere and also visible were pomegranate, orange, lemon, hazel and other fruit and nut trees. As they drove higher on to a road on the lower slopes of the mountains they saw thin forests of beech and chestnut interspersed with slopes of Mediterranean scrub; it in turn, gave way to rocky arid slopes deeply scored by flash floods which had dug their own ravines and removed any topsoil, and left them devoid of vegetation.

Leaving the main road, the Fiat drove uphill for few miles passing a village and some cultivated land with cattle and sheep sheltering beneath trees and a few orchards where peasants could be seen tending the trees.

The road dipped in a small valley and then ascended over a small rise; before them it could be seen terminating where a stone wall some fifteen feet in height spanned it and stretched either side for over one hundred yards. The wall was interrupted by an archway over the road and a large barred gate stopped further progress. Mario stopped the car at the gate and an armed guard looked out at him. He opened the gate and motioned them through after Mario had identified himself.

Having driven through, the guard closed the gate behind them and went to a small stone guardhouse situated inside the wall and telephoned their arrival to the villa towards which they drove.

"What is this place?" asked Rory.

"Thees ees the villa of Signore Luigi Furari. He ees the Big Man and your host while you are on the Island. And that," he said pointing to a big stone house which came into view as they rounded a bend in the road, "that ees hees villa, or perhaps I should say *uno castèllo*."

The large three-storied building was surmounted by a shallow sloping tiled roof of the old Roman style. The windows on the outside were small and most of them had their wooden shutters closed, presumably, Bernadette thought, to protect the rooms from the heat of the Sicilian sun. The road along which they had driven from the perimeter of the estate was lined with tall pines and the vegetation on each side was obviously better watered than other aspects of the island that they had seen. The road led directly to an arched gateway built into the villa and two stories in height. Two iron gates opened as the Fiat drew up to one side of the archway and two men, one armed with a submachine gun walked to the car and looked inside at the occupants.

"*Ciao, Roderigo,*" said Mario, addressing the guard who peered into his window.

"*Ah, Mario, mio amico, buon giorno. Come sta?*"

"*Benissimo—e lei?*"

Roderigo smiled, "*Benissimo, grazie,*" and, looking at the two strangers said, "*Banditti Irlandese?*"

Mario laughed, "*Forse. No, terroristi Irlandese.*" Then he opened the car door and on alighting requested Bernadette and Rory to do so. They stepped out and he again addressed Roderigo.

"*Permetta che presenti a Rory O'Higgins e Bernadette Malone.*" And turning to Rory and Bernadette said, "Thees ees Roderigo Sicarus. He isa the right-hand man of Signore Furari and willa look after you from now on." Roderigo shook hands with Rory and then kissed Bernadette's hand and bowed slightly.

With a strong trace of a Sicilian accent laced with garlic, Roderigo said, "You are both very welcome. I hope your stay in Sicilia will be a happy and interesting one. I am in charge of your training but we will get down to details later." He signaled to an elderly gray-haired servant and a buxom middle-aged woman dressed in black, who were standing just inside the gateway. "Meanwhile I will get Alfredo and Isabella to take your luggage to your bedrooms and when you are ready come down to the dining room. Isabella will show you the way."

Sextus opened the trunk of the car and handed the two handgrips to Alfredo and Isabella who looked pleased on discovering both were light to carry, and, smiling at Rory and Bernadette, led the way to their respective rooms.

As they walked through the entrance to the villa, the size of the building became more apparent. In the center was a raised pool with marble walls delicately carved. There was a marble bowl supported by three graceful female figures in its middle from which a fountain played. A few slender cypresses were artistically arranged to form four small groups around the pool, which was itself surrounded by a grassed area interrupted by stone paths. Marble benches adorned each corner of the grassed area and shrubs, and nearby flowers were planted. A paved path encompassed the perimeter of the courtyard and a cloister with Greek colonnades was present along each wall. The villa itself was built in the form of a square, each side being some two hundred feet long. Above the cloisters were two galleries, the upper being roofed. They both noted that although the windows on the outside of the building were small, those on the inside were large. Shutters were still present but with the shelter of the balconies and roof, they were not necessary to keep out the sun.

"This makes an ideal fort," remarked Rory to Bernadette.

"Maybe it has been used as such in the past," she replied, and then added, "and in the present, too."

Alfredo and Isabella took them to their rooms which were situated on the third floor. Each was comfortably appointed and well furnished, and they both got the impression that Luigi Furari was a wealthy man.

That impression was confirmed when they were introduced to him after having settled in. Roderigo had met them and escorted them to the ground floor where they walked along one of the cloisters to halt at the door of Luigi's office. He had knocked and was ordered to enter, and on doing so found the Mafia boss dictating a letter to a tall blonde woman with Greek features. She was seated at a computer and taking down his words at dictation speed. He looked round at them as they entered and then walked towards them extending his hand and in American English with a trace of an Italian accent addressed them with charming smile.

"Ah. So Bernadette Malone and Rory O'Higgins you have arrived at last. Welcome to Sicilia." He bowed slightly as he kissed Bernadette's hand and shook hands lightly with Rory.

Luigi was a man past middle age. The black hair of his earlier years was iron-gray. Turned sixty years, he had a spare figure which still denoted agility and considerable physical strength. Of swarthy complexion, his face showed several scars from wounds acquired during his very active criminal life. With his slightly aquiline features, one's attention was drawn to his deep-set eyes with their almost black irises and which had a hard penetrating look about them. This impression was enhanced by his possessing thin lips which suggested he could be capable of ruthless cruelty. Both of his new guests got the impression that here was a man not to be trifled with let alone crossed. Later they were to learn that his American English had been acquired during frequent visits to the USA where he had a powerful following in various rackets involving organized crime. Ostensibly the enterprises were legitimate, but bribery, extortion and the elimination of competitors kept him wealthy and free from unwanted legal inquiry into his business activities.

Despite his recurrent traveling across the Atlantic he never suffered from jet-lag. This was partly due to his physical fitness and also to the fact that he traveled on Concorde; he looked upon the fare as legitimate expenses in an illegitimate business. Later the two Irish terrorists were to learn that Luigi's family had not always been wealthy, but with the advent of the 1939-1945 war, American strategic planners had thought up the idea of enlisting the Mafia to help the Allied cause; this had resulted in the sending of money and arms to Sicily among other places. From that start the Furari family had considerably benefited and, in addition to the American arms, they had managed to obtain German weapons which had been acquired, as the weaponry had not been collected, once hostilities had ceased.

However, Luigi was not content with old weapons when sophisticated guns were available, and he and his followers enjoyed the results of modern research and development in the armaments field. This was due to the manufacturers' strong desire to export arms to countries that would have been better off, had the resources spent in propping up power-mad leaders been used for home industries and feeding their hungry populations. However the state of the world's poor was of no great interest to the Luigi clan, except that poverty made bribery and extortion all the easier.

The first two days in Sicily were spent in getting to know parts of the Island where their training would be carried out. Bomb-making from garden fertilizer and weed killer was already a well practiced art with both Rory and Bernadette. It was new techniques with more powerful explosives and detonating devices in which they were more interested. The smaller the devices the easier it would be to conceal and plant them. The latest explosives difficult to detect and reliable timing devices were all to be practiced with. In addition, powerful rifles for sniping at long range and night vision devices were all on the training agenda. Even techniques for holding up pursuers were to be included, and they both looked forward to commencing the course proper. It was later that they discovered they would be participating in a training exercise that would have unanticipated results.

■ ❑ ■ ❑ ■

It was a coincidence that Parker opened his apartment door a few seconds before Caria. He had his hand on the shared street door handle when Caria opened her apartment door and emerged into the small hallway. She looked better made up than usual, and wore clothes more suited to traveling than she normally wore for her occupation at the Londinium Club. Parker looked at her quizzically, then said. "'Allo, an' where do yer fink your goin'?"

"Ain't none o' your bleedin' business, mate. I got a few days orf."

"'Oo sed so?"

"Ma. I ain't no good ter the customers once a munf an' it's abaht time yer knew it. Didun't yer muvver tell yer nuffink abaht the birds an' the bleedin' bees."

"Very funny."

Both Caria and Parker noticed the postman deliver the letter almost at the same time. Mail arriving at their apartments was not a daily occurrence and naturally their curiosity was aroused. They shared a joint letter box which was situated beside the front door of the apartments and Parker, standing by the street door, was able to reach the mailbox first. As he stooped to pick up the letter which had fallen to the floor, he heard Caria walk forward out of curiosity; he suddenly whistled in surprise.

"Wot is it? Whose it for?"

"It ain't fer you mate, it's fer Eve."

"Wot. Who from?"

Parker looked at the left hand corner of the envelope and read the sender's address.

"Well, stone the crows! It's from 'er bruvver in America. De Vere-Smythe won't 'arf be pleased wiv this."

chapter twelve

Richard yawned. He had been up for nearly two hours and noticed a slight lightening in the sky. In addition to that, there were signs the avian dawn chorus was beginning. He was sitting in his study re-reading data he had entered in his computer. He was puzzled by several cases of superior limbal keratitis, a disease of the outer eye that had appeared in the hospital clinic. One would expect vernal conjunctivitis at this time of the year—allergic conditions were the run of the mill as far as he was concerned. He had carefully gone over a differential diagnosis of each case at the hospital and there had been no error. The patients had complained of a foreign body sensation, burning, pain, and a mucoid or mucopurulent discharge. They had also experienced a blepharoptosis or a strong desire to keep their eyes closed. He was not unduly worried about two of the patients, for they had experienced the condition before. Their condition spontaneously recurred and prior occurrences had lasted for weeks in one case and for years in the other.

The patient he was more concerned about was one who had keratoconus. This distortion of the cornea meant that in order to keep her job it was essential for her to wear contact lenses. The senior optometrist had first brought her to his notice during the out patients' morning clinic. The upper palpebral conjunctiva, the skin situated beneath the lid, had shown a fine velvety hypertrophy. He had observed that the papillae or little nodules had coalesced and remained small. This ruled out the beginnings of medium or giant papillary conjunctivitis. The upper conjunctiva was hyperemic, excessively red, and mildly keratinized or dry in the ten o'clock and two o'clock regions.

The optometrist had pointed out the thickening of the upper limbus, or edge of the cornea and white of the eye. The area showed that rose bengal accentuated punctate staining more so than the yellow fluorescein. He had been correct in his diagnosis.

Richard recalled taking scrapings from the affected areas of the conjunctiva which showed dryness or keratinization of the epithelial cells, a mixed polymorphonuclear-monocytic cellular response, and also mucus. One problem was that the aetiology of superior limbal keratitis (SLK) was unknown, and swabbing the affected areas with a solution of silver nitrate had helped, but the contact lenses should be discontinued if the condition was to improve. The keratoconus or distorted cornea had not reached the normal stage for a corneal graft, but that could be brought forward. However, he did not intend to carry out that operation until the SLK had cleared and that was an unknown factor. The question was how to speed up the treatment and prevent a recurrence of the condition.

He rose to his feet and went into the kitchen, heated some water in a mug and walked into the garden. The dawn chorus was now increasing as the sky brightened along the eastern rim. He walked down the dew-strewn path towards the rockery, stopping at the pond to admire the sunrise as he sipped from the mug. The opening lines from a Shakespearean sonnet entered his mind as he stood there:

> *"Full many a glorious morning have I seen*
> *flatter the mountain tops with sovereign eye,*
> *kissing with golden face the meadows green;*
> *gilding pale streams with heavenly alchemy . . . "*

His reverie was abruptly stopped by a rustling in the hedging behind the rookery. He froze and half turned his head in the direction of the noise, wondering who it was. It flashed across his mind that someone was watching the house, having discovered that Eve was living there. He felt hot and cold as he thought of the children and Dawn being exposed to danger because of his affection for his cousin. If there were someone watching him then he would have to act normally. What if the person were armed?

The thought made him feel uncomfortable but he knew he was a perfect target and there was nothing he could do in his defense. He stood stock-still, gazing into the pool as the goldfish rose to catch gnats skimming the surface. Were anyone watching him, they would think he was keeping still in order not to disturb the fish. There was a further rustling in the hedging, and out of the corner of his eyes he saw the head of a small deer suddenly poke through. His immediate reaction was to burst out laughing at its appearance and at his own fears. His outburst no doubt frightened the deer more than he had been, for it disappeared quicker than it had appeared, and he heard its movement through the small copse as it fled.

As he returned to the house, he again reflected on the possibility that the people looking for Eve might trace her to his home and then his wife and children would be in real danger. The more he thought about the situation the less he liked it, but what could he do? Should he ask his cousin to find another hiding place for her? If he did so he would upset his cousin and Eve for that matter. She had now been with the family for several weeks and it was convenient having her to help with the home and children. The children were very fond of her and she got on well with them all. Another point was that she was found to be very trustworthy. He had been assured that the chances of her being traced were virtually nil. She did not come from that area and no one but Sean and the police knew of her whereabouts. Perhaps he was worrying unnecessarily. In a few months' time she would marry Sean and then she would be his responsibility and move somewhere else.

He started to prepare some porridge when Dawn entered the kitchen. "Hello sweetheart, you're up early," he said, putting his arms around her. She gave him a kiss and hug in response. He was about to mention his doubts about Eve staying when she interrupted by saying, "And how long have you been up, Richard?"

"About two or three hours. You appeared so fast asleep when I rose—I hope I did not disturb you?"

"Your overactive mind chasing away Morpheus again, I suppose." Then she said, "No, you did not disturb me," and added, "What's the problem this time? I hope John did not see another ghost?"

He smiled at that suggestion and went back to his previous thoughts. He suddenly realized that if he voiced his fears he might cause Dawn unnecessary worry, and so launched into a description of his clinical research. Dawn listened while she prepared the breakfast table. Soon they both heard the children and Eve stirring, and the dog came running downstairs from John's room, sat by the garden door and made a slight whining noise, her usual request to go out.

"Time to spend a penny eh, Poppet?" said Richard and Poppet walked out of the door, sniffed the air and suddenly shot off down the garden barking loudly.

"What has she seen out there?" asked Dawn.

"Probably the deer I saw earlier. They are beautiful little things. We must see if we can train her not to chase them, although I doubt they will come back after her little caper."

Within a few minutes Poppet returned and tapped on the glass door with a paw, signaling that she wanted to come in. Richard interrupted his preparations and ladled some dog food into her bowl, which she emptied eagerly.

It was a typical morning scene in the Rutherford household. The children had fended for themselves with their ablutions and dressing, and they entered the breakfast room ready to tuck away happily everything placed before them. It was an informal affair, but Eve was always impressed with the fact that both Richard and Dawn did not tolerate bad table manners and eating habits. She could see the wisdom of this for it meant that the children would be comfortable in any society.

Richard usually left before seven thirty in order to arrive in adequate time at the hospital, for he started operating at eight. Dawn left next and then Eve with the children, dropping off Jennifer and John at their school and then Jean at hers a quarter of an hour later. Before she left, Dawn had spoken to Eve: "The weather report mentioned light rain this morning, but if the ground is dry enough this afternoon, Len will be along to cut the grass."

"Oh, good. I expect he'll want his usual cup of tea," Eve replied, quite pleased with the thought of seeing him again. Len Barker was in his late sixties and had grown up on a farm in the Essex countryside. He and Eve had a farming background in common and she enjoyed his company. When he had his tea she always joined him and was well entertained by his reminiscences and anecdotes. His knowledge of local history was encyclopedic and he was a mine of country folklore and information. He also enjoyed teasing. Absolutely fearless, he was so adept at keeping a serious face and leading people on that Richard had presented him with a large wooden spoon one Christmas. He was particularly popular with the ladies and although he lived alone in the village, being a widower, he always had plenty of visitors to his home where he enjoyed holding court in the driveway of his house.

That morning, after leaving Jean at her school, Eve drove to the Catholic church. Father Brendan was taking the class of potential converts or catechumens, as he correctly called them, for their instruction. She was enjoying the course immensely, and some of the knowledge she recalled from her Protestant upbringing in the Church of England. She sat in the small vestry with five other catechumens and listened attentively to his lecture. He had been discussing Saint Peter and the part he had paid in the foundation of the Roman Catholic Church.

"When he was released from imprisonment by King Herod, Saint Peter fled to Rome and there founded the Roman Catholic Church. By placing his hands on his successor and with it the Holy Spirit, he passed on the apostolic blessing to all succeeding popes. The pope is therefore the direct successor of an apostle of Jesus who, as you know, was the Son of God." Father Brendan paused and looked at the class and, noting that they were all paying eager attention, continued, "In the New Testament one can see the words of Christ: 'He who hears you hears me.' This was the authority for his disciples to teach his message in his name. This commission to his disciples is also the direct authorization of those followers to teach in his name. And so by the laying on of hands and the initial commission to his disciples by Jesus Christ, the Roman Catholic Church is the true authority for the teaching of the Word of God. Remember those words of Christ to his disciples, 'He who hears you hears me.'"

With her quick mind and good memory, Eve had no problem retaining all that was being taught. She found herself wanting Father Brendan to go more quickly and he soon realized that she was brighter than any other member of the class.

This pleased him considerably and he gave her texts to learn and extra work to study at home. He realized that such an intelligent convert would be an asset to the church. It also crossed his mind that when she and Dr. Sean O'Neill were married they would be in a position to have a considerable influence in their community. With the prospect of them having a large family there would be more children born into the faith.

In turn, Eve was eager to make progress as quickly as possible. She was driven by an honest desire to find purpose in existence, to become purified from the taint of prostitution which she abominated and, perhaps most of all, to be in the position to become Sean's wife. She found her love for him increasing with the passage of time. Frequently, when thinking of him, and that was most of the time, she would find her heartbeat increase and other thoughts subordinated—it took a considerable effort of will to drag her mind back to her task at hand.

On returning from the church, she sat in the sun lounge at Bracken and quickly scanned her notes. It was early afternoon and the sun had dried the morning's rain from the lawns. She could see Len sitting on the small tractor mower at the far end of the garden, cutting the grass. He was near the copse and shrubbery and the noise of the tractor mower was not intrusive at that distance. She watched as he occasionally disappeared out of sight behind the graceful weeping willow beside the pond. From where she sat, one could only be aware of the pond by the sight of the strongly growing bulrushes and lilies that flourished beside it.

To its left side, she could discern the small cypresses, heather and other plants that grew richly on the large rockery. Her gaze was again drawn towards Len as the tractor mower emerged from behind the graceful weeping willow. It took four hours to cut the lawns in the back and front of the house, and when he had finished the back lawn she always invited Len into the sun lounge for a cup of tea. As she anticipated, he would not finish the back for an hour and a half at least, so she occupied her time with revision.

She glanced at her notes and started to daydream of Sean. Then, suddenly realizing what was happening, smiled, and forced herself to concentrate on her reading: "The Roman Catholic Church recognizes the Bible as the word of God and that tradition is the word of the church. The Roman Catholic Church is the living teaching authority of Christianity."

"I wonder what Dad would have thought about that," she mused. Then went on, "This authority is called the Magisterium. The church is the deposit of revealed truth, faith and morals. It was the first Vatican Council that stated historically, 'Human reason has but a distorted idea of God and an imperfect idea of moral order. In order to understand the true nature of the divine and of correct moral order, God revealed himself to mankind through Jesus Christ. In order to bring this about, the Immaculate Conception occurred through the Holy Spirit. God therefore reveals himself to mankind as the Father, Son and Holy Spirit: the Holy Trinity.'"

The Holy Spirit, she remembered in her Protestant teaching had been referred to as the Holy Ghost, and that reminded her of the private conversation she had had with Father Brendan after the lesson. She had informed him of the ghost she had seen in the garden. He had questioned her very searchingly about what she had seen and raised doubts as to the nature of the vision. Her persistence that it had not been an hallucination nor a dream had convinced him that she sincerely believed in what she had seen.

"What did it look like?" he had asked.

"Like a woman in long robes."

"Has anyone else seen this apparition?"

"Yes, John has. Well no, not directly. One evening I heard him call out to his father that there was a ghost in his room."

Father Brendan had thought carefully in silence for a few minutes before advising Eve. "It would appear to me that you have had a revelation that there is a spiritual world. This is a confirmation of your faith and you are one of the fortunate few to be so blessed. I advise you to keep this revelation to yourself but let me know if you see the figure again. I wonder if it is one of our blessed saints who has appeared to you in a vision or . . . ," he paused and said in almost a whisper, "or even our blessed Virgin Mother herself." And then he quoted, "Lord, now lettest thou thy servant depart in peace according to thy word; for mine eyes have seen my salvation."

She had left the church feeling strongly moved and convinced that she was now glimpsing at the wonderful reality behind life and the universe. Going back to her notes she read, "Christ was conceived by the Virgin Mary and this was the Immaculate Conception.

158   Adamant Eve

The doctrine of the Immaculate Conception is a dogma of the Roman Catholic Faith. Among other dogmas of the faith are Christ is the true Son of God. The Douay Version of the Bible is the correct translation."

Eve pondered on that. She now had a copy of the Douay Version but had also retained a copy of the King James version which had been given to her as a child by her grandmother. She had enjoyed reading it with its beautiful use of the English language and the aura of poetic truth which had impressed itself on her when quite young. She did not find the Douay Version so enjoyable, but perhaps the aesthetic appeal was unimportant compared with the correct interpretation of the word of God.

The sound of the lawnmower was louder now and intruded into her reflections. She looked up and saw that Len had reached the center of the lawn, which indicated that she still had plenty of time to complete reading through her notes before she had to make tea. She looked back at her notebook. "The church recognizes that as well as the New Testament, the Old Testament is also the word of God, and therefore the church existed before the New Testament. The hierarchy of the church are the pope and the bishops and they are the organs of the teaching authority of God on earth. The pope himself is the leading teaching authority of the church and through God's guidance he is infallible. By declaration of the first Vatican Council, the infallibility of the pope applies to teaching solemnly in the area of faith and morals."

Eve paused on reading that. Had she not read something about the Borgia family and Rodrigo Borgio or, to use his Spanish name, Rodrigo do Borja Y Doms, became Pope Alexander VI and was corrupt? She recalled that her father had mentioned something about him. Perhaps she should ask Father Brendan but, on second thoughts, she would ask Dawn or Richard as she would have a week to go before attending her class again. She read on about the bishops being authentic teachers in their own dioceses and the declaration of an ecumenical council and the assembly of bishops.

Now I must get this teaching order straight, she thought, and read: "The bishops' teaching is known as ordinary teaching; a solemn declaration of an ecumenical council is extraordinary teaching and the most solemn type is a papal declaration—that one is ex-Cathedra from the throne. But that must apply to bishops, too, for they have the most important church in a diocese and that is a cathedral church or one with a throne."

She recalled from her school days that definition of cities: cities were towns with cathedrals, so they were the centers of the Christian dioceses, and immediately started to daydream about being married to Sean in a cathedral.

The mower could now be heard very loudly and she looked up to see Len driving it round the side lawn to the front of the house. She knew it would take him another three quarters of an hour to finish the front lawn and put the machine away.

She noted that the object of the church teaching is faith and morals. "Faith means belief in revealed truth and 'morals' means the moral principles underlying moral judgment and behavior in any area of human conduct."

Well, that is pretty straight forward, she thought, and then paused at the next paragraph. "A moral judgment includes the prohibition of contraception for it is contrary to the laws of nature. In the teaching of the faith, contraception is universally wrong."

I must talk to Sean about this, she thought. I want to have children but not too many. No wonder Catholics have large families. It also reminded her of a discussion Richard and Dawn had where Richard had commented that there were far too many people on the planet for the earth's resources, and the starvation and wars for living space, or "lebensraum" as the Germans referred to it, were a direct result of overpopulation. He had also commented on the large families encouraged by the Muslims and other faiths like the Mormons in America. He had emphasized that the crime in large cities was associated with overcrowding, among other factors such as a breakdown in family discipline, drugs, unemployment and a decay in social and moral teaching in schools and homes. Dawn had mentioned the Malthusian doctrine where the population would always be too great for the food supply. The regular news reports of starvation and wars seemed to confirm their remarks.

All these recollections troubled Eve and made her feel that she was being tempted by doubts about her chosen faith. Then her mind went back to her wonderful revelation and her deep love for Sean. Whether the former or the latter was stronger in influencing her she did not know, but she determined to complete her studies and conversion. For her, that was to be her immediate course of action, and silently she prayed for strength, guidance and the will to put aside all distractions, temptations and deviations from the course she had set herself.

As she finished praying, Eve heard the noise of the mower suddenly increase as Len drove it round the side of the house on his way to the outhouse where it was kept. This was the signal for her to switch on the kettle, and she rose and did so. She had already prepared a tray with two mugs and some biscuits and small cakes beforehand and as soon as the kettle had boiled she quickly made tea and carried the tray out into the sun lounge. Within a few minutes Len came out of the outhouse and strode across the patio into the doorway, his big muscled frame revealing the great physical strength he possessed. His close-cut silver hair contrasted with his ruddy complexion.

"And how are you today, my dear?" he asked in his broad Essex country dialect.

"Fine thanks, Len. And how are you?"

"All the better on seeing you, Eve."

She laughed at that remark. Len was almost old enough to be her grandfather and she knew that his remarks, even if personal, were meant in a light-hearted way and without ulterior motive.

They both sat down at the table and she handed him a mug of tea that she had poured. He helped himself to a biscuit and nibbled at it while she poured her own mug. He commented on her having it without sugar and milk and she informed him that in the north where she came from as well as in Scotland, it was customary to drink tea her way. She added that it was only in the south of England where the people spoiled tea by contaminating it with milk and sugar.

"So you think we're an uncivilized lot down here, do you?" said Len with a grin.

"If the cap fits, wear it," Eve teased him in turn.

"I tell you, we were civilized down here when you lot up there were still running about in animal skins an' painting yourselves with woad." And so the persiflage went on until tea was finished and it was time for Len to go. At this point Eve always handed him his earnings in an envelope prepared by Dawn and accompanied him round to the front garden. She liked to walk on the freshly mown lawn and smell the clean-cut grass.

They stood on the driveway at the front of the house and Eve had her back to one of the open gates. As they stood there, while Len commented on one of the shrubs needing some fertilizer, he looked towards the open gate and watched two men approach them. Eve looked up from the shrub as Len remarked, "I wonder what these two blokes want?"

Eve turned round and both the men were now quite close to her. They wore sunglasses and dark trilby hats, and both had tanned complexions and could have been taken for Italians. One was carrying a bulky attaché case under his left arm and unclipped the lock and slipped his hand inside while he looked at both Eve and Len. Then he addressed Eve, speaking with an American accent.

chapter thirteen

"I want you to circumcise my baby."

Sean looked at the woman seated before him with disbelief. She was from west Africa and of Negroid extraction.

"You want what?" he said, seeking to give himself time to think of a course of action and looked at the baby girl her mother was holding on her lap. She was a lovely little Negress with black curly hair, and he saw her rich brown eyes regarding him. His hesitancy was misunderstood by the mother.

"I want my baby circumcised. My husband tells me that the operation can be done free on the National Health Service. He is a student and we cannot afford to pay."

Sean was at a loss for words for a few seconds. Although he did not agree with it, circumcision for males, that was one thing, but for females it amounted to what was technically known as female genital mutilation (FGM), and unnecessary mutilation it was. And the way it was generally practiced in Africa with unhygienic and crude tools, many infants developed septicaemia or tetanus.

The mention of Mrs. Ezzetti's husband, Chakawa, reminded Sean that he was indeed a student and had come to England on a scholarship to read for a Master's degree. They were a likable enough couple and she had given birth to a girl named Fatima a couple of months before. "Why do you want this done?" he asked.

"We are Muslim and it is part of our faith and a tradition in our tribe."

Whether it was a practice of the Muslim faith was something he would ask Dr. Bannu Sind about. That such customs existed in Africa he was aware. He had seen several Muslim women who had gynecological problems as the result of FGM, and he always referred them to the hospital. In any case, they usually asked to see a woman doctor when they felt anything related to feminine sexual matters was involved, and there were no women doctors in the practice. Meantime, he decided to play for time by saying. "We do not perform these operations at this surgery and I am not so sure that the National Health Service covers it. I shall make inquiries at the gynecological department at the hospital and will have one of the staff contact you." And at that she had thanked him and left.

When he finished the morning surgery he sat in the dining room awaiting Dr. Bannu Sind and thinking back on his morning's work. Sean was having to see more Muslim patients than he had expected because the numbers were increasing. He realized that he would have to know more about their faith and practices to cope properly and understand their thinking.

He had noticed that several women would come into the surgery showing bruises. He had not attached too much importance to that at first, for the odd Caucasian displayed bruising and bullying husbands existed in all walks of life. He had learned that it was not always wise to inquire how marital physical traumas had been acquired. He did learn that one wife had been beaten because she had gone shopping without wearing her veil, and of another who was beaten because she had given birth to a girl when her husband wanted a son. The women usually said nothing probably because they feared getting more. It was true the Caucasian patients would sometimes leave their husbands and sue for divorce, but to his knowledge no Muslim in his practice had done so. Again, he thought to himself, there was no doubt he would have to learn more about Islam. At that point Dr. Sind entered the room and sat down heavily at the table.

"What a morning," he said. "I could do with a holiday."

Sean laughed at this, for it was only a month or so since his colleague had returned from a holiday in Pakistan. "Been busy, eh? Well, it has been the same for me. And that reminds me. One of my patients, Mrs. Fatima Ezzetti, wants me to carry out FGM, and I'm damned if I will. In my opinion, not only is it unnecessary but unethical. In any case, with the economies on the National Health Service that we are bound to follow, it cannot be done." He looked at Bannu Sind inquiringly.

"You are right about the NHS not catering for it, but as for being unethical that is a matter of opinion. Are the Ezzetis from West Africa?"

"Yes. She mentioned something about it being a tribal custom and also implied that it was a Muslim religious practice. Is it?"

"The Koran does not encourage the procedure, but there are many who consider it a religious duty. Would you like me to see her?"

Sean paused before replying, wondering what his colleague had in mind. He knew that FGM takes one of three forms. The mildest was senna circumcision where all or part the clitoris was removed. This resulted in the complete loss of sexual pleasure when intercourse took place. Another form, excision, was removal of the clitoris and all or part of the inner vaginal lips. He felt the worst was infibulation where the clitoris and inner and outer vaginal lips were cut away and then the two sides of the vulva were sewn together leaving only a minute opening for blood and urine.

"You are not thinking of carrying out this barbaric procedure are you?"

Bannu Sind looked at his colleague pensively and pursed his lips.

"If I don't carry it out then when these people go back to Africa they will have it done locally. It will probably be performed by untrained personnel, probably using a razor blade, with no precautions against infection and you know what risks they run." He paused and added, "The people can pay privately."

"But surely this mutilation is not only unnecessary but unkind to the baby in the long run, and I still think it is unethical. After all, we are here to save life and diminish suffering."

"I said ethics is a matter of opinion. What we have to consider here is the long-term effect on the infant. If I don't do it someone else will, and that could be a real health hazard. Another point is that it is not illegal in this country."

"Would you take someone's arm off if they asked you to?"

"I don't think that is a fair argument. Male circumcision is carried out routinely in all countries. Come to think of it, the practice goes back to pre-historic times. The early preference of a stone knife rather than a metal one is an argument in favor of its great antiquity. To my knowledge there are no ethnic barriers to its distribution and I read somewhere that the only exceptions were the Mongols, the Finno-grian and the Indo-Germanic speaking peoples. It is part of the Jewish ritual on the eighth day as part of Abraham's covenant with God. It is also part of Muslim ritual as you know. Of course it is performed less with Caucasian males, but it is still a common practice. Do you think that male circumcision should also be stopped?"

"Yes, I do. After all I can understand it being necessary in countries where washing of the genitals is not a daily routine, but in countries where daily hygiene is the rule then it is completely unnecessary."

"How many males really take care of themselves? Have you not noticed that despite notices in public toilets to wash one's hands after using the toilet, many men don't bother. How many then bother to keep their genitalia clean? You know that it prevents the condition of smegma, and another thing—in India where the Muslims practice ritual circumcision, they have far less cancer of the penis than the Hindus who do not, and with Jews cancer of the penis is a rarity."

Sean reflected on his colleague's argument and then replied, "I can see the point regarding males, but for females it has no medical merit. I appreciate it is an old and widespread practice, and may make some men happier about the chastity of their wives, but I can still see no medical reason in its favor and in my opinion it is still barbaric and unnecessary."

"Look Sean, you like others to respect your religious practices and must therefore respect the practices of other faiths. Regarding male circumcision, in my religion a man cannot enter paradise, or heaven, unless he has been circumcised. Did you not know that?"

"No."

With a twinkle in his eyes Bannu Sind said, "It seems to me that it would be beneficial for you to read the Koran as you are having to see more Muslim patients. You might then get a better idea of the psychology of the people you have to deal with."

Sean looked at Bannu Sind then grinned, "OK, I'll do that. And I'll tell you what I think of it when I've finished." That was the end of the conversation but the beginning of knowledge that opened Sean's eyes to a different world.

Back at his apartment Sean phoned his cousin. He wanted to find out how Eve was and at the same time ask if he could borrow the copy of the Koran that he knew his cousin possessed. His cousin answered the phone and evinced amusement at Sean's request.

"Don't tell me you are considering conversion to Islam?" he had said with a chuckle. "You are not thinking of a pilgrimage to Mecca instead of Jerusalem are you?"

Sean took the ribbing in good part and then explained to Richard his reasons for the request. Richard listened attentively and commented that to achieve his goal of understanding Islamic patients he would benefit more by reading not only the Koran but also on the life of Mohammed and on the cultures of the Mashriq.

"The Mashriq, what is that?"

"That is basically the whole of the Middle East, the area where Islam developed and is largely practiced. I have a very good article on it in one of my encyclopedias and it is only about half a dozen pages, so you will still have time to spend with Eve who, incidentally, is standing right beside me. So I'll hand over the phone and exeunt." He chuckled and, handing the telephone to Eve, left the room.

"Hallo, sweetheart, how are you today?"

"Fine, Sean, but I am missing you."

"Don't you worry, Eve. It's reciprocal, but I guess we both have to be patient. Are things going alright at the church?"

"Oh, yes. What I have to learn is easy and Father Brendan is very helpful. He is such a mine of information and has given me extra reading matter as I am getting ahead of the class."

"Oh good. So you are not just a pretty face, darling."

"Oh, Sean. By the way I could not help overhearing Richard mention about Islam and Mohammed. What was that about?"

"Oh, don't worry about me reading on Islam. I want to understand the Muslim patients better than I do. I am having to see more of them due mainly to relatives settling here from Pakistan. Dr. Bannu Sind cannot cope. Incidentally, tell Richard that I shall pick up a copy of the Koran and one on the life of Mohammed tomorrow. There are still five days before I can get to Bracken so I will use what spare time I have meanwhile. However, I would like to read his article on Middle East culture so I hope you won't mind that intrusion on our time together."

"Not at all, sweetheart. But don't get converted to Islam while I am working so hard on the Catholic faith," Eve added teasingly.

"Don't you worry, Eve. I shall never lose my Christian faith any more than I shall lose my love for you." Then he added with a chuckle, "Maybe I will be able to convert Bannu Sind to Christianity when I understand more about his religion." And so the lovers chatted for a while before reluctantly saying good-night.

The following day after evening surgery, Sean went to a local bookshop and had no difficulty in obtaining the two books he wanted. The shop catered to the Muslim, Hindu as well as the indigenous Caucasian population. He was rather surprised on the shortness of the Koran and, being a fast reader, glimpsing through it, realized that it would only take a few hours to read. The same applied to the work on the life of the prophet. He made his purchases quite happily and went to his apartment, cooked his evening meal and sitting down to eat wasted no time to read.

He learned that the Koran in Arabic meant "the recital" and was a collection of sayings and writings in some 114 short chapters. Apparently they had been written on any available material and had been put into book form on the prophet's death. To Muslims the Koran, or Qur'an in its other spelling, was the true and infallible word of God and is a transcript of a tablet preserved in heaven or paradise, to use the Arabic translation. The word was revealed to Mohammed by the angel Gabriel and apart from a few verses where the prophet or the angel speaks, the speaker throughout is Allah.

In the preface he learned that Mohammed made a habit of retiring into a cave for solitary prayer and meditation. One night the angel Gabriel came to him and said, "Recite!" According to Muslim tradition Mohammed was asleep or in a trance when the vision occurred. He asked the angel, "What shall I recite?"

After the order was repeated three times, Gabriel said: "Recite in the name of your Lord, the Creator, who created man from clots of blood. Recite! Your Lord is the most Bountiful One, who by the pen has taught mankind things they do not know." Sean read quickly and the Islamic message became clearer. Apparently the Jews corrupted the scriptures. Christ was another prophet and by pretending he was the son of God and worshipping him they, too, corrupted the scriptures. God, or Allah, is the founder of the Islamic faith and Mohammed was his true prophet. The true religion had been previously preached by Abraham and it was Mohammed's duty to bring humanity back to the right path from which the Jews and Christians had sadly strayed. God said: "We have made a covenant with you as we did with the other prophets, with Noah and Abraham, with Moses and Jesus, the son of Mary. A solemn covenant we made with them, so that Allah might question the truthful about their truthfulness. But for the unbelievers he has prepared a woeful punishment."

Sean was disturbed by what he read. In the chapter or sura, called "The Cave," it was clearly stated that the Christian belief in Christ as the Son of God was a falsehood: " . . . and admonish those who say that Allah has begotten a son. Surely of this they could have no knowledge, neither they nor their fathers; a monstrous blasphemy is what they utter. They preach nothing but falsehoods."

Other things he read shocked him too, and he made a list of some of the revelations: "Men have authority over women because Allah has made the one superior to the other, and because they spend their wealth to maintain them. Good women are obedient. They guard their unseen parts because Allah has guarded them. As for those from whom you fear disobedience, admonish them and send them to beds apart and beat them. Then if they obey you, take no further action against them. Allah is high and supreme." So that was why he had noticed bruises on the female patients.

Sean read on: "If one of you (men) cannot afford to marry a free believing woman, let him marry a slave girl who is a believer . . . In the Name of Allah, the Compassionate, the Merciful . . . Men, have fear of your Lord, who created you from a single soul. From that soul He created his mate, and through them He bestrewed the earth with countless men and women." More confirmation that women are subordinate to men, he reflected.

"Give orphan (girls) the property that belongs to them. If you fear that you cannot treat orphans with fairness, then you may marry other women who seem good to you: two, three or four of them. But if you fear you cannot maintain equality among them, marry one only or any slave girls you may own."

My God, Sean thought, slavery is approved of in the religion of Islam. "You are forbidden to take in marriage married women, except captives whom you own as slaves. Let those who would exchange the life of this world for the hereafter, fight for the cause of Allah; whether they die or conquer, We shall richly reward them . . . He that leaves his dwelling to fight for Allah and His Apostle and is then overtaken by death, shall be rewarded by Allah. Allah is forgiving and merciful . . . Seek out your enemies relentlessly. If you have suffered, they too have suffered: but you at least hope to receive from Allah what they cannot hope for. Allah is wise and all-knowing.

"As for those who have faith and do good works, We shall admit them to gardens watered by running streams, where, wedded to chaste virgins, they shall abide forever. We shall admit them to a cool shade . . . Believers you have an enemy in your wives and children: beware of them. But if you overlook their offense and forgive and pardon them, then know that Allah is forgiving and merciful . . . No misfortune befalls except by Allah's will. He guides the hearts of those who believe in Him . . . Allah has knowledge of all things."

Sean continued to read into the early hours of the morning and also the following day after he had completed a few domiciliary visits and surgery. He gathered that at one stage Mohammed had respect for the Jewish and Christian faiths and the Jews were known as "The People of the Book." He came to physical blows with Jewish tribes on several occasions. In the year 626 the Jewish tribe of al-Nadir was reduced and expelled. A year later the Jewish tribe of Qurayza was raided by Mohammed and some 800 men beheaded with the exception of one man who embraced the Islamic faith to save his life. All the women and children were sold as slaves. Two years later the Jews of Khaybar were reduced. Was that the beginning of the centuries' old antagonism of Jew and Arab, he wondered?

An analogy between Jewish and Arab history, and that of Irish Protestant and Catholic history came to his mind. Historically the Jews had occupied Israel and had left. They had returned relatively recently and the Arabs naturally objected. The Scottes had occupied part of Northern Ireland and left to conquer Scotland. Later they had returned and the displaced Catholics had naturally objected. Admittedly the British had occupied a disunited Ireland, but they had initially been provoked by the constant raids the Irish had carried out on the British mainland.

Another analogy crossed his mind. All parties whether Jew or Arab, or Protestant or Catholic Irish had resorted to terrorism in recent years to try to gain political ends. As always with terrorism, innocent people suffered, and always in the end the only solution was to get down to talk and work out a political solution. Winston Churchill had put it so well when he wrote: "It is better to jaw jaw than to war war."

One thing struck him as odd about the Qur'an. Mohammed had clearly used war as a means of spreading his message. In the final chapter titled "Prohibition," Allah had spoken to Mohammed saying, "Prophet, make war on the unbelievers and the hypocrites and deal sternly with them. Hell shall be their home and evil their fate." However, Allah was constantly being depicted, or rather stated, as being merciful. He again read the exordium from the Qur'an: "In the name of Allah the compassionate, the merciful. Praise be to Allah, Lord of the Creation, The Compassionate, the Merciful, King of the Last Judgment! You alone we worship, and to You alone we pray for help. Guide us to the straight path, The path of those whom You have favored, Not of those who have incurred your wrath, Nor of those who have gone astray."

He continued his reading on the life of the prophet Mohammed and found himself understanding the Qur'an better; it was clear that the religion was introduced into the Arab tribes at a time in their cultural history when they were ready for a change from the narrow idolatry that they had hitherto practiced. Their religious paganism made poor showing beside the other more developed religions of Zoroastrianism, Judaism and Christianity with whose followers they came into contact through trade and their nomadic way of life.

However, Islam appealed to them where other religions did not and there were several reasons for its great success with the Arab tribes. First, Mohammed's personality, his charm and convincing manner of speaking had an effect on all who met him. In his immediate vicinity perhaps ten thousand or more were completely certain of his being the messenger of God that he claimed to be. With his success in battle more distant tribes looked upon him as a potential ruler and as he grew more powerful, deputations of tribal chieftains visited him and became converted. He thus became the most important political figure among the tribes.

Although the Arabs were easily able to discard their pagan goddesses, they clung tenaciously to their customs. Being a desert nomadic people they displayed hospitality to strangers, knightly honor and barbaric ruthlessness when engaged in blood feuds. Unlike the Christians, the messenger of Allah did not ask them to love their enemies. On the contrary, when it came to revenge, if they forgave their enemies it would please Allah, but they were entitled to avenge themselves on them.

The fact that on winning battles Mohammed and his followers acquired booty and could take or sell their captives as slaves, was a real material incentive and not just the promise of heaven for all true believers. And the fact that there was only a single monotheistic god with whom they could be in direct contact through prayer, must have been a great incentive for these simple tribal people.

A few days later Sean had the opportunity to put his reactions on his reading to Dr. Bannu Sind. They were lunching together and Sean broached the subject mentioning his surprise at the Muslim attitude towards slavery and a number of other aspects that had come to his attention. His colleague listened carefully and even got Sean to show him the relevant passages in the Qur'an.

"I don't think you will find any Muslim country nowadays where slavery is permitted. One must realize that at the time of Mohammed slavery was practiced and continued until the last century in many countries until the British stopped it. Of course it may well take place in parts of the world where law is not enforced, and in some societies there are many people who are virtual slaves because of economic servitude. However, one should not judge today's practices by those of yesterday.

"Islam has many merits which include the concept of a single monotheistic God, unlike the trinity of Christianity and the polytheistic gods of Hinduism. In this, Allah is similar to the Jehovah of the Israelites. In the Qur'an you read that Mohammed instructed believers to treat their wives kindly and give them what is their due. He told his followers to do good deeds such as helping the poor and show mercy towards their conquered enemies."

"But Mohammed massacred the men of a Jewish tribe," Sean protested, "and made slaves of the women and children."

"Mohammed made several pacts with the Jews of Medina for joint defense of Medina against his foes. The Jews repeatedly broke faith and betrayed the pacts, and that is why he carried out the massacre. Prior to that he had put the Jewish tribe on equal footing with Muslim tribes. Both Jews and Christians had been invited to cooperate on the basis of monotheism."

"Yes," said Sean, "on that point I notice when an enemy was conquered he was offered freedom if he became converted or offered tribute, otherwise he was put to the sword."

"True, but that does not apply anymore. We are living in the twentieth century not the ninth. One should not focus on issues which have become modified with time. There are several ways of interpreting the word of the prophet as there are of interpreting the sayings of Jesus. We have Sunnis and Shiites, Druzes and Baha'is and you Christians have Greek Orthodox, Roman Catholics, Protestants, Lutherans, Wesleyans, Mormons, Jehovah's Witnesses and each interprets their holy books their own way.

"I think one of the most important aspects of Islam is the moral aspect and the application of law as part of one's religion. From the former, look at the value placed on family life. In contrast, permissiveness and the breakdown of family institutions in Western societies stands out in great contrast."

"I don't think that can be laid at the feet of Christianity. I think the breakdown is more due to economic and materialistic factors. As a Catholic I greatly value family as an institution and do not hold with divorce, as you Muslims do."

"The rights of the individual are considered where laws permit divorce and this is the modern view in western society. It is true that in some Muslim societies backward-looking rulers do not permit wives to divorce their husbands, but many societies feel they have the right to reinterpret the Qur'an as far as law is concerned. For example, the basis of law in Turkey is Swiss family law; in India and Pakistan the system is basically English law."

"But what about the practice of polygamy?"

"Regarding polygamy, Syrian reformers consider that one must show evidence of ability to support a second wife before permission by courts is granted. In Tunisia, polygamy is prohibited. In any case most Muslims do not have more than one wife simply because they cannot afford more than one."

"I understand the practice of child brides is still carried out?"

"Many Muslim countries no longer allow child brides. Only the old fashioned interpretation of law called the Shari'ah is practiced in Arabia and perhaps a few places in Africa, and that is subject to change."

Dr. Sind paused and then added, "Sean I feel you make the same mistake that many others do in that as the Muslim way of life is different from yours it is something to fear. Mohammed spoke of the goodness and power of Allah. Man should respond to his goodness with generosity and responsibility towards his fellow man especially towards the poor and with fair dealing in business. A whole way of life has been built on the Qur'an and that includes law as well as religion; it is hardly surprising that it is the fastest-growing religion in the world."

At that point the discussion ended and Sean felt he needed time to reflect on the conversation, and, when the opportunity occurred, to speak to Richard about it. He thanked Dr. Sind and returned to his apartment.

That weekend Sean arrived at Bracken late on Saturday afternoon. He was greeted by Eve who kissed him passionately. "I could hardly wait for you to arrive. Although I keep very busy the time between seeing you seems to drag. I do love you, darling."

"And I you, sweetheart. How have things been going?"

"I had a great shock last Thursday. I was just seeing Len off when two American men came up to us. When they addressed us with their American accents I thought they were sent here by Mr. de Vere-Smythe." Sean paled on hearing that and asked, "Who were they?"

"They were members of the Mormon faith who were here on a missionary visit. They left some tracts with me, but I must admit I felt very frightened at first."

"Are you sure they were genuine?"

"Yes. Len found out that they had visited other villages and one of them had been this way a year ago, so I am sure we have nothing to worry about."

Sean thought about Eve's answer and relaxed. The fact that one missionary had been there two years before dispelled any fear that Eve's cover had been exposed. His reverie was interrupted by Jennifer who came running into the room chased by her dog.

"Hello, Uncle Sean, Poppet has come to say hello to you." Poppet did so by jumping up at Sean when Jennifer embraced him. He spent a short while playing with Jennifer and the dog before going to greet Dawn and Richard who were busy in the kitchen.

"What do you think of Eve's scare with the Mormons?" said Dawn after embracing him. Sean smiled wryly, "I feel guilty for bringing Eve here, in that any of you have reason to be worried."

"Don't think on those lines," interjected Richard. "I know that if our positions had been reversed you would have done the same thing for us. But I can see the funny side of Eve being scared by Mormons."

At that point Jean had entered the kitchen and hearing the last part of Richard's sentence asked, "What are Mormons, Daddy? Are they aliens from outer space?" At that question they all burst out laughing.

"I doubt they would be very pleased to hear you say that."

Dawn interrupted by saying, "They are a religious order which has over three and a half million members. The religion was founded in America by a man named Joseph Smith. He claimed to have been given some gold plates by a resurrected being, or angel. He translated these into a book called the Book of Mormon, claiming that the plates were written on by the prophet Mormon and describe the history of a group of Hebrews who migrated to America from Jerusalem about 600 B.C. Over a period of time they increased in numbers and split into two groups, the Lamanites, who lost their beliefs, became savages and were the ancestors of the American Indians, and the Nephites, who built cities and were a cultured people. At about 400 A.D. the Lamanites killed all the Nephites after Jesus had appeared to them and taught them. His teachings were written on the gold plates and the son of Mormon named Moroni, also made additions. It is claimed that these plates were buried for 1,400 years after which they were given to Joseph Smith."

"Oh, that's interesting," said Jean. "Where are they now?"

"Don't ask me, Jean. I understand they have disappeared. Actually they may never have existed, for some non-Mormon critics claim that the book of Mormon is based on a lost novel written by a clergyman, but that has not been proved. Others think it was written by Joseph Smith."

"How can it be true, Daddy? Mummy told me that the Amerindians traveled to America by way of a land bridge across the Bering Strait about 12,000 years ago."

"Your Mum is right. Actually it could have been earlier, between slight warming of the earth during the glacial epoch. Anyway, modern excavations show that the ancestors of the Amerindians were present thousands of years before 600 B.C."

"So the Book of Mormon cannot be true."

"No."

Jennifer took that all in and asked, "Why do people believe in something that is not true?"

"That is easy to explain. If they are not taught anything else but one thing they will generally accept it as true. But generally Mormons are law-abiding citizens and are industrious, so their faith does no harm to others."

"But if they go round telling fibs about history that cannot be the right thing to do!"

"They are not the first and no doubt will not be the last to lie about history," said Dawn. "The Russian communists wrote false history and now that the regime has collapsed, they are having to rewrite their history books all over again. It would have saved a lot of trouble if they had written the truth in the first place."

Richard looked at Sean and commented, "After all your research on Islam you are now getting a dose of Mormonism." Then he added, "Variety is the spice of life eh, Sean? You don't happen to have any Mormons in your practice as well do you?"

Sean shook his head, grinning. "Not to my knowledge, but fortunately patients do not have to state their faith on our records unless they wish to—but sometimes I think it would help."

"You are probably right. However, I must say that I think you were right in reading the Qur'an and studying Islam. I did the same thing several years ago, Sean," Richard said. "I do not think one can know enough about any aspect of one's patients' outlook which will help one understand them and improve one's clinical approach. I have even read about Hinduism, Parseeism and Buddhism for my own enlightenment and pleasure as well as in order to understand others better. It is a pity that comparative religion is not taught compulsorily in schools."

"I don't think many religious authorities will approve of that idea."

"Probably not."

Dawn interrupted the conversation, "Come on you two, I think we have had enough on religion and you are now starting to talk shop. We have two hours before dinner so who would like some tea?"

■ ❑ ■ ❑ ■

Eve lay in bed thinking about the weekend and felt very happy knowing that Sean had been there. It had been a very pleasant two days. They had been planning to go sailing on Richard's yacht for at least two weeks during the summer holiday and Eve knew that Sean would be able to join them for several days. He had not been in his practice long enough for a long period of leave, but he seemed to get on well with his partners and they did not object to him having the odd long weekend off, especially as the practice was always quieter during the summer holidays.

It had rained on Sunday and they had stayed indoors for most of the day after mass. Sean had related to Eve the information he had gleaned from his studies of Islam and Eve had taken it all in, happy just to be beside him. But when she thought about the conversation and that of the previous night when the Mormons had been discussed she felt some disquiet. She knew that there were many other faiths apart from Roman Catholicism and she wondered how one alone could be right and all the others wrong. She desperately wanted to become a true believer in the faith that would result in her marrying Sean, and she also felt deeply that when she had finished her course and was fully accepted into the faith, she would feel pure once again and the stain of prostitution would be a thing of the past, never to rear its ugly head again. How she longed for that moment, but on learning about other faiths she felt a degree of uncertainty about Catholicism. She decided to pray and, as if in answer to her prayers, she knew that all she had to do was to express her fears to Father Brendan. With that happy thought she fell into a peaceful sleep.

■ ❏ ■ ❏ ■

It was later in the middle of the week that Eve was on her way back to Bracken that she decided to break with routine. Dawn had mentioned to her a village called Cogglesham which was quite pretty and well worth a visit. Eve had dropped off the children at their respective schools and had done some shopping. She felt it would make a change to have a mid-day meal out, for she usually had that at home and alone. The rain of the last few days had given way to bright sunshine once again and she felt her spirits uplifted. With the help of her AA road atlas she had no problem in finding her way to Cogglesham and found the village quite entrancing. She had visited an old medieval building, looked at several antique shops and visited the church. Although a Church of England building, she had gone inside and enjoyed the quiet religious atmosphere, had prayed silently, and felt an inward peace that seemed to penetrate to the very core of her being.

Heaven must feel like this, she said to herself as she left the church and walked out into the sunshine. Eve made her way towards a restaurant she had passed earlier and had decided to lunch there. She entered through the glass entrance door and past a counter where cakes, and bread on salvers were on display. A waitress smiled invitingly at her and led her into the dining room towards a table. "I'm afraid we are rather full but if you don't mind sharing a table with this lady we can serve you."

Eve responded by saying, "I don't mind at all," and looked at the occupant of the table who simultaneously looked up at Eve. With a sinking feeling in her stomach she found herself looking into the dark brown eyes of Caria Crompetta.

chapter fourteen

Caria drove as fast as she dared along the A12. She had looked forward to getting away from the Londinium Club and her day had started badly. Despite the sunshine she could not get worrying thoughts about Eve from her mind. It was the letter of course; the letter from Eve's brother in the USA. She'd had a row with Parker and had been defeated—or rather left in the limbo—and she did not like that. It had started when he had picked up the letter and said he was going to hand it over to de Vere-Smythe.

"You wot!" she had said forcibly in surprise.

"I sed I fort Mr. de Vere-Smyve would be interested in this. And anyway," he added, "It ain't none o' your business."

"And it ain't none o' yours eiver. You would be a rotten sod ter give Eve's bruvver's address ter de Vere-Smyve. Yer know wot would 'appen ter Eve if the nasties got 'old of 'er if she contacts 'er bruvver."

They both stood glaring at each other in the hallway as sunlight filtered through the stained glass windows above the front door.

"Why doncher give it ter me," said Caria. "No one will know it came an' yer won't 'ave nuffink ter worry abaht."

Parker thought on her request, then suddenly said, "Wait a minute. We've got ter fink abaht this. Let's see wot the letter sez." And at that he opened the door of his apartment and went inside. Caria followed, although she had not been invited. She seldom entered his apartment for she saw enough of him at the Club, and there was no love lost between them. However, on the rare occasion she did go in she was struck by the tidiness and cleanliness of the place. His parents had brought him up in a clean and tidy home and had made him participate in keeping things tidy and that habit he had never lost. She always felt surprise at the number of books he had, which stood out in sharp contrast to the mediocre number of women's magazines that she possessed, and they were mainly concerned with fashion. He had numerous works and magazines on racing and form, and she knew he did well at the local bookmakers or turf accountants, as they euphemistically termed themselves. His wealth of reading material reflected the fact that his parents had not possessed a television set for some time after they became the fashion, and also to a natural curiosity which had not been satisfied with his somewhat restricted schooling.

As she entered his living room she saw that he had switched on the kettle, and surmised that he intended to steam open the letter in case De Vere-Smythe considered it might possess information he would rather keep concealed from Parker. Actually, Parker would have been hard put to give an excuse for opening the letter in this way, for the real reason was that he was in the habit of approaching everything in a way that always left his tracks covered.

Caria waited and simmered down while the kettle steamed up. Within a few minutes Parker was holding the letter over the spout, and they both watched the envelope unseal as if by an invisible hand. Parker released the kettle switch which he had been holding down to maintain the boiling of the water and moved towards the table situated in the center of the room. He quickly withdrew the letter from the envelope and silently read it to himself.

"Well, wot does 'e say?"

"You read it," he replied, handing the letter to Caria and she did so with a certain amount of relief.

"My Dear Eve, I have not heard from you for some time and am wondering how you are getting on. I must apologize for not having written before but I have been very busy with my work despite the general recession and, as you know, what little spare time I have is spent at night school. Actually, the law studies are coming on well and I hope to graduate next year, but it is all time-consuming.

"I expect your job as a hostess keeps you busy and as you are relatively new, there may be much to learn. I would like you to write and tell me more about it as soon as you have the opportunity. At least you are working which is fortunate in these difficult times. Please drop me a line as soon as you can, or even a postcard will do. Take care. Your loving brother, David."

Caria looked up at Parker when she had finished reading, remarking, "Well, she ain't wiv 'im anyway an' that's a relief."

Parker answered with a nod. He, too, was relieved although the thought did cross his mind that the letter could have been written to throw anyone off the scent, assuming he knew of Eve's whereabouts. But, on second thoughts that appeared unlikely. Were that the case it would have been wiser not to have written, for the last thing he would have wanted was to notify Eve's pursuers of his whereabouts. It seemed certain that Eve's brother was unaware of both her hiding place and her late occupation. Another thought was at the back of his mind. Subconsciously Eleanor had made a greater impression on him than he cared to admit to himself. He wanted to see her again and the fact that she was a distant relative of Eve's troubled him.

He was shaken out of his thoughts by Caria saying, "Well, wot are yer goin' ter do wiv the letter? Are yer goin' ter 'and it over ter Smyve?" and it was his reply that had riled her.

"I'll fink abaht it. Nah you buzz orf," and at that he had pointed to the door adding, "'An that's the way aht."

"You rotten sod. Let me 'ave the letter."

"No! I told yer I'll fink abaht it, an' I mean it. 'Ow long are yer goin' ter be gorne for. No more than two days I 'ope."

"Well, it will be free, it's just started."

"Orlrite, I'll 'ang on ter it till yer get back. Does Ma know yer are goin' ter be free days an' where yer' orf to?"

"Yus o' course she knows, yer twit, an' where I'm goin ain't none o' your business."

On that point Parker was not worried, for he knew that Caria had too much tied up in her apartment and also that she did too well in her occupation to abandon both.

But Caria did not give up easily. "I still fink yer should give me the letter or burn it."

"I told yer I'll 'ang on ter it till yer come back. Nah 'oppit!" And at that he had pushed her out of the door and closed it with an air of finality.

Wrapped in her thoughts, Caria was woken from them by noticing a police car about forty yards ahead. Glancing at her speedometer she realized that she was going fifteen miles per hour over the speed limit. She suddenly braked and swerved to the left to get behind a car which was just to the rear of the police car. The driver of a car which had been pressing to pass from behind her blew his horn and shot past her. As he did so he raised a finger at her and sneered. Three minutes later she had the pleasure of seeing the driver pulling up on the side of the road with the police car slowing down. She stuck her tongue out at the driver as she passed and his look of fury made her feel better. "That'll teach you yer saucy sod," she mouthed as she drove past comfortably within the speed limit.

The sudden excitement coupled with the diversion of her thoughts from her worries made her realize that she felt hungry. She had eaten no breakfast and had probably an hour to drive before arriving at her destination. Noticing a sign indicating a village called Cogglesham, she maneuvered the car into the slip road and turned left towards the village. She drove down a country lane with hedgerows, trees and fields on either side and before long entered the village. There were few parking places available in the old-fashioned street and she eventually found one near the village church. She had seen a restaurant-cum-patisserie as she drove down the village high street and she made for it on foot. Walking along pavement she passed a local tavern, then stopped to look in several antique shops admiring some of the objects on display. Many pedestrians passed her, a few hurrying and others sauntering, occasionally window shopping or just admiring the quaintness of the village. This was interrupted by a slight sinking feeling in her stomach which indicated to her that she really was hungry.

The restaurant was across the road at a corner which she had to cross, and, as she stepped off the pavement, a car turned the corner. She felt slightly faint and missed her footing, falling in the path of the car. A passerby screamed, "Look out!" and as she heard the screeching of brakes she felt two hands grab her around her waist and lift her bodily from the path of the braking vehicle. As Caria felt herself lifted she was suddenly jerked up into the air as her rescuer jumped to avoid himself from being run over. My God, she thought, this bloke must be strong, and then she felt herself being lowered to the ground and stood with trembling knees trying to regain her composure before turning to look at her rescuer.

"Are ye alroight?" a deep masculine voice with a strong country accent sounded in her ears. She did not answer for a few seconds and still felt the hands around her waist supporting her. Other passersby stopped to console her and the driver of the vehicle pulled up a few yards down the road and walked back to where Caria was standing. She was a motherly-looking woman of middle age and beneath her country tan looked a little pale with shock.

"Are you alright, dear?" she inquired and Caria replied, "Yes, fanks."

Then the lady looked at Caria's legs and remarked, "I'm afraid you have grazed your right knee. Would you like to come home with me and I'll clean it up for you? It really should be attended to straight away for there is the risk of infection."

"Oi think that would be a good idea miss," said the man who was still behind and supporting her. Caria turned to thank him and he released his hands and held her by her left elbow to steady her. She found herself looking at the broad chest of a man wearing an open-necked shirt. Looking upwards to his face, she noticed strong handsome masculine features. He must have been at least six feet two inches tall and his ruddy country complexion contrasted with a shock of curly blonde hair. He was gazing down at her with a genuine expression of concern and looking into his light blue eyes she felt tongue-tied and paled again.

Both the man and the car driver noticed this and he said, "Come on, miss, I fink ee 'ad better go wiv the lady. She is the district nurse an' ee couldn't be in better 'ands." At that Caria allowed herself to be escorted to the car while the small group of onlookers dispersed, and the driver opened the door for her and seated her on the back seat. As she relaxed, the nurse addressed her rescuer.

"You had better come along too, Barney. I must say you were quick off the mark. I doubt if many people could have acted so fast. I think this young lady and I owe you a great debt."

"You're right there, Mrs. er—I mean, nurse," Caria replied softly.

"My name is Mary Collins. Call me Mary. And your rescuer is Barney Buntingford."

Caria looked at Barney who had sat down on the passenger seat in front of her and turned his head to look at her. He smiled and she felt her heart melting as she again gazed into his blue eyes. She managed to whisper her thanks, and sat back with her eyes closed wondering what had come over her.

It did not take long before the car drew up outside a thatched cottage where Mary Collins lived, and Barney escorted Caria inside while Mary obtained some medicaments to attend to Caria's knee.

"I am afraid your tights are ruined my dear," she said. "Perhaps you had better take them off so that I can clean this knee properly. Barney, you go into the kitchen and put the kettle on. I think we can all do with a cup of tea."

Barney nodded and left the living room and while filling the kettle heard Mary call out to him, "The cups and saucers are in the cupboard above the stove and the spoons in the drawer beside the fridge."

"OK," he called back.

"What's your name, dear?" inquired Mary as Caria rapidly removed her damaged tights and gazed down at her blood-caked knee.

"Caria," she replied and winced as Mary cleaned the abrasion with some antiseptic.

"When did you last have a tetanus injection, Caria?"

Caria reflected for a moment and then said she thought it must have been about ten years ago. "Then I'd better give you one now. Do injections worry you?"

Caria shook her head and rolled up the sleeve of her left arm in preparation for the injection. She showed no emotion as Mary rubbed surgical spirit on the skin, inserted the needle and gently pushed home the plunger of the syringe. Placing a plaster over the puncture she remarked, "Well, Caria, you're a brave one. You certainly have earned your cup of tea." At that Barney called out saying that tea was made. "Good. Bring it in Barney; Caria looks respectable now."

Caria did not feel respectable with her knee bandaged and she knew she looked a little pale despite her careful make-up. She watched Barney as he brought in a tray with three cups of tea, a jug of milk and a bowl of sugar on it. Placing it on a small occasional table he looked at Caria and gave her a warm smile that made her melt again. She was thinking to herself, what a lovely hunk of man, much better than the blokes she had to put up with at the Club.

"So. Yere name is Caria; that be noice. Do yere take sugar an' milk?"

"Yus please, er . . . "

"Call me Barney, Caria."

Mary noticed Caria's hesitancy and surmised she must be suffering from post-traumatic stress. "Just relax and drink up your tea, dear, and you'll feel better," she advised Caria and, as an afterthought she added, "Have you eaten today?" Caria shook her head. "I thought as much. You young girls will worry about keeping slim. Would you like me to boil you an egg and have some toast with it?"

Before Caria could reply Barney interrupted with, "I ain't 'ad lunch yet. How about ee comin' wi' me to the village an' you can 'ave a meal at the Pantry," he said, naming the restaurant.

"Oo, that would be very nice. But fanks for the offer, Mary. You bin very kind to me."

"You are welcome, dear. I am only too thankful that things were not worse, thanks to Barney here. As you are both hungry I'll drive you to the village as soon as you have finished your tea."

To Mary's surprise both Caria and Barney finished their tea well before her and both also refused a second cup. Then, with a woman's intuition she guessed why, and with an inward chuckle, took the teacups to the kitchen, and said, "I'll sort them out when I return. I imagine you are both starving. Let's go." And with a professional air of authority she ushered them both to the car and returned them to the village. During the journey Barney invited her to join them but, to the relief of both Barney and Caria, Mary refused.

At the Pantry Caria spent more time listening and Barney talking than eating. He told her that he was twenty eight years of age, and worked at a firm owned by his father who was a local builder. Unlike many builders, despite the recession, business was good for they did an honest job and believed in quality. He managed to glean from Caria that she worked as a hostess at a very posh gentleman's club in London. She embellished her story stating that she was concerned with administration arranging accommodations, luncheon and dinner functions, etc.

He was impressed with her skills, thinking she must be very bright to hold such an important position at her young age. He gathered from her accent that she was Cockney born and bred, but did not realize that with such diction it did not fit in with the class tradition that a "posh" club would demand from a hostess handling people of importance. As it was, he was so enamored with her looks that he would have believed her had she claimed to be related to royalty. So they both sat at their table, oblivious of the world around them until eventually the waitress placed the bill on the table and asked if they wanted anything more.

Shaking her head, Caria suggested they pay separately for their meals, but Barney insisted that he pay and produced his credit card.

"I'd rather pay for you, 'cos you saved my life, an' it's the least I can do."

"No," Barney replied. "Oi 'm payin' for lunch, but if ee really want ter thank me, then let me see ee again." Caria looked at him and her heart melted once more. "I'd love that, but . . . " Then she thought of how difficult it would be for her to get away from the Club as frequently as she would like, and had visions of what had happened to the previous occupant of her apartment when she had decided to leave. Life could be very difficult. However, she realized that she would be staying with her friend at Walton-on-the-Naze which was only a couple of hours away by car. She had arranged to stay with her for two nights and would have to return via the same route to London. She felt like suggesting she see Barney the following day, but realized that she needed time to think over the sudden passionate feelings she was experiencing. She was levelheaded enough and too experienced with men to give way to what could be a temporary infatuation. She needed time to think and reflected that a couple of days with her friend would help her to get things in better perspective.

"'Scuse me if I go an' pahder me nose," she said and headed for the ladies room, returning after a short while.

On receipt of the bill, Barney looked at his watch and exclaimed, "Oh Lord, it is twenty past two and oi 'm late for the office. Can oi give ee a lift anywhere, Caria?"

"No fanks. I gort me car dahn the road."

"Well, le me escort ee to it."

"Well, fanks. Coo, you are a real gent. There ain't many o' them arahnd naha days." They walked towards the church where Caria had left her car and Barney pressed her again about seeing her. "Won't ee let me 'ave your address, or telephone number?" he entreated, then added, "When can I see ee again?"

Caria was silent for a while then replied, "I'll tell yer wot. I'll see yer at the Pantry restaurant the day arter termorrer say 'arf past twelve. I got ter stay wiv me friend until then." Then she looked up at him and gave him the most bewitching smile she could muster. This had the effect of making him feel as if he were floating on cloud nine. She found her car keys and he stooped to open the door for her. As she was about to step in she surprised herself by suddenly putting her arms round his neck and kissing him. "I can never fank yer enuff fer savin' me life." Then she quickly slipped into the driving seat before he could respond.

Barney closed the door almost automatically, feeling in a daze, and Caria opened the car window. "Fanks again!" And as she fastened her seat belt said, "See yer Barney the day arter termorrer." Then she drove off as he waved good-bye, feeling that the day after tomorrow would be an eternity in coming. He retraced his steps through the village to his car thinking to himself that this was it. Many girls had been interested in him mainly for his good looks, but he had not responded. The thought of marriage with its responsibilities had not appealed to him. He had been very keen on athletics and had taken courses in judo and karate, becoming a black belt in both.

This time, however, his interest in the opposite sex felt far more than transitory. He started to recall holding her in his arms and her kissing him as he drove out from the pavement. The loud blast of a car horn shook him out of his reverie and he braked suddenly as another car drove past. "Good Lord, this won't do," and he pulled himself together and carefully drove to his office endeavoring with some effort to keep his mind on his driving.

■ ❑ ■ ❑ ■

Caria had more success than Barney in controlling her feelings. She had been in love when younger, and had got over that when the object of her affections suddenly discovered he preferred male company to female. Her experience with men later had not encouraged her to respect any of them. She had endured bestiality and had become hardened to it, but it paid and she had learned how to look after herself. It had been a tough school but she had determined to get all she could out of the life, make as much money as she could, then leave the racket before it ruined her looks and health. She knew she could not go on forever.

She had seen many women in the oldest profession age prematurely, and the specter of AIDS, syphilis, gonorrhea or other nasty diseases was always at the back of her mind despite regular medical examinations. Meeting Barney made her wonder if the time was near to seriously consider making the break. She knew that could be dangerous and her life could be in jeopardy if she made a false move. She would have to be patient. And there was another thing: Barney was clearly interested in her, but how seriously was difficult to assess. She knew that she would have to see him several times before she knew if their mutual attraction blossomed into something deeper and, what was more important, lasting.

Caria drove on with her spirits uplifted by her meeting Barney, the thought that she would see him again within two days, and by the brilliant sunshine that illumined the verdant and colorful glory of the countryside with the splendor of early summer. The vehicle sped along the A12 and after passing Colchester she drove towards Walton-on-the-Naze, passing through the picturesque village of Wheeley and then Thorpe-le-Soken. Soon she could see the waters of the Naze to her left and beyond them the entrance to the River Orwell with the dockside cranes of Felixtowe raking upwards. The church at Walton with its square Norman tower became visible and soon she drove into the town to find her friend's house.

It was odd how they had met, she thought. Her friend's father had been in Italy during World War II. He had been in an infantry regiment and had been captured by the Germans after the fall of Monte Cassino. During an Allied bombing raid, he had managed to escape and a friendly Italian farming family had hidden him in an outhouse. The tide of fighting passed and he had been rescued by a Polish platoon after two weeks of hiding. During that time the daughter of the farmer had brought him provisions and they had fallen in love. When the war was over he had returned to Italy and they had married. They had settled in Walton where he had managed a successful garage and his wife Rena had given birth to a daughter whom they named Forenza. They had taught her Italian which she spoke fluently thanks to frequent holidays with her mother's relatives in Italy.

Caria had been taught Italian by her father and one day when out shopping she dropped a bottle of milk in a supermarket. At that she had let forth a stream of expletives in Italian, and Forenza, who had been standing nearby burst out laughing and responded in Italian. From then on their friendship ripened and Caria had attended

Forenza's wedding. Later Forenza and her husband had moved to Walton-on-the-Naze, he being employed in the Coast Guard. They now had two children, a girl aged three and a boy aged five who attended school locally. Caria only occasionally saw them, but her friendship with the family was deep and they were always pleased to see her on the rare occasions of her visits. She had told them the same story about her occupation that she had related to Barney, and Caria was comfortable with the assurance that she was believed.

Forenza had just arrived from collecting her son from school when Caria's car drew up outside the house. They embraced, greeting each other warmly. Caria had stopped at a village en route and purchased some small toys for the children, and, after they had all settled inside, she produced a small doll for Candida, who was usually called Candy, and a small boat for the son Michael. On producing them the children had whooped with joy and Michael immediately asked if they could go to the beach to float the boat in the sea. However, with the promise that they would go shortly, Forenza prepared tea and, despite the excitement of the moment, the children's appetites were unaffected.

The tea lasted longer than normal due to Caria and Forenza catching up with news. The conversation continued on the way to the beach, and was only interrupted when Caria helped Michael and Candy to build a sand castle with a moat, in which Michael happily floated his little yacht. Caria helped to make it move by blowing on the sails, much to the children's delight, and their excited exclamations turned to shrieks of laughter when Caria overbalanced and fell with her arm in the water. Then Forenza produced a ball and they all played at throwing and catching, after which Caria romped with both children until they sat out of breath, exhausted by their efforts and laughing with joy. And so two hours were spent happily on the beach until Forenza decided it was time to go home. This they did, both Caria and Forenza taking turns to carry Candy who was feeling tired after her exertions. Despite the physical effort it did not prevent the two adults from continuing their conversation.

Later, Forenza's husband Jack arrived from his turn of duty at the coast guard station and he greeted Caria affectionately. He was a broad-shouldered man of medium height with brown hair and the healthy looking tan that accompanies those exposed to maritime wind and weather. He had kindly light brown eyes which would sparkle as he played with the children or joked with Forenza and Caria. Caria had great regard for him from knowing that he was a good husband to Forenza and a good father to the children. She also knew that he had been a crewman in the local lifeboat and had taken part in several rescues of the crews of vessels in distress, some in the appallingly dangerous steep seas that the North Sea could brew. He also had several parchments of commendation and a medal for bravery he had shown in carrying out rescues at sea. Caria had received this information from Forenza, for Jack never mentioned them.

It was the following night as she lay in bed, that Caria reflected on the happiness she found in her friend's home and the promise of happiness should her relationship with Barney deepen. Of course there was work with children, but providing they were brought up sensibly the rewards were inestimable and, in any case, that was what life was about. The family had found contentment, and that was a rarity in a society where material values and aggressive competition appeared to be the philosophy.

There would be problems for her of course. She had her apartment with its small mortgage, and more worrying was breaking her ties with the Londinium Club. She shuddered at the thought of what had happened to Anna and Tornilla. She knew that should she try to get away a similar fate would await her and that thought reminded her of Eve. So far nothing had been heard of her. It was doubtful that she was in the USA and probable that she was still in England. Even now Eve might have been found and killed, and that thought filled Caria with a feeling of dread and an unpleasant flutter in her stomach. She also felt twinges of guilt, for she was mainly responsible for Eve taking the course she had, and Caria had not realized how unsuited Eve was for the role she was expected to perform. With her elation slightly dampened by the memories of Eve, Caria fell asleep troubled by dreams involving her newfound happiness, her struggle to find a way out of the dilemma of her occupation and her conscience over Eve.

■ ❏ ■ ❏ ■

The following morning Caria said good-bye to the family. She had enjoyed herself more than she had expected and, although anxious to get away to meet Barney, wished she could have stayed longer. After saying good-bye with the promise to return as soon as she could manage it, Caria drove out of the town and retraced her route to Cogglesham. So keen was she to meet Barney again that she drove faster than the speed limit, but kept a wary eye out for police patrols. She had noted a police rest stop en route to Walton and she made a point of slowing down as she neared it. It was as well, for a police car was stationed there and she thanked her lucky stars for her quick Cockney mind and good memory. Due to her desire to see Barney she arrived half an hour earlier than the appointed time.

Noticing that the Pantry restaurant was gradually filling she decided to sit at a table, and explained to the waitress that she was expecting a friend. The waitress recognized her and remembering that Barney and Caria had been in there two days before, escorted Caria to a small table and brought her a cup of tea with which to quench her thirst while she awaited the arrival of Barney.

The restaurant filled rapidly after that and it was another waitress who, not knowing that Caria was awaiting Barney, directed Eve to her table. It was difficult to establish who was the more surprised at the meeting. They both recognized each other simultaneously and both their jaws dropped in surprise.

"Well, stone the bleedin' crows!" exclaimed Caria as she endeavored to get over the shock.

"Caria!" Eve could only say as she felt a shock of fear in her stomach. She paled and felt so faint that she grabbed the edge of the empty chair to support herself. Noticing this and recovering from the surprise more quickly, Caria stood, took Eve by the arm and assisted her to sit at the table.

"'Ere, sit dahn, luv," she said kindly and, unable to resist, Eve sat on the chair and looked at Caria. Suddenly she looked around the room to see if other members of the Londinium Club were present, and Caria, noticing it said, "No need ter worry, Eve, I'm by meself—there ain't no one from the Club 'ere, honest. 'Ere, 'ave a swig o' char," and she offered Eve her own cup indicating the side from which to drink. Eve took a gulp of tea and gradually recovered from the shock.

"What are you doing here, Caria?"

"I'm waitin' ter meet a boyfriend. Look, Eve, yer don't 'ave ter worry. No one knows I am 'ere an' wots more, I don't want 'em to. I'm goin ter git aht o' the Club as soon as I can. The bloke wots goin' ter meet me 'ere, well, 'im an me, we've clicked. If they know wot I am goin ter do at the Club they'll kill me. The trouble is that I got a mortgage on me flat an' a lot o' money tied up in it. I gotta fink of a way ter sell it wivaht Nosey Parker rumblin' me."

Eve looked at Caria taking it all in and felt that Caria was telling the truth. She had not forgotten that Caria had helped her when she was at her wits' end. She also believed that Caria, as well as herself, had been deceived by Parker's pretending that she had killed the black man. But Eve was still worried.

"Is your boyfriend coming here?" Eve asked, wondering if a trap had been set for her. Then she realized that she was being alarmist as Caria nodded.

"Yus Eve, 'e'll be 'ere any minute. I would like yer to meet 'im jest ter see that I am genuine an' on the level. An' listen, Eve. I ain't gonna tell anyone I've seen yer, honest. I want ter git away like you—really."

Eve had been looking at Caria's eyes carefully while she was speaking and again concluded that Caria was being honest. Her thoughts were interrupted by Caria adding. "Oh, by the way, a letter arrived for you this mornin' from yer bruvver in Boston. 'E wants ter know if you are orlrite. It said 'e adn't 'eard from yer an' wants yer ter write, but I fink I wouldn't if I woz you. Parker opened the letter an showed it ter me. I tried ter git it from 'im but 'e wouldn't let me 'ave it. 'E sez e' might turn it over to de Vere-Smyve."

Eve reflected on that new piece of intelligence and realized that Caria's advice not to write to her brother was sound. If he thought she was missing then he would act genuinely in trying to trace her and that would throw any pursuers off the scent. She had no doubt that in the long run her brother would be traced by the people she had escaped from, and if he honestly did not know where she was they would probably leave him alone.

"Listen, Eve. I don't want ter know where yer are stayin', but I would like ter see yer again. I will be back in a munf, an' we could meet at the Shepherd an' Dog Pub dahn the road. The date will be on the fifteenf an' I'll be there at eleven o'clock in the morning."

"I'll see," said Eve, and at that point the waitress came over and asked Eve if she was staying and if so, she would get another chair. Eve replied that she would collect some sandwiches at the bar counter, said good-bye to Caria, rose from the table and walked to the bar. As she ordered sandwiches she saw Barney enter. He walked over to Caria without hesitation and took her hands in his.

When she saw the look on both their faces whatever doubts she had had about Caria vanished at that instance. It was clear to her that they were both in love and she quickly collected her packet of sandwiches, paid and slipped out of the restaurant unnoticed by Caria. As she drove out of the village she saw the pub indicated by Caria, and resolved to think carefully before deciding to meet Caria there. She felt she needed to confide in Sean and Father Brendan before making that decision.

She still felt uncomfortable at Caria having seen her, so she drove off in an opposite direction to the village where she resided. She turned off the main road and noticed that a car with two occupants also turned off. This alarmed her and she again took another turn before she realized that she was not being followed. Eventually she arrived back at Bracken and ate only one sandwich, having lost her appetite at the turn of events. Soon it was time to collect the children and this she did and brought the three of them home.

The children were very hungry and Eve let them finish her sandwiches while she prepared tea. While doing so she asked Jennifer what she had done at school that day. Jennifer in reply mentioned several subjects that the teacher had taught and then had read from the Bible the story of Adam and Eve.

"She said they were the first Man and Woman."

"That's silly," John joined in. "The first man and woman were not Adam and Eve were they Eve?"

Eve smiled. "Well, Father Brendan says they were and I think they must have been if he says so."

Jean then joined in the conversation. "Daddy says that we don't really know who the first man and woman were but the first woman was probably evolved in Africa due to a mutation."

"A mutation, Jean?"

"Yes. We change because of slight alterations in our genes. Daddy said that we are a species of animals called *Homo Sapiens sapiens* and that we are a sub species of *Homo sapiens* who evolved from *Homo Erectus*."

"You mean your daddy thinks we are just animals like other animals?"

"Yes, but we have bigger brains and so we are much more clever."

"You don't think God created mankind then. You don't think man is a special creation?"

"No. I've heard Daddy and Mummy talking about mankind and God and Daddy thinks God is one of several gods thought up by people in the past to explain why the universe exists. I heard him say that when men in the past were wondering about nature they thought there were lots of spirits behind everything that happened, and later the spirits evolved into lots of different gods and then into one all powerful God."

"I think there is a God," said Jennifer, "'cos how else would the universe get here?"

"I think you are right, Jennifer. Did your teacher read about the creation of the world and the heavens?"

"Yes, and it must have had a beginning—everything has a beginning."

"And an end, too," interjected John who did not want to be left out of the conversation.

"We don't really have an end when we die, John. We have a soul and that goes on forever; it is eternal."

"How do you know that?"

"Because after Christ was crucified and died, he returned to this life in a spirit or soul form and that proves we have a soul. Anyway, I have seen a spirit and so I know." Eve was about to add that John had seen a ghost or spirit when they were interrupted by Dawn opening the front door. Jennifer and John immediately ran out to greet her, and Eve decided to bring up the subject with John another time.

It was later after Richard had arrived home that Jean mentioned the subject of creation and Adam and Eve. She and her father were alone, for Jean had gone into his study to get a book while he sat at his desk making notes in his diary. He listened attentively to Jean's account of the conversation.

After Jean had finished, he pointed out that many of the Biblical stories were just myths to explain the origins of mankind and the creation of the universe. "They were thought up by men in the past who knew nothing of science and the scientific method. Many people believed the stories, for there is more than one, until the last century when Charles Darwin and Alfred Russell Wallace put forward the theory of evolution."

"But Eve and Jennifer's teacher say the Bible account is true," and as Jean was speaking Eve walked through the open door tapping on it as she entered.

Richard gave her a warm smile and said, "Come in, Eve, we were just talking about the Bible stories of creation and the first man and woman. Come and sit down."

Eve was pleased to be included in the conversation and, on Richard's request quoted what she had learned from Father Brendan on the subject. When she had finished speaking Jean commented, "There you are, Daddy, Father Brendan believes it the true account so that is three to one."

At this observation he laughed and said, "So I am outvoted eh, Jean?" Then he added, "Now, you do not really know if Jennifer's teacher believes the Bible stories. She takes Jennifer's class for religious instruction and later will be quoting from the Koran, the Bhagavatgida, the Torah, and various Buddhist books, and as these religious works do not all agree, then you cannot claim that Jennifer's teacher believes everything she has to teach."

He turned to Eve and remarked, "I was just telling Jean that modern scientific evidence shows that mankind evolved from lower forms of life and that the universe probably came into being about fifteen billion years ago in what is called the 'Big Bang.'"

"The 'Big Bang?'" queried Eve.

"Yes. That is a name coined by Sir Fred Hoyle, the British astronomer, about the theory that the universe suddenly came into being all that time ago."

"How can scientists claim that when there was no one about then?" asked Eve.

"Well, there are two main pieces of evidence. The first is that the galaxies, that is collections of stars varying from forty billion to four hundred billion stars, are almost all moving away from each other. This is called the recession of the galaxies. If you go backwards in time they must have been closer to each other, and the further back you go the closer they get until they all coalesce to the same spot in space-time. The other piece of evidence lies in the present temperature of the universe's background radiation. At the beginning of the 'Big Bang' the universe was very hot for all matter would have been colliding, and when anything collides so the temperature is raised. Well, calculation of the speed of recession of the galaxies shows that the temperature left over now, after the 'Big Bang', would be about two degrees Kelvin. Zero Kelvin is -273.13 degrees Centigrade. Under normal conditions water boils at a 100 degrees Centigrade or 373 degrees Kelvin.

"As the universe expanded so the temperature fell from one hundred thousand million degrees Kelvin to the present temperature which is three degrees Kelvin. Two astronomers measured the present temperature and found it the same as predicted in the theory of the 'Big Bang'."

Eve listened to Richard's explanations and felt uneasy. If what he was saying was correct then the Bible must be wrong. She had learned a great deal from Father Brendan and was finding a degree of security and self-confidence from his teaching that brought her happiness. Her priest had assured her that the Bible was the word of God and this she had begun to believe. On top of that she knew that her future lay in her devotion to Sean and to the acceptance and firm belief in the Roman Catholic faith.

As with the encounter with Caria earlier, she resolved to speak to Father Brendan after the lesson at the church the following day. Two shocks that jolted the very fabric of her belief were more than enough for one day. She thanked Richard for his explanations and left the room.

Later Richard and Dawn were undressing for bed and Dawn suddenly put her arms around Richard and murmured, "Darling, I love you so much, sometimes it hurts."

He immediately responded, squeezing her close and kissing her tenderly. As they slipped off the last of their clothes he again held her close and then, holding both her hands in his, stepped back and looked at her admiringly. "You know, sweetheart, you have the most beautiful figure I have ever seen."

Dawn laughed and teasingly responded with, "And how many women's figures have you admired in this way?"

"One," he replied, and pulling her close gently slapped her on the buttocks saying, "That's for being cheeky!"

"Well, it's the right place," Dawn responded, and then she squeezed him close and pulled him off balance so that they both fell on the bed laughing. She ran her fingers through his hair kissing him and he lightly ran the fingers of his right hand up and down her spine pulling her on top of him. It was then that they made love happily and passionately until they uncoupled, lying on their backs panting from their exertions.

Dawn rested her head on Richard's shoulder, snuggling up close to him. As they lay there, Richard recalled that Eve had been rather quiet after the conversation in the library-cum-study and he mentioned it to Dawn. When he had finished explaining the conversation and Eve's reaction Dawn told him to be more careful.

"You must not say anything that upsets Eve, Richard. She has so much to worry about at the moment, not being sure that the people after her will find her or not. She has had a pretty rough ride in life, and her only hope lies in her faith and marrying Sean."

Richard started to speak, but Dawn put a finger to his lips and added, "I know what you are about to say, dear. You had no intention of hurting Eve by raising doubts in her mind and, what is more, you do not want the children to grow up with ideas that are both obsolete and untrue. Am I right?"

Richard put his arm around her and laughed. "You read my mind you clever so-and-so." He paused. "But I am concerned about the children; I want them to have an accurate understanding about the reality of existence and not have disproved dogma cluttering up their minds. And Darling, I think you feel the same way."

"Of course I do, but if what you say makes Eve lose her faith and confidence you will do her irreparable damage."

"I agree. Jean also told me that Eve had seen a ghost or spirit and that is something I cannot agree with. First of all, I don't think they exist, but if Eve convinces the children that they do they might be frightened, and that would not be good for the children's peace of mind. When I was young I was frightened dreadfully by a nurse telling me ghost stories, and it was years before I could walk in the dark alone. Even now I can have the occasional nightmare involving the terrors of my childhood dreams and fantasies; yet I know that they are harmless recollections and laugh to myself when I awaken and realize what was happening in my sleep. I will not have the children scared unnecessarily."

"Come on, Richard, I think you are exaggerating."

"I do not think so. And I must think of a way of letting Eve know that I disapprove of the ghost nonsense at least. You know John had a fright a short while ago and we do not want another occurrence."

"The trouble with you Richard is that you make people think and people do not like to think; so please be careful and don't hurt her."

He removed his arm from under Dawn's shoulders and kissed her goodnight, but they both felt that their difference over Eve had spoiled their lovemaking. Then a thought crossed Dawn's mind which left her feeling worried; she lay on her back staring upward at the ceiling before drifting into a disturbed slumber.

chapter fifteen

Parker sat in his comfortable armchair with the footrest extended and looked again at the racing fixtures for the following day. He was doing his best to relax for it had been a busy day. He had carried out delivery of some packages for Boss but with his acute awareness of the moods of others, had realized that the picture of delivery and receipt was changing. He was always careful to ensure that he was not followed, and carefully drove to new delivery rendezvous which he would often change at the last minute. He sensed that some of the contacts were not as careful as he, and had a suspicion that they were either being watched or followed, to the meeting points. He had made a point of getting to any rendezvous very early and always placed himself in a position to observe it undetected; this had paid off. Twice during the past six weeks he had seen a car containing two or three men arrive at the meeting place and stay there apparently keeping it under observation. He had not waited to meet the next link in the chain of crime; instead he had left and later endeavored to make contact, but had not done so until well after the appointed time.

The shadows of the night filled the deserted street as he looked out of his apartment window; recollections of the day's efforts displaced the thoughts of racing from his mind. He had managed to deliver his packages that day but had a feeling that he had been watched. He always wore dark glasses, often a false mustache or beard, a low-fitting hat and a bulky but lightweight raincoat when on an assignment involving the distribution of the packages. He appeared a short but bulky man to any onlooker; however, had they seen him in his normal attire they would not have recognized him as a very slim and lithe but short man. But despite his care, his disguises, his frequent changes of pick-up places and his arriving early to note any suspicious observer, he had the feeling that the game would not last much longer. He wondered if the police were getting wise to the racket or whether some other gang was trying to muscle in; either was not to his liking. He had not mentioned his suspicions to Boss. He realized that Boss might think that he Parker, was endeavoring to get out of the organization and he knew that such a suspicion in Boss's mind would result in Parker shaking off his mortal coil prematurely.

And then there was the letter from Eve's brother David; that letter troubled him.

To deliver it, or not to deliver it—that was the question. Whether it was wiser to hand it to Boss or just destroy it was not as simple as it seemed. Of course Boss knew nothing of the letter, but the mob, Boss's connections in the USA, were bound to find Eve's brother, and if he revealed to them that he had written to Eve's address at Caria's apartment then Boss would want to know why he had not been informed. Of course, letters could go astray, but there would always be the lingering doubt in Boss's mind that Parker or Caria, or both, had kept the communication from him.

"No," Parker said to himself, out loud, "it ain't worf the bleedin' risk. I ain't goin' ter stick me neck aht fer Eve." Then the recollection that Eve had tricked him and led him a merry dance when she had thrown him off her track when he was following her, came flooding back to his mind, and reinforced his intention to give the letter to Boss. And that he did the following day, but not until after Caria had returned.

With her meeting of Eve fresh in her mind, it was Caria who approached Parker. "Ave yer destroyed the letter yet?" she asked, with little ceremony.

"Nah I ain't. I'm gonna give it ter Mr. de Vere-Smyve." And he preempted Caria's expostulation by quickly explaining his reasoning behind his action. Caria listened in silence, not completely convinced.

"Eve's bruvver David will 'ave the 'eavies arter 'im, you know that."

"Listen yer twit. As they will know 'er bruvver don't know where she is, they'll 'ave ter wait before they take action. I bet wot they'll do is watch 'is mail box an' git any letter from Eve that way. Alternatively they'll watch 'is 'ouse an' git Eve if she turns up."

"I still fink we should burn the letter," said Caria, thinking of Eve and the possibility of her being upset should the "heavies" put pressure on her brother.

"Well I ain't. An' anuvver fing, I ain't stickin' me neck aht fer Eve even if you want ter act daft." And with that parting shot, he terminated the conversation and left for the Londinium Club.

"You rotten sod, I 'ope yer fall froo yer . . . " but the words were lost on Parker who had slammed the front door as he exited.

Parker was almost as good as his word, almost that is, for he did not take the letter to de Vere-Smythe, instead he took it to Boss. As far as Caria knew, de Vere-Smythe ran the Club for shareholders. She was unaware that of the employees, only he, Slioghan and Parker knew that Boss was the brains behind the organization. She knew that there were shadowy figures in the background, but associated them with hired killers and gangsters.

Boss's face was expressionless when Parker entered his office and handed him the letter, but Parker noted a slight widening of Boss's eyelids when he saw the return label with David Eden and the address. He wasted no time and slit open the envelope with a wicked-looking letter knife he kept on his table. He rapidly read the contents and copied the address on to a note pad. Then he rose from his desk and quickly typed out a cover note on his computer and, on pressing two keys, the printer sprang to action. Retrieving the cover note from the printer he handed it and the letter to Parker and said, "Get Mr. de Vere-Smythe to fax these to Dermot O'Rourke in Boston."

Parker nodded and left the office without further delay. En route to the Club he read the cover note from Boss and noted with satisfaction that O'Rourke was instructed to approach David Eden carefully and not arouse his suspicions. It was obvious that Boss was assuming that Eve was not with him and that the best strategy was to wait until she either contacted her brother or turned up in person. Parker considered imparting that information to Caria, but recalling her antagonism said to himself, "Why the 'ell should I? She can bleedin' well stew as far as I'm concerned!" And with that reflection he dismissed such thoughts from his mind.

■ ◻ ■ ◻ ■

Eve prayed with fervor and deep sincerity. She kneeled before a statue of the Virgin Mary with her hands clasped together, her fingers pressing into the backs of her hands, her eyes closed and her head bent forward in supplication. Before the statue several candles burned, and among them was one that she herself had lit. She could feel the slight warmth from them as they radiated their small heat in all directions. She had at first noticed the odor of evaporated wax which temporarily overcame the sweet smell of incense in the church, as one of the candles flickered out, but now she was oblivious to any sensation as her mind was totally engrossed with her devotions.

She prayed with such concentration and intensity that she remained immobile save from the gentle movement of her breast in rhythmic respiration; she was almost as still as the statue that stood before her. And this was noticed by Father Brendan as he walked quietly along the aisle to the high altar. When he reached it he kneeled and prayed and then went to the back of the church where several catechumens sat awaiting instruction. With her devotions finished Eve, too, walked to join the others and the lesson for that morning commenced.

It was after the hour's instruction was over that Eve asked Father Brendan if she might talk to him. He was always ready to listen to any of his parishioners and particularly so Eve, who always had a sensible question or problem to bring to his attention. Eve told him of her having seen Caria and that Caria wanted to meet her again. Father Brendan was already acquainted with Eve's background and her having encountered Caria came as no surprise to him. In response to her requesting his advice he suggested he would think over the situation and let her know later.

"You must be cautious Eve, but as Caria appears to have turned over a new leaf and is intending to leave this hotbed of vice, you must have compassion on her. She may even be seeking spiritual comfort and moral support in her endeavors to quit the dreadful life she is leading, and seeing her again may give her the encouragement she needs. Let me think this over." He paused, and noticing Eve's slowness to leave asked, "Is there something else you wish to discuss?"

Eve nodded and then mentioned Richard's talk on creation, the first humans and the Bible stories of Adam and Eve. Father Brendan questioned her for clarification on various aspects of Richard's discourse and then said, "I feel I should see Mr. Rutherford. I do not want your newfound faith to be jeopardized. I shall phone him and arrange to see him." And noticing the worried look on Eve's face, he added, "Don't worry, Eve, I shall be very diplomatic and discreet," and he took her hand in his, patted it and said, "God bless you, my dear."

Eve felt much happier when she left the church than she had before entering; whether this was due to her praying, or unburdening herself to Father Brendan, or to both she did not know but she drove back to Bracken feeling that a weight had been lifted from her shoulders.

That evening with the family all home, save for Richard who had been delayed at the hospital to carry out an emergency operation, Dawn announced that they were all going sailing for the weekend. Eve looked forward to that but her expectations were dashed when Sean phoned and said he would not be able to get along until early Saturday evening. Richard was anticipating arriving home on Friday evening and the plan was to board their yacht *Aurora* on that very same evening. With other yacht owners in the sailing club of which he was a member, they had planned a sail across the Thames to

Ramsgate on the Saturday, returning on the Sunday. An early start on the Saturday was essential in order to take advantage of the tides. Eve realized that Sean would not be able to come and, as her desire to see him far outweighed her interest in sailing, she elected to stay at the house and forego the trip.

"You will be quite alright alone on Friday night, Eve?" Dawn had asked when she had been apprised of Eve's decision.

"Yes, thank you, Dawn. I feel so safe and secure here that I shall have no fears of being alone at night."

But when Friday night arrived, and Eve lay in bed alone in the house, she felt somewhat uneasy. Later, after the family had departed for Burnham-on-Crouch, Sean had telephoned her after she had eaten her evening meal. They had spent some time on the phone, to the delight of British Telecom, and finally had rung off with Sean promising to get over as early on the following day as the demands of his practice would allow him. Comforted by this, Eve had prepared for bed and sat for a while reading until her eyelids began to feel heavy. She then put down her book, switched off the light and fell into a deep slumber.

As the sleep pattern altered from the nadir so she lay in bed half awake. She suddenly felt the loneliness of the house and seemed to hear a slight creaking of the stairs and then a noise on the landing and then sensed that someone was opening her bedroom door. She tried to rise but her limbs felt too heavy. She sensed a man standing over her with a sneering salacious expression on his face and then she saw the red pulsating devil's horns shape on his forehead. She tried to scream and then she was out of the bedroom, running down stairs, out of the front door and running, running, running down the lane with the sneering man chasing her shouting in a rough Irish voice: "Stop you bitch—I've paid good money for you!"

Then she tripped and felt herself falling over a steep cliff into a gaping chasm of nothingness below. She put out a hand to arrest her fall and touched something solid. It proved to be the bedside lamp and she fully awoke from her nightmare and switched on the light. With its bright glow filling the room she rapidly recovered until she heard a noise just outside her door. A shiver ran down her spine until she realized it was Poppet. With a sigh of relief she rose, opened the door and let in the dog. Normally it slept in Jennifer's room and Eve had left the dog in the kitchen before retiring; no doubt it had felt lonely and hearing Eve's distressful breathing had pawed at the door for admittance.

Eve felt less affected by her dream as she sat in bed, with Poppet lying beside the door in an attitude of relaxed comfort on the thick bedroom rug. However, she was still worried by the memory of the man who had so cruelly deflowered her. She realized that it would take time to push that traumatic experience into the deep recesses of her mind, where she hoped it would be forgotten to upset her no longer. Eventually she fell into a troubled sleep to be woken later by the dawn chorus and the whining of Poppet who wanted to go outside to answer nature's call.

That day went fairly slowly for Eve although she kept very busy. She had prepared a good meal for Sean and herself and looked forward with mounting excitement to his arrival. This was earlier than expected and announced by Poppet barking at the window as she heard his car draw up in the driveway. Eve ran to the front door to greet him and opened it as he alighted from the car. Poppet ran out ahead of her and jumped up to lick Sean's face as he bent over to stroke her. However he did not encourage her to slobber over him and held her down as he petted her.

As Eve walked quickly up to him he took her in his arms and remarked, "I shan't object to you kissing me, darling," and at that they held each other close while Poppet tried to draw their attention in her direction. Eventually she succeeded, and they all made their way indoors feeling that living was wonderful, savoring the aura of happiness that only deep love could bring.

After Sean had settled in his room they both went for a swim, for the day was still warm and in any case the pool was heated. It was a large circular affair about five feet deep and Sean enjoyed chasing and diving after Eve. They exercised together this way for almost an hour, and then after showers dressed comfortably for dinner, a meal Eve had prepared prior to Sean's arrival and completed cooking after the swim.

They decided to eat in the sun lounge which gave them a full view of the garden. Before leaving Dawn had given Eve a bottle of Hock to drink with their meal and after having eaten sat hand-in-hand finishing the wine and watching the evening shadows slowly lengthening on the lawn. "Let's go in the garden and see to the dishes later," proposed Sean after their glasses were empty. Eve readily concurred and they walked happily across the patio and on to the soft green lawn as two local house martins dived overhead. They strolled by the pond, stood gazing at the gold carp just discernible in the dusk and then sat on the comfortable swing seat beneath the weeping willow. They watched the water lilies close their flowers as a few water boatmen skimmed across the surface of the water. The evening was tranquil and, as the shadows continued to lengthen, they admired the blues and purples of the flowers on the rookery which contrasted more so with the darkening greens in the twilight.

"How beautiful it is here," said Sean. "I only hope we can have a place like this in the country when we are married and I have my own practice. I think Richard and Dawn are very lucky." He paused and then added, "Of course, they have both worked hard for it all—and still do for that matter." Eve squeezed his hand and murmured her assent. His mentioning the prospect of their becoming married had triggered her response more than the compliment to Dawn and Richard. Sean responded to her signal of love by putting an arm round her, drawing her close to his side and kissing her passionately.

"By heaven, I do love you, Eve," he whispered in her ear, as she clung to him and yielded to his embrace. He had his left arm around her shoulders and his right around her waist as he pulled her closer. Their lips met once again in a sensuous searching kiss; their pulses began to quicken as did their breathing rate and they both felt their desire for each other mount. Eve began to tremble as Sean slid his hand down from her waist and to her left thigh moving it to slowly slide under her thin summer skirt.

Eve suddenly felt a moment of panic and tried to break free but Sean gripped her more tightly and pursued his intentions more forcibly as she struggled. He was fully aroused, his desire for her matched by his ardor. Eve managed to disengage her lips from his and said, "No, Sean. Oh, please, no." She struggled again as he paused slightly in his efforts to fulfill his natural animal desire and attempted to smother Eve's protests with more kisses on her lips. But she moved her head and pantingly said, "Oh, please, Sean, we must not do this until we are married. We both know it would be a sin."

He relaxed his grip slightly and gave a panting reply to her pleading with, "But we can get dispensation in confession."

His grip on her relaxed just sufficiently enough for Eve to break free and stand up and he sat still on the seat surprised and shocked at her refusal of his awakened libido.

"Please, Sean, I can't.—We mustn't. Please. Not yet. Not until we are married. If we give way now you will have no respect for me and I will lose my respect for you."

He rose and extended an arm to take hold of her hand. "But Eve we can get dispensation and I will not lose my love for you."

Eve moved back and shook her head. "Please, Sean." Her beseeching voice arrested his intention to hold her tightly and fulfill his strong desire to take her by force. "Please Sean, oh please be patient. I have embraced your faith and by following the Holy Law I will be cleansed from the sin I was forced into."

Sean raised his arm and moved slightly towards her and she reacted swiftly by moving back a foot or so. She started to sob, "Oh, please do not make me lose the only chance for dignity and forgiveness that will enable me to become your wife and gain your respect. I love you so deeply that I fear I may lose you if you lose your respect for me."

"But . . . "

She shook her head—Eve was adamant.

Sean felt the coolness of the night now that the twilight had given way to nightfall. He felt frustrated, and breathing hard walked past Eve in angry strides towards the house. Eve watched him go feeling torn between her love for him and the fear that by her refusing him he would no longer love her. With trembling knees she walked back to the swing seat and sat down to recover her composure. There she sat sobbing in the dark until a bat fluttered nearby and startled her. She began to feel chilly, rose from the seat and slowly walked back to the house; but as she approached the patio the outside lights flooded the area with brilliance and Sean emerged from the sun lounge door. He walked slowly towards Eve as she stepped onto the patio and hesitated at seeing him emerge from the house.

"I'm sorry, Eve," he said. "It was wrong of me to try to make you give way to what we both know was wrong. You are right. I should not have been so weak. I do love you deeply and was overcome with desire for you."

They approached each other and he took both her hands in his and kissed them. Looking up into her eyes he saw the tears still wet on her cheeks and then, murmuring, "Oh my dear, I am sorry," produced a tissue from his pocket and gently wiped them away. Eve smiled a little at his action and then made no resistance as he put an arm lovingly round her shoulders and escorted her to the open door.

Back in the sun lounge they both cleared the remaining dishes from the table and proceeded to the kitchen. With plates, and cutlery placed in the dishwasher, Eve washed the cooking utensils while Sean dried and put them away. With the chores completed they watched a video of *Fawlty Towers* which Eve had chosen. In view of the event in the garden she felt that something lighthearted and genuinely funny would be both appropriate and perspicacious. Her ploy worked and Sean forgot his earlier emotional upheaval watching the antics of Basil Fawlty.

They had no problem in kissing each other good night. Sean had given Eve a hug and told her that she was wonderful and that he loved and respected her more than ever; with that they had both gone to their respective rooms while Poppet lay down in front of Eve's bedroom door as if on guard.

Eve lay in bed and as usual, read a little after saying her prayers. She put her book down and lay in the dark thinking about her having resisted Sean in the garden. She knew in her heart that she had been right but she still felt that she had thwarted him and that frightened her. She longed for him to make love to her but knew that to give way prematurely could sow the seeds for a broken marriage later; that she could not bear. Sean was her only hope in the world save for her newly-found religion, and it was he who had led her to the faith. She gradually drifted off to sleep wondering if she should have allowed him to.

As she lay there she seemed to sense Sean enter her room, and with the lifting of the covers slip into bed beside her. She felt her desire mounting and they made passionate love, their orgasms coinciding. Then Eve awoke.

She was alone and her desire for Sean had vividly manifested itself in a dream. She sighed; oh, how she longed for him. She heard the church clock chime two, clambered out of bed and walked to the door. Opening it quietly she saw Poppet outside and the dog raised its head at the slight noise. She stepped silently over the sleepy animal and walked towards Sean's bedroom and paused before his door.

chapter sixteen

Eve sat in the confession cubicle and heard Father Brendan's gentle voice from behind the curtain. "You say you had this lascivious dream and then went into the corridor with the intent of rousing Dr. O'Neill and giving way to the desire he had demanded of you earlier?"

"Yes, Father."

"Did you give way to this temptation?"

"No. As I placed my hand on the door handle of his bedroom I seemed to hear an inner voice within me which said, 'Eve this is sinful; be patient and remain pure in the sight of the Holy Father.' I knew then that my longing for Sean to make love to me must wait until we are married, and then it will have the Holy Father's blessing."

"You are quite right, Eve, and you are to be commended for not giving way to temptation."

Having concluded her confession, Eve received absolution and left the cubicle feeling buoyant and optimistic for the future. She genuflected towards the altar as she crossed the aisle and paused a few moments before the statue of the Blessed Virgin; there she looked at the beautifully molded face and seemed to feel a power of love emanating from it. She crossed herself, left the church and walked to her car.

It was a warm day and only a few small cumulus clouds looking like fluffy balls of cotton wool, drifted slowly across the azure sky. She entered the vehicle and drove out of the car park into the main road, carefully wending her way through the busy traffic and avoiding the odd jaywalker. On glancing into the rear mirror she noticed a Bentley with a man at the steering wheel whose face looked strangely familiar. As she drove across a junction the traffic lights changed and the Bentley was left behind.

Eve continued on her journey and her feeling of happiness remained with her. What a wonderful world it is, she thought to herself as she pulled into the driveway of Bracken and alighted from the car. As she closed the door, the Bentley she had seen earlier entered the driveway and pulled up behind her. She saw a man get out who was about six feet tall with thinning dark hair. He walked towards her with a spring in his step and extended his right hand when near her.

"You must be Eve," he said, and at that Eve suddenly realized why his face looked familiar: She could see an older Richard standing before her, with his kindly yet clever face and a strong personality which indicated a person of both courage and leadership. She raised her hand and he gave her a firm handshake and smiled warmly. Eve responded saying, "And you must be Dr. Gerard Rutherford. Dawn told me you would be staying for a few days."

"Well, how do you do, Eve, and please call me Gerard."

"How do you do, Dr. Rutherford, er . . . I mean Gerard." They both laughed, Eve a little awkwardly for she realized that she felt somewhat awed in his presence as she had done on first meeting Richard.

"I am sorry I was out earlier," Eve remarked as they both made their way to the front door. "Don't let that worry you, Eve. I made better time than I expected thanks to the excellent motorways and the new Dartford Bridge. The bottleneck at the tunnel has now disappeared."

Eve opened the front door and on entering asked if Dr. Rutherford would like some tea or coffee. "No. Just hot water, thanks." His response hardly surprised her for it was the sort of answer his son Richard would have given. It was to be expected that they both showed no signs of adiposity and kept very fit. Eve had learned that Gerard Rutherford was a retired physicist and his wife had died from cancer several years earlier. She had understood from Dawn that they had been a very devoted couple and had given their two sons and daughter a very happy home and a good education.

She found it difficult to believe that he was sixty-eight years old, for he looked at least ten years younger. Apparently his interests were numerous and even included single-handed sailing. Jean had remarked how surprised she and her brother and sister had been to arrive in their yacht at Ostend Harbour and have "Grandpa" tie up his yacht beside them. He had sailed from Plymouth a few days before and purely by chance had met up with them.

Now he had come to stay for a few days to fix a CCD camera to the telescope that he had originally designed and built for Richard. Eve had seen the moon through the instrument and had been amazed at the sight of the craters, mountain chains, rays, valleys and rilles on its stark surface.

She mentioned this to Gerard and he asked, "Have you seen a galaxy?" Eve shook her head.

"Well, if it is clear tonight we will look at the Andromeda galaxy. It consists of some two hundred thousand million stars and is two point three million light years away from us." Then he stopped talking abruptly and grinned, "Am I boring you with statistics?"

Eve shook her head. "No, I have heard Richard and Dawn talking to the children about astronomy, among a host of other subjects, and I enjoy learning new things."

"Well, I enjoy learning new things too, Eve, but I shan't start a lecture now. Instead I'll go and get my bag and take it to my room," and he rose from his armchair, thanked her for the drink and left the room.

Eve had been warned that she would have a busy weekend ahead of her. In addition to Richard's father staying, several friends would be coming for some musical evenings. Eve had met one woman who played the violin beautifully. She was a Jewess in her sixties and had been born in Germany in the 1930s. Her family had fled to France before the war broke out and had lived in Paris. With the defeat of France in 1940 the family had gone to the Free French Zone. At that time, Rachel Steinberg was fourteen years old and a staunch believer in Zionism. Eve found her very friendly that weekend and had learned how she had escaped from France to Spain when the Germans overran the Free French Zone of Vichy, France.

"We were staying in a town near Bourges and I had been out shopping and was on my way home. I saw some French police with a small bus outside my home and my parents and family were being ordered into the bus. I was running past the table of a roadside cafe when a woman grabbed me by the arm and told me to sit down. 'You must not go over there or you too will be arrested and taken away.' 'What is happening?' I asked, but I sat down for I was very frightened. She replied, 'All Jews and gypsies are being deported to Germany to be sent into the concentration camps. Hitler has ordered the Vichy Government to use its police to round them up.'

"There was a young man sitting with the lady and they both took me away to hide for fear that I too would be arrested. The man was a pilot of a Hawker Hurricane that had crashed in France and he had escaped from a prison camp and was on his way to England via Spain. Later I learned that the Vichy French government had rounded up over 70,000 Jews and gypsies. My family was taken and they were all murdered, being gassed in the concentration camp at Dachau. It has made me bitter against the French and also against religion, for no amount of praying prevented the wicked acts that have been perpetrated against a people supposedly chosen by God for their having recognized Him first."

At that point Rachel had been interrupted by her husband who had been sitting beside her. "You must not feel too bitter, Rachel," he had said, taking her by the hand and squeezing it. "I don't think the present generation of French can be held responsible for the atrocities permitted by the Vichy Government."

"No, perhaps not, but they know nothing about the way their fathers cooperated with the Germans. They are fed with stories about how their fathers all fought in the French Resistance when the only Frenchmen in it were the Communists and that was because they wanted the guns to start a revolution after the war was over."

Rachel's husband interrupted again. "Some of the French Resistance did take action once the Allies landed in Normandy. And another thing, don't forget that for collaborating with the Germans, French leaders of the Vichy government like Laval and Marshall Petain were condemned to death after the war was over, although Petain's sentence was commuted to life imprisonment. But come on, Rachel, one should not dwell on the past."

Eve looked at him as he spoke. Dawn had told her that he was the English airman who had helped Rachel out of France. He had escaped thanks to an Englishwoman who had been married to a French count. Both had organized a group of French and others who had formed a network of people to assist escapees. But despite her husband's remonstrance, Rachel wanted Eve to know how bitter she felt about losing her family.

"I know Harry, but the French are told that the British ran away from the Germans at Dunkirk. Actually, they are not told the truth. The British were fighting between the Belgians and the French and fought well, but suddenly the king of the Belgians surrendered to the Germans and they immediately took advantage of the left flank of the British army being exposed. They tried to get behind the British army which had to retreat in order not to be surrounded. The Germans broke through in the Ardennes and the French Army collapsed on the British right flank and they had no choice but to fall back to Dunkirk and Calais. Had they not done so they would have been completely surrounded. I know that the French army resistance at Lille helped to slow the German advance but by then it was impossible to retrieve the situation. Thank heavens a third of a million British and French soldiers escaped to form the nucleus of a new army."

Harry looked at Eve and smiled. "Please excuse Rachel letting off steam. Her memories of those terrible events can never be forgotten. Man's inhumanity to man is something too many people have to contend with even to this day. One need only think of the Khmer Rouge and the activities of President Saddam Hussein. The world is ever producing its tyrants, megalomaniacs and arrogant people who think they are chosen to right the world's wrongs as they see them and think fit. Ultimately, they become power-mad and have to be removed by force."

On hearing this, Eve thought to herself that if only everyone accepted Christianity with its message of love and compassion, there would be no more wars and people would be able to live in harmony.

It was after dinner when the children had gone to bed that the family and guests assembled in the drawing room. More guests, some teacher colleagues of Dawn, arrived and Eve sat with them to listen to a performance of Schubert's "Trout" quintette and Chausson's piano concerto. Her taste for classical music was widening through hearing so much in the Rutherford home. She felt strongly how shallow so-called "pop" music was and that "rap" music was primitive to the point of being antisocial and pathetically degenerate. A friend of Richard's had been in the pop music business, and had described it as a racket where young people and immature adults were conned into buying recordings through slick publicity and pandering to the ordinary individual's appreciation of simple hypnotic rhythms.

The first quintette made her feel very happy with its buoyant beats and pretty melodies. With the second work, by Chausson, Eve felt transported into a world of such melodic and harmonious beauty that it seemed as if it reached into the very innermost depths of her soul. She had been moved once before when Sean had sung with deep feeling and expression, but that paled in comparison with the emotion the music aroused in her this time. She wondered if such beauty was a special gift of God to the composer.

That night Eve sat in her bed thinking what a pleasant evening it had been. Had Sean only been present, too, it would have been perfect; but she had enjoyed the music and the conversation. Richard's father, Gerard, had kept his promise after the other guests had departed. He had taken Eve to the observatory and aligned the telescope to the Andromeda Galaxy. What she had seen had at first puzzled her when he showed her a photograph of the galaxy with stars present in it.

"I can't see any stars, Gerard. It is just like a pale oval mist."

"Not a bad description. Someone wrote many years ago that it resembles 'a candle shining through a horn.' But you won't see individual stars in a spiral galaxy with this telescope, Eve. You see it is not big enough to collect enough light to magnify the stars with a sharp image and one has to take photographs and enlarge them to get more detail. The important thing is that you have seen an 'island universe,' that is, a galaxy or collection of millions of stars which revolve round a common center of gravity."

"I heard Richard explain to the children that we live in a similar galaxy and that the Milky Way is part of it."

"You are quite right, Eve. Our planetary system with the sun in its center, is part of our galaxy and all the stars you can see are also part of it, except those in galaxies outside ours. There are probably some two hundred thousand million stars in our galaxy and probably as many galaxies in the universe."

"Do you think that there is life elsewhere in the universe?"

"Yes, Eve. I feel certain there is, although it cannot be proved yet. The sun is a G2 spectroscopic type star and there must be thousands of millions of them among all the galaxies. In fact, one of the nearest stars to ours is of the same type. Recently another planetary system has been found and it is probable that all stars have planetary attendants unless they are blown away when the stars become supernovae. Meteors have organic molecules as part of their structure and I do not think that this planet is the only one with life on it as far as the universe is concerned. I do not think that we are unique; to do so smacks of self-flattery and sheer conceit."

"The size of it all fills me with awe. I just cannot imagine it and quite honestly find it all frightening."

"I would not let that worry you, you are not the first. The French astronomer Laplace wrote of how the silence of eternal space frightened him. I wonder how he would have felt if he knew what we now know about the age of the universe, about quasars and black holes etc. He would certainly have been overawed as you are."

"Richard also mentioned that the universe probably started some fifteen billion years ago in a 'Big Bang'. How could it have appeared out of nothing and suddenly filled space?"

"It did not happen quite that way. As far as science takes us back into the past there was no space, no time and no matter or energy. Suddenly matter or energy, which are the same, with space and time appeared. There cannot be one component without the other. All came into being simultaneously."

"This is the creation referred to in the Bible."

"Not really, Eve. If you read the three Bible stories on creation carefully you will find that the events portrayed in the Bible creation stories are nothing like the scientific explanation. For example, just take the first verse in the first chapter of the Book of Genesis: 'In the beginning God created the heaven and the earth'—and incidentally, all that in six days. Well, the universe started about fifteen thousand million years ago. The earth is only four thousand six hundred million years old. I could work my way through the whole of the Bible accounts of creation and show that they were just guesses about the origins of the universe and nothing like the reality."

Eve had felt somewhat disappointed at Gerard's statement but did not feel knowledgeable enough to argue. She had, however, felt secure enough to ask, "As scientific theory shows that the universe had a beginning, was it not created by God?"

Gerard had looked at Eve and paused before replying. He had been told a little of Eve's history and wanted to be careful not to say anything that would shake her faith or deviate her from her course. On the other hand, he was too honest to deceive her with ideas that he knew or felt could not possibly be true.

"Belief in God is a very personal thing, Eve. I have often asked myself what God is and apart from thinking that 'It' is the creator of the universe, have not got any further. The truth is, if there is a Supreme Power, Being, or whatever you like to call it, whatever it is is far beyond anything we can imagine or comprehend."

"Don't you feel that there is something powerful beyond this universe?"

"I don't know if that question is valid; I mean, I wonder if it makes any sense. You see all we know and are capable of knowing is of this universe. How can we speculate on something beyond it when our experience and imaginations are limited to this universe?"

Gerard paused and directed the telescope to a pair of binary stars which had one component a brilliant emerald green and the other a bright red. Eve looked at them and gasped, "Why, they are like two brilliant jewels!" she remarked, admiring their beauty. "It amazes me that one can understand what they are and yet they are so far away and inaccessible."

Gerard smiled. "It is odd when you come to think of it, Eve. This jelly-like substance in our heads enables us to comprehend the universe around us. Just imagine it. This gray matter, this brain weighing about three pounds is the center of our universe. My body carries it around and, at its command, transports it to wherever is physically possible for the body to go. It is a wonderful memory bank, calculator, producer of complex ideas, inventor of new machines, composer of music and poetry, full of reflexes and inherited data which enable the body to survive the stresses and strains of existence, puzzling why life and the universe exists, finding and inventing many solutions, appreciating that in time many more riddles of existence will be solved and understood except perhaps the ultimate one."

"And what is that?"

"If the universe was created, who created it, why was it created and for what purpose."

"The Bible says . . . "

"I know what the Bible says, Eve. I have read it from cover to cover and find it a mixture of history, mythology, poetry and guesswork."

"Father Brendan says the Bible is true. It is the revelation of God and so gives us an understanding and sense of purpose of the universe and for existence."

"He is entitled to his opinion Eve and I to mine. As I remarked before, he speaks of God but do we really know what God is? At this point, faith has to take over from logic and for myself I do not find it satisfying. To have faith in something completely unknown, which one can only surmise exists and which may well be just the product of one's imagination seems hardly logical and is not necessarily being honest."

"I do not think I can accept that," said Eve. "I feel that we do have an idea of what God is. The Bible says clearly that man was created in God's image and Jesus calls God His Father and the Father of mankind."

"You say God created man in his own image. Personally, I feel the reverse is true. Man has created God in man's image and I do not think it much of a compliment to God—assuming there is one. One only has to think of the terrible atrocities being committed by mankind at this very moment to realize that any resemblance between God and man is no compliment to God. And one other thing: one should not forget that the Bible was written by men and not by a God; nor was it dictated by a God."

"But belief in the existence of God explains why the universe is here."

"It may be a reason but it is not an explanation; in reality it only does what man has been doing ever since he started thinking about existence. He ascribed to spirits, demons, devils, gods and God what he did not understand. In order to find a rational reason for explaining the phenomena of nature, man imagined there were spirits being the cause. Later the spirits became gods and eventually a supreme God transcending others became the first cause. This is the theory of causation. The trouble with that theory is that if one cause follows another and one works one's way back to God as the first cause, then who created God? Once man started to think scientifically then the multiplicity of spirits, demons and gods vanished; there was no need for them. What it boils down to is pushing back the frontiers of knowledge and attributing to a God what is unknown. If man exists long enough to explain everything, or perhaps to have a theory of everything then God, or perhaps the concept of God, may become redundant.

"However, I doubt that stage will ever be reached no matter how clever our descendants become. I mentioned earlier the French astronomer Laplace. When he described to Napoleon Newton's theory of gravity and how the planets moved round the sun, Napoleon asked: 'And where does God fit into this?' Laplace replied: 'He doesn't.' Divinity is not necessary to explain scientific matters.

"As things are now, I know that the universe exists and have a pretty good idea how life has evolved but as far as the ultimate question is concerned, that is, why does the universe exist, it is still an enigma. Of one thing I am sure: if there is God then God has no parameters."

"I feel the Bible has the answer."

"And what is that Eve?"

"God is love."

Gerard was about to say, "Perhaps you might ask Richard what he thinks of a loving God," then he thought the better of it and said, "Well, maybe."

He looked at his watch. "Good Lord. It is past midnight. Perhaps we have had enough of stargazing tonight, Eve," and at that they carefully covered the optics of the telescope and closed the observatory.

Walking back along the pathway to the house Gerard had put a hand on Eve's shoulder and in a kindly voice said, "You must not let my views on God and the Bible affect your own ideas, Eve. We are all entitled to our opinions and who knows which are right? You must be guided by your own gut reaction—by that I mean what your heart of hearts, or the innermost core of your own being tells you is right."

Eve sat in bed reflecting on the conversation with Gerard and the events of the evening. Despite the small doubts he had put into her mind regarding the Bible, she felt her faith deepening in a God who cared enough about humanity to send his Son to be sacrificed by men to show his compassion for mankind. For her it revealed that God did exist and cared for the results of his creation. She fell contentedly asleep in the middle of her prayers.

■ ❑ ■ ❑ ■

Boss sat at his desk and looked out of the window facing the river. The sky was slightly overcast and the windows were still wet with droplets of rain that had fallen earlier. He absentmindedly watched two seagulls in flight as he mentally ruminated on several problems that demanded his attention. He had returned the letter from Eve's brother marking it, "Return to sender. No forwarding address."

He smiled cynically to himself as he recalled writing on the envelope; at least that was true. He also realized that Eve was not with her brother. His informant in Boston had been quite certain of that. Her brother's house had been kept under observation; the odd visit by a pseudo salesman and also more importantly a telecommunications engineer, had confirmed that David Eden was the only occupant. Boss smiled again as he thought of how easy it had apparently been. By the simple expedient of cutting the telephone cable, one of the Mob's workmen at the telephone engineers department had gained entry when David Eden's housekeeper was at home. She had legitimately let him in and he had left a "bugging device" suitably placed which enabled henchmen to listen in at any time to all conversations that took place in the house.

It was obvious after a week that Eve was not present; only the voices of the housekeeper, David and some American friends had been heard. Eve was certainly not there. No doubt David Eden would start making further inquiries after her but that was in the future. No, the chances of her being in the USA were small. He would have to hope that one of his contacts in the UK found her unless she had managed to get across to France.

He watched seagulls wheeling down in a steep dive towards the river. A pleasure boat with tourists on board had attracted the birds which no doubt were hoping for some tidbits to be thrown overboard. They were not disappointed. A child threw a half-eaten sandwich into the water and the leading bird immediately dived at it while another rapidly caught up and tried to snatch a morsel for itself.

Seeing the vessel reminded Boss that the following week *Erinyes* would have to be at sea to pick up another consignment of drugs. He had received intelligence that the container vessel was en route to Hamburg and would be collecting a consignment there. With the fall of the Iron Curtain the route of drugs through Pakistan across Eastern European countries and into Germany was very easy. Collecting the packages at sea was also easy, but one had to be careful outwitting the British customs officers. So far the method he had perfected had worked successfully. Often his vessel was searched but as there were no drugs on board on each occasion the customs officers had always drawn a blank. In any case, the relatively frequent visits of *Erinyes* to the continent of Europe had enabled him to get to know some of the officials and they were always friendly.

Boss looked at the calendar; the pick-up would be a week from today, so he would have Eoin Slioghan, Parker and Bounce ready to report on board in three days. That should give them adequate time to be across to Ostend and on station when the freighter arrived, weather permitting. Weather permitting—that was always the unknown factor. He had once lost a consignment due to inclement weather, but that was just hard luck.

There was a more important matter that now needed his attention. There had been talk of real peace being discussed between the IRA, the Dublin Government, the British and the Northern Irish and he did not like the way things were going. John Major, the Prime Minister of Great Britain, and Albert Reynolds, the Irish Prime Minister, had issued a joint declaration in December of the last year. The IRA had been invited to the conference table providing that they undertook to stop violence.

The idea of stopping violence did not appeal to Boss although it did to some of his colleagues. He wanted to see complete surrender of the Protestants in the North to Eirrean rule. He wanted to see the Catholics rub the Protestant noses in the dirt the way they had made Catholics second class citizens under the Stormont Government in the past. It was true that since the British Government had dissolved the Stormont Government and ruled from Westminster, the lot of the Catholics in the North had improved immensely and the economy of the country was better than it ever had been, thanks to the British taxpayers.

But the improvements were not good enough for Boss; he wanted revenge for both real and imagined wrongs, and he intended to get it. It was some six months now since the peace initiative and some handy stalling was still going on with requests for clarification. Boss knew that some of his colleagues were sincere and might well go to the conference table and he frowned at that thought. Then he suddenly grinned when he reflected that he could rely on the activities of Protestant fanatics to continue the violence and play right into his hands. He could trust fellow Irishmen to keep up the temperature whether they were in the IRA or members of the so-called Ulster Freedom Fighters—there would always be some hot-headed fanatic to stir things up.

Apart from his political views, Boss had further very good reasons for "keeping the pot boiling" as he neatly put it. He was running his own personal racket and he had no desire to see the voluntary funds he received from the USA disappear. He guessed that if a peaceful solution to the Irish problem was found then that lucrative source would trickle to nothing. Of course the drugs paid, but there were always attendant risks, and carelessness on the part of the chain of distributors could spoil that little game. The Club barely paid but it was excellent cover. No, he did not want to have his own personal interests interfered with by a successful peace initiative.

Boss looked again at the river. The tourist vessel had long disappeared round a bend and a big barge carrying sand and gravel was making its way down stream, probably bound for the River Orwell, he thought. A river bus was plying between ports and a police launch bounced in its wake as it carried out a routine patrol.

Boss picked up one of the phones on his desk. Seeing the vessels on the river reminded him that he had better get the crew notified of the forthcoming voyage of *Erinyes*, a voyage that was to have completely unexpected results. For it was later during the voyage that Parker, looking through his binoculars, was so startled that Boss noticed it. In turn he brought his binoculars to his eyes. "Well, well, well . . . " he chuckled.

chapter seventeen

Richard listened attentively to the gentle voice of the man seated in the armchair opposite him. He, too, was comfortably ensconced in a similar chair and sipped some orange juice as he heard the arguments put distinctly yet courteously to him.

"You see Dr. Rutherford, I am very much concerned with her spiritual welfare as well as wanting her to have a happy and normal life, free from the sin and sadness of her past."

As Father Brendan spoke, Richard Rutherford could hear the background noise of road traffic passing outside the presbytery. He recalled that several days before, Father Brendan had requested to speak to him about Eve. To a certain extent he had not been surprised, but nevertheless, he felt a priest was hardly in a position to even hint to him how he should behave towards a young woman who had the hospitality and refuge of his home.

Of course she was also a well-paid employee, but she was treated like a member of the family and the only thing the priest could complain of was that his catechumen was being informed about the truth and reality of existence; if this contradicted religious dogma and misinformation, then that was too bad. Father Brendan had offered to call at Bracken but as Richard often passed the presbytery on his way home he had volunteered to call there instead.

Richard dragged himself away from his earlier somewhat cynical and critical thoughts and concentrated on what Father Brendan was saying. It was true, as Dawn had pointed out previously, Eve was in a very vulnerable state of mind. Her religious instruction was giving her hope and the prospect of a happy future and anything which questioned her beliefs, or contradicted what was being taught to her, could disturb the very foundation of her faith. Her state of mind appeared to be fragile and he, Richard, did not desire to disturb that fragility and so destroy the peace of mind that she had found and wished to retain.

Richard looked intently at the ascetic face of the priest. There was no doubt in Richard's mind that Father Brendan was sincere. There was also an air of sanctity in his face that impressed Richard as it did all who met him. Here was a man who was absolutely certain of his faith and whose mind was at peace with the whole of creation. Was it the shape of his face, his quiet yet convincing manner of speaking, or just the strength of his personality that gave him that aura of, for want of a better word, "spirituality?" Richard wondered. At least he is a man I can respect, Richard thought to himself before replying to Father Brendan's comments.

"I fully appreciate your concerns over Eve and I recognize her need for a strong faith that can give her a sense of security and purpose in life. Apart from that, I am very fond of my cousin Sean, and I want to see him achieve the happiness he too desires."

Father Brendan smiled and nodded, "I do not doubt that. I understand that your views on the Bible have caused doubts in Eve's mind and although I appreciate that we are all entitled to our opinions, she is in a formative state of mind where anything that undermines her faith could have damaging consequences."

"Please understand, Father Brendan, I do not take religion away from anyone. I appreciate that many people have very hard lives and need something like religion to cling to. Many people find this world, let alone the universe, too complex, and may not know enough to understand it. One would be cruel to deprive them of the only comfort they have, even if it is a simplistic explanation of what it is all about."

"You think that religion is a simplistic explanation of the nature of the universe?"

"Yes, I am afraid I do."

Father Brendan smiled at that reply. "Well it may be so, but not all humans are given the gift let alone the opportunity, to understanding the complexities of this universe and for ordinary mortals God reveals Himself in a way that can be understood. We cannot all be and, come to think of it, Isaac Newton believed in God."

It was Richard's turn to smile. "That giant of physical science was a product of his environment and time. He had religion instilled into him when he was young and very impressionable. It is hardly surprising that he expressed belief in God."

"You have no such belief in God?"

"In order to understand the question would you please define what you mean by God?"

"To my understanding, God is the ultimate Spiritual Being and Creator of this universe whose nature is beyond our comprehension. As Newton put it, 'This Being governs all things, not as the soul of the world, but as Lord over all . . . As a blind man has no idea of colors, so have we no idea of the manner by which the all-wise God perceives and understands all things.' And again Newton wrote: 'We have ideas of His attributes, but what the real substance of anything is we know not.'"

To hear Father Brendan quoting Isaac Newton surprised Richard considerably for he knew exactly where the passages had originated.

He could not resist asking, "So you have read Newton's 'Principia Mathematica'?"

The priest smiled at the question and shook his head. "No, I am afraid not. I was shown Newton's writing on God by a fellow student from the Natural Philosophy Faculty when I was at Theological College. Newton wrote a page and a half on God and was obviously a firm believer."

"Yes, I too have read it, for it occurs in the General Scholium in Book Three entitled 'The System of the World.' However, I did not come here to have a discussion on theology, but as I appear to have let myself in for it I hope you will not mind if I make my views plain."

"I would appreciate your doing so, for although my faith will never be shaken I am always open to learning and, in any case, I shall be very interested in your views, especially as you are a man whose calling helps relieve mankind from suffering in a very practical way."

"What I have to say may not meet with your approval, and I will be honest with you as I believe you to be honest with me. But before giving you my views I would like you to understand that as you are concerned about Eve, so am I concerned about my children. They too are young and impressionable and some of the ideas Eve has put to them are not only incorrect but misleading. I feel it important that my children get knowledge and especially facts that are accurate as possible at the outset. That is why Eve has heard me make statements she finds contradict her religious teaching."

Father Brendan inclined his head. "I appreciate your concern and respect your point of view, although I doubt anything Eve learns from me can cause any possible harm to your children." Then he added, "But please continue, I do not wish to interrupt."

"You have asked me my views on God. How can one give views on something about which one knows virtually nothing? It would appear to me that one invents the concept of God to account for the existence of the universe and if that God is good then one attributes to the deity all the good things in life, that is, all the things that please one. Newton did this in his writing on the subject.

"For myself, I am agnostic. I do not pretend to know whether or not there is a creator of the universe. I recall attending a committee where we had a very tricky project to try to bring into being. Having heard the views of colleagues and looked into the practicalities of it all, I voiced my opinion by saying that, 'This is like looking for God: You don't know what you are looking for, you don't know where to look and even if you found It you probably would not even recognize It.'

"Please do not misunderstand me. What I am saying is not a matter of debunking God, but being honest to God. For all I know there may well be a God, but if there is then I would not call the creator a loving God, which is what I understand Christians claim."

"Why so?"

"Because there is so much suffering in the world."

"The suffering is due to mankind."

"How can this be so? All sentient organisms suffer; pain is part of the nervous system."

"The suffering in this world is due to Adam and Eve's original sin. Until mankind is cleansed of sin it must suffer."

"I find that argument illogical. What about the suffering of all living organisms? Did mice commit original sin to be tormented by cats? Did a wildebeest commit original sin to undergo the anguish of fear when being chased by a lion, and then have the pain of its body being broken, its throat ripped open and the agony of a horrible death?

"Frankly, I feel that the idea of original sin is an insult to the idea of a benevolent and merciful creator. If one's grandfather broke the law, should one's parents, one's self, one's children and their children all be made to be punished for the grandfather's transgression? The idea of children and future generations being punished for the folly of a forbear is abhorrent and I consider that idea an insult to the deity."

"You must not forget that God, too, suffered. He sent His only beloved son to suffer for the sins of mankind."

"Look, I don't want to sound cynical, but quite frankly surely the God you mention had something better to do."

"What do you mean?"

"Pain and suffering are part of nature. Organisms experience it because we have evolved that way in order to survive. If one did not experience pain one would go on damaging one's body without being aware of it. Any God, especially if that God created the universe, would be aware of the fact that pain and suffering are part of nature and unless he was a masochist, he would not want to create a son to undergo what he had put there in the first place?"

"I am aware that pain is a natural thing. By suffering, I would interpret that as suffering of the immortal soul for transgressions against God's holy law."

"That, I feel, is shifting the goal posts. However, be that as it may, what is this sin that your faith places so much emphasis on?"

Father Brendan looked at Richard with an air of kindly patience and explained, "Sin is the transgression of God's holy law which is moral law. It is the word of God and can be found in the Ten Commandments. There are seven capital sins: pride, covetousness, lust, anger, gluttony, envy and sloth. Murder is a cardinal sin. Unnatural vice, oppression of the poor and defrauding laborers of their wages are also serious sins."

"This holy law sounds like a commonsense set of rules for living and can be found in many faiths and secular laws for that matter. Christ said, 'Do unto others as you would have them do unto you,' but Confucius said the same thing some five hundred years before. Buddha taught that one should avoid killing any living creature, stealing and committing adultery. He also advised one to appreciate the tranquillity of mind by speaking the truth, that is, be free of deception, avoid duplicity, avoid abusing others, be free of idle talk, avoid anger, avoid ignorance and show compassion to all.

"I myself feel compassion to my fellow men and that is why I chose my profession."

"The feeling of compassion for one's fellow men is a gift from God."

"I do not think so. I think it is genetic and stems from the long period in man's evolution when he was a tribal animal. Come to think of it, we are still tribal animals."

Richard looked at a clock situated on the wall behind Father Brendan. "Good Lord, is that the time? I hope you will forgive me for terminating our discussion. Clearly we cannot agree on everything, but at least I feel we understand our viewpoints better. I also hope that you will rest assured that I shall take care not to have Eve upset and deviated from her course."

Father Brendan smiled. "I appreciate what you have said. I would add that although we differ in our viewpoints, I have enjoyed talking to you and hope it will not be our last meeting. I must admit I was curious to know what you meant by saying that compassion is genetic and would have liked you to elaborate on that."

Richard rose to his feet as he spoke. "I shall be happy to discuss that with you at another time. Perhaps you would like to come to my home one evening and we can participate in a friendly debate over some suitable refreshment. I shall give you a ring and we can arrange a mutually convenient time."

Father Brendan rose and saying, "I would very much like that and look forward to it," escorted Richard to the door and they parted amicably with a handshake.

As Richard drove home he recalled a verse from the Rubaiyat of Omar Khayyam: "Myself when young did eagerly frequent doctor and saint, and heard great argument about it and about: but evermore came out by the same door as in I went."

■ ☐ ■ ☐ ■

There was considerable excitement among the children when Richard got home. Their summer holidays had arrived and they were preparing for a week's sailing on *Aurora*. Each of them was sitting at an occasional table in the lounge with a pencil and paper making a list of clothing and items they were to take on the yacht.

"Are we going to sail to Holland?" asked John.

"Possibly," Dawn replied. "It all depends on the weather."

"Can I bring Castor and Pollux with me?" asked Jennifer, referring to her two pet mice.

"Course not, silly," Jean interjected. "They will get seasick."

"Daddy can give them an anti-seasickness pill, can't you, Daddy?"

"That has a practical difficulty, Jennifer. Judging the dosage would not be easy and if I made a mistake you might be attending their funeral."

"Ooh, that would be fun," said John enthusiastically. "We could have a burial at sea. Just imagine two tiny little coffins sliding into the water underneath the Red Duster."

"Don't be horrid, John. How would you like to die from a seasickness pill and be buried at sea?"

"Well, he'd certainly make a bigger splash than Castor and Pollux," said Jean unfeelingly.

"I'd like to bring Poppet. Would you like to come sailing, Poppet?"

"If we go to the continent we cannot bring Poppet, Jennifer. On return we would have to leave her in quarantine and that would be for six months. Len will take care of her and Castor and Pollux."

"Couldn't we hide her in one of the lockers, Mummy?"

"If you did that and got caught you would go to jail for six months and Poppet would still be in quarantine."

"Let's do," said John. "Then we would not have to put up with Jennifer's jokes for six months."

Eve listened to the banter with amusement and a little misgiving, wondering what it would be like being confined to the yacht for a week in close proximity to the children. However, she need not have worried; Richard decided not to sail to Holland as a ridge of low pressure was to be present for three days. This meant that the North Sea would be very rough and so they confined the sailing to short voyages along the coast with visits to places of interest inland. Eve would have enjoyed it more if Sean had been able to spend some time with them, but he was unable to leave the practice.

It was late one afternoon when they boarded *Aurora* at Burnham. Eve was quite impressed with the way Dawn and Richard organized the children and supplies. As the yacht was moored in midstream in one of the lines of yachts, they were conveyed to her by a small ferry boat and, as they were frequent users the ferryman knew them well. With obvious practice the children climbed from the ferry to *Aurora*. Dawn and Eve boarded, and then Richard handed the kit and food supplies to Dawn and Eve. It did not take long to get everything stowed carefully.

"Everything in its place and a place for everything," Dawn told the children who were well aware of the need to keep the vessel tidy for comfortable living in a confined space. Eve had been given a Royal Yachting Association booklet entitled "Competent Crew" some weeks before and had read it through carefully. She found the information of inestimable value during her stay on the yacht. It whetted her appetite for more knowledge regarding sailing and she determined to take the competent crew course and examination when the opportunity occurred.

She had learned from the children that both Dawn and Richard held Yachtmasters certificates and that knowledge was of some comfort to her later when they experienced rough conditions. Her confidence was further improved when Dawn conducted her carefully over the vessel and showed her the various features of the yacht, and Richard organized several drills including fire drill, man overboard and abandon ship. He also got Eve and the children to raise and lower the sails.

On helping to prepare dinner aboard that evening, Eve discovered the advantages of a pressure cooker on a yacht. The temperature had cooled slightly with dampness in the atmosphere and their appetites were best satisfied with hot food. They retired early in preparation for an early start in the morning to take advantage of the tide.

Eve lay on the comfortable bunk in her cabin and listened to the gurgling of water as it streamed past the yacht. Although they were still at the mooring she felt tired after all the excitement and exertion. Thoughts of Sean crossed her mind and she wished that he could be on board. A motor cruiser passed alongside and she felt the gentle rocking of *Aurora* in the passing wake.

She realized how different things were since she had run away from the Londinium Club. Meeting Caria had been a shock and she still wondered if it was wise to see her again. If by chance Caria had found her, what were the chances of Parker or Mr. de Vere-Smythe finding her? The thought disturbed her and there was another thing: she had not contacted her brother and he would be worrying about her. She knew from Caria that he had tried to contact her but realized the wisdom of not notifying him of her whereabouts; she would be safer and if the Mob, as Caria called it, traced him, he too would be safer. It had not been an easy decision for her to make for she was very fond of her brother, but despite agonizing over it she knew there was no other way.

With those thoughts on her mind she decided to pray and ask God to keep her brother safe from her enemies. She appreciated that apart from praying there was little else she could do. With her prayers concluded she felt less worried and fell asleep assisted by the gentle rocking of the yacht.

Eve was woken in the morning by a knocking on her cabin door. She opened it to see Jennifer standing outside wearing a pirate hat.

"The captain said he will make you walk the plank if you don't show a leg."

Eve looked beyond Jennifer into the saloon and saw Dawn smiling and preparing breakfast. "Don't you believe a word of it, Eve."

"No, you will get fifty lashes instead," John piped in, not wanting to be left out of the conversation.

"John, that's enough," and addressing Eve, Dawn said, "sorry about that, Eve. I hope you slept well?"

"Yes, thanks. I'll get dressed and give you a hand."

Eve quickly washed and dressed and joined the family as they sat round the breakfast table. It was a comfortable and spacious saloon, the vessel being thirty-nine feet in length with an eleven-foot beam. There were three separate cabins and two heads which gave a considerable degree of comfort for a fast cruising yacht. The saloon could also be converted to sleep three although Richard and Dawn preferred not to crowd the vessel.

Eve discovered she had a good appetite that morning. She had slept well and now looked forward to the day's voyage. They had enjoyed a breakfast of oatmeal, eggs and fruit and after assisting clearing up, Eve prepared to go on deck.

"Put an extra pullover on, Eve," said Dawn. "It will be fresh outside. I know you can swim, but our clothes are heavy and Richard makes it a rule to wear life-vests when out at sea unless one is wearing a swimming costume."

Up on deck the strong salty smell of the sea surrounded them and they felt the coolness of the air. Eve looked around her and saw the lines of yachts stretching upstream. The north shore was dominated by the large building of the Royal Corinthian Yacht Club, and she noticed the picturesque brick houses and the odd tavern lining the river beyond. It being midweek and early in the morning, there were only few other vessels being prepared for sea.

With the strong ebbing tide *Aurora* was pointing upstream in the opposite direction to which they intended to go. Although Richard had started the engine they hoisted both jib and mainsail. Dawn watched with interest as the vessel started to sail upstream responding to the southwesterly wind. On Richard's command, assisted by John, she let go the mooring rope attached to the buoy and they sailed slowly upstream for a few yards. As Eve and John made their way back to the cockpit, Richard spun the steering wheel to port while Dawn loosed the mainsheet. The foresail was still tightly sheeted to starboard and as *Aurora* swung the backed sail rapidly pushed the bow round to port until they were pointing downstream. Having been previously prepared for the maneuver Dawn tightened up the mainsheet while Jean slackened the starboard jib sheet. With Dawn then quickly tightening the port jib sheet the yacht responded, cleared the vessels moored on either side and sailed rapidly downstream assisted by both wind and tide.

The tide was ebbing fast and an hour was to elapse before it turned. Richard intended to take advantage of it to carry them towards the Whitaker Beacon. Dawn had shown Eve the Admiralty chart before departure and she, with the children participating, took an interest in marking the route on the chart and entering in the deck log the times of passing buoys and landmarks of interest en route.

As low water was approaching they kept strictly to the deeper part of the river and estuary. Mud and sand banks rose on each side and the low mass of Foulness Island was considerably extended eastward, it being a spring tide. Dawn was making a note in the deck log of the vessel passing the outer crouch buoy when Jennifer excitedly called her up on deck.

"Come and see the seals, Eve." Putting her pencil carefully in its slot on the navigation table, Eve mounted the steps and emerged into the cockpit to see Jennifer pointing to starboard. She looked in the same direction and saw a number of black seals lying on the exposed Foulness sandbank. Dawn handed her a pair of binoculars. "How many do you think there are, Eve?"

Adjusting the focus of the instrument to her eyes, Eve counted thirteen.

"I counted twelve," piped in Jennifer.

"I counted thirteen. You missed a baby one," John interjected.

Eve looked carefully and counted again. "Sorry, Jennifer, I make it thirteen, but you were not necessarily wrong."

"How's that?" John having initially looked pleased, then frowning when he suspected that he was not right after all.

"Well, John, what is a dozen?"

"Twelve."

"And therefore Jennifer counted a dozen." John nodded at that.

"Well, what is a baker's dozen?"

"Thirteen!" said Jean quickly.

"So we were both right," giggled Jennifer.

"Very funny," John pulled a face. "But that's cheating."

Eve looked forward and trained the binoculars on a tall yellow and black buoy situated about two miles ahead. "Is that the Sunken Buxey buoy?"

Dawn replied, "Yes. You can see the twin cones pointing upwards?"

"Yes. I remember seeing that type of buoy in the almanac and it is a north cardinal buoy. We have to go north of it."

"See, Mummy, Eve has been doing her homework," said Jean who was also scrutinizing the buoy with another pair of binoculars.

"You'll be a first-class navigator yet," Richard joined in the conversation. "Would you like to steer for a spell?"

Eve nodded happily and on taking over the helm repeated the compass course after Richard. "Zero-six-zero. Aye, aye, captain," she said, entering into the spirit of the occasion while Richard and Dawn encouraged the children to adjust the sails to take full advantage of a slight change in the wind direction.

Aurora was now sailing on a broad reach and Eve felt exhilarated as the vessel responded quickly to the helm. The sun had broken through the slightly gray sky and the landscape was suddenly filled with a welcoming brightness. As she steered so she soon felt in complete control of the new action of steering and she was pleased when Richard remarked to Dawn, "It looks as if we have a born helmswoman in Eve."

Any misgivings Eve had previously felt about sailing rapidly disappeared as the yacht sped on its way, and she knew that she was going to enjoy the novel experience. She looked around, confidently keeping the vessel on course by feel, and watched the patchy shadows of the clouds speed across the water leaving sparkling reflections in their wake. To her right side the long bank of Foulness Sand lay bare; to her left the Buxey Sand stretched ahead, bare and glistening in the sunlight. Looking beyond it to the north she could see the exposed Dengie Flats and the low tree-lined Essex Coast lying low on the horizon. She noticed a square building standing out beyond the shoreline and recalled that the landmark was the Bradwell Atomic Power Station. They would be sailing closer to that later in the day when they reached the River Blackwater.

They had passed the green Buxey Buoy to port when Richard addressed Eve. "Steer closer to the Ridge Buoy, Eve," he advised. "With this being low water and a spring tide there is a risk of running aground on this course. When we reach the buoy keep it to starboard and steer zero-seven-zero."

Eve repeated the course and steered towards the red can-shaped buoy she could see about a mile and a quarter ahead. They were still sheltered from the effects of the wind on the water by the Buxey Sand which was now fully exposed. The wave height was quite low although the wind had increased slightly in strength. Eve could feel the vessel heeling and she heard Richard say to Dawn that he would wait until they were clear of the Whitaker Beacon with more sea room before taking in two reefs of the mainsail. He did, however, reduce the foresail using the roller reefing.

It seemed only a short while when *Aurora* passed the Whitaker Beacon which marked the end of the Foulness Sand. Once beyond it the vessel felt the influence of the open North Sea although the wind was blowing offshore, it having veered since they left the mooring. Richard pointed out the shallow areas to port as the vessel sailed past them.

"When we have gone another mile steer zero-three-zero; Dawn and I will slacken off the main sheet and let the main fly. We will then take in two reefs; the jib will keep her going forward and give you adequate steerage way."

Eve nodded and repeated the new course to be followed then added, "How shall I know we have gone another mile?"

"I shall take a bearing on the Ridge Buoy and the Whitaker Beacon and tell you when." Then addressing Jean and John said, "Come on, you two. Jean, you note the bearings on the chart. I'll take a bearing of the beacon and John, you take a bearing of the buoy."

It was not long before the bearings were taken. "I make it two hundred and forty," announced John, and Richard called out two hundred and ten while Jean plotted them both on the chart under the watchful eye of Dawn.

"Time to turn, Eve," and she brought the bow of *Aurora* to point in the direction ordered as Dawn came up on deck.

Dawn let go the mainsheet and the sail swung out towards the starboard side and shivered in the wind. She then quickly clambered on the coach roof and, as Richard lowered the main halyard, she hooked the tack of the sail to the reefing hook and then went to the end of the boom to complete the slab reef, while Richard tightened the halyard. With a signal from Richard, Jean and John tightened the main sheet with the winch handle while Jennifer hauled on the rope and then they neatly coiled the sheet and stowed it into the side locker.

Eve felt the vessel heel to starboard as the mainsail worked the wind and the speed of the yacht increased. Steering on the course given she could see a mile and a half almost directly ahead, the Swin Spitway buoy. The wind was now fully on the beam and she felt invigorated by the spanking pace of *Aurora* as she seemed to fly through the water. Dawn looked at her and saw the excitement on her face. "Good fun, isn't it, Eve?"

"I'd no idea sailing could be so exhilarating, Dawn. If I had known I would have come before."

There was more fetch when the protection of the Buxey Sand was lost and with the strong wind against the flowing tide, the waves were breaking and an occasional wave shot a cascade of water over the bow to hit all those standing in the cockpit. They all put up their hoods except Jennifer who wanted to keep her pirate hat on.

"Put your hood up, Jennifer," Jean advised her.

"No—I'm the pirate captain."

"You'll lose it in this wind," Jean responded.

"No, I . . . "

But it was too late. A gust caught the hat and whipped it off Jennifer's head. Fortunately Richard was standing behind her and it struck him on the chest which arrested its flight just long enough for him to grab it before it flew overboard.

"Well, young pirate," he said, "do you want to walk the plank or put your hood on your head?"

Jennifer sheepishly turned her back to the wind and covered her head with her hood and then tightened the draw string making it secure.

With Eve still at the helm, *Aurora* sailed through the Spitway and then headed northeast into the Wallet. Once steadily on course, Dawn relieved Eve at the wheel and they sailed for an hour before reversing their direction and, after taking another reef, tacked all the way to the River Blackwater. They passed as close to Clacton as the depth of the water permitted and Eve noticed some strange round buildings surmounting the low cliff. Pointing them out to Richard, she asked what they were.

"They are small forts built during the time of the Napoleonic wars when this country was expecting an invasion by the French and are called Martello Towers. Fortunately, the defeat of the French and Spanish fleet at Trafalgar put a stop to that tyrant's plans. This area of the coast has had many defenses built throughout history, for there are many inlets and small rivers into which invaders could sail, often without detection. Also, it has always been a favorite haunt for smugglers."

"Many of our ancestors came to Britain through Essex," said Richard, joining in the conversation. "Brythons, Kelts, Romans, Saxons and Danes all came this way looking for plunder or land on which to settle their excess populations. There is an old English poem called 'The Battle of Maldon' which commemorates the defeat of the English by the Danes and it took place there in the year 991.

"Race preys on race even to this day; one sees it with the Arab and the Jew, the Tutsi and the Hutu, to name but a few. It is still the struggle for the survival of the fittest. Such is the sad state of the human race throughout the world. The Malthusian Doctrine is probably true. Perhaps the Gaia theory is correct: the mother earth is a self-regulating body; where organisms proliferate in numbers beyond the capabilities of support by their environment they will be reduced either by starvation or warfare."

"Come on, Richard," Dawn interrupted. "We're on holiday; let us forget the morbid matters of the world."

For the next two hours they tacked westward into the River Blackwater. Eve went below assisted by Jennifer to plot the course, but began to feel the effects of the bouncing of the vessel in a confined space. She quickly went back up on deck to the cockpit where Dawn noticed her pallor.

"I think you should steer, Eve; it will make you feel better. Keep your eyes on the horizon. Richard has decided to take in the sails and we will motor the rest of the way to Maldon." Eve was grateful for the advice and her feeling of nausea gradually disappeared as they continued upstream. They made their way past the Bradwell Atomic Power Station, and the Bradwell Marina. The sky was overcast and the wind continued to increase and occasional squalls of rain fell, but now they were protected from the strength of the wind by the steep wooded banks of the river.

Before passing Osea and Northey Islands, Richard relieved Eve from the helm and, aided by the tidal flow, carefully steered the vessel through the narrow navigable channel where the only deep water was to be found, although the river extended nearly half a mile on each side. They rounded the bend off Chigborough and after leaving the stretch between the northwest bank and Northey Island, *Aurora* entered Maldon and moored on the quayside above two spritsail Thames barges. On having made the mooring ropes secure, the whole crew repaired to the saloon as another squall descended. As Richard entered, a large motor cruiser passed by, heading downstream, taking advantage of the high tide to pass through the narrow navigable passage to the sea.

Inside the cabin, Richard showed Eve how to operate the Weather Fax and she was surprised to see the rapidity with which the weather map was printed out. Dawn explained, "That indicates the low is passing across the North Sea and high pressure is over the Azores moving slightly north. We should have a sunny day tomorrow and good weather for the next three days at least."

This piece of news was welcome to Eve who had wondered how she would feel after several days of bad weather in the confined space of the yacht. She had listened to one of Jennifer's jokes: "Did I tell you about the boy who wondered where the sun went at night?"

"No, Jennifer."

"Well, he walked for miles and miles until he came to the sea."

"Oh. What happened then?"

"He stayed up all night and then it dawned on him."

Eve smiled and then John said, "You should eat something, Jennifer."

"Why?"

"Because you'll have your mouth full and won't be able to tell any jokes."

However, Eve need not have worried. After a somewhat late lunch, the rain stopped and they all went ashore to explore the town.

Maldon has often been described as the "Pearl of the Estuary Towns of Essex." Situated at the head of the River Blackwater with its picturesque marshes, islands and wooded banks, it is a safe haven from the storms that beset the more exposed and shorter estuaries. A charming market town, the site was occupied in prehistoric times and the present burgh was established by the Saxon King Edward the Elder in 916. In the Domesday Book of 1086, Maldon was referred to as "terra regis," a royal town. Later, Henry II granted the borough its first charter in 1171. For the lover of ancient architecture and historical monuments, Maldon is one of the most rewarding towns in East Anglia.

Three towers dominate the skyline of the town: All Saints' Church which stands at the highest part of the High street, is situated on the site of the most ancient part of the town; Saint Mary's Church, historically the oldest and recorded in 1056 which stands by the waterfront and the Town Hall. This latter is an interesting old red-brick building called the Moot Hall or Darcy's Tower. Built in the 15th century as the "Moot" or meeting place for discussion, it contains a fine collection of old charters dating from the reign of Edward I to George III.

It was to explore these ancient edifices and enjoy the atmosphere of antiquity that the crew of *Aurora* sought respite from the exertions of sailing in an adverse wind. They walked along a short stone-paved esplanade among large numbers of tourists, and ascended the main street admiring the old buildings and shops. Eve and Dawn in particular enjoyed window shopping. They admired the Blue Boar Hotel with its Georgian frontage. On inquiry they learned that much of the building dated from the fourteenth century when King Richard was on the throne. Across the yard there are parts of the fine old inn dating from the early thirteen hundreds which was built of Essex oak and Essex clay before bricks came into general use.

They stopped to admire the All Saints' vicarage with its exposed timber frames and entered the church with its quaint triangular tower and its numerous traceried windows. While the Rutherfords trod slowly and quietly inside the building admiring its shape and structure, Eve felt an overwhelming desire to pray. She entered a pew and knelt, crossing herself in an act of humble contrition.

When Eve had finished her devotions she found the family waiting outside the church door. They expressed a wish to visit the Moot Hall which lay a little west of St. Peter's Tower along the High Street and Eve cheerfully agreed. As they proceeded the sun came out and the roadways began to dry rapidly in its warmth. They found the building without difficulty, recognizing it by its overhanging clock.

"This is the Moot Hall some rooms of which are still used as a Court Room, Council Chamber and a Muniment Room."

"What is a Muniment Room?" queried John.

"That is a room in which documents are stored. If we go up the stairway we can see the town and the coastline."

"Oh, let's do that," chorused Jean and Jennifer.

"I think it is a moot point whether we should all make that effort," John volunteered. The response was several groans and an immediate move to enter the building. They went slowly through the building and in particular admired the collection of old charters displayed on the walls of the Muniment Room. Eve and Dawn were taken with the charter granted in the reign of Henry IV with its decorative illuminations, and also those of the sixteenth century for their exquisite penmanship. From there they mounted the stairway to the top of the building.

"Oh, what a lovely view," exclaimed Jean. "One can see for miles!" And it was so. Beneath them lay the town and the stone bridge over the Blackwater which was once called the Panta. Like the Horatii of Rome, three East Anglians held the bridge against invading Saxons for a brief spell but unlike one of the defenders of Janiculum, all perished. Further downstream below the bridge, *Aurora* lay moored to the jetty and stood clear with her spring mooring ropes secure.

To the south they could see the River Crouch and to the east the sea was clearly visible. Richard looked to the east and recognized the cabin cruiser that had passed them earlier. It appeared to be heading towards the Belgian coast and was throwing up spray in the sea that was still affected by the movement of the depression that was now dissipating over the continent.

The following day *Aurora* set sail for Walton-on-the-Naze where they anchored in the afternoon in the Naze. The whole crew went ashore in the dinghy and played on a strip of sand for a while, then went to the town, shopped and took the children to enjoy the entertainments provided on the pier. Dinner ashore was welcomed by both Dawn and Eve who had attended to most of the meals on board ship.

The third day they sailed to explore the Rivers Stour and Orwell and the River Deben the day after. The most northerly destination was the River Ore and Aldburgh, the Old Borough to the Saxons. During the sixteenth century the town was an important fishing and commercial port as well as a shipyard. However, a large source of prosperity to the local inhabitants lay in smuggling and, for entertainment, outwitting the excise men. From Aldburgh, the whole crew went to the village of Snape to where a concert was being held in the evening. Eve was delighted to visit the Maltings Concert Hall in the village of Snape. It was the first time she had the opportunity to attend the celebrated Aldburgh Festival. She had read of the Festival having been founded by Benjamin Britten, Peter Pears, Eric Crozia and Imogen Holst, all of whom had lived in Aldborough. That night they all went to their bunks tired yet delighted to have had a very satisfying musical experience in novel surroundings.

On the morning of the last but one day, *Aurora* motored to Brightlingsea, for the high pressure system that had followed the previous bad weather resulted in little wind. It was not without a certain amount of hazard for there was fog in the morning. However, the vessel had radar and Eve and the children enjoyed using it to assist conning the yacht to Brightlingsea. The next day there was a very light breeze and they sailed lazily down the Essex coast. With a full main and genoa set they were among a large number of yachts following the coastline. The sky was a deep blue and the sun shone warmly. This tempted all the crew to adopt bathing costumes and sunscreen ointment. Richard had been watching the sky a little inland above the verdant cliffs. He pointed out to Dawn and Eve the small cumulus clouds that were slowly developing.

"We had better take in two reefs of the main and shorten the genny."

Eve was surprised to hear that order, for there was little wind. However, she assisted him and the children to carry out the orders while Dawn steered. With the sail changes accomplished, *Aurora* sailed more slowly than ever and Jennifer commented on the other vessel in the flotilla overtaking them. Eve looked around and saw only two other vessels reducing sail. Noticing the puzzled look on her face, Richard pointed to the small clouds forming a line just inland along the coast.

"You see those clouds?" Eve nodded. "Well, they are due to hot moist rising air and that will suck in a breeze from seaward. It should be with us quite quickly."

They had only ten minutes to wait when they saw to seaward a disturbed surface on the sea. Within five minutes the wind increased to fifteen knots and apart from the two vessels and themselves, all other yachts in the flotilla were turning into the wind and lowering sail. Having been prepared, *Aurora* and two other yachts sped ahead of the remainder of the vessels and Jennifer and John cheered excitedly. At a spanking pace they left the Wallet, through the Swin Spitway and along the Crouch estuary where they enjoyed high tea while the yacht, assisted by the breeze and flowing tide, sailed towards Burnham being steered with the autohelm.

As the wind was with the tide, Richard had set the genoa with a whisker pole and the main with a preventer. As a result, the vessel was very steady and they all enjoyed the meal sitting at the table rigged in the cockpit. Eve sat beside the hatchway with her back to the bulkhead and watched a large motor cruiser coming up astern to gradually overtake them.

"That is a smart looking vessel," remarked Dawn as the motor cruiser drew alongside. They all waved as it passed and they noticed two figures in the steering housing looking at them with binoculars.

"I guess the sight of two shapely ladies is the cause for their interest," grinned Richard. Eve blushed and ducked down while Dawn laughed and said, "Flattery will get you anywhere Richard." He was still smiling when he remarked, "Odd name that vessel has. It is called *Erinyes*. I wonder what that means?"

chapter eighteen

"*Entrare mi amici.* Please come in and sit down." Bernadette and Rory entered the spacious office of Signore Luigi Furari and seated themselves on the comfortable chairs indicated by him. "Roderigo tells me that you have done well and benefited from the training." They both smiled at the compliment. "I was very interested to learn that you are both very accurate with the mortars. That is good." He regarded them with his penetrating black eyes. "You are happy with the new bomb-detonating devices?" Both Rory and Bernadette nodded; the new devices were good and virtually foolproof. Furthermore, the new explosives and fine shrapnel bombs could cause more devastation and injuries that were difficult to treat. They both felt very satisfied with all they had learned and practiced.

Addressing Rory, he added, "Your skill in field work and being able to take full advantage of cover is outstanding. Well, we are going to put you both to the test with a real situation. It will make a fitting and exciting end to your training here. You leave Sicilia the day after tomorrow."

Luigi Furari paused and looked at both their faces intently before continuing. Their lack of expression reassured him that his next announcement would not be adversely received.

"There is a villa which is occupied by people that are hostile to our *famiglia* and business interests. You will prove the value of your training and appreciation of our hospitality by participating in the *eliminazioni* of that *famiglia*. You comprehend, *si*?"

Both Rory and Bernadette looked interested. They were now such professional killers that any qualms about taking innocent lives were nonexistent and neither had a conscience about such activities. Rory recalled the statement he had read made by O'Connor, the IRA leader and organizer of terrorism in Ireland in 1918: "We may make mistakes in the beginning and shoot the wrong people, but bloodshed is a cleansing and sanctifying thing and the nation which regards it as the final horror has lost its manhood." He smiled inwardly thinking that at least he had not lost his manhood. Then he brought his mind back to pay attention to Signore Furari and with Bernadette nodded his head in agreement to the proposition.

"Ah, good. Roderigo will outline the plan of attack to you all after you leave here. You and eight of my men will leave at three o'clock tomorrow morning and will be taken to the villa."

He rose, indicating that the audience was at an end, and they both followed suit as he gave them a slight bow and showed them to the door. As they left the office they found Roderigo waiting for them in the corridor.

"So you are going to assist our *famiglia* with a little enterprise." It was more of a statement than a question. Both Bernadette and Rory looked at him a little warily. "We do not appear to have much option."

Roderigo laughed. "You do have a choice. You can either assist or have our padre read you the last rites." He laughed at his little joke and conducted them both to a small conference room; there they met four men who they already knew from their having participated in their training.

The room was set up with a map of the whole island on one wall, and some maps of the countryside in which the villa was situated, as well as detailed plans of the villa. There were also photographs of the villa and grounds taken by helicopter from the air.

As Roderigo spoke, both Bernadette and Rory began to take a professional interest in the plan he outlined. He started by stating the object of the enterprise: to leave the villa uninhabitable and liquidate all the occupants. No one was to escape. In all, the briefing lasted an hour and a half and was finished by lunchtime, after which all of the participants enjoyed a siesta, and later retired to bed early.

Bernadette and Rory were aroused at two-thirty in the morning and the cadre departed promptly at three. It took nearly an hour and a half to reach the road where they disembarked from the two Land Rovers owned by Luigi. They walked the rest of the distance and took up their positions just before daybreak. The air was warm and they knew that a hot day lay ahead. Roderigo was in charge and wasted no time in getting his force to carry out the preparatory activities.

Villa Strattoni was situated on the top of a cliff which, being vertical, made it almost impossible to attack from the sea. There was only one road leading to the villa and that was always guarded. Like Liugi Furari, Storsi Strattoni had profited from the WWII supply of arms but he had not been as successful as his arch enemy. Prior to that world war, the ancient feuding between the two families had been bitter but relatively mild in the toll of lives.

Since the war, their extortion rackets had overlapped and there were clashes whenever the opportunity occurred. However, during the last few years there was a temporary truce, due to the Italians on the mainland starting to take real action against the Mafioso. Although mutual tolerance was now practiced, treachery could be expected at any time. The one who struck first needed to be thorough, for the authorities were beginning to take an interest in the successes against the Mafioso on the mainland and this was not in the interests of the Mafia families in Sicily.

Luigi had one big advantage over his rivals: there were a number of members of the local police who were able to turn a blind eye to his activities and also act as part of his intelligence service. Their cooperation was assured by indirect financial reward and the threat of direct action against loved ones and dependents. The latter was seldom resorted to, for Furari was so successful and astute his bribes outweighed any reward the police were likely to get for reporting his activities to higher authorities. In any case the rank and file of the law-keepers did not know who among their superiors was in the pay of Luigi. So it was not surprising that when the attack on the Villa Strattoni occurred, the police were noticeably absent and somewhat tardy in taking action when reports of the raid started coming in. Apart from that, it also suited them to let the Mafioso eliminate each other, for when the authorities reached the position where direct action against criminals was viable there would be fewer of them to deal with.

Rory's first assignment was to place explosives in a small conduit under the road leading from the villa. This demanded his field skills, for the Strattonis as well as the Furaris took advantage of modern technology and used infrared night vision instruments. He crawled behind cover to reach the conduit and carefully inserted the plastic explosive. He anticipated a powerful and shattering explosion having prepared a mixture called C4. With the radio-firing mechanism attached and operative, he carefully crawled away from the site ensuring that no part of his body was exposed so that its heat could be seen by guards at the villa. He rejoined his fellow assassins without a sound and was quietly congratulated by Roderigo on his accomplishment.

The plan of attack was straightforward. Two mortar teams each consisting of two persons, were to position themselves to enable them to pitch mortar bombs onto the villa. Initially they would fire incendiaries at all the buildings and set them on fire. They would then follow with high explosive bombs which would not only kill but render firefighting impossible. One team would then attach explosives to the southern end of the surrounding wall and breach it. With sub-machine guns the storming party would enter and kill anyone left alive after the mortar bombardment. Prior to that action and after they were all in their respective positions, Roderigo knew that the leader Signori Strattoni and eight of his men would be leaving the villa at seven-thirty that morning. A special meeting had been arranged by Luigi Furari at a mutually agreed spot, to confer about some business arrangements and action to be taken if the polizei took heart from the successes of anti-Mafioso activities on the mainland.

Two men were assigned to detonate the explosives under the road and also shoot any survivors. With half of Strattioni's fighting force out of action, Luigi anticipated that Roderigo would have a relatively easy task to eliminate the rest; and he did.

At the time expected, the gates of the wall surrounding the landward side of the villa opened and a Fiat followed by a large Alfa-Romeo emerged. Bernadette had been assigned to the northern mortar team and Rory to the southern. From their positions both could see the departure of the vehicles from the villa. They watched fascinated as the automobiles separated by the short distance of ten meters approached the conduit. They had gathered speed and were traveling at about fifty miles per hour when the Fiat reached it. The explosive was detonated just as the vehicle passed over the top. The ground erupted with an ear-shattering bang as the radio signal set off the explosives. The Fiat leaped into the air somersaulting forward as its petrol tank exploded, its occupants being killed instantly. The Alfa-Romeo caught the blast as it ran into the Fiat—the front of the vehicle was shattered and lifted to somersault backwards and land upside down. Hardly had the debris from the explosion fallen when the two men lying in wait sprayed a volley of bullets inside. But they may as well have saved their ammunition; at that moment the fuel tank exploded and any chance of survival, had it existed, disappeared.

The sound of the explosion was the signal for the incendiary mortar bombs to be lobbed onto the buildings within the compound, a task which both Rory and Bernadette performed with consummate skill. Their training had been very thorough. Within a short space of time the villa and all the outbuildings were aflame and then the high explosive mortar bombs detonated with bangs, followed by screams from the wounded. Smoke and flames rose accompanied by debris as each bomb exploded.

Two members of the Strattoni mob started to fire back at their attackers, but they were hampered by not knowing exactly where their enemies were. All they accomplished was to give away their positions and this resulted in one of Roderigo's marksmen, armed with a sniper's rifle, picking them off. From that point all opposition seemed to cease and Roderigo ordered the breaching of the wall. In this he displayed his skill as a tactician. Instead of storming through the breach as soon as the debris from the explosion had ceased falling, he instructed Rory to lob two mortar bombs just inside. The resultant shrapnel achieved the desired result of killing two defenders and badly wounding another.

When at last the attackers entered through the breach in the wall, most of the defenders were either dead or wounded. The attackers had opened the gap at one end of the compound, and on entering, spread out, with four on each side of the buildings which were in line. They riddled with bullets any of their enemies who showed signs of life. Meantime, Bernadette lobbed several more mortar bombs between buildings and at the far end of the compound; these ensured that anyone hiding there would stand an excellent chance of either being killed or put out of action before the attackers reached their positions. The defenders now consisted only of a few women trying to protect their surviving children.

Amidst smoke and flame the attackers shot them one by one. At one point two terrified, shrieking children broke away from their mother and ran towards the low wall beside the cliff. One boy had a neck artery ripped open with a bullet and the stream of blood that shot from it drenched his sister. The frantic mother ran screaming after her children and then scooping them both up in her arms jumped over the wall hoping to find shelter on the narrow edge of the cliff top between the wall and the sheer drop. As she leaped over the wall, one of Roderigo's men shot her in the back—she missed her footing and she and her two screaming children fell the two hundred feet into the sea.

Roderigo felt proud of himself after the attack was over; it had all been too easy. His plan of attack had worked perfectly and his small force had experienced no casualties. He and the rest of the gang searched the compound and ensured that no one remained alive. The whole operation had been completed within an hour of blowing up the two cars. His only disappointment was that there was little loot to retrieve, for the fires had gutted all the buildings and effectively destroyed anything of value inside. Not all members of the Strattoni Family could be accounted for, but it was realized that many had perished in the buildings, either killed by the mortars or burned to death.

Rory was amused to note that several of Roderigo's men crossed themselves when they viewed the corpses. He had long since ceased to perform that observance, although the habits and superstitions of his early religious training and practices still dwelt deep down within his mind. It was long since he had rationalized his actions. He was now so much in the habit of killing and so hardened to it that he no longer felt the need to hunt for arguments to justify doing what he wanted to do, or believing what he wanted to believe. His hatred for the Protestants in Northern Ireland and the British, despite the latter trying to protect the common people against the excess of the gunmen of both sides, was so strong that rationalization of his actions was not now necessary.

Bernadette had never needed to rationalize her actions in committing murder and the maiming of innocent people. The constant brainwashing of herself and her brothers and sisters by her mother served to justify any action that she undertook. Although she had been brought up as, and still was, a staunch Roman Catholic, she did not relate the Christian principles to her nefarious activities. Her mind completely dissociated the two conflicting concepts: on the one hand of Christian compassion coupled with forgiveness and "turning the other cheek," and on the other hand the very antithesis of cold-blooded murder. Seeing the dead corpses of women and children left her completely unmoved.

Despite their different mental approaches to their activities, both Bernadette and Rory had one thing in common—they both enjoyed the excitement of their chosen profession. Like Boss, they too were not happy the way things were going politically. There was talk of the IRA stopping the killing, accepting the invitation by the British and Irish governments to the conference table and participating in trying to find a solution to the Irish problem. This did not appeal to them any more than it did to Boss. Another problem for them was that Boss was doing very well with his occupation and rackets. They did not have his advantages.

"Time to go," Roderigo addressed both Bernadette and Rory who had been watching four of Roderigo's men throw the corpses into the still-burning buildings. He noticed their attention to the proceedings and laughed, "*Cremazione senza prezzo.* We all get away now *rapidamente*. I have sent Alphonso and Sextus to bring the Land Rovers as close as they can. We leave before the *polizia* helicopters arrive."

The victors needed no further prompting and all rapidly left the enclave and made for a copse away from the villa and near the road. They passed the two burnt-out vehicles with their charred and blackened corpses still confined to their *màcchina* coffins. A small wisp of smoke ascended from the remnants of both vehicles and the smell of burned petrol and flesh floated in the air.

They reached the copse and rested under the shade of the trees while they waited for the two Land Rovers. Roderigo looked back at the villa, "Some, how you say, real estate will be going *buòn merca-*

to." He laughed at his own joke then congratulated everyone on the parts they played so well in the very successful operation. They were on their way back to the Villa Furari when they saw a police helicopter pass along the valley in the distance. The delay had been well arranged thanks to a few palms being well oiled. By the time a fire truck arrived at the villa it was only necessary to hose down smoldering ashes; most of what was combustible had lost its oxidative qualities and was charred or just hot cinders. Even the corpses had either been completely incinerated or rendered unrecognizable.

It was later in the day that Luigi Furari congratulated them all on their masterful tour de force and, after a late siesta, the entire company celebrated with a dinner followed by entertainment and a party. It was also a farewell party for the two IRA members and Luigi honored them in a speech. "You *Irelandese* have learned your lessons very well, *con perfezione*. You are *molto professionisto*. You leave tomorrow and we wish you both good fortune in your future enterprises."

Both Bernadette and Rory were pleased, not only with the praise from the Mafia boss and the thoroughness of their training, but also with the arms and explosives that were to be loaded on the container to take back with them to the United Kingdom. They both felt that their time in Sicily had been very productive, and the excitement and novelty of the combat in which they had participated was a fitting end to their stay in the country. The following day they joined the *El Arabiyana* on the first leg of her voyage to Hamburg. As before they would abandon the vessel at a previously arranged rendezvous with the motor cruiser *Erinyes* in the North Sea. They both looked forward to meeting Boss again and continuing their campaign. Meantime they would relax during the voyage; life was very pleasant for them.

■ ❑ ■ ❑ ■

In London, Boss was feeling very pleased. During the morning Ma had succeeded in tracing the address of the owner of the yacht *Aurora*, and he was engaged in instructing Parker to check on whether the woman he and Parker had seen was actually Eve. He recalled the incident with considerable satisfaction. With Slioghan at the helm, Parker had been standing beside him in the wheelhouse of *Erinyes* and had been idly surveying vessels with binoculars. He, Boss, had noticed Parker stiffen suddenly when he trained the binoculars on the yacht on their port bow. He recalled saying, "What is it, Parker?"

Parker had thought quickly for he was sure he had recognized Eve. He was of two minds as whether to tell Boss or conceal his suspicions, but knew he had better be careful in what he said. "I fort I saw . . . ," but he had hardly begun the sentence when Boss had quickly taken another pair of binoculars from the rack and was focusing them onto the yacht.

"Well, well, well; of all the luck of the Irish."

By that time the vessels were fairly close and they could see the two women among the crew waving to them. Fortunately for Boss and Parker they were in the shaded wheelhouse and were not clearly seen by Eve. Due to the position of the sun and Eve sitting next to the bulkhead in the cockpit her face was in shadow, but despite that Boss was fairly sure it was Eve.

"So here is the address. You will go there today and check that Eve is staying there. If she is not, find out where she is. I am sure it was her on the yacht."

He looked at the clock on his desk. "You will probably be back late tonight, so report to me first thing in the morning."

Parker nodded and muttered, "OK, Boss." He did not relish finding Eve but knew better than to fail on a mission ordered by Boss.

■ ❏ ■ ❏ ■

Parker looked at the address and then at the AA atlas. The house was situated in a small village in Essex, and he reckoned it would take two hours to get there even with the new motor roads permitting faster traveling. On leaving his house he realized that fast travel did not apply to London and its vicinity; he was well and truly caught in the rush hour and, when driving through Barkingside, the engine began to falter. Despite coaxing, it eventually stopped and he had no alternative but to phone the Automobile Association for help. Due to the heavy traffic and other emergency calls, it was an hour before the breakdown vehicle arrived and Parker was not feeling in the best of moods.

"I'm afraid I will have to tow you to the nearest garage, sir," the AA mechanic had said. "It looks like a computer part that has failed. There is a garage nearby and I can get you there in five minutes."

Parker nodded his head. "Looks as if there ain't no alternative. Git on wiv it, mate," and he helped the mechanic to attach a towing rope and then entered his vehicle.

The AA mechanic had been true to his word, for it took only five minutes to reach the garage. There a helpful mechanic quickly diagnosed the problem and phoned to the car distributors for a spare part. There Parker came up against another unexpected delay. The part was available but it would take two to three hours to reach the garage. He inquired about hiring a vehicle but there was none available. On learning of that he looked at his map again and noticed an underground station nearby. "I can git back ter London on train from Barkingside station can't I?" he asked the mechanic who nodded the affirmative.

"Wot time do yer close, mate?"

"Not 'til eight o'clock"

"Good, I'll try ter be back by then, if not first fing in the morning."

It took him only ten minutes to reach the station, and he watched as a train came in and disgorged many passengers. A number of them collected their vehicles from the adjacent car park. This time his luck was in. A young woman parked her vehicle and went to the station. He saw her board a train bound for London and guessed that she would not be back for several hours. He walked up to the vehicle and, removing a sheet of plastic from his pocket, slid it down between the window lock and the metal work of the driver's door. The lock clicked open. Quickly getting inside, he reached beneath the dashboard where a small group of wires was situated and with his pen knife cut two and then joined them together. The engine started immediately.

Blimey that was easy, he thought, grinning to himself. Parker drove happily eastward, passing through Lambourne End, Brentwood and Billericay before going deeper into the Essex countryside. He eventually reached the village and discovered that each dwelling was individually named. However, this did not deter him. With his usual patience and persistence he drove through, looking at each house name. Light was beginning to fade when he eventually found Bracken. It was almost at the end of one of the four roads in the village which ended at a field. He drove past and parked his stolen vehicle near another house beyond, having noted that a small lane ran down one side of the Bracken property.

He knew that finding out if Eve was inside the house would not be easy, and decided to walk down the narrow lane and view the house from the rear. He was aided in this respect by the edge of the garden being lined with thick lawsoniana which grew to about twenty feet in height and provided excellent cover for anyone wishing to survey the garden and house. Again luck was with him. He saw three men sitting on chairs on a large patio situated at the back of the house. The patio was well-illuminated with overhead floodlighting and the men were obviously engaged in discussion.

Parker was too far away to hear them distinctly but he could see that they appeared very interested in the subject of the conversation. He was wondering how he could get to look inside the house, when he stiffened in surprise as Eve walked out of one of the patio doors carrying a tray of drinks. It was a warm evening and the air was sultry and humid.

"Gor blimey, stone the crows, talk abaht bleedin' luck." He took another look at her as she placed the tray on an occasional table and then decided to get away while his luck held. As he made his way back along the lane to the road a dog emerged from the house onto the patio and sniffed the air. She must have either heard or scented him for she started barking and ran towards the trees in his direction. Parker moved fast and, on emerging on the road, ran towards the car. He heard both a man's and Eve's voice calling the dog, and the name sounded like Poppet. As he approached the car he turned and looked toward the dog, which hesitated as Parker stood his ground. On seeing it hesitate he quickly entered the car as the dog approached, still barking.

Parker started the engine and switched on the headlights as a man emerged from the lane calling the dog. Parker then drove towards the man with the headlights fully on rendering the man's vision temporarily useless. He then drove at a moderate speed past the man who held the dog. He felt that the owner of the dog would imagine that the vehicle had emerged from another driveway adjacent to where he had parked. As Parker drove on he looked back in the rearview mirror and noted that the man and dog were walking back to Bracken.

Parker grinned to himself as he left the village—it had all been too easy. Outside the village he stopped and looked at his map again. By driving through Billericay and Shenfield into Brentwood, halfway through the latter he could turn north and cut across country towards Barkingside. On leaving Brentwood he looked at the clock on the instrument panel and noticed that the time was getting on for eleven. The journey had taken longer than he had expected and he realized that he would not be able to collect his car until the morning. "Daft twit," he said out loud, berating himself. He decided he would either have to find a station with a line to London, or drive there.

He was now on a country road and stopped to look at his map again. As he did so two cars drove past him and he followed them at a distance of about one hundred yards. They warned him that his luck had run out. As he turned a corner he saw that both vehicles had stopped and the first was illuminated by the headlights of the second. Two policemen were standing beside the first and questioning the driver. Parker realized that it was a police checkpoint and that they were probably looking for the very vehicle he was driving.

"Oh, sod it," he mouthed and immediately turned his car and drove off in the opposite direction. As he drove off he looked back and saw one policeman looking in his direction and speaking into a portable phone. He realized that he would have to get rid of the car without delay and recalled that he had passed a field with a gate a mile or so behind.

He switched off the lights as he approached the gate and then, after quickly alighting to open the gate, drove into the field. The field was surrounded by trees and tall hedging and he stopped the vehicle in a position where it could not be seen from the road. Taking a tissue from a box in the instrument cupboard, he carefully wiped all traces of his fingerprints off every area he knew he had touched. He even had the presence of mind to run back and close the gate, before crossing the road and walking alongside a hedge to the other side of a field to avoid the roadblock. He guessed that if he skirted the roadblock the police would not look for him in that direction, and in that he was correct. He crossed to the other side of a field adjacent to the road and quietly made his way towards Barkingside but knew that it would take several hours to get there.

Once well past the police roadblock he rejoined the road and felt walking easier than it had been in the field. He was feeling hot, due partly to his exertions and the warmth of the night air. He realized that when he did get out of the country, getting transport in the early hours of the morning would not be easy; he would either have to find somewhere to stay or walk on until he found a night taxi service. Of course a telephone directory would supply the latter information but then he had to find a telephone.

The decision was made for him by the sudden flash of lightning followed by thunder and a deluge of rain. Within minutes he was drenched to the skin. He had little choice but to continue walking for the road ran between fields. Visibility had decreased to few yards and only the frequent flash of lightning illuminating the way enabled him to keep his direction. The lightning also enabled him to find unexpected shelter for as he passed a cottage he saw a caravan situated in an adjacent field. Wondering if it was occupied he approached it carefully and looked through a window which had the curtains drawn back.

As lightning flashed he was able to see clearly inside and realized that the caravan was unoccupied. As he expected the door was locked, but locks did not deter Parker for long. His pocket knife had several useful gadgets, one of which enabled him to unlock the door and thankfully get inside out of the driving rain. Before closing the door he looked towards the cottage and noted that it was obscured from sight by the trees. The odd flash of lightning lit up the interior of the caravan sporadically and it enabled him to inspect it in detail. He noticed a cooking stove and heater, both worked by natural gas. He opened several drawers in the kitchen area and found what he was looking for, a piezo gas lighter, but before lighting the gas stove or heater he closed all the curtains as a precaution to prevent light being seen from the cottage despite his earlier observation of its position. His first attempts to ignite the stove failed and he realized that the gas had been turned off. He opened the cock on the pipe but no gas came through. Following the pipe he saw that it led outside and surmised that the cylinder was kept there for safety reasons.

Although the rain continued to batter the roof, he did not allow it to deter him but went outside and found the cylinder. He located the cylinder screw and on turning it counterclockwise felt, more than heard, a slight vibration as the gas flowed through the pipe. He quickly reentered the caravan and thankfully lit the gas heater and gas stove. What he needed more than anything else was a hot cup of tea and this he made as quickly as he could, using powdered milk substitute with plenty of sugar. He also found some shortbread biscuits and chocolate cookies that had been left in an airtight tin.

Feeling better for the food and drink he stripped and, after wringing out his soaked clothes arranged them to dry over the heater. The night had cooled considerably with the rain showers and he searched in the bedroom for blankets but found instead two sleeping bags. He put one on the bed and got into it shivering slightly, then he looked at his watch; the time was a few minutes after two o'clock.

"Time for a spot of kip before dawn me lad," he said to himself. He felt drowsy as he gradually warmed up in the sleeping bag. As he began to doze off he thought of his clothes drying and hoped that they would be fully dry by the time he awoke. "That gas orter do the trick, at least I 'ope so." He felt sleepy and as he began to doze off the word "gas" persisted in his mind. Gas! He began to snore and disturbed himself, muttering in his sleep, "Gas!" carbon monoxide . . . ventilation . . . He snored again and began to dream.

chapter nineteen

Sean opened the door of his apartment and sniffed the welcome smell of dinner. His housekeeper had been there in the morning and had left a stew fully prepared in the slow-cooker. Although it had been a warm day he was hungry, having been very busy in the surgery as well as carrying out domiciliary visits. With people taking holidays during the summer, he had expected the demands on the medical services to have diminished. But this was not so. The demands on his services were not always genuine and this irritated him. There were a number of patients who were playing on virtually nonexistent ailments in order to avoid working. His refusal to give certificates in non-genuine cases had resulted in several of the patients on his list requesting to be seen by his colleagues. They had initially laughed at this, but also told him not to be so fussy.

From the surgery office he had brought home a social security benefits booklet to peruse. A number of patients had made demands for certain benefits to which he was not sure they were entitled, and so he had decided to improve his knowledge on the subject. He had been surprised at the number of pages, some eighty in all, and also the number of benefits. He was also surprised to see that a free telephone inquiry service was available not only in English, but in Chinese, Punjabi, Urdu and Welsh. He had mentioned this to Dr. McMurrough who commented, "They will be adding Irish and Cornish next."

There were so many benefits available that it obviously paid to not work and indeed, despite the recession, there was every encouragement to live on taxpayers' money and not bother to seek work. Being a Catholic he did not approve of abortion and contraception. He considered that self-control before marriage, was the best way of preventing people having children before they were responsible enough to provide for them. And that was a point that did annoy him.

The government took away money from those who worked and gave to those who did not, which was tantamount to an obligatory charity. He knew that there was a growing feeling among taxpayers that the welfare mothers should not be bringing yet more babies into the world for society to clothe, feed, house and medicate. He had heard some patients remark that they felt that people who live on public charity should have an unlimited right to add more children to the welfare rolls. There were too many young unmarried mothers about and the fathers often were absent.

As Richard had said when the subject had cropped up, "People of all races should support the children they bring into the world and should not have them until they are in a position to do so." It was all very well living off the backs of others, but one had a duty towards society as well as to oneself. As it stood, instead of "Laughing all the way to the bank," many were "Laughing all the way from the welfare office."

It was hardly surprising that the country was slow in getting out of the recession. He also realized that it was a self-perpetuating system, for the greater the demand for benefits, the more civil servants would be required to run it. This meant that any reduction in benefits would not be desired by those in office, so the country was slowly being made bankrupt by a system which sounded very humane and compassionate in theory, but was wrecking the country and increasing poverty and hardship in the long run.

Sean laughed to himself when he thought of the politicians who claimed credit for their government giving the benefits. He knew that the government gave precisely nothing. The taxpayers were those who gave. He had no feelings against those who had worked and made their contributions into the social services; they deserved the benefits for they had earned them. It was those who had paid nothing and had no intention of doing so to whom he objected. They lived on the backs of others and he felt that they should contribute towards society and not just take from it. There were exceptions, of course, but they were actually very few.

It particularly annoyed him that with child benefits so easily available, people were encouraged to have children and have them supported at the taxpayers' expense and also that abortions were freely available. This made colossal extra demands on social security and it was not surprising that some of the major hospitals were being forced to either close or reduce the number of services. The system could not go on much longer and was close to bankruptcy.

Sean had been serving his meal while thinking about the social services, and sat down at the table to make the most of the excellent stew. He had hardly eaten two mouthfuls when he was interrupted by the telephone. He had left it on the answerphone and did not lift the receiver until he heard his sister's voice requesting him to phone her as soon as possible. She sounded upset and this worried him, so much so that he lifted the receiver and switched off the recorder.

"Hello, Morag, what's the trouble?"

He heard Morag sobbing at the other end of the line. "Oh, Sean . . . " She could hardly get the words out. "Oh Sean, Morgan and Eamon have beaten up Gordon!"

"What?" He could hardly believe what she was saying. "Why? What for?"

He heard her sob again. "I'm never going home again, Sean."

"Wait a minute, Morag. Just pull yourself together and tell me what happened." He heard her crying and waited patiently.

"I'm sorry, Sean. I know I must pull myself together, but I feel so angry I could kill them."

"OK, Morag, now please put me in the picture. What happened?"

"I went home with Gordon to introduce him to the family and they made him welcome."

Sean had met Morag's fiancé and liked him immediately. An accountant by profession he was industrious and owned a flourishing accountancy business. Sean knew that he would make Morag a fine and loyal husband and she would never want with him. He liked his dry sense of humor, trained logical mind and the fact that Gordon and Morag were deeply in love with each other. Gordon's welcoming handshake and open honest face had impressed Sean and he knew that with Morag and Gordon married, he not only would have a brother-in-law he could trust, but a friend for life. And that made it all the more difficult to understand the antagonism that his stepbrothers had shown towards Gordon.

Was it because he was English? he wondered. But then he dismissed that thought. His cousin Richard and his family were all English, and they had been made to feel welcome on the rare occasions that they had visited Ireland. On second thought, Morgan and Eamon had not shown enthusiasm during the visits and his stepfather had been reserved. However, his mother had made them welcome. Then he tore himself away from his thoughts and listened to what Morag was saying.

"Mother made Gordon very welcome and step-dad and the boys seemed friendly enough. They reacted to Gordon's charm in a positive way and offered to take him out to the local pub one evening."

"What happened to make them do what they did?"

"Apparently they had several pints of beer and Irish whiskey, although Gordon is not a drinker and managed to keep to a pint of ale. Well, on the way home Gordon let them know that he was a Protestant and they then both set on him and badly beat him up in a cowardly way. As they were walking home Morgan suddenly punched Gordon in the solar plexus and, as he doubled up in agony,

Eamon punched him on the nose and then they knocked him down and kicked him. They shouted at him telling him that their stepsister was not going to marry a Protestant bastard and an English one at that."

Morag started sobbing again and Sean interjected saying, "Listen, Morag, I'll go . . ."

But she interrupted. "Sean, I am never going home again. I know it will hurt Mother, but while those two animals are in the house I shall keep away from it."

Sean felt pained but understood Morag's reaction. It must have been a terrible decision for Morag to make for, like Sean, she loved their mother dearly.

"Morag, I'm going to go over there and see if I can persuade Morgan and Eamon to apologize. After all, they both had too much to drink you said?"

"They did, but they did not show any repentance afterwards."

"I want to go over there to see Mum anyway for she must be very upset by all that happened."

"She is, but I've made up my mind."

"How is Gordon now?"

"He has recovered, but he had to have his nose reset for those bastards broke it."

"Good God!" and the thought crossed his mind: "Is he going to sue them for assault?"

"No. I wish he would, but he feels it would upset Mum and me. His only comment was that it was an interesting experience and an introduction to life in Ireland that doesn't warrant repetition. You know how dry his sense of humor is."

"Has it affected his relationship with you?"

"Apparently not, thank God. He still wants to marry me and says that I am not responsible for the narrow-mindedness of my relatives."

Sean was relieved to hear that, for he was genuinely fond of Gordon and did not want to lose his friendship. He would rather Gordon had been a Catholic if only because he wanted any of their children to be brought up in the faith, but he knew that Morag could not have a better man for a husband.

"Look, Morag. I'm going over there as soon as I can, perhaps in a few days. I'll let you know how I get on. I am particularly concerned over Mum. She must be shattered by it all."

At that the conversation had ended, and Sean looked back at the table at his meal which was now getting cold. He did not feel so hungry after the unexpected news and inwardly cursed his stepbrothers for their appalling ignorance and viciousness. He felt ashamed of them. It was true that the Celts had always had a reputation for fighting; every history book showed that. A visit through Ireland showed fortified churches and dwellings, not just the usual castles found elsewhere. All these fortified places were built, not so much to defend the country from invaders but to protect the occupants from the predations of their own neighboring countrymen. The veneer of civilization did not appear to have much substance on Morgan and Eamon. Thank God there were others who did not share their bigotry and stupidity.

He picked up his plate from the table and, covering it with another, put it in the microwave oven to warm up. Inwardly he was seething with anger, and suddenly laughed out loud when he realized that he had better cool off before eating if he did not want indigestion. He walked to the window of his apartment and looked across a small esplanade which separated it from the river. It was a calm warm evening and the river was busy with traffic. Tourist vessels, river buses and an occasional coastal barge plowed their way through the water. He saw several seagulls swooping down for tidbits and watched pedestrians ambling along the esplanade.

One young couple was leaning over the balustrade, their bodies in close proximity and arms tight around each other. He thought of Eve and then guessed that through having to go to Ireland he would miss seeing her for about two weeks. This did not make him feel any better towards his stepbrothers. His thoughts were interrupted by the "ping" of the microwave as the power switched off. He walked back to the kitchenette, donned some oven gloves, retrieved the hot plates from the microwave, dispensed with the upper plate and placed the remaining one on the table. He sat down for a few minutes, relaxed, said a short grace and crossed himself before starting to finish his meal.

Three days later he was on his way to Ireland.

■ ❑ ■ ❑ ■

"Dad, I would like to introduce you to Father Patrick Brendan." Gerard rose to his feet and extended his right hand to the ascetic-looking figure who had entered the room. They both smiled and shook hands warmly.

"How do you do, Father Brendan. Call me Gerard."

"Thank you, Gerard. My name is Patrick, as you know. Eve has told me about you and I have looked forward to the pleasure of meeting you."

Richard interrupted at that point. "It is a warm evening. Perhaps you would like to sit outside on the patio."

"Why thank you. You have a beautiful garden and I cannot think of more pleasant surroundings." Father Brendan and Richard left the lounge and walked through the French doors to the patio where they seated themselves on the cushioned garden chairs.

Bird song could be heard from the copse at the far end of the garden and some rooks were busily croaking their evening chorus in a nearby oak tree as they prepared to settle down for the night. Two house martins swooped overhead catching their evening meal on the wing. The sun was setting in a blaze of crimson; there were long shadows on the lawn. In the still of the evening the air was warm, and they could smell honeysuckle as it slowly wafted in their direction from a nearby shrub.

"What a lovely place and a beautiful evening. We get splendid sunsets here in Essex."

"Yes, you are quite right, Patrick. I imagine it is due to the fact that we are east of London and the dust haze from the city scatters the blue rays of the sun's spectrum but allows the longer red rays to come through."

"Well, Richard, whatever the scientific explanation, the beauty makes me think it shows the handiwork of God."

"Odd you should say that. Dawn wrote a poem on that theme once and used almost the same words at the end."

Father Brendan looked at Richard and smiled. "I would like to see that."

"I can get it for you now. Perhaps this is just the time to read it."

Richard rose and left the priest and returned with a small notebook containing Dawn's poems. He sat down and thumbed through the pages and found the one he sought.

"Here you are." With the appropriate page open he handed the small book to Father Brendan who read:

> *Sunset.*
> *I walked with silent footsteps in the glade*
> *relaxing, now that my day's work was done.*
> *I stopped beneath an oak tree in the shade*
> *and watched with wonder at the setting sun.*
>
> *As dusk fell the rustling leaves were stilled*
> *of birch, beech and all forest trees around.*
> *Once noisome day was now with silence filled*
> *and darkening shadows spread across the ground.*

Before me a smooth grassy meadow lay,
which stretched for half a mile into the wood.
A lone couple wandering hand in hand,
I could just discern from where I stood.

The sun in glorious splendor then withdrew
as the minutes all too soon sped quickly by,
leaving in its stead an azure hue
with roseate tones reflected from the sky.

A nightingale sang with melodious song
as I stood entranced beneath a tree,
but it did not sing alone for long,
an owl began its mournful melody.

I saw the church tower high upon the hill,
its masonry quite reddened in the light
and, as the shadows lengthened all around,
its spire and shape soon disappeared from sight.

The gravestones were all slabs of crimson hue
and beyond them rose a crescent moon,
their presence on the hillside brought to mind
the sun would set on all of us too soon.

One day my turn will come to part this life
and when my ashes are then laid to rest,
I hope that those I loved will be aware
that though I made mistakes I did my best.

Though much evil stalks this world today
and conducts terror with a mighty rod,
as if to drive satanic thoughts away,
did that sunset show the hand of God?

Patrick Brendan handed the book back to Richard commenting, "What a lovely poem; it reveals feeling for nature, humanity and cosmic piety. Your wife must be very religious."

"I am afraid she isn't, although like myself she used to be."

"It may be that you both still are. The appreciation of beauty and awe at the wonders of nature is to my mind part of religious feeling. Einstein mentioned that feeling, and he also believed in God."

"I think one should qualify those comments about Einstein. The God he believed in was not a personal God; indeed he was quite scathing about his children having to be taught orthodox Jewish religion. In his biography by Philipp Frank entitled, *Einstein, His Life and Times*, he said: 'I dislike very much that my children should be taught something that is contrary to all scientific thinking.' And he recalled jokingly the manner in which school children are told about God: 'Eventually the children believe that God is some kind of gaseous vertebrate.'"

"I read somewhere that he said: 'Science without religion is lame, religion without science is blind.'"

Richard thought for a moment then replied, "Yes, he did say that, but its meaning can easily be misunderstood or misinterpreted if taken out of context. My father will probably recall the whole quotation."

"Your father is not joining us?"

"Well, I thought that as we are going to have a discussion on some matters of mutual interest, you might feel a bit outnumbered if my father were here."

Father Brendan smiled. "I don't think I will be unduly worried. I doubt the number of people present can affect truth."

"A good point." He stopped and then added with a grin, "I see you have started the discussion already."

Father Brendan smiled back. "Just warming up. Your father is a retired physicist I understand. I have no doubt he would add much of interest to the discussion. Please ask him to join us."

"Alright, I will. Incidentally, what would you like to drink?" Richard added, noticing Eve walking onto the patio.

But before Patrick Brendan could reply Eve went up to him. "Oh, Father Brendan, how nice to see you. Richard said you might be calling."

He rose and shook hands with her.

"Yes. Richard invited me to do 'battle,' metaphorically speaking, of course. But I gather that for verbal battle one must lubricate one's larynx," and looking at Richard he said, "A glass of white wine would be welcome."

"Let me see to that, Richard. What can I get you?"

"Grape juice, please, and would you mind asking my father to join us?" Eve nodded and left while both the men seated themselves again.

The priest looked admiringly at the statues lining the left side of the lawn leading down to the rockery, which was covered with small cypresses interspersed with heather and numerous mountain plants.

He noted the paved walkway around the pond and the graceful weeping willow which stood just beyond it. Beneath the willow was a bench, no doubt a good trysting place for those so inclined, he thought. His reflections were interrupted by the appearance of Gerard whose upright stance gave him a somewhat military bearing, a habit or legacy of the time he had spent in the army.

"Come and sit down, Dad. Father Brendan has decided to take both of us on."

"As I said earlier, please call me Patrick. Father Brendan is so formal and I do not feel that formality is necessary."

Here Gerard joined in. "Quite right, Patrick. Thank you, I shall do so."

As Eve put a tray of drinks and homemade cakes on the table and then left the men to their conversation.

"I see you are both teetotalers," Patrick observed.

"Well, in the main," Gerard remarked, "I once read that alcohol reduces the number of brain cells and, as we start to lose them at the age of twenty-five anyway, I want to hang on to what I have got left."

Father Brendan laughed. "I understand one has trillions of brain cells, so I doubt that alcohol in very small quantities will do much harm. I am also led to believe that a small amount of wine is good for the heart."

"Yes, I have read something to that effect, but I don't feel inclined to put it into practice, so I'll have to drink your health in grape juice."

Richard smiled at that remark and commented, "At least both the drink and toast are healthy."

They sat sipping at their glasses for a few minutes and then Richard broke the silence addressing his father. "Patrick and I were discussing Albert Einstein's attitude towards religion, and Patrick quoted Einstein saying, 'Science without religion is lame, religion without science is blind.' Do you recall the rest of the quotation?"

Gerard Rutherford smiled and nodded. "Yes. In the autumn of 1940 he sent a letter to a conference held in New York to discuss what contributions science, philosophy and religion could make to American Democracy. He entitled it 'Science and Religion.' In it he said: 'The main source of conflict between the spheres of religion and of science lies in the concept of a personal God. It is the aim of science to establish general rules which determine the reciprocal conceptions of objects in time and space. It is mainly a program, and faith in the possibility of its accomplishment in principle is only founded on partial success. But hardly anyone could be found who would deny these partial successes and ascribe them to human self-deception . . .

'The more a man is imbued with the ordered regularity of all events, the firmer becomes his conviction that there is no room left by the side of this ordered regularity for causes of a different nature. For him neither the rule of human nor the rule of divine will exists as an independent cause of natural events. To be sure the doctrine of a personal God interfering with natural events could never be refuted, in the real sense, by science, for this doctrine can always take refuge in domains in which scientific knowledge has not yet been established . . .

'To the sphere of religion belongs the faith that the regulations valid for the world of existence are rational, that it is comprehensible to reason. I cannot conceive of a genuine scientist without that profound faith. The situation may be expressed by an image: science without religion is lame, religion without science is blind.'"

"Well, Gerard, I must congratulate you on a remarkable memory. It is clear that Einstein did not believe in a personal God, but at least he recognized the importance of religion and the existence of God."

"Quite so, but if I have read correctly, his attitude towards religion was a mystical feeling towards the laws of the universe, what he called the cosmic religious experience felt by a scientist discovering new facts about nature. He also included belief, in the Judeo-Christian tradition, of the free and yet self-responsible development of the individual. To my mind this includes self-discipline and moral obligation towards one's fellow men—that is towards society as well as to one's self and immediate family. The great American scientist Robert Millikan put it so well when he said: '. . . The task of religion . . . is to develop the conscience, the ideals and aspirations of mankind.'"

"Many scientists like myself regard religions as social institutions evolved to encourage stability in society; a code of moral and social behavior; a refuge for those who need comforting and are satisfied with a simplistic explanation of the universe and mankind's place in it. They can give hope and a sense of purpose despite their claims being tendentious and in the wrong direction. But believers can be exploited and the room for fanaticism can cause and still causes untold misery and unhappiness."

"This is true," commented Patrick. "Every institution is open to abuse. Man's inhumanity to man is the underlying factor. I fear original sin is with us all. However, religion, especially the Judeo-Christian, enables individuals to have the self-discipline and sociability to live in harmony with their fellow men. And I would add that prayer and confession play a very important part in enabling believers to rid themselves of worry and guilt, and become pure again in the sight of God."

"You know, I think that . . . " Richard interrupted, then, noticing the expression on his father's face, apologized. "Sorry, Dad, I did not realize you had not finished."

At that Gerard continued. "Just one thing, Patrick. You did say that Einstein believed in God."

"Yes. He is quoted in saying that, 'I cannot believe that God plays dice with the world.'"

"I recall reading that in his biography and in other reports. He also said that, 'God is sophisticated, but he is not malicious.' When he made these statements his biographer wrote he was using the term God as a figure of speech and not in a theological sense. He found it difficult to accept the statistical conception of physics in that the element of chance exists in nuclear activities."

"Was he right?"

"No, I am afraid not. Chance reigns and plays a prominent part in the sub-atomic world. There is also much random behavior elsewhere in nature. However, having said that, I would add that with the development of chaos theory, much random behavior in nature is now known to possess hidden patterns governed by mathematical rules and geometric forms. I feel that the last word on the subject has yet to be written and may take many years before it is."

"Well, this is all very interesting," said Richard, "and I feel that many people assume that because well-known and especially intelligent persons mention God, one must accept them as being a good judge of the existence of a creator. Actually fame and intelligence are no proof that the person is correct in their judgment. And what is more, the tenacity of one's beliefs is no proof of their validity.

"One must work out one's beliefs oneself and not have them dictated by others. However, I digress. You have brought up several points which I feel warrant comment. Dad, you mentioned the value of religion in society. To my mind religion is but a phase in the evolution of human thought and development.

"It would appear from anthropological finds that the phase of hunter—gatherers included a predisposition to religious belief. In those primitive tribal cultures burial customs, hunting rituals, fertility rites, animism, spiritism, shamanism, sorcery, magic, and other social customs no doubt evolved.

"When mankind moved from the phase of hunter-gatherers to more complex societies, that is to nomadic and agricultural, then further rules for cooperation were required especially with the growth of towns and cities. To ensure co-operation, laws reinforced by religion developed. Through dominance, tribal leaders supported by elders held power with the hunter-gatherers. With the improvement in food abundance, tribes became larger and leaders not only made laws but medicine-men and shamans developed into priests, and so tribal religions developed into national religions. Man had developed a gregarious and cooperative nature as well as a religious and superstitious one, and so it was easy for leaders both civil and religious, to take advantage of their subjects and retain power.

"It is possible that organized warfare started around this time due to the increase in numbers, encroachment on established territory, inter-tribal rivalry and the ambitions of leaders. The superstitious interpretations of dreams which the Australian aborigines call 'dream-time,' may well have led to the idea of an afterlife, a spirit or soul, and this has been used by leaders and priests to deceive their followers into doing their bidding by risking their lives in warfare or losing them in religious fanaticism.

"No doubt *Homo sapiens* have always wondered about nature, and superstitious explanations were conceived which in time gave rise to the more organized religions we have today. It is possible that hundreds of religions and religious leaders have risen and fallen since mankind started to think about his place in nature. As Statius wrote, 'It was fear that first made gods in the world.'

"Patrick, you mentioned the Judeo-Christian tradition. This tradition with its emphasis on compassion is laudable and one of the best social ways to live, but a good way of life is not confined to the two faiths that have developed from the tradition. There are many other stable societies where compassion exists that have never heard of Christianity or Judaism. One only need think of the North Amerindians, many of whom lived in societies where tolerance and consideration for the environment as well were practiced.

"Christianity is no guarantee of tolerance, compassion or decent social behavior. The shocking terrorism practiced in Ireland by both Catholics and Protestant Christians is hardly an advertisement for Christianity. Moslems share the same deity through the ideas of Abraham and Moses. Of course their religion is more belligerent, but generally they do have stable societies. That and the Zionism with the Jews, has not prevented both groups of believers from committing acts of terrorism against innocent people. And one of the tragedies is that due to the words of Mohammed in the Koran, with promises of Paradise to come, it is easy to brainwash young people into committing murder of innocent people and blowing themselves up at the same time."

Richard went suddenly silent as Eve came onto the patio again. "Sorry to interrupt," she said. "Dawn wonders if you would like another drink?"

Father Brendan smiled in acquiescence. "Yes, please, Eve. That wine is very palatable."

"You having the same, Richard?" asked Gerard, adding, "I can get them."

As Richard nodded, Poppet walked through the door, went up to Richard and wagged her tail. He bent forward to stroke her, when she suddenly growled and then ran barking towards the side of the garden near the house.

"What is it, Poppet? Have you heard a deer or a mouse? Come back!" he called, but Poppet found her way through the hedge and they could hear her barking as she made her way along the lane into the road.

Richard stood up. "I had better see what is upsetting her. Excuse me," and he walked to the side gate and, opening it, entered the lane and walked rapidly towards the road. He called again to Poppet who was barking at a car which was approaching from the direction of the cul-de-sac. Blinded by the headlights he could not see the driver as it went past. He noticed from its speed that the driver was in no hurry. Poppet continued to bark and went to chase the vehicle but Richard managed to restrain her and walked her back to the house.

Retracing his footsteps and returning through the side gate, he walked back to the patio and found Eve with Patrick Brendan looking questioningly at him. "There was a car in the road and it was probably either a neighbor or the driver had taken a wrong turn," he explained to Patrick and to Eve who was looking anxious. "We often get people at this end of the road who fail to notice the road sign indicating that it is a cul-de-sac."

At that point, Gerard returned bearing a tray of drinks and the men settled down to continue their discussion as Eve left.

"Now where were we?" said Gerard.

"I was about to comment on the value of prayer and confession," Richard volunteered. "Prayer and meditation appear to me to be very similar except that prayer is addressed to a deity. And as for confession, it is very similar to sessions with a psychiatrist or psychologist."

Patrick Brendan shook his head. "No, I do not agree with that, Richard. Prayer is a direct communication with God, the mother of God or one of the holy saints. With confession one opens one's heart to God and begs forgiveness for one's sins or transgressions of God's holy law."

"The practice of confession puts great power into the hands of priests and is open to abuse. I have read of priests in Ireland who held confessions for IRA terrorists and gave them absolution after they had committed murder."

Father Brendan interrupted again. "If that is true then those priests betrayed their trusts."

"I am sure it is true, for it is recorded in a well-written book on the IRA. However, there is another point I wish to bring up. The crux of the matter is the question: What is God? Or perhaps I should ask, what is your definition of God, Patrick? You see, unless I understand that then we could be talking at cross-purposes."

"This I appreciate," Patrick replied. "The Christian definition of God is that he is the creator of the universe and that he is love. The Bible confirms this."

Gerard joined in then. "May I comment on your statement that God created the universe? As a physicist, I have taken considerable interest in the origins of the universe. Present evidence suggests that the universe is about fifteen billion years old. Space, time and matter suddenly appeared."

"You mean were created," interrupted Patrick.

"No, I mean appeared. To create something one needs time. Now the theory of relativity, which has been well-tested, shows clearly that time, space and matter are all related and one cannot exist without the other. Before the universe appeared neither time, space nor matter existed, so where was the time for creation?"

To that Patrick replied, "An omnipotent power could have done this. I have no doubt that God is not governed by the laws of physics and is therefore capable of creating the universe. What is more, the Book of Genesis appears to be confirmed by modern science. I recall in 1951 that Pope Pius XII in an address to the Pontifical Academy of Sciences in Rome referred to the 'Big Bang' theory. He stated that everything seems to indicate that the universe has in finite times a mighty beginning."

"I remember that," said Gerard, adding, "I also recall a conference on cosmology organized by the Jesuits in the Vatican in 1981. There the current Pope said it was all right to study the universe after the 'Big Bang', but not the 'Big Bang' itself for that was creation and therefore the work of God. That statement put many scientists in mind of the fate of Galileo, when the Catholic Church condemned him for his observations of the position of planet earth regarding the sun. Steven Hawking in his book *A Brief History of Time* makes some amusing comments on that. In addition, he makes the interesting observation that if the universe has no boundaries in space nor boundaries in time, there would be no need for a Creator.

"However I think the universe has boundaries in space and time, or perhaps I should say space-time, and this is bound up with the beginnings of the universe. But let me clarify that for you. The scientific reasons for the sudden appearance of the universe and its not having existed forever are firstly, the recession of the galaxies. All galaxies or groups of galaxies are moving away from each other. Space is gradually being stretched. We are living in an expanding universe. This was predicted in Einstein's relativity theory, and confirmed by Edwin Hubble with his measurements of the galaxies in the nineteen twenties. If one goes back in time, all the galaxies would be closer until one reached the stage where they were much closer together and initially space-time was reduced to a single point or singularity.

"The second reason is that the universe must have been very hot at that stage and has been cooling down ever since. Remnants of this heat have been measured and they conform very well with theory. A third reason is entropy, the second law of thermodynamics. This states the universe is running down; things gradually become more disorderly with the passage of time; there is a gradual loss of heat or a consumption of energy and, if the universe exists long enough it will die a 'heat death.' Eventually the stars will use up all existing energy.

"Another reason for the universe to be finite in time is that if it were not and had it existed forever, then we would see light all round us, for stars emit light and they exist to the uttermost depths of space. This last idea posed a puzzle known as Olber's paradox."

"Well, Gerard, you seem to have given every reason for the universe to have been created at some time in the past and not satisfactorily proved that it was not created by God. Everything and every action has a cause and God was the first cause. To my mind, God is a contingent being. I would add that the universe clearly has design and mankind is the ultimate purpose of God's design."

"I cannot let that go," intervened Richard. "The idea that the universe was created for mankind, appears to be either a piece of conceited assumption or sheer lack of recognition of the fact that mankind has evolved, as have all other organisms on this planet. We are not a special creation but the result of evolution. Furthermore, it may well be that life exists on other planets and when found will prove that the universe was not made for us."

It was at this point in the conversation that Eve sat down in an armchair in the music room. It being a warm night the windows were open, and she could clearly hear the conversation of the three men seated on the patio. Earlier she had left Dawn who was busy marking exercise books. She had intended to read but her concentration was taken from her book by the sound of Richard's voice, and what he was saying disturbed her. He in turn was unaware that he was being overheard by her.

"Christ said, 'In my Father's house are many mansions.' This allows for life elsewhere in the universe," Patrick observed.

"There is no evidence that Christ knew anything about modern cosmology, and as he spoke in riddles half the time one can make what one likes out of his sayings. Whatever one construes on ambiguities proves nothing," Richard countered.

"Christ spoke in parables, not riddles, and did so to enable the people of his time to understand his message which was the Word of God."

"I find this idea of revelation and the 'Word of God' untenable, Patrick. As *Homo sapiens* have existed for at least some hundred and fifty thousand years then why did not God reveal himself to them earlier? Why wait until less than four thousand years ago? The earliest 'revelation' for the Judeo-Christian and Islamic faiths is that recorded of Abraham. That date's approximately the early second millennium B.C. I do not doubt that he was an historical figure for archaeological finds support this—that God revealed himself is another question. Personally, I think Abraham invented Jahweh to keep the Jewish tribe cohesive; later, Christ and Mohammed adopted Jahweh."

"Here we cannot agree, Richard. I am sure that mankind is a special creation and that God revealed himself. The universe was created for man and God created it out of love for mankind. That is the Christian message. The description of creation in the Bible closely resembles the findings of modern physics. The fine balance in nature of the appropriate atoms, chemicals and, I understand, the physical constants cannot have occurred by chance. Were they not arranged in the way they are then life could not have developed in this universe, and it would have been devoid of life."

"I do not find that argument logical. Had the universe not been arranged as it is and evolved as it has, then we would not be here to observe and marvel at it. This is the anthropic principle of Brandon Carter. One can hardly talk of other universes when they cannot be observed. The universe certainly is a wonderful thing, but that is no proof that it is the work of a loving God. Furthermore, your view that the Bible supports modern theories on cosmology and vice versa is not logical."

"In Genesis, God said, 'Let there be light,' and I understand the theory of the 'Big Bang' states that photons of light dominated the mini-universe and for that matter there are one hundred million photons to every atom to this day."

"With respect, this type of argument I find dishonest. The Bible and description of creation in Genesis is supposed to be the word of God. Now God says, 'Let there be light' and we find light at the beginning in modern theory. The Bible also says everything was created in six days. It wasn't. It also says that man was made out of clay and Eve was made from the a rib of Adam. We know that cannot have occurred, for man existed long before the time of creation of Adam according to careful examination of the biblical time scale. God appears to be telling the truth on the one hand and telling lies on the other."

"The story is an allegory, Richard, to explain the creation to the people of the time. The six days should really represent three billion years each, which makes it fit in with modern physical theory."

Richard shook his head. "This is ridiculous. Again one is twisting dogma to fit in with modern theory. If each day represents three billion years what happened to the seventh? Has God and the creation been resting for three billion years, for that is what the Sabbath must amount to? To take things out of context and pretend that things are not what they are to suit religious dogma is to use the techniques of a dishonest attorney at law; win your case by hook or by crook; the truth doesn't matter."

Gerard could see that the discussion was getting heated for Richard and decided to intervene. "I would like to enter the argument before we go too far past your views on the anthropic principle, Richard. I would point out that physical theories of the universe are still theories, the validity of which depends on experimental proofs. In order to make sense of measurements and data about the universe one has to make a model of the universe into which the data fits. Models of the universe are not necessarily descriptions of reality. Stephen Hawking, among other scientists, writes about a theory of everything; they think that the complete unification of quantum theory and relativity will provide it. Personally I think this is premature although the superstring theory may provide the answer.

"In reality, in our minds we have a synthesis of the universe around us as given by our eleven or more senses. This is especially true of the micro and macrocosmic, that is, quantum mechanics and the astronomy. Our minds are not in direct contact with the universe or our environment but our senses receive data from external reality. Our cerebral synthesis is close to reality, for were it not so, *Homo sapiens* would not have survived or evolved. However, we cannot appreciate or visualize the inside of an atom yet, simply because what goes on there is in no way similar to our immediate environment. One can only appreciate the microcosmic because experiments show that the activities revealed experimentally follow mathematical rules. The same applies to the macrocosmic when one deals with the origins of the universe and the possibility that other universes exist. *Homo sapiens* have existed for such a short time that we are only at the beginnings of understanding the nature of the universe."

"Well, Dad, I understand what you are saying from the physicist's point of view. There is still much to explore in physics, but as far as evolution is concerned, we have reached the stage where we know with certainty that *Homo sapiens* have come from other organisms and is just another species." Richard looked away from his father and towards the priest.

"Patrick, reverting to your earlier remark that mankind is a special creation and that God has revealed himself, we must beg to differ. As Dad mentioned, *Homo sapiens* have existed for a short time, possibly one hundred and fifty thousand years. It seems ridiculous to me that the universe, which came into being some fifteen billion years ago was created for us only. Like all other organisms on this planet we have evolved and come into existence by chance. The evidence, whether from the record of the rocks, the vestiges of our anatomy and physiology and its similarities to, and the genetic or DNA relationships with our distant cousins the apes, establishes without doubt our origins.

"During the course of evolution our predecessor hominids have become extinct and we in turn will have the same fate. One hopes that the next mutation will be progressive and not regressive. Mankind is the result of evolution. Evolution applies to everything. I think it was Hipparchus who stated 'Panta re,' everything changes or flows. And he was right."

"You are correct there, Richard," said Gerard breaking his silence. "The only certain things in life are change and, for that matter, death. However, we must not get morbid."

"I won't. But to revert to the point. Evolution applies to religion as to everything else. The way the Catholic Church has altered its claim that the earth is at the center of the universe, and the way the several stories of Genesis were originally accepted as the true word of God but are now used as allegories by some theologians, and the way the church and other churches are jumping onto the modern physics bandwagon shows that the various religions, churches or faiths undergo evolution. They have to adapt to the new knowledge as organisms have to adapt to the environment, or go under.

"The Judeo-Christian and the Islamic faiths are committed to creation because of the stories in Genesis. It was taken as literally true until Galileo showed it wasn't. It has been altered to suit modern cosmology but modern cosmology could be wrong. There are strong grounds for a revised theory of continuous creation. What will the three faiths do if that occurs; change the goal posts again?

"It is a current fashion to use modern physics to put new life into established religions. This is shifting the goal posts, because of the human weakness of attributing to a deity or the Deity, things that are not understood. This is the 'God of the Gaps.' The various religions, especially the Christian, do this constantly as I have illustrated. What is the truth about Jesus Christ?"

Father Brendan answered the question which Richard had posed mainly for himself to clarify. "There is no doubt that Jesus was and is the only begotten Son of God who was born to take away the sins of mankind and reveal that God cares for us."

Richard shook his head. "He is accepted as the Son of God by Christians. Neither Zionists nor Muslims agree with this. Buddhists do not accept a God anyway. Who is right? Obviously no one. We do not know the nature of God or even if there is one. Any definition is man-made and pure guesswork. I do not believe the prophets, because their revelations can more easily be accounted for by self-deception and hallucination, which is partly the result of thinking on fixed lines for a period of time.

"Anyone can have a revelation, for the Mormons are right in claiming that revelation is an ongoing thing. All one has to do is concentrate one's thoughts on the deity, spirit, angel or whatever; go into isolation, or join a group of other believers; pray or meditate, fast, lose sleep, and soon one will see one's spirits, ghosts, hear voices and feel the presence of the 'unearthly.' This can be brought about more quickly by the use of hallucinatory drugs such as the sacred mushroom, mescaline and lysergic acid, etc. Actually, many shamans in South America use these techniques. The truth about it is that nothing 'spiritual' occurs. What takes place is changes in the brain which appear to be real experiences but are in reality hallucination—a mental virtual reality.

"Every religious leader underwent a similar pattern of living and contemplation before revelation. Buddha meditated then received 'enlightenment.' Christ went into the wilderness, was tempted by the Devil and resisted his blandishments. Mohammed retired to a cave and had his vision of the angel Gabriel informing him that he was the messenger of God. Zoroaster is also believed to have retired from all human company to meditate and pray before his vision. Like Mohammed, Zoroaster had the idea of a monotheistic deity, only his was conceived some five hundred and fifty years before Christ. Like Jahweh being the tribal god of the Hebrews, his god was a tribal god and the Allah of Mohammed was initially the tribal god of the Arabs."

It was Father Brendan's turn to shake his head. "Again, I cannot agree, Richard. There is only one God, and he keeps in touch with humanity through prayer and revelation to show that he cares for mankind. When praying to God one achieves rapport and communication spiritually with God. God's response is to give one an inner calm."

Richard could not accept that explanation. "In my opinion the feeling of inner calm is more accurately accounted for by accepting that it is due to the functioning brain and part of sensation. One can get feelings of inner calm, ecstasy and relaxation by prayer, meditation, hypnosis, positive thinking and taking drugs. Technically, if I may quote Candace Pert, 'Emotions are neuropeptides attaching to receptors and stimulating an electrical change on neurons.' Religion takes advantage of people's natural fears in order to bolster its power, jumping on the current scientific bandwagon, grasping at any scientific straw that can be used, even by twisting its meaning, to lend apparent support to its questionable dogmas.

"Religions all differ in the interpretation of the originator's preaching. In the Islamic faith there are many different sects, for example, the Shiites, the Sunnis, the Druzes, etc. In Christianity there are the Roman Catholics, the Eastern Orthodox Church, a multitude of Protestant faiths, Baptists, Methodists, Congregationalists, Jehovah's Witnesses, Mormons, etc. As I have remarked before, all claim to have the word of God, except the Buddhists. But even there adherents often go to war and kill their fellow men despite their faith.

"Regarding Catholicism and science, whatever the claims pertaining to creation, the crux of the Catholic faith depends on belief in the Immaculate Conception, therefore the divinity of Christ, the promises of Christ regarding the Kingdom of Heaven and the return of Christ from the dead after the crucifixion. It also depends on the Creator being a personal and loving God, and also hinges on the value of prayer.

"No amount of science supports any of these beliefs. The Immaculate Conception is considered to be a blasphemy by the

Muslims as written in the Koran, and the Zionists ignore it. In any case it is not the only case of divine fertilization of a human ovum in mythology. There is the story of Zeus disguised as a swan to seduce Leda. Christ claimed he was the Son of God and no doubt believed it. He stated, 'I am the way and the truth and the life. No man can come unto the Father but by me.' This is a tremendous claim, for there must have existed and exist, millions of human beings who have lived and live, who have never heard of Christ and therefore cannot enter the 'Kingdom of Heaven.' When asked what the Kingdom of Heaven is, Christ replied, 'The Kingdom of Heaven is among you.' Frankly, I interpret that as meaning it is purely a state of mind brought about by having faith and belief in him.

"As for there being a personal and loving God, it is something for which I cannot find evidence. This may be a beautiful world and a very happy one for some, but it is a very hard and unhappy one for many. Nature is red in tooth and claw and all the evidence points to the struggle for survival of all organisms. Pain is built into organisms as part of the survival kit. All living organisms compete and are disposable containers for their genes. And, except for the lowliest single-celled organisms, all feed on other organisms to exist, causing pain and suffering. Is this therefore what is meant by a loving God where pain and suffering are intentionally built into his creation?

"I see in my work many people who suffer dreadful diseases through no fault of their own. Cancer alone can put them through sheer hell for years. Is this the work of a loving God?

"In addition to pain, the higher organisms can undergo sheer terror before death. Witness a wildebeest being hunted by a lion; a deer being gradually strangled by a boa constrictor; and on the human scale, a group of Palestinians in a mosque being machine-gunned by a Zionist fanatic; or a group of Zionists being terribly maimed by a Muslim fanatic's suicide bomb; an informer being tortured by an IRA member before being murdered. So much for the evidence for a loving God.

"Man is not a special creation; we are the result of evolution and the laws of nature apply to man as to all other self-replicating organisms on this planet.

"The Christian claim that their God is love may account for the immaculate conception, but frankly that is a misconception."

"That is a bit below the belt, Richard," interrupted Gerard.

Richard frowned and said, "I'm sorry and apologize if I have caused offense, Patrick, but I find the idea of God becoming a sperm donor ridiculous. Another thing, if God has to keep interfering with nature it could not have been created as good as is claimed in the Bible in the first place.

"As for the value of prayer, if soldiers on both sides before a battle pray to God for protection, did God turn the other way for the losers? There is an old Indian simultaneous equation regarding the value of prayer and it runs like this:

> 'Work plus prayer equals crops
> work minus prayer equals crops.
> Add the two together and prayer equals nothing.'

"Prayer may have a considerable value for those who obtain comfort from it, but I doubt it is a form of spiritual radiotelephony. I feel many believe that the supreme being who rules the universe can be bribed to alter his decisions by prayers and solicitations for personal preference."

Father Brendan and Gerard had listened to Richard's outburst in complete silence. When he had finished Patrick Brendan quietly said, "With your attitude towards religion, Richard, it would appear that religion should not be taught."

"On the contrary, Patrick, religion should be taught. But students, especially the young, should not be confined to one faith or philosophy and told that it is the only truth. They should be exposed to all faiths, that is, learn comparative religion.

"They should also be taught how religions have evolved and the bad as well as the good things about them. Knowledge should never be hidden no matter how unpalatable, and should always be given at the right time. I want my children to grow up with a very broad education including religion, for that way they will get a sense of mankind's place in nature and will be able to make better judgments in life."

"Regarding the value of religion in morality, I do not need religion to know how to behave civilly to my fellow men, or play my part in my obligations towards society to enable it to run smoothly. From the purely logical standpoint I know that I must contribute towards society as well as take from it. I do not need religion to give myself a clear conscience. My conscience becomes clear by being honest with myself as well as with others.

"There is another thing. Christ claimed he was the 'Son of God.' As I said, I have no doubt he believed it. But why should God reveal himself as a man? Why not a woman? It gives one the impression that the God of the Bible was being a bit sexist."

Eve heard Father Brendan's voice in defense of his faith. "Richard, it is clear from the New Testament that God appreciates the suffering on this earth and sent his only begotten son to share our suffering. He therefore, too, has suffered. He did this out of love and compassion for us and therefore made the greatest sacrifice. Man is made in God's image."

"Well, Patrick, if man is made in God's image then why are there so many imperfections and vestigial remnants in humans? One of the commonest physical complaints is back pain and that is due to *Homo sapiens* having evolved from forebears who walked on four legs. The upright stance has also resulted in problems for women by so altering the pelvis that childbirth is hazardous. Intelligence in our species can vary from the super intelligent to the morons. There are many defective humans born and I have even seen a Cyclops in the pathology museums. We are a species among other species and not a special creation.

"Frankly, I think that because we fear death, we have created God in man's image, and if there is God, then it is not much of a compliment. As far as God sending his only begotten son to suffer as well, then that smacks of masochism. But seriously, whatever power there is behind the universe I doubt that power can be as narrow-minded as all religions that claim him imply.

"I was in the USA recently and saw a newspaper with one page devoted to advertisements for various religions ranging from Catholic to crazy ones. Many were contradictory. I felt tempted to put an advertisement in the paper saying: 'To all who read this: your faith, and your faith alone is the correct one; all other faiths are wrong. This universe was created some fifteen billion years ago purely for your faith to be practiced.'

"It seems to me a bit of cheek and conceit to claim that God created the universe all that time ago so that he would be recognized by us human beings, the intelligent results of his creation. It seems to me that we flatter ourselves because we need some compensation for an innate sense of insecurity. This sense of insecurity I term the Principle of Insecurity and is part of our survival kit. Another part is the Territorial Imperative. The sexual factor is also there because our genes must be passed on to form the next generation. I do not think we have souls but are virtually biological robots. It would be nice to think otherwise, but I can find no convincing evidence to the contrary."

Patrick looked at Richard and smiled. "So you do not think we have souls, Richard?"

"Where is the evidence?" Richard quickly retorted. "I have attended seances and nothing has happened."

"But ghosts, the spirit or soul of men and women have been seen and recorded throughout history. Christ himself came back from the dead to reveal himself to his disciples and so prove that we have souls."

"I do not believe in ghosts and, as I was not present at the resurrection, I cannot judge the validity of the gospel story. However, I think the appearance of ghosts, souls or spirits is more logically accounted for by hallucination."

It was then that Eve recalled seeing the vision in the garden and John calling out that there was a ghost in his room. She immediately rose and opening the French doors on to the patio, walked through and approached the men. On hearing her approach they fell silent and turned their heads in her direction.

"I am sorry to interrupt, but I couldn't help overhearing your remarks about the soul. I have seen a spirit here; John has also and I think you may have done so, Richard."

"What!" Richard voiced in surprise.

To lend support, Patrick Brendan interjected, "Without betraying trust, Eve informed me that she saw a spirit in your garden not long after she came here and I understand you and John saw the same apparition in his bedroom."

Richard looked at Eve and, noticing that she looked pale, smiled to try to put her at ease. Gerard rose and offered Eve his chair. "Come and sit down, dear," he said in a kindly voice.

"So we have a family ghost?" Richard said inquiringly. Then suddenly he snapped a thumb and finger saying, "I think I know . . . but you tell us, Eve. Was this not long after you came here?"

"Yes," said Eve a little tremulously. "I was looking out of the window one night and there was a full moon. I was thinking about something and looked at a statue for a while. When I looked away I saw a figure like the statue and she floated about the garden and gradually disappeared."

"Was that the night John called me saying there was a ghost in his room?"

"Yes, Richard. Didn't you see the ghost, too?"

Richard laughed. "In a way, yes, but neither John, nor you and I saw a real ghost."

"But I did see the figure for some minutes and I was not dreaming."

"I am sure you saw the figure, Eve, and that you were wide awake. But it was no spirit."

"Then what was it?"

"You had been looking at the statue for some time and the figure appeared immediately wherever you looked in the garden?" he queried.

Eve nodded in reply.

"Eve, what you saw was the after-image of the statue on your retina. What happened was that you had been staring at the statue for some time and the retinal pigment had become bleached. This chemical rhodopsin has to regenerate and while it does so an after-image is visible. You must have stared at the statue for some time for the after-image to have lasted so long."

Eve had looked crestfallen but then suddenly brightened. "But John saw a ghost in his bedroom."

Richard shook his head. "No dear, he thought he did, but I shall tell you what happened. You recall it was the night of the full moon?"

Eve nodded, saying, "Yes."

"Well, when I entered his room I stood at the door and asked him where the ghost was and he replied, 'It is right beside you.' I asked, 'Where, John? He said, 'On your right hand side beside the closet.'"

"I looked and could only see the stained wood of the closet cupboard; so I walked over to John and sat beside him on his bed and then I saw the ghost. Actually it looked most eerie, for it was six feet tall and as broad as a man. As I thought it was a real spirit I suddenly realized that it was a reflection of light through the bathroom window. I said, 'Speak spook,' but no spook spoke. And I explained to John what the apparent apparition was. I then got up and closed the bathroom door and the reflection disappeared. Joking aside, I was quite disappointed for when I first saw the reflection I thought there must be something in a spirit world after all."

Richard paused and saw tears welling up in Eve's eyes. "I am sorry Eve to have embarrassed you and perhaps disappointed you."

Eve just whispered, "Excuse me," and, quickly rising from the chair, walked into the house and ran past Dawn upstairs. She looked up to see Eve looking on the brink of tears and rose from her chair as Richard entered the room.

"What happened?" she asked Richard. He explained about the ghost conversation. Dawn gave Richard a look of annoyance and shook her head. She quickly followed Eve and, running upstairs, called her name as Eve was about to enter her bedroom.

"Oh, Eve, don't be upset. Richard did not mean to embarrass you. He was just giving a scientific explanation to what you saw.

Remember, he thought the reflection seen by John was a ghost at first."

Dawn put an arm around Eve's shoulders and, producing a tissue, dabbed her eyes.

"I made a proper fool of myself to you all and to Father Brendan."

"No, you did not, Eve. You only told of what you saw and genuinely believed. What is more, John firmly thought he had seen a ghost and that is why he called Richard into his room."

She stopped dabbing Eve's eyes and said, "Come on now, no harm has been done and you did not make a fool of yourself. No doubt tomorrow you will laugh at it all." Eve managed to summon up a half-smile and kissed Dawn.

"You are so wonderful to me. I do appreciate your kindness and friendship so much."

Then she paused and added, "Perhaps I should go and apologize to Father Brendan for misleading him and to Richard and Gerard for rushing out."

"Don't worry, dear. You go to bed and I will speak to them. In any case, Father Brendan would not think an apology necessary I am sure. He appears to me to be a very understanding man and Dad and Richard would not think an apology necessary. You go to bed and don't worry any more about it. Good night, dear." And at that Dawn kissed Eve on the cheek and closed the bedroom door.

Eve walked over to her bed, took off her dressing gown, threw it on to a chair and climbed into bed. She sat there for a while and heard the men and Dawn go inside and close the patio door. She lay down and thought about the snatches of conversation that she had heard previously while she was undressing for bed. It was of Richard's condemnation of religion that she had heard the most and he had sounded so convincing that she started to cry again. "Oh God, what if all I have been taught and believed in is false. Oh God, what shall I do? Surely Father Brendan cannot be wrong in everything."

She then thought of the "ghost" and went hot and cold with embarrassment and disappointment. She started to weep quietly again and tried to pray, but could not concentrate. A poem she had once read came to her mind:

> *Sometimes when I gaze around,*
> *it seems*
> *that the world*
> *once full of dreams*

*has lost its lure
and each day
I do miss my way;
as though some other hand
has willed
that my dreams
shall never be fulfilled.*

She felt that the world was tumbling down around her and the security she so unconsciously wanted in life was fading away. She silently sobbed herself to sleep feeling wretched and abandoned.

chapter twenty

He had a sensation of floating and felt he could hear disembodied voices far off. He seemed to recollect that someone had been shaking him, but that seemed to be replaced by something pressing around his face, and then the floating sensation recurred. He kept feeling giddy and disoriented and there seemed to be something across his body holding him down. He vaguely tried to move but felt too weak to do so. Far off in the distance was the noise of a vehicle engine and he could feel vaguely as if the ground were shaking and vibrating his whole body. He tried to move again but experienced vertigo and seemed to float upside down, then round and round in circles. And his head ached! Oh, how it ached! He had never experienced a headache like it before; it throbbed and felt as if there was a tight band around his skull boring into his temples.

He tried to open his eyes but the effort seemed too much for him and it made the pain increase. Then he felt the weights being taken off his chest and legs and being lifted and placed on a bed, or was it a bed. He felt himself moving but this time there was only a little vertigo and he was dimly aware of bright light above, shining through his closed eyelids and waxing and waning as he floated along on his bed. He lost consciousness again.

Parker swore. "Christ. My bleedin' 'ead—Oh Gawd, wot 'it me?" With great effort he opened his eyes and his surroundings gradually came into focus. He found himself lying in a room clinically spotless, and gradually surmised where he was when a nurse walked in through the open door leading to the corridor. He shook his head in disbelief and wished he hadn't. "Oh, Gawd, me 'ead don' arf ache."

The nurse came over to him and smiled. Then he heard a masculine voice beside him say, "So you have woken up at last, Mr. Parker. Thank heaven for that."

Then the nurse chipped in. "You had us all worried, you know."

Parker attempted to move, then pulled a face as he felt the headache become more manifest. He looked to his side in order to locate the source of the masculine voice and jumped when he saw a uniformed police constable sitting there.

"Wot the 'ell's goin' on?" But before the constable could reply, the nurse said, "Now don't go upsetting our patient. I want the doctor to see him before you start asking questions."

Then she turned to Parker. "You have had a nasty dose of carbon monoxide poisoning and must take it easy." She noticed him wince as he moved, "I am going to get the doctor to see you and we'll get something for your headache. You will probably be better off sitting up. But just relax for the moment while I get Dr. Linmann." She abruptly left the room, and Parker closed his eyes and tried to relax but it was easier said than done. Returning a few moments later, Parker opened his eyes on hearing Dr. Linmann's voice.

"So you've decided to rejoin the land of the living," he remarked in a jocular voice and then proceeded to examine Parker. After sounding his chest, heart and lungs and looking into his eyes with an ophthalmoscope. Parker was relieved to hear him say, "Hm . . . It looks as if you are OK. You know you have had a very narrow shave and," he added, "don't make a habit of it. You might not be so lucky next time."

During the course of the examination Parker had to sit up and groaned a little putting a hand to his head. "Still aches does it? Don't worry. Nurse Henderson will give you a couple of tablets to get rid of that pain. I'll see you after lunch and by then you should feel much better. Just stay sitting up." And at that, assisted by the nurse, he rearranged his back rest and pillows leaving Parker in a more comfortable position. He and the nurse left the room and Parker closed his eyes.

At first he wondered how he had got there then gradually recollected lying in the sleeping bag in the caravan. Carbon monoxide poisoning! He knew enough about that to appreciate what had happened. He had left the gas on to dry his clothes and the carbon monoxide produced by combustion had built up, gradually poisoning him.

He realized he was lucky to be alive and guessed his life had been saved by the owner or someone noticing that the caravan was occupied. He was later to learn that the owner had taken his dog out very early in the morning and the dog had alerted him to Parker's presence. As soon as the owner opened the door, felt the warmth and saw the gas on he suspected someone was in there. He had found Parker and tried to arouse him but to no avail. He had the great presence of mind to open the windows and switch off the gas and leave the door open to keep a constant draft of fresh air circulating through the caravan. On finding that Parker was beginning to breathe more regularly he had returned to his house and phoned for an ambulance and also reported Parker's presence to the police.

Parker kept his eyes closed not so much for relief but in order to think before the constable started to ask him questions. He realized that he could be charged with breaking and entering. As he had done no damage he could not be charged with theft and, in any case, he would voluntarily make amends by offering to pay for the gas used, repairing the lock and having the sleeping bag dry-cleaned. His main worry was finding an excuse for having been there so late at night and if the police associated his presence with the stolen car. He did not know which hospital he was in but hoped it was not too far from Barkingside. He decided to say nothing about his car having broken down, but concocted a story to the effect that he had been to Southend for the day and had caught a train back to Brentwood, and it being a warm night he decided to walk back to London. Unfortunately he had been caught in the rainstorm and decided to seek shelter, which was true. From then on the police would have deduced what had happened.

He opened his eyes and looked at the constable who looked up from a copy of a magazine he had been passing the time with. "Feeling any better, Mr. Parker?" the constable inquired.

"Yus mate—er fanks."

Nurse Henderson entered carrying a glass of water and a small container with two pills in it. "Here we are, Mr. Parker. Take these and you will feel as right as rain in a short while." He accepted the two small capsules readily, put them straight into his mouth and drank a good mouthful of water to wash them down. Through sitting up his headache had begun to feel easier and his normally buoyant spirits began to return. He handed back the glass to the nurse. "Fanks, Flo," he said, alluding to Florence Nightingale and endeavored to raise a smile. The nurse gave him a good-humored look.

"That's the spirit, Mr. Parker. Now I must get on and meantime I'll leave you to entertain this gentleman in blue." And with a chuckle she left the room.

Parker and the constable looked at each other then simultaneously burst out laughing. "Alright mate," said Parker, "I suppose yer want ter know jest wot I wos doin' in the caravan?"

The policeman nodded and reached for his notebook, then paused, saying in a kindly voice, "Do you feel up to it?"

Parker replied, "Yus," and launched into the story he had dreamed up to establish why he had broken into the caravan. He also added that he was willing to pay for any damage done. The policeman made notes as Parker related the story and asked, "Are you willing to make a statement?"

"Yus o' course, mate."

"You realize that anything you say may be used in evidence against you?"

"Yus."

The constable was silent for a moment. "You know, Mr. Parker, if you have a clean record I doubt if there will be any charges. However, that will depend on the station sergeant." He rose from his chair and walking towards the door said, "I'll be back in a minute."

Parker responded, saying, "Orf ter chat up the nurse?" The officer grinned and promptly left the room.

Parker's head was beginning to feel better and he also felt his strength returning. It crossed his mind to get dressed and leave the hospital, but then he realized that firstly, he did not know where his clothes were and secondly, the police would have found his wallet and identified him. He guessed the constable was phoning the police station to let the officer in charge know that he Parker, had recovered from his ordeal. No doubt he would also be finding out if Parker had a record. Parker relaxed when that thought crossed his mind. He had no criminal record; he had always been too careful and had never been caught. His cogitation was interrupted by a domestic entering his room.

"Like a cup of tea, sir?" she asked.

"Not arf," he replied thankfully, and added, "An' two spoons o' sugar. I could do wiv a bit o' energy, luv." She left the room and he could hear her outside the door busy with the tea trolley. She reentered bearing a cup of tea and a couple of biscuits. "Here you are, sir," she said cheerfully. "You must have come in this morning. Are you going to be here long?"

Parker shook his head. "Nah, I don' fink so. Jest popped in fer a cup o' tea." The domestic gave him a sideways glance. "Oh, yes."

"Yus." And he drank a mouthful. He paused for a moment, pretending to savor it and commented, "Nice cup o' char, luv. Worf all the effort o' comin' in. 'Ave ter do it agin' sometime as long as yer 'ere ter make it."

"Pull the other one," was her response as she left the room.

Parker enjoyed the tea and took his time drinking it but had finished when the constable returned.

"Wot, visitin' time orlready," Parker queried jestingly. The constable sat down and ignored the repartee. He was in a hurry, having learned that Parker had no record and that a decision of whether or not he was to be charged was to be made later. The police had Parker's address from the driving license they had found in his wallet. All the constable needed to do was to check Parker's credentials by questioning him about where he lived, and getting him to sign a statement which he read out to him and asked Parker to read in turn before signing it. Parker had no quarrel with that and happily signed it.

"Incidentally," said the constable before leaving, "the owner of the caravan is willing to drop charges providing you pay for the damage as you suggested. He happened to be in the station when I phoned in my report. An officer will contact you to let you know the result of the police decision on whether or not you are to be charged. Where are you going from here when the doctor says you can leave?"

"I'll be orf 'ome."

The constable nodded. "Well, as far as we are concerned you are free to go, but you must report to your local police station after you get home. OK?"

Parker nodded. "No need ter worry, mate. I won't be 'oppin orf on a world cruise."

The officer looked at him and held out his hand. "As the doctor said, don't make a habit of it."

Parker took the proffered hand with an odd feeling. He had always regarded the police as enemies who were out to stop his somewhat unlawful activities, and to have a member of the force showing him even a mild degree of affability made him feel uncomfortable.

"Fanks, mate. I won't tike any walks in funderstorms agin."

The constable nodded and left the room.

Parker had walked around his room after the officer left and knew that his strength was returning rapidly. He ate all the food that had been brought to him in the lunch hour, and by late afternoon the doctor returned to examine him again.

"You're as fit as a fiddle Mr. Parker," he said. "What did you come in here for, free bed and board?"

"'Ere," Parker retorted. "Wot d'yer fink I pay me national 'elf contributions for?"

"I knew it. Have you tried walking?"

"Yus an' fank Gawd me 'eadache's gorn."

"Good. I'm going to give the nurse a letter for your own doctor and I want you to see him in the morning. Anyway you are free to go and," anticipating the questioning look on Parker's face Dr. Linmann added, "The nurse will bring in your clothes. Be careful in the future." And with that parting shot he left the room.

The nurse entered shortly afterwards bearing a bag in which all Parker's clothes had been inserted and left him to get dressed, returning after he had finished with the letter for his own general practitioner. He left the hospital thanking the nurse and doctor for their attention and hired a minicab to take him to Barkingside. He managed to collect his repaired vehicle just before the garage closed.

There had been a problem with the fuel injector, and it having been replaced the vehicle was functioning well. He settled his bill with a credit card, and drove slowly back to the city reflecting on the events of the last twenty-four hours. It was early evening and the rush hour was over, but he took his time driving. The experience of having nearly lost his life had a sobering effect on him and he did not like it. His philosophy had always been that although aware of his mortality, and that everyone had to face death one day, he was in no hurry. He realized that his mode of life had enough risk without adding to it and he felt himself having second thoughts about the web he had spun for himself by choosing to serve Boss.

"Boss!—Oh, gorblimey," he reflected, "I gotta report ter 'im." It was still early evening, a little after seven and he would have to phone Boss as soon as he got home. He sighed and drove on steadily.

It was around that time that the police found the stolen car.

■ ❏ ■ ❏ ■

Sean sat in a window seat of the aircraft as it sped over the English countryside. It was a bright sunny day and the fields were a patchwork of green, brown and yellow, their conterminations clearly marked with hedgerows. Here and there small woodlands and copses stood out in a deeper green, while an occasional pond, lake, reservoir, stream or river would sparkle in reflected sunlight. He watched cars like minute ants coursing along the roadways and was thankful he was not having to drive to Ireland and use the ferry. Flying was much quicker and almost as economical, possibly more so in view of the time it saved.

He glanced at his watch and noted the time; the plane had left Stanstead airport an hour and a half late and he was not feeling very pleased. Apart from that he felt tired for he had experienced a busy week and needed the break. It would be good to see his mother again but he was not relishing meeting his two stepbrothers. He wondered what he would say to them and wondered more so what they would have to say to him. He interrupted his reverie as the plane gradually gained height and flew through some thin clouds which partly obscured the ground below. He picked up the newspaper that had remained unfolded on his lap and glanced at the headlines. He turned the front page idly and looked over the second page. He stiffened as his eyes read a headline: "IRA KILLERS OF MOTHER BARBAROUS."

He noted that the news following the headline was written by an Irish correspondent of the *Daily Telegraph*. He read with feelings of loathing.

"The 'barbarous savagery' of an IRA gang who shot dead a young mother, claiming she was a police informer, was condemned by a priest at her funeral in the Lower Falls area of West Belfast yesterday. Fr. Luke McWilliams told mourners at St. Paul's Church that the community had been 'revolted' by the killing of Mrs. Caroline Moreland, thirty-four, whose body was dumped a few yards from the Irish Border at the weekend.

"Mrs. Moreland, a mother of three children aged between ten and fourteen, was vice-chairman of the West Belfast Muscular Dystrophy Association and had raised thousands of pounds towards the cause after her brother had died from the illness, he said.

"'That was the kind of person Caroline was, a straightforward, direct person who said out straight what she thought, a caring person who did a lot of good and eased pain and suffering for others,' Fr. McWilliams added. 'This makes her death and the vile manner of her dying all the more shocking and distressing.'

"Her friends called on all Protestants and Roman Catholics to attend the funeral in protest, expressing their 'outrage and abhorrence of her brutal abducting, torture and killing.'

"The IRA alleged that Mrs. Moreland had been working as an RUC informer for the past two years, a claim that has been disputed by her friends."

Sean put down the paper in disgust and the expression must have shown on his face for he heard a voice beside him say, "It is a terrible business is it not?"

Sean looked at the passenger sitting beside him and noted the concerned look. In response Sean shook his head and sighed, "When will those animals grow up and stop the unnecessary bloodshed?"

The passenger who earlier had introduced himself as Father O'Mallon tut-tutted. "Sometimes I am ashamed of my fellow Irishmen. There seems to be the devilish streak in some of them that is so obscene; Christian values such as compassion become foreign to them. I read about Mrs. Moreland and if I say I express my condemnation and disgust it is because I cannot find adequate words to condemn this barbarity. Such people are the sons of Satan."

"One must not condemn a whole people for the sins of the few."

"No, I don't do that. The victim of the IRA savagery was a good person and most of our compatriots are of the same fine caliber, but there are too many who seem to delight in causing pain and suffering to innocent people because of some imagined wrong in the past or for very doubtful political ends." Father O'Mallon paused and added, "I am a Catholic priest and would like to see a united and peaceful Ireland, but even so we have no right to force the Protestant North to join us if they do not want to. And especially through bloodshed," he added. "To bring about a united Ireland by coercion is to fly in the face of freedom and democracy."

Sean nodded, "I fully agree with you." He sat back and looked out of the window. "We seem to be flying over Anglesea."

The plane roared on and he noticed the mountains of Wales far to the left and the Isle of Anglesea lay below. The Irish Sea lay beyond it and he could clearly discern a ferry crossing to Ireland. He knew the plane was going to be late and decided to spend the night in a bed and breakfast near Dublin. He would drive to Ennis where the family home was the following day. He had arranged to hire a car and would collect it at the airport.

Although it was the holiday season he anticipated he would find a B&B without much difficulty and he was not disappointed. He had driven for about half an hour from the airport and reached Kildare; there he found a neat clean-looking house which had a vacancy notice for bed and breakfast displayed. The hostess welcomed him and offered him tea. He sat in a small lounge in which a television set was placed for guests' use. A commercial traveler who introduced himself as Pat, was watching the news when he entered and he politely asked Sean if he minded. "Not at all," Sean had replied and he too sat down and watched. The news included a report on the forthcoming meeting of Sinn Fein, the political wing of the IRA. They were to debate the peace initiative—the Downing Street Agreement—arranged by the British Prime Minister John Major and the Irish Prime Minister Albert Reynolds, and launched seven months earlier. Pat commented, "If Sinn Fein do not agree to join the peace initiative, they will be the only republican nationalist party that does not." Sean agreed.

Their viewing was interrupted when the landlady brought in tea for Sean. He thanked her and started to pour a cup when his attention was arrested by another news item. A lorry containing two tons of explosive had been seized at the Lancashire ferry port of Heysham; the fertilizer-based device contained all the ingredients for a live bomb and could have been primed for detonation in five minutes. It had arrived from the Ulster port of Warrenpoint. It was suspected that the channel tunnel was the prime target for this latest IRA device. Sean and Pat looked at each other and shook their heads. "Is there no end to their devilry?" Pat commented, more by way of a statement than a question. "I sometimes wonder," Sean had replied. And later that night he reflected on the conversation.

After watching the news he had walked to a restaurant and had an evening meal. His mind was too occupied with his thoughts about what he was going to say to his step-brothers to pay much attention to savoring his meal. Later in bed he could hardly remember what he had eaten and smiled to himself at the thought. He wondered if he could make either one of them see reason and felt depressed at the thought that his visit would be a waste of time. His only consolation was that his mother would be glad to see him. And she was.

"Why Sean, 'tis wonderful to see you." She had put her arms round him and hugged him and had tears in her eyes. He had arrived in the early afternoon and his stepfather and both stepbrothers were out, so he and his mother had two hours to themselves.

Sean told her that Morag sent her love and was terribly sorry not to want to return to Ireland. Their mother already knew this and was reconciled to the idea. She had liked Morag's fiancé and was very happy at the thought of their marrying, despite his not being a Catholic. She told Sean that she hoped Morag would come and see her even if they could meet away from the house and that there would be no risk of her coming across her stepbrothers. Sean did not consider it likely, but kept that thought to himself.

His mother then changed the subject and he told her about Eve. He had previously only mentioned to his mother that he had met a girl he wanted to marry. His mother asked for more details. He spared her the knowledge that Eve had been tricked into prostitution and that she was in hiding from her former employers. He told his mother what a lovely and beautiful girl Eve was and also that she was studying for conversion to the Catholic faith. The latter information pleased his mother who was devout in her faith. She had been a little disappointed that Gordon was a Protestant, but the news that Eve would soon become a Catholic seemed to make up for it. She felt reassured that at least some of her grandchildren would be Catholics, and this thought was a very comforting one to her.

It was later that the two stepbrothers returned. Sean stood up as Morgan and Eamon entered the room. They both stiffened in surprise when they saw Sean, and Morgan reddened as if guessing why Sean was there. A line from Shakespeare came to Sean's mind as their body language indicated. They "started like a guilty thing upon a fearful summons."

"Hello, Morgan. Hello, Eamon," he said somewhat flatly. Both the brothers nodded and looked at each other. There was an uncomfortable silence for a moment and then their mother broke it saying, "I'll go and get tea ready," and left the room. Sean was glad to see her go. He had told her previously that he did not want her to be present when he spoke to them. She had wanted to be there to give him moral support but he had demurred at that. She knew that he was quite capable of looking after himself should the need arise, but doubted that there would be any violence. She guessed that Sean would tell them what bigoted savages they had been in acting as they had done, and Sean did so; however he started off quietly enough by asking them why they had behaved so badly to Gordon.

Morgan, the more intelligent of the two said little and was obviously embarrassed, but Eamon was defiant. "Who the bloody hell do you think you are talking to me like this?" he yelled. "Just because you are a doctor you are not God Almighty." This lack of logic in Eamon's reasoning did not surprise Sean.

"I don't want Morag to disgrace the family by marrying a Protestant and a Brit at that," he had yelled. Sean was glad that his stepfather had not yet returned. "I tell you, Sean, if that bastard comes here again I'll kneecap him."

"You'll what?"

Sean raised his voice in surprise. He had so far kept his voice down, but the idea of his stepbrother carrying out the vicious punishment on Gordon that was practiced by the IRA infuriated him. He closed his mouth to control himself and glared at Eamon who glared back defiantly.

"I've kneecapped people before and I'll do it to that bastard if he comes here again." Sean realized from the reply that Eamon was more dangerous than he had imagined. He knew he was not bright and very bigoted but had no idea how far he had gone in his narrow-mindedness.

"Are you in the IRA?" Sean asked heatedly. Eamon opened his mouth to speak and then realized that he had given himself away. By way of a response he walked towards the door and then, turning round, spat back at Sean, "It's none of your damn business." He paused and then added, "You had better be careful, Sean." And with that parting threat he abruptly left the room.

Sean started to go after him and then Morgan said, "Don't, Sean. You won't make him alter his mind and he is dangerous."

Sean looked at him for fully a minute before speaking. He realized that Morgan was right, and felt frustrated that Eamon could not appreciate that he had acted in a non-Christian manner.

"What about you, Morgan? Are you in the IRA?" Morgan shook his head. "No, but you know it is dangerous to ask questions like that, Sean."

Sean fell silent again. "Do you really think you were justified in beating up Gordon?"

Morgan looked away from Sean's gaze and then, as if finding courage looked back and said somewhat lamely. "I suppose I had too much to drink, but I still think it is a disgrace to our good Catholic family's name if Morag marries a Protestant Brit."

"Your cousin Richard is a Brit and he is not a Catholic either."

"That's different. He is really your cousin by blood so he doesn't count." Sean took this statement in and realized that Morgan also was too bigoted to think rationally. He then asked, "Does not the message of Jesus mean anything to you, that one should have compassion and love for one's fellow men?"

"Of course," said Morgan, "but not for Protestants. They sin against God by denying the authority of the Catholic Church."

It was at that point that Sean gave up the idea of rational conversation, and decided that his hopes of getting the brothers to apologize to Gordon and Morag were completely dashed by a wall of blind bigotry and sheer pig-headedness.

"I only hope that God will forgive you," was all he could say.

The following day he spent with his mother, taking her out to lunch and driving down to the coast. He had invited his stepfather but he had declined the invitation. They had a pleasant time together and Sean realized that his mother was not completely happy. He asked her why and she told him that his stepfather was kind enough to her in his way, but his ideas which he had imparted to his boys upset her. He suggested that she should consider leaving, at least for a while, but she would not think of it. She believed in the sanctity of marriage and the duty of a wife towards her husband and family. He could not dispute this for his views on marriage were similar. At least she was in touch with him and Morag, although she had been told she would not see Morag in Ireland again. She was happy at the thought of his being able to come and see her and excited at the thought of Sean getting married. "You must bring her over here to meet us," she had said. At which Sean had replied with a laugh, "I'll wait until she is converted first." But the association of ideas suddenly left a bitter taste in his mouth.

He left the following day and drove to the airport feeling somewhat sad. He had accomplished very little with his stepbrothers, but at least he had cheered up his mother and for that his journey had been worthwhile. He returned his hired car and purchased some

Irish and English newspapers to read on the plane. This time the aircraft departed as scheduled and he sat back to relax and make the most of the journey. It had rained a little when they left the airport, but the plane flew above the clouds into bright sunshine and that revived his spirits. The clouds gradually cleared as they flew over the Irish Sea and he could see the Isle of Man clearly to the north. He admired the scene for a while and then remembered the newspapers.

His feelings were not improved when he read: "More than forty people were injured yesterday when the IRA fired three mortars, containing 600 lbs. of explosives in all, at a police station in Newry Co Down. Two soldiers suffered serious head and neck wounds . . . thirty-nine civilians, young children, including a two-year-old girl and an elderly woman, were treated in Newry. Most of the civilians were injured when one of the mortars missed the base and landed in a nearby street before 9 A.M." He put down the paper in disgust.

Turning to the *Irish Times* his eyes opened wide as he read the headlines: "Sinn Fein decision seen as effective rejection of the Joint Declaration." He read on and to his consternation learned the Sinn Fein had thrown away the one hope for peace in Ireland. So the unnecessary terrorism and murders were to continue. He looked at the other paper and learned that the reaction of all the political parties, including the pro-nationalist parties had been one of criticism of the Sinn Fein's rejection of the only hope for peace. He read several commentaries to the effect that the political wing of the IRA had distanced themselves from all other parties. It was obvious that all sane Irishmen wanted the peace initiative to proceed and by rejecting the initiative Sinn Fein had not understood the mood of the people.

Sean sat back in his seat and put down the newspapers on the folding table in front of him. Will they never learn? he wondered.

■ ❏ ■ ❏ ■

Parker sat in his living room with a copy of the *Sporting Times* unread on his lap. His interview with Boss had left him with a feeling of unease. Boss had looked very pleased when Parker had informed him of Eve's whereabouts; that is as pleased as Boss ever showed. He was not one to betray his feelings with facial expressions. "Well done," he had said and went on to listen to further detail from Parker. When he came to the revelation that Parker had been interviewed by a policeman in the hospital, Boss's face seemed to harden a fraction. "You say you had an interview."

"Yus, Boss. I 'ad ter sign a statement sayin' why I woz in the caravan."

Boss had looked at Parker without blinking and that made him feel uncomfortable. It was the way Boss questioned Parker that made Parker realize that all was not well. It was obvious that Boss was concerned that Parker had not given any other information away and Parker had reassured him that he, Parker, was not a "grass" or "copper's nark."

"I know when ter keep me mahf shut," he had said, and Boss's soft Irish voice saying in reply, "Yes, I am sure you can," had not sounded convincing. Boss had told him to take three days off to get over the poisoning and Parker was relieved at that, but his instinct suggested to him that Boss no longer trusted him.

He knew he had no real grounds for that suspicion but if Boss considered him a risk then he, Parker, would be pushing up daisies before too long. And then there was the matter of Eve.

Eve troubled Parker's conscience. He did not think he had one until he had met Eleanor. She had given him a degree of respect and dignity that was new to him. Meeting her had been a turning point in his life although he was reluctant to admit it even to himself. Eleanor was distantly related to Eve and, by finding Eve and informing Boss of her whereabouts he had effectively and personally given her a death sentence.

"Oh, sod it!" he said out loud when the realization of his activities and position became clear to him.

He was interrupted from his thoughts by the ringing of the telephone. I wonder 'oo the 'ell that can be, he mused as he picked up the phone.

"'Allo," he said, and then repeated his phone number.

The feminine voice at the other end of the line sounded familiar. "Hi, Bert. How are you? It's me, Eleanor."

chapter twenty-one

Boss sat in his office alone. Parker had just left and Boss needed time to think. He had a number of things on his mind and wanted to cogitate on them before deciding upon action. So Parker had found Eve—good. He had considered having her eliminated quickly, but figured that she had not been to the police regarding the Londinium Club. Had she been, then it would have been either raided or kept under observation by the police before now, but it had not. Certainly there had been no sign of police snoopers. It might be that she was afraid to talk or that she had done so but was not believed. The club was used by people in high places and it would not be the first time that evidence was suppressed because of the risk of scandal.

As for Eve Eden, there was no hurry; he would have her removed from the scene by either Rory or Bernadette. They were both on their way back to England and would have no problem in kidnapping Eve. She too would be dumped overboard in the North Sea and no longer be a risk.

Parker had done his job but Parker had been careless and been interviewed by the police. Boss did not like any of his minions to be interviewed by police. What compounded his concern was that Parker had again to report to the police. Of course it was straightforward. He had committed a trivial crime and might or might not be charged. However, the charge did not worry Boss, it was the fact that Parker would then have a criminal record and that could cause problems should he run foul of the police in the future. Apart from de Vere-Smythe, Parker was the only member of his employees who knew Boss's true identity. Neither knew of his IRA connections; apart from Rory and Bernadette there were two other members in his cell. If Parker was getting careless then he might need to be removed. However that, too, could wait, for he would need to be replaced and there was no immediately suitable substitute.

There was another thing on Boss's mind that was causing him concern. The British and Irish prime ministers had started the peace initiative and it did not appeal to him. The Downing Street Agreement had included inviting all interested parties to the conference table. The only stipulation was that the terrorists lay down their arms and denounce violence. The British had made the great concession of recognizing the words "United Ireland." The Irish Prime Minister had made the considerable concession that unification was to come about by free vote in both Northern and Southern Ireland.

He did not like Albert Reynolds' decision; it amounted to the Protestants having a veto on the decision of unity. He thought of the announcement in the December of the previous year and grinned inwardly when he recollected the IRA's response—shooting a young British soldier by sniper fire as soon as it had been announced. That showed the British that the IRA had the power to dictate their terms. It had all been too easy. Shooting a Brit gave the American Irish fund subscribers the impression that the war was against the British when it was actually against the Northern Irish; the stubbornness of his fellow Irishmen the Protestants, had prevented unity in the first place over a hundred years ago and continued to do so.

Boss smiled again when he recalled the yelling pedagogue protestant Irishman in the British Parliament, who had shouted that to negotiate with the IRA was a betrayal. He considered that person was unintentionally one of the best allies of the IRA in that his belligerent attitude and rabble-rousing technique put the Protestant cause in a bad light and gave ammunition to its opponents.

Boss and his immediate associates did not want a negotiated peace. They wanted total surrender by the Protestants in the North and the satisfaction of the Catholics doing to them what they had done to the Catholics. He wanted total revenge as he saw it. He hoped that the IRA would be able to ferret out the Protestant terrorists in the UFF and the other groups and shoot them all. The merciful aspects of Christianity did not matter. As a Catholic he could always find a priest to give him dispensation in confession and anyway, he had his doubts about religion and afterlife. Whether there was or was not a heaven or hell, he wanted the Protestants and Brits to get hell on earth.

There were other reasons why he did not want peace by negotiation. Should it be achieved then the futility of all the killings would be obvious to any intelligent observer. That would not do the IRA image much good. And they needed a good image, especially in the USA. The funds from America had kept a large part of interested parties living in comfort. Where funds were given voluntarily—he smiled at that word—there was no check on the amount and the taxation authorities had no idea of the sums involved. Arms were very cheap to obtain and there was a very nice surplus to keep a few organizations supplied with adequate voluntary income. He had long realized that any cessation of funds from the USA would mean that the gunmen would have to negotiate for peace in Ireland and that did not suit him one bit.

Boss was doing very nicely from the drug side too, and all these unofficial sources of income helped to supplement the takings from the Londinium Club. That establishment barely paid its way with legitimate income, but it was an excellent front and had such powerful clients it was worth keeping going. It was also a useful source of information: the odd blabbermouth Member of Parliament; the odd overconfident businessman; the occasional visiting diplomat all provided useful information skillfully obtained by the manager Mr. de Vere-Smythe whose charm and discretion they found irresistible.

Boss grinned again; no peace, thank you, the rackets were running very nicely. And as for innocent bystanders getting killed or maimed, as long as they were Protestants or Brits they were expendable.

His mind went back to the recent turning down of the peace initiative by Sinn Fein. It suited him but there was an uncomfortable rumor in the "grapevine" that the reaction of the general public and all the other parties in the Irish Parliament, the Dail, had so isolated Sinn Fein that they were likely to change their minds. In addition there had been talk of the Sinn Fein being able to isolate three Catholic dominated counties of Northern Ireland by negotiation at the conference table and get them to join Eire. Things did not look so good. Perhaps another bombing could be arranged to stir things up a bit; maybe a bank or post office robbery. The extra funds would come in handy anyway.

Another thing had been brought to his attention which involved Caria Crompetta. Some regular clients had complained to de Vere-Smythe that she was not performing as well as expected; that would not do. Apparently she would take time off at every opportunity and drive east to Essex. Was she in contact with Eve, he wondered? It would be as well to find out and have her followed next time she departed. He phoned de Vere-Smythe and instructed him to ensure that Caria was followed. De Vere-Smythe had said he would make it so and Boss then got on with other commitments.

De Vere-Smythe spoke to Donna Ke Babe asking when Caria was due to have a day off. In reply to the question she said, "Tomorrow." De Vere-Smythe knew that Parker had another two days off to recover from his poisoning. He winced when he realized that the only person available to follow Caria was Bounce. He knew Bounce was not bright but he saw little of him and felt he would be able to do the shadowing job. He phoned Donna and told her to send Bounce to him straight away and Bounce arrived within two minutes.

"Come in," de Vere-Smythe called out in response to the knock on the door. Bounce entered without hesitation, walked across the carpet to seat himself on the chair indicated by de Vere-Smythe.

"I have a job for you, Bounce," de Vere-Smythe said affably. Bounce waited for the instructions, not because he was eager to hear them but because he could not think of anything to say.

"You are to take a hired car tomorrow and follow Caria Crompetta. You are to shadow her and find out who she meets. Do you understand?"

"Yeah, Mr. de Vere-Smyve. Yer want me ter follow Caria an' find aht 'oo she meets."

"Quite right. Very good," said de Vere-Smythe. At that Bounce stuck his chest out with pride. He was unused to praise. He was instructed to report to Donna early in the morning and collect the car. She would accompany him and leave him waiting for Caria's car where he would not be easily noticed. That would ensure that he got off to a good start.

De Vere-Smythe made Bounce repeat his instructions twice more and then dismissed him. He also sighed and crossed his fingers.

■ ❏ ■ ❏ ■

Eve unlocked the front door and entered the hallway feeling in good spirits. She had taken the children to school and now had to see Gerard who had agreed to follow her to the local garage. Her car required servicing and he would follow and then give her a lift to the church. She heard him practicing his cello and liked the cheerful music that flowed from the music room. He, Dawn and Rachel were to play Mendelssohn's first piano trio and Gerard was playing the cello part. He was a better cellist than Jean and Eve looked forward to the performance.

Another reason for her feeling happy was because she had woken in the night feeling the need to pray. The prior evening she had fallen asleep crying because of the doubts about her faith planted there by Richard's outburst against religion. She had prayed hard and then fell asleep. In the morning she had woken in brilliant sunshine and felt not only rested but uplifted by her prayers, feeling that they had been answered.

She entered the music room and Gerard looked up at her and smiled. "Well, young lady, are you ready?" he said, stopping playing and rising from his seat.

Eve nodded. "Yes, please. I am sorry to interrupt you."

"No need to be. Perhaps you would like to leave now while I put my cello away. I'll meet you at the garage." Eve acquiesced at this and went to her car. He heard her drive off as he finished putting the cello and bow in the case. Fifteen minutes later he arrived at the garage and had only to wait a minute for Eve who was speaking to the mechanic. As soon as she had finished she opened his car door and sat beside him.

"What time will it be ready?" he asked.

"Two o'clock," she replied.

"Ah, good. I understand you finish at the church at twelve-thirty, so I'll treat you to lunch and we can pick up the car afterwards."

"That's very nice of you. Are you sure I am not putting you out?"

"Oh, terribly," Gerard replied, "but don't worry, I can take it."

Actually he had arranged to take Eve to the church, leave her there while he did some shopping and then collect her at noon. His reply was not unexpected. He enjoyed indulging in banter and she was used to it, although sometimes she was uncertain if he was serious or not. But in any case, she had found him to be a kindly man and could not imagine him hurting or hating anyone.

Eve suddenly thought of Sean and how he had fared on his visit to Ireland. She would know the following evening, of course, for he had promised to phone her as soon as he returned. Sean had mentioned the beating up of Gordon and she could not imagine why people could hate so much to act so badly. Gerard glanced at her, wondering why she was so silent.

"A penny for your thoughts?" he asked.

"I was thinking about hatred. Have you ever hated anyone, Gerard?"

Gerard grew silent and there was a long pensive pause before he replied. His mind went back to the time when he was a second lieutenant in the parachute regiment in the British Army. With hundreds of others he was dropped in France on D-Day in World War II. He visibly shuddered at the thought of that experience.

With his company he had been accidentally dropped away from the intended area. He had been horrified to find himself descending into a long ditch filled with water and, unknown to him, pointed stakes lay just below the surface. He heard several men in his platoon scream as they drowned or were impaled on the stakes. He had been lucky. He had spilled some air from his parachute which enabled him to drop near the edge of the ditch. He had unbuckled his harness just as he had struck the water and had twisted his body towards the bank. His right foot had landed on top of a pointed stake the tip of which was about three feet below the surface. He had always been a quick thinker and as he felt his boot hit the stake, so he bent his legs, dampening his fall and kicked himself towards the side of the ditch. At the same time he whipped off his helmet to save weight. His hands struck the vertical wall of wet clay and he felt them slide as he struggled to get a handhold. He went below the water and kicked hard again, rising to the surface spluttering.

Somehow his right boot found a hold in the wall and he stuck his fingers in the clay and, with the initial impetus, rose enough to grab grass at the top of the bank. A tussock of grass came away in his left hand but he felt his boots again getting a hold and he grabbed again. This time the grass held and he rested for a second before gingerly starting to pull himself up the bank. At this point he was still covered with the parachute canopy which had settled around his head and was slowly sinking in the water. He realized he would have to get out quickly if he was to avoid being dragged under by its weight. Preparing himself for a final heave he heard the sound of running footsteps and voices. He froze in fear. The footsteps stopped just above him and he hung precariously with the parachute still covering him.

"*Il y a un autre ici. Vitement!*" On hearing the French voice he called out, "*Assistez moi, s'il vous plaît.*"

He felt the parachute being pulled aside and two men grabbed his arms and hauled him out of the ditch. "*Merci. Vous êtes les Résistance Français?*"

"*Oui. Venez avec nous, vitement. Les Bosches sont la,*" one of the men pointed.

"*Ou sont les soldats Anglais?*"

"*Votre soldats sont dans le bois. Venez promptement.*"

He followed the two Frenchmen who led him to a small copse where, to his relief, he found the company sergeant major and the remains of his platoon. He had lost half his men in the drop, mostly drowned but some shot by the Germans. He was glad to find the company sergeant major who was a short stocky man, absolutely fearless and as tough as nails.

It took them two hours to locate the rest of the company and glider troops. It was *then* that he learned to hate. A number of glider pilots had obviously been captured by the Germans. With their wrists tied behind their backs they had all been forced to kneel and were then shot in the back of the head.

"I shall never take another prisoner alive," swore the sergeant major, and Gerard learned later that it was so. He felt the same way, but it was later that he learned to hate not just the Germans but also a nation of their victims, and it was many years before he overcame his hatred.

One of Gerard's brothers had landed in Normandy and was on the ridge with the British forces that drove back the 21st Panzer Group and so ensured the success of the D-Day landing. It was on the ridge that his eldest brother was killed and that made him hate the German nation.

His second brother was killed in different circumstances. He was serving in the Eighth Army and had fought at the battle of El Alamein. The winning of this battle by the British had ensured that the Germans did not overrun Egypt and Palestine. Had they done so, all the Jewish settlers would have been murdered as their fellow Jews were being murdered in Germany.

His brother had been wounded in the battle and invalided to the UK. On recovery he had gone to serve in Palestine and helped to keep the peace between the Jewish settlers and the Arabs. Ironically the Jewish leader Chaim Weitzmann was a friend of Winston Churchill and Churchill had promised him that the Zionist dreams of a national Jewish homeland would be realized as soon as the war ended. Unfortunately, young men who had escaped from Germany and their conquered countries considered that they had the right to carry out a campaign of terror against the British, hoping to influence them. This backfired on the terrorists and although Chaim Weitzmann had some of the terrorists shot, the remnants continued their campaign of terror, killing British soldiers, civilians and Arabs.

Unfortunately, his second brother was killed after the UK had handed its mandate to the United Nations to arrange for a Jewish state. The terrorists with Begin at their head, continued their murderous campaign and sent letter-bombs to British politicians hoping to influence them. Like the IRA the Jewish terrorists did not realize that threats and murdering innocent people would not deter the British from seeking a fair solution to the problem. As it was, the United Nations, pushed by an American government strongly influenced by the Jewish lobby and with USA funds, made the final decision.

Gerard was so long recalling the events to himself that Eve felt uncomfortable. They had arrived at the church and she could see that his eyes were moist as he remembered the deaths of his brothers. She took his left hand in hers and, feeling full of compassion said, "Oh, I am sorry, I am afraid I upset you."

"Your question opened up memories of the past. I must admit that my experiences made me hate the German and Jewish peoples. I have grown past hatred since then and no longer condemn nations, peoples or ethnic groups for the stupidity and absolute moral decadence of certain individuals who conceitedly imagine, and deceive themselves, that they have the right to kill innocent people to achieve their questionable political ends. Not only are assassins morally wrong but also are their leaders. Terrorists are not freedom-fighters although they pretend to be. They are just cold-blooded murderers who care nothing for the people they murder. They don't give a damn for the anguish and suffering they inflict on the loved ones left behind to mourn.

"Those I find most sickening are the religious types. For example, the Catholics and Protestants who are supposed to believe in Jesus Christ; the Zionists who are supposed to believe in Jahweh and the Muslims who are supposed to believe in Allah—'Allah the most mighty and merciful' as stated in the Koran. Their priests and rabbis forgive the criminals and the mullahs encourage them in their evil acts. How people will twist religion to suit their own political ends, or perhaps just selfish ends, makes me despair for the human race."

Gerard paused and looked at Eve. "I'm sorry. I should not have said that. Although I was a soldier for a time because I had to be, I hate war and killing. I lost two fine brothers because of evil megalomaniacs who can never be adequately punished for their wicked crimes."

Eve continued to hold his hand and he squeezed hers and then withdrew his. "Time to go into the church, Eve. Please give my kind regards to Patrick Brendan. I'm off shopping and will pick you up at twelve." And with that Eve alighted from the car and walked to the church.

■ ❑ ■ ❑ ■

Gerard looked at his surroundings. The cafe was quite old-fashioned with its dark wooden pew-type seats which enabled four people to sit in pairs in virtual seclusion. He was thankful that the wooden sets were cushioned and comfortable to sit on. Edwardian drapery lined each side of the bay window with square-leaded lights that separated the room from the street. That window put him in mind of eighteenth century architecture and he realized that the building dated from that period. He had finished his shopping by eleven o'clock and decided to have morning coffee and relax before returning to the church to pick up Eve. He had been sitting there for a short while drinking tea and reading a copy of *The Times*.

The news was not very cheerful. The fighting was still going on in Bosnia; the Americans were threatening to invade Haiti to depose a tyrannical oligarchy; AIDS was spreading throughout Africa; the recession was still causing jobs to be lost; a Jewish terrorist had killed over forty innocent people in a mosque in Palestine.

"God, what a cheerful world," he said half out loud and heard a voice opposite say, "I beg pardon, are you addressing me?"

He suddenly realized that a woman had occupied the pew opposite him while he had been reading. "I am so sorry, I am afraid I was talking to myself. I did not realize you were there."

"Oh, that's all right. I sometimes talk to myself although I have heard that it is the first sign of insanity."

He noticed the twinkle in her eyes as she made the remark and he responded with a smile. She appeared to be a woman in late middle age but what was most noticeable was her rich chestnut hair which fell to her shoulders. He wondered if it was artificially colored for there was no sign of gray. She smiled at him again and he responded saying, "Well, if it is I no doubt qualified for a mental home years ago. But joking aside I was reading the news and only thinking that the world is in a hell of a mess."

He paused and then remarked, "But on reflection I suppose it always has been."

"You don't strike me as being a permanent pessimist," she volunteered.

"I'm not really. Life has a great deal to offer and I find it generally pleasurable and exciting. So I shall thank you for taking me out of my earlier line of thought."

At that point the waitress arrived at the table to take the woman's order. Gerard was amused to see her eyeing a tray of cream cakes. She suddenly realized he was looking at her and guessed what he was thinking. "You are wondering if I am going to be led into temptation?"

"It did cross my mind," he answered.

"Well, you are dead right I am," and she pointed to a milk chocolate eclair. "I will have that one and tea, please," she said to the waitress.

Gerard looked at her figure and noted that it had reached a Rubenesque stage. "There appears to be enough cholesterol in that éclair to float a battleship, but it does not appear to worry you."

She interpreted that remark as a compliment on her figure. "Oh, how very gallant of you." Gerard realized he had been misunderstood but decided to refrain from enlightening her for she seemed a little too informal for a stranger. "Do you always pay compliments to strange ladies?"

"Only if they deserve them," was his quick retort, and on that she warmed towards him. He glanced at his watch noting that it was half past eleven. He had finished his coffee and decided that although early he would go to the church and wait for Eve there, not wanting to get on too friendly terms with the stranger. "As a matter of fact I am on my way to meet a lovely young blonde."

She looked a little nonplused and suddenly laughed and said triumphantly, "Your daughter or granddaughter, of course."

But at that he shook his head and the woman looked a little disappointed. "It can't be your wife?"

He shook his head and she colored a little.

"No, not a relative and I can tell she is quite beautiful. So please excuse me and it was nice to meet you." The woman colored more so and tried to smile, and he left, glad to depart without getting involved. His memories of his late wife were too strong in his mind for him to want to risk close friendship with a member of the opposite sex and, in any case, it had not been two years since his wife had died of cancer and he preferred to be alone although he sorely missed her. Apart from that, since he had retired he had continued studying and researching into several subjects in which he had been interested for many years but had never had the time to devote fully to them. What with his interest in music, sailing and several research projects his time was fully occupied and he did not feel the need for feminine company.

A short walk brought Gerard to the church, and he entered to encounter Father Brendan who recognized him straight away. "Ah Gerard, welcome. I presume you have called to collect Eve. She is still with Father O'Connor. Perhaps you would like to come into the vestry?"

"Why yes, thank you, Patrick—and it is nice to meet you again."

Gerard followed Father Brendan along one of the aisles and through a side door into the vestry. "I hope I am not interrupting you on other more important matters?" Gerard asked on being motioned to a chair.

"No, not at all. I could do with a break for a few moments. Would you care for some refreshment?"

"No, thanks. I have just had coffee, but don't let me stop you."

Father Brendan smiled and shook his head. "I shall be having lunch with Father O'Connor soon."

Gerard looked at him and thought of the conversation between them and Richard a few nights earlier. "Oh, Patrick, I would like to apologize for Richard's somewhat emotional criticism of religion. I feel he put his viewpoint too forcibly."

"There is no need to apologize either on that score or on his behalf. I respect him for his argument and beliefs are sincere. I actually found his arguments and yours very interesting. Modern science appears to be getting closer to proving the existence of a creator than it has since before the discoveries of Isaac Newton. Richard was certainly not wanting to win debating points."

"Well, that is magnanimous of you. I regret he did upset Eve."

"Yes, Gerard, that did occur to me, but he was not responsible for her having overheard our conversation and I am sure had no intention of upsetting her. In any case, I do not think it had a lasting effect on her. She has reached a stage where her faith is able to overcome all doubts."

"Although I do not have her faith I am glad of it for her sake, for she needs a sheet anchor in life and her religion certainly provides one. Of course, most religions provide that for many people who find life not only difficult to cope with but otherwise pointless and incomprehensible."

"I agree, Gerard. Incidentally, I hope you will not mind my observing that you have a very sympathetic approach to religion and yet I gathered from our conversation the other day that you are agnostic."

"You are quite right. I am agnostic."

"You don't believe in God at all in any way, shape or form?"

"No. I did once and even considered the priesthood, especially after the war when I was stationed in Germany in the Army of Occupation. Thanks to our side getting the atomic bomb first I did not have to go to fight the Japs as well. Had it not been for the bomb I doubt I would have survived, but I digress. I had time to study comparative religion and also read Tom Paine's *The Age of Reason*. It all made me realize that no faith could be right.

"I have always wanted to find an answer to the ultimate questions such as: Was the universe created and if so, when? What purpose is there for the universe's existence? When will it end or will it exist forever? Is religion necessary for people to live in harmony together? What is mankind's place in nature and is there any part of us that still exists after death and do we have a soul? And, of course, the ultimate question: Is there a personal God and/or Creator of the universe? All these questions have been on my mind since I was a child and got an idea of the immensity of the cosmos."

"Have you found any of the answers, Gerard?"

"Actually I have. I first looked for them in religion to no avail. I then turned to philosophy and again got negative results. My next step was metaphysics but the guesses of metaphysics needed empirical substance. It was not until I turned to science, at first general science and then specializing in physics that I found the answers to most of the questions."

"You have not found them all?"

"Oh no, of course not. I have found very satisfactory answers regarding the origin and end of the universe; of the nature of mankind; the reasons for our existence; whether or not we have a soul and whether some part of us exist after death; and whether there is a personal God."

"You appear to have come a long way, Gerard, and have answers to the questions most thinking people ask. You did give me some inkling of your views the other night but if I am not being impertinent I would like to hear your evidence and logic behind the answers you have found."

Gerard inclined his head slightly and was about to speak when Father O'Connor entered the vestry. Both Patrick and Gerard stood up and Patrick said, "Gorry, I would like to introduce you to Dr. Gerard Rutherford," and turning towards Gerard said, "This is my good friend and colleague, Gorry O'Connor."

Both men shook hands and exchanged the pleasantries of introduction.

"Gerard has come to give Eve a lift home. I gather she is ready?" Then looking at his watch remarked, "I had no idea the time had flown so rapidly."

"Eve will be with us in a minute. I left her at prayer," Father O'Connor said and added, "I hope I am not interrupting you; you seemed to be deeply engrossed in your conversation."

Patrick smiled and replied, "Yes, we were but it was time for us to be interrupted." And then addressing Gerard added, "I would be most interested to hear your answers to the questions you put. I have my own, of course, but unless they can stand the light of honest open inquiry and comparison with other viewpoints then their validity is open to question."

"I would be pleased to have a talk with you again, Patrick. I shall be leaving Richard's home in ten days, so if you can spare say one lunch hour we can continue where we left off."

"Good, Gerard. Perhaps I can give you a ring and we can consult our diaries. Now I wonder what has happened to Eve?"

■ □ ■ □ ■

Eve lit the candle, placed it in the candlestick and then knelt before the statue of the Virgin Mary. She crossed herself and then placing her hands together, with fingers tightly clasped prayed fervently: "Oh Holy Mother of God, hear my prayer."

Although she had recovered from doubts about her faith a few days earlier, had attended confession and received dispensation, she still felt the need for forgiveness for having had the uncertainties in the first place. She prayed with deep concentration, so much so that she became completely oblivious of all else around her. "Forgive me, Holy Mother, for having doubts. I know Father O'Connor has given me dispensation and I humbly accept that with all my heart. I beseech you, Holy Mother, please favor me with the strength to no more doubt or question Our Savior's Holy Word."

And as Eve prayed so she felt an uplifting of her spirits so strongly that a feeling of ecstasy seemed to flow throughout her whole body. She experienced a mysterious contact and dialogue with the Virgin Mother herself. Her body seemed to lose all sensation and seemed as if it were floating and suspended from the ground. To her wonderment she clearly heard a gentle motherly voice saying to her, "Have no worries, Eve. You are forgiven and the Holy Spirit will always be with you and guard you from all doubts and the Love of God will keep you pure in His Sight."

Eve heard the words so clearly that she opened her eyes and looked at the beautiful face of the statue in front of her. She felt that the face was looking directly at her and that there were visible tears of compassion. She closed her eyes again and within herself was convinced that she had heard the voice, and fervently thanked the Holy Mother of God for speaking to her and for her vision.

After crossing herself, she rose from her prayers, genuflected towards the statue and walked down the aisle. She turned and this time bowed towards the altar, and then saw Father Brendan and Dr. Rutherford walking towards her. They noticed the flush of excitement on her face.

chapter twenty-two

Runt Parker entered the lobby of the hotel and looked around. His light gray suit and a red, blue and gray matching tie gave him a well-dressed appearance and his black suede shoes with thick soles and uppers increased his height by an inch and a half. Although not naturally vain, he always took pride in his appearance and had he paid more attention to his diction in what was the most snobbish of countries, he would have got much further on in life. It was fortunate for him that Eleanor came from Oregon which was one of the more egalitarian of the states in the USA. It had been pioneered by settlers who had to run the gauntlet of the Oregon Trail and that had served to weed out the weak and timid. The original pioneers had to work together to survive, as had the Indians they had conquered and deprived of their hunting grounds. This had resulted in a society where all were considered equals and this was well-demonstrated by the lack of formality in speech, manners and dress of the inhabitants.

She had little time for snobbery and judged people by their characters and reliability. Of course there was class distinction in the USA, and that mainly on the Eastern seaboard, but the class distinction there, as elsewhere, depended upon one's bank balance. Eleanor was from the professional classes and therefore enjoyed a comfortable income. She had considerable experience in life and was not easily hoodwinked, and perhaps her only weakness was that she was of the motherly type as Parker was to learn. He looked around and spotted Eleanor engaged in reading a magazine and sitting on an elegant couch in a small waiting area to the right of the entrance. Walking towards her he passed a large mirror strategically placed, to give the appearance of greater size to the lobby. He glanced in it as he passed and noted his unusually smart appearance and wondered at his being there.

It was not without some considerable reflection and misgivings that Parker had decided to meet Eleanor. In view of his experience with women early in his life, he had decided to keep clear of any attachment and the possible hurt that could come with it. Furthermore his mode of making money and his lifestyle was not conducive to being shared with anyone. Perhaps unconsciously, what had decided for him to respond to Eleanor's invitation was his gut feeling that time serving Boss and the Londinium Club was running out and meeting Eleanor was symbolic of a change in the course of his life.

He had not liked the look in Boss's eyes when he had revealed details of his interview with the police. Boss's face had remained expressionless but Parker had noticed a slight narrowing of Boss's eyelids. He knew that Boss was perfectly capable of removing any potential threat to his organization and his own security. But perhaps he was worrying unnecessarily. He would wait and see if he was to be charged; the crime was piddling but involvement of any of his minions with the law was not something Boss tolerated. Boss was against the law, but was very aware of the possibility of one of the few employees who knew he was behind the organization, spilling the beans inadvertently. Parker was one of the few and a trusted one, but Boss was aware that people could succumb to threats or even change in their loyalties.

But the unconscious desire to seek a change in his lifestyle was not the only thing that had influenced Parker's decision to meet Eleanor again. She had given him something no other woman had and that was a feeling of self-respect. She made him feel more than just a quick-witted con man and a stooge for a master criminal, a Jekyll and Hyde character who was feared but one did not cross. He liked Eleanor for her appearance which he found pleasing, and the way she showed friendship for him and appeared to trust him. He had got over the idea of robbing her and as he still had two days before he had to report back to the Londinium Club, felt it could not be better than to spend them in showing Eleanor some of the interesting sights that he had grown up with and knew so well.

Eleanor glanced up as Parker approached her and stood up, "Hi Bert, how nice of you to come." Her pleasant voice with its pronounced Oregonian accent brought back memories of the happy time he had spent in her company in Yorkshire. He started to put out his right hand to shake hands when she leaned forward and hugged him in the American fashion common among friends. He was a little surprised but being quick-witted hugged her in return.

"Luvverly ter see yer agin, Eleanor. 'Ow did yer travelin' go?"

"I've had a very interesting time but I shall tell you all about it at lunch time." Then she added, "I could have done with you as a guide."

"Well, if you like you can 'ave me as a guide in London. I know it like I know the palm of me 'and."

"Do you really have time?"

"Yus, as I told yer on the blower, I got a couple o' days orf an' I kin show yer lots of interestin' places."

"Oh, that's wonderful. In return I would like to take you to a musical. Have you seen *Miss Saigon*?"

"No," said Parker. "Never met 'er."

Eleanor laughed. "It's a musical show, silly."

"Yus I know. Jest pullin' yer leg."

"Would you like to see it with me?"

"Yus. Fanks very much," he replied with as much sincerity as he could muster. Musical shows did not appeal unduly to him, although he had enjoyed *My Fair Lady* mainly because of its Cockney connections. He had read Shaw's *Major Barbara* on which the musical was based and felt like correcting the author had he been alive, for Cockneys would not have said "Not bloody likely," but "Not bleedin' likely."

But it was an academic point to which he had given but fleeting attention. His main concern now was to take Eleanor to various places of interest in the city and he suggested they both have coffee or tea while they planned a tentative itinerary. Eleanor warmed to the idea and they both sat on the settee sipping their beverage while Parker made a list in a small notebook.

"I do want to see Buckingham Palace and have a tour inside. And we must not forget the Tower of London and the Crown Jewels, and Westminster Abbey, and Saint Paul's Cathedral and the Old London Bridge with the walkway at the top."

At that point Parker intervened. "I fink yer mean Tower Bridge, luv. The Old London bridge is in America."

"Oh, so it is." Then she paused and recommenced, "I would like to see Hampton Court Palace, the National Gallery, Trafalgar Square, Hyde Park and Hampstead Heath . . . "

"Woah, nah Eleanor. Yer will 'ave ter be 'ere fer weeks if yer want ter see all them fings an' 'ave time ter enjoy 'em. I'll tell yer wot. When do we see *Miss Saigon*?"

"Tomorrow afternoon."

"Good. In that case we kin start wiv Buckingham Palace an' I' tike yer on ter as many uvver fings as we kin git ter terday an' termorrer."

"That will be OK by me, Bert."

"Right, so let's git cracking," and at that they rose and walked towards the lobby.

"Is Buckingham Palace very far away, Bert?"

"Nah, we could walk there in abaht twenty-five minutes, but if we can git a cab it'll save time."

"I wonder if they can ring for one at the reception desk?"

"Yerse, no problem. There are plenty of cabs abaht an' minicabs, an' they all 'ave radio phones." And at that Parker walked up to the receptionist at the desk and requested her to phone for a cab.

She looked down her nose when she heard his broad Cockney accent and asked, "Are you staying here, sir?"

"Nah, luv, but this American lidy is."

On recognizing Eleanor Fletcher the receptionist smiled and promptly ordered a cab. "There is one on its way and it will be here in about a minute, Mrs. Fletcher," she said addressing Eleanor, after putting down the phone. Parker ignored her, took Eleanor by the arm and, escorting her to the door, said in the receptionist's hearing, "Bit of a toffee-nose that one." The receptionist blushed, realizing that she had made a mistake in addressing Eleanor and it was too late to rectify it.

They had hardly arrived at the pavement's edge outside the hotel when a black London taxicab drew up. The driver looked at them and asked, "Mrs. Fletcher?"

Eleanor nodded and Parker opened the door for her and, as she entered, said to the driver, "Buckingham Palace, mate."

To which the driver replied, "Goin' there fer elevenses wiv the Queen?"

"Nah, Princess Di'. 'Er Majesty is at Sandringham wiv the Dook." Then he entered the cab and closed the door, but before sitting down leaned forward and said, "Drive straight there, mate, an' if yer dunno 'ow to I'll tell yer." At that parting shot the driver acknowledged by nodding his head, put the cab into gear and entered the stream of traffic.

"What was that all about, Bert?" asked Eleanor.

"I jest told the cabbie ter drive by the shortest route ter the Palace. Some of these blokes tike a rahndabaht route ter put up the charge. This bloke knows I am on to the game so we won't be overcharged."

"You're a useful person to have around, Bert," Eleanor commented gratefully, at which Parker felt very pleased.

Despite the heaviness of the traffic they arrived at the Palace in just over ten minutes and Parker paid off the cabbie notwithstanding Eleanor's attempt to do so. Arriving at the west wing, they joined the queue of tourists waiting to enter on the tour. While moving along slowly, Parker told Eleanor that the reason why the Palace was now open to the public was because of the fire that had occurred at Windsor Castle. The Queen was trying to raise funds to pay for the cost of repairs.

"I read about that at home. It was big news at the time," Eleanor remarked.

"Do yer get a lot o' news from England in the USA?" queried Parker.

"Yeah, Bert. There has been a lot of publicity over the failure of the marriage of Prince Charles and Princess Diana. All very sad. As an Englishman what do you think of it?"

Parker paused before replying. He recalled his parents' loyalty to the royal family and also that of an uncle of his who had served in the Brigade of Guards in WWII. They all thought highly of King George VI and Queen Elizabeth, the present Queen Mother. They had personally seen them on numerous occasions walking among the people during the German blitz on the city which had lasted on and off almost the length of the war. He remembered his father telling him the King intended to fight should the Germans invade, and had a shooting range erected in the back garden of Buckingham Palace and practiced daily shooting with both revolver and machine gun.

Eleanor interrupted his reflections as they continued moving towards the ticket office. "Penny for your thoughts, Bert."

"Oh, sorry, Eleanor. I was jest finkin' 'ow popular the Royalty was in me parents' time and what a mess the present lot 'av made of it. The Queen does 'er job but 'er kids are like a lot o' spoilt yuppies. I fink they've turned the royal family inter a soap opera."

"That's true, one gets the impression that Britain's Windsors have pioneered a new category—tacky royalty. I must say that my friends in my home town think more of Princess Di' than of Prince Charles."

"I ain't surprised. Washing 'is dirty linen in public makes 'im look a bit of a wimp. We call 'im the Prince of Wails. In 'is job yer've eiver got ter do it properly despite personal feelin's or git aht."

"Do think he will become king?"

"Dunno. The Queen is still goin' strong an' could well carry on fer anuvver ten yers."

At that remark they reached the ticket office and Parker paid the entrance fee despite protestations from Eleanor. "The treats on me luv," he said.

"We should really go Dutch, Bert. I can't let you pay for everything,"

"Fink nuffink of it, Eleanor. You must be me guest in me 'ome tahn."

Eleanor looked at him and smiled as they entered the ornate building. "Then I shall pay for lunch, and no argument."

She became quite excited as she donned the headset of a guide tape. Walking through the first room into the quadrangle Parker heard her utter "wow" a number of times. She stood open-mouthed when they entered the Ambassadors' courtyard and saw the imposing Palace surrounding them. She tugged at his arm excitedly when they descended the Grand Staircase with its highly ornate gilded balustrade and white walls with their friezes edged in gilt with the colorful paintings of royalty. They stopped and gazed at a tall bronze statue of Perseus holding the head of Medusa before descending the staircase.

"Mustn't look at the head 'e's got in 'is 'and or you'll turn to stone," Parker remarked to Eleanor's amusement.

After descending the stairs on the plush red carpet, Eleanor's jaw dropped as her eyes caught the magnificent doors of the Guard Room and on entering the room she "wowed" so loudly that Parker laughed. She caught his expression and commented, "Did you know these doors were made by George Harrison and Samuel Parker, Bert? I wonder if Samuel Parker was a relative of yours?"

"Dunno abaht that. Could a bin." He paused and added, "Arter all, if we go back far enough we are all related—even ter the monkeys." He grinned, making Eleanor respond with a smile and an old-fashioned look.

"What a fabulous chandelier," she remarked looking at the splendid glass ornament hanging from the ceiling. Turning her gaze from it to the ceiling itself, she stood admiring the etched glass and gold squares in the half cupola above the semi-tambour wall, at each end of which stood a white marble column surmounted with gold Corinthian capitals.

"Isn't that a beautiful statue of Queen Victoria. I see it was made by John Gibson in 1847. That must have been in the early part of her reign."

"Well, she looks young enough at any rate," observed Parker who had been distracted from his thoughts wondering how much money all the splendor had cost. He noticed Eleanor looking at the other side of the Guardroom—she was admiring the statue of Prince Albert, the Prince Consort.

"My," she said, "He was a handsome man. German wasn't he?"

"Yus, that's right, but 'e wus one o' the gooduns. 'E 'elped the queen a lot so I've read an' froo 'is diplomacy even stopped us Brits gittin' involved in the American Revolution."

"You mean when he modified the ultimatum to the USA after a British ship was illegally boarded and two southern American citizens removed?"

"Yus, that was it."

Eleanor's eyes opened in surprised admiration. "Well, fancy you knowing that about American history, Bert." Parker laughed, "Don' fergit it is British 'istory, too."

From the Guard Room they entered the Green Drawing Room, the central apartment on the west side of the quadrangle. Eleanor looked around interestedly and noted the gilt chairs and sofas covered with green silk.

"How do you like the green wall panels and the matching furniture, Bert?"

"Dunno. Seems a bit cold ter me."

"Do you think the color is puce?"

"I suppose so but it looks more like puke ter me."

"Oh, Bert, it doesn't look that bad," Eleanor replied and they moved into the Throne Room.

"Wow! What a beautiful ceiling," exclaimed Eleanor, enraptured by the richness of its ornate decoration. "Stars, roses, crowns, coats of arms with leopards, harps, lions—why they are just magnificent. And look at those winged victories supporting the throne arch and the friezes depicting scenes from the War of the Roses, Bert."

"Yerse. Luvverly, Eleanor," he replied trying to muster enthusiasm. He had been wondering how much money it had cost the taxpayers to pay for the Palace and its contents. But Eleanor had not noticed the slight lack of enthusiasm in his voice and continued in her fascination and appreciation of the room.

"And look at those two beautiful thrones," she rattled on enthusiastically pointing in the direction of the dais with its rich burgundy drapery and canopy edged with a gold fringe. "I see one has E.R. and the other P. monogrammed in the order of the Garter, Bert."

"So it 'as. Must admit it's a funny place to wear a garter on the back of a chair. Still, there's no accountin' fer taste. Jest jokin' o' course. Y'know, they were the thrones used in the coronation ceremony in Westminster Abbey in 1953."

"Well, whaddaya know."

They took in the sight of the thrones used in earlier coronations and the gilded trophies displayed on either side of the throne canopy which are reputed to have come from King George IV palace, Carlton House.

Eleanor's fervency for all she saw continued throughout the tour, and some of her excitement rubbed off onto Parker and he became less cynical in his thoughts. They passed through the picture gallery with its priceless paintings on display, the east and west galleries and entered the dining room where Eleanor bubbled over with admiration and enthusiasm.

"I'd love to dine here, wouldn't you, Bert?"

Parker laughed. "Oh, yus. Fat chance o' that, though. Daht I' even git inter the kitchen let alone upstairs. Maybe if I win Ernie an' donate a million ter charity I mig git an invitashun."

"Ernie?"

"Yus. The state lottery, but I ain't 'ad any luck wiv it. I do much better wiv 'orses. The odds are much better."

From the dining room they entered the blue drawing room and Eleanor was fascinated by all she could see. She pointed excitedly to the twenty-four paired columns, painted to look like onyx and surmounted with more gilt Corinthian capitals. Then her attention was drawn to the ornate ceiling and, having feasted her eyes on its splendor, pointed to the sculptured reliefs of Shakespeare, Spencer and Milton, identifying them to Parker and asking him if she was correct.

"Yus, very good."

"Really, Bert, this is better than Hearst Castle," Eleanor enthused, "and it has real history behind it in addition," and she commented on each item that caught her eye. Her fervor had not diminished when they entered the music room which brought forth another "wow" from Eleanor which made Parker wonder if Americans knew any other expression of enthusiasm and delight.

The resplendent bowed room with its black imitation lapis lazuli columns, the contrasting red and gold draperies, and especially the ornate domed cupola ceiling brought several animated comments from Eleanor. The sparkling chandelier suspended from the center of the ceiling, the grand piano with its black and gold casing and unusual single column central leg were not lost on her. And her animation was obvious when with other tourists they walked through the white drawing room and the Bow Room, another splendid design of John Nash who was the favorite architect of King George IV and who had been responsible for most of the design work they had seen.

On leaving Buckingham Palace they were guided through the gardens on the way out to Grosvenor Gate and Grosvenor Place. There Eleanor turned to Parker saying, "Oh Bert, that was wonderful. My friends back home will be envious when I tell them and show them the guidebook. I must be careful not to lose it," and at that remark she slipped the book into a large carrier bag.

"Would yer like me ter carry that bag fer yer?"

"I can manage, Bert, but thanks all the same," and she gave him a smile that made him feel elated. "Where do we go now, Bert?"

"Well, if yer feel like a walk we kin go dahn the Mall, froo Admiralty Arch ter Trafalgar Square. The National Gallery is on the norf side, an' if yer feel like a bit o' grub we kin go ter Piccadilly."

"Oh, that would be lovely, Bert, but I must take a photo of one of the sentries outside the palace." And happily complying with Eleanor's wishes Parker led her to the front of the Palace where she obtained a clear view of one of the sentries standing in front of his sentry box. Eleanor adjusted the zoom lens in her camera to obtain a long-distance shot and pressed the button. As she lowered the camera she noticed a small squad of soldiers led by a sergeant marching towards the sentry. Her camera clicked again and again as she recorded the changing of the guard.

"What luck," she remarked to Bert and added, "I notice that the guardsmen have the buttons on their tunics arranged in pairs. Is there any reason for that?"

Bert recalled his uncle who had served in a guards regiment explain that the Footguards Regiments had buttons arranged in order of their founding and seniority.

"Ackshully the Grenadiers 'ave their buttons spaced evenly, the Coldstream's 'ave them arranged in pairs, the Scots Guards in frees, the Welsh Guards in fours an' the Irish Guards in fives."

"Well, waddaya know!"

She then pointed to a large monument with several stone figures and a central plinth surmounted by a winged statue made of gold and glinting in the sunlight. In answer to her query Parker informed her that it was a memorial to Queen Victoria and the statue was that of Victory. Eleanor eyed the tall statue and then looked at the figures below it.

"That must be Queen Victoria, Bert."

"Yus, that's right. 'Er in orl 'er glory. An' those bronze statues look pretty good, too."

"Why yeah, they are beautifully made. And aren't those tulips lovely?" Eleanor exclaimed, her gaze wandering to a large lawn with thousands of tulips arranged in beds. Then she allowed him to guide her across the road to the Mall where they walked, chatting cheerfully, along the pavement in brilliant sunshine to Admiralty Arch. The light gray pavement reflected back the sunlight and Eleanor donned sunglasses.

"Don't you have sunglasses, Bert?"

"Nah, the sun don't bovver me."

"You should protect your eyes in bright sunshine, Bert," Eleanor said in a motherly voice which he heard with mixed feelings. He had learned to be independent and had always made his own decisions which affected him personally. These thoughts, however, did not last long and rapidly evaporated as Eleanor's mood of excitement again became contagious when she saw a small detachment of The Household Cavalry riding along the road. Her camera was produced with a degree of rapidity that amused Parker and he smiled as she took several photographs in rapid succession of the smartly blue-uniformed young men riding easily on their chestnut horses, each holding the reins in his left hand while the right held a saber resting on his right shoulder. Their brightly polished steel breastplates and helmets adorned with brass emblems and a central spike from which hung a tassel of silver-white horsehair, sparkled in the sunshine.

"What handsome young men," Eleanor exclaimed rapturously, and Parker felt a little envious of their youth, height and masculine appearance.

They passed the odd group of tourists en route to the Palace which lay behind them, but so engrossed were they in their conversation that they hardly noticed them until they nearly bumped into a group of Japanese tourists. The broad road with its light traffic lay to their left and Eleanor's attention was brought to the park which lay beyond it.

"What a lovely park, Bert. Does it have a name?"

Bert drew his gaze across the road and nodded, "It's called Green Park and on our right is St. James Park."

Eleanor laughed. "You know, Bert, I have been looking in your direction and did not notice it. What beautifully kept lawns and all those trees make it look very cool and attractive."

Bert noticed the couples and small groups of tourists.

"Yus it is. An' there's a very nice lake in the middle of it, but if yer want ter see orl those uvver fings we don't 'ave time ter stop." He paused. "What would yer like ter do?"

"We'll carry on please, Bert. Maybe we can see a park tomorrow," she added and they continued along the mall, past the Admiralty Building and through the imposing Admiralty Arch. As they proceeded through, the vista of Trafalgar Square opened up before them.

"Wow!" exclaimed Eleanor as she took in the view. "Why it is just as the picture books show. There are the magnificent lions and on the top of that Grecian column it your great naval hero Lord Nelson. How high is the column, Bert?"

"Oh," Bert replied, having done his homework from a guidebook the night before, "The column is 185 feet in height an' 'is lordship 17 feet. Must say 'e is a bit bigger than 'e was in real life. 'E was abaht my 'ite."

"I read a lovely story about him and Lady Hamilton—it was called *Emma*." She sighed. "They must have been deeply in love for him to have flown in the face of convention and have her live with him at his home. Still I must admit I felt sorry for his wife when I read the story." Eleanor sighed again. "I suppose when you are deeply in love you will do anything to be with the person you love. That happened to your King Edward VIII, the duke of Windsor and Mrs. Simpson. Do you remember that, Bert?"

"I remember readin' abaht it; I warn't arahnd when it 'appened. Still, me mum tol' me abaht it an' 'er feelin's were wiv the dook. Me dad fought the opposite—still, none of 'em are arahnd nah so wot difference does it make in the long run I wonder?"

They walked along the pavement among a jostling crowd and, crossing two roads to the eastern side of the square, went directly over to the square itself. As they entered, a crowd of pigeons flew around them and landed at their feet. A man selling peanuts approached them.

"Peanuts ter feed the pigeons, lady?" he inquired.

Parker pursed his lips and gave him a hard look commenting, "Looks ter me as if they git fed enough. Why arf of em look too fat ter fly."

"Oh, don't be unkind, Bert," said Eleanor rebuking him. Then, addressing the vendor, accepted a small bag of shelled peanuts and gave him a coin saying, "Keep the change."

He thanked her and gave a triumphant look at Parker who said to Eleanor, "Nah yer've done it. Still make the most of it. If yer 'old a few in yer 'and they'll take 'em direct."

The birds recognized the action of opening a bag of nuts, an action they had no doubt been conditioned to with many a tourist, and flocked round both of them in droves. Eleanor stooped, holding a few nuts in her open palm and two pigeons braver than the rest ensured they disappeared quickly and then turned their heads with one eye looking up at her imploringly, expecting more. They were not disappointed and it did not take Eleanor long to part with the contents of the bag, the birds rushing and squabbling for the tidbits as each handful hit the paving stones.

"Well, that wos yer good deed fer the day, Eleanor. It'll keep our little fevvered friends 'appy." Eleanor laughed happily and they wandered across the square towards a group of people sitting on the flagstones beside one of the fountains and looking down and out.

On questioning Parker about them he stated they were probably unemployed and many just slept in the open at night.

"What, here in the square, Bert?"

"Nah. They doss mainly arahnd Charing Crawss Station. Yer don't see so many 'ere at this time o' the year. A lot of 'em go dahn ter the West Country mainly Cornwall. They all draw social security so beggin' ain't necessary."

"I have noticed a lot of street musicians, but we have beggars in Oregon. I have seen a number who have a written sign reading, 'Will work for food.' The depression has hit some people hard."

"Do they git social security?"

"Yeah, Bert, but I suppose a little extra is welcome. What annoys me is that people can enter the country and get all the benefits from the social security system without having had to work for them. This is very unfair on the taxpayers."

"Yus, I suppose it is. Anyway, there's the National Gallery in front of us. We can 'ave an hour in there before gettin' some nosh."

"Nosh? What's nosh, Bert?"

"Grub, tucker, y'know, food."

At that Eleanor complied and they crossed the square, taking advantage of the traffic light crossing to enter the imposing building of the National Gallery. Eleanor was intrigued by the check on her handbag and the carrier bag containing the booklet on Buckingham Palace that Bert carried for her. She had noted the security checks at the palace and was therefore not surprised. Parker had informed her that these arrangements were necessary in view of terrorist activities perpetrated occasionally by the IRA and Muslim fanatics.

She enjoyed the hour spent in the art galleries especially when she saw the works of Turner and Constable, and was particularly thrilled on seeing Constable's *The Haywain*, having a small copy at her home. The quiet and relaxed atmosphere in the galleries was welcome after the roar of the city's traffic and the hustle and bustle of pedestrians, many too much in a hurry to admire the many places of interest in the friendly metropolis.

They lunched happily together after their visit to the gallery and then walked a short way along the Strand before turning on their way to the embankment. Parker was feeling particularly happy; he had enjoyed the meal, the sun was shining and he was in the company of a woman who was not only genuinely interested in him but respected him. In a buoyant mood he began to sing: "Let's all go dahn the Strand, 'ave a banana, ain't life jest bleedin' grand."

"What was that you sang, Bert?" interrupted Eleanor, uncertain if she had misheard amidst the noise of the traffic. Parker suddenly wondered if Eleanor had been offended by the use of the word "bleeding" and had no desire to shock her as he often tried to do unsuccessfully to the hostesses of the Londinium Club. He had early realized that the crude and risqué stories he often reveled in at the Club were not for Eleanor.

He quickly replied, "I was jest singing an old music hall song, 'Let's all go down the Strand' and some of the words are 'ain't life jest bloomin grand.'"

Eleanor laughed and looked at him, wondering if she should tell him that she had heard the original word sufficiently, then decided not to. It was obvious that he considered her feelings and she felt flattered. Not that she was a prude. She had heard far worse and although she did not use expletives, heard more than enough through the media not to be shocked by anything. Instead she asked, "Why is this street called the 'Strand,' Bert? The strand is a beach beside water or the sea."

Bert was once more delighted to show off his knowledge and replied, "This used ter be on the side of the river. The land was reclaimed but the name stayed. The side of the river is now the Embankment, an' there it is in front of us."

They had turned from the Strand into Craven Street and, as they progressed alongside Charing Cross Station, the river and Embankment came into view.

"Oh, Bert. Gee. The river looks more wonderful than the picture books show."

They crossed the road at the traffic lights and stood beside the low stone wall of the Victoria Embankment. Parker noted that the time must be about half an hour after high tide for the river traffic was moving faster towards the bridge to their left than vessels emerging. Eleanor looked across to the Riverside Walk admiring the stone embankment there and the two rows of trees lining each side of the esplanade. Her gaze wandered upstream to the large buildings of London County Hall, an imposing stone edifice once the power center of greater London—now its authority emasculated by the greater independence of its boroughs.

Eleanor turned her head further upstream and suddenly pointed excitedly, "Look, Bert, there's Big Ben!"

"Gorblimey, so it is, luv. It ain't run away arter all."

For his banter Eleanor's response was to give him a token shove, at which he diaphanously pretended to show pain and which resulted in a peal of laughter from her. But his acting did not last long. His faced creased into a broad smile and he blithely said, "Let's go an' 'ave a closer look, luv." And at that they both walked along the

Embankment towards the Palace of Westminster, like a pair of excited schoolchildren on an outing.

As they progressed along the pavement Parker explained that Big Ben was the name of the Bell at the top of the Clock Tower, and it had been named after Sir Benjamin Hall, the Commissioner for Works. "That bell weighs fourteen tons an' even 'as a four-foot crack in it."

Eleanor's rapt attention to Parker's discourse made him feel he was in his element and this gave him greater pleasure than he had experienced for years. He racked his brains for all the information he could recall about the Palace, and expounded to Eleanor that it was the Mother of Parliaments containing within its walls the House of Commons and the House of Lords; that there was a gilded throne for the Queen in the House of Lords which she used at the State Opening of Parliament every November.

"Quite a posh do that is, Eleanor. Lots of pageantry an' the locals an' tourists love it."

"My that is interesting, Bert. I suppose that your House of Commons and House of Lords is similar to our House of Representatives and Senate House in America."

"Yus, I fink it is, but your president an' our prime minister are elected in different ways. The prime minister is chosen by the party in power."

"Yes, so I have read, Bert. Our president is elected by the people which I think is a better system, but a term of four years is too short."

"Why?"

"Because during the second half of the term the president is preparing for the next election. And another thing, the practice of putting into office only party members leaves much to be desired. Still, we won't talk politics, it's bad enough listening to politics and politicians in any country." Parker agreed there, sharing the common view in Britain that politicians were the lowest form of animal life. Had he been an American he would have added that lawyers had precedence as Eleanor informed him later.

They ascended the broad stone steps leading from the Embankment to Westminster Bridge at Bridge Street and looked up at Big Ben as its powerful bells chimed three o'clock. Eleanor instinctively raised her camcorder to capture the magic moment and Bert smiled inwardly at her excitement. He conducted her to Parliament Square from which vantage point she was able to admire the greater view of the Palace with it majestic yet restrained Gothic style. It drew admiring remarks from her, so much so that it was not until Bert brought her attention to another imposing building that she realized it was one she also wanted to see.

"Westminster Abbey, how wonderful. Is this where the Kings and Queens are crowned?" Bert nodded and conducted her across the square and to the entrance into the Abbey. He had not been inside a place of worship for many years. His parents had taken him to visit the Abbey and St. Paul's Cathedral in his teens but he had not appreciated the ambiance. His main interest then had been to see how far a paper dart would fly when launched from the pulpit into which, unseen, he had managed to climb.

With other visitors, tourists and a few faithful, they entered the ancient Abbey welcoming the soothing silence in contrast to the turmoil of the traffic outside. On glancing around the walls, Eleanor was impressed by the hallowed atmosphere—so much so that she went to a pew and knelt to pray. Parker followed her example in walking to a pew, but without her sanctity; his sole object was to sit down and rest his feet after all the walking he had done so far that day. He had no time for prayer and with his mode of living, had he given it thought, it was doubtful if divine assistance would have been forthcoming had he asked for it.

Her devotions completed, Eleanor sat back from her precatory position and smiled at Parker. This he returned warmly and then they rose simultaneously from the pew and, at her suggestion, walked along the aisles admiring the stained glass windows, the 17th century choir screen containing a monument to Isaac Newton, the tall stone supports rising to the vaulted roof, and, in the King's chapel, the royal tomb with effigies of Henry VII and Elizabeth of York guarded by stone lions and angels.

Eleanor felt she had been transported back through the centuries. She learned that the Abbey had been consecrated in 1065 and every monarch since William the Conqueror in 1066 had been crowned there except for two: Edward V who was murdered in the Tower of London and Edward VIII who abdicated in 1936. She admired the shrine of Edward the Confessor, a king who had been made a saint in 1161. She was particularly impressed by the tomb of Queen Elizabeth I, about whom she had read so much. The massive stone canopy supported by ten black columns rested above the stone likeness of the virgin queen.

If Parker began to tire of the Abbey he did not show it, but he was relieved when Eleanor had her fill. He suggested that they take a river bus downstream and visit the Tower of London. Eleanor happily complied with his suggestion and enjoyed both the river trip and the visit as much, if not more than her visit to the Abbey. The red

Tudor costumes of the Beefeaters and the guardians of the tower brought forth the remarks of "quaint" and "cute."

They joined the throng of tourists all gazing at the various aspects of the castle and paused at the Traitors' Gate. Parker explained to Eleanor that it was through this gate that traitors and prisoners were often brought by boat from the river. "I bin told that anyone who came in this way never got aht alive. Most of 'em 'ad their 'eads chopped orf."

"How horrible. There must be a lot of ghosts here," Eleanor said feelingly.

The White Tower, so named when it was whitewashed in 1241, is a "must" for visiting. Eleanor learned that it was built by William the Conqueror to overawe the citizens of London, although they had opined and shown their loyalty to the Norman monarch. It impressed Eleanor when she looked up and saw the frowning battlements towering above them. They joined the queue for seeing the Crown Jewels. Eleanor viewed them with an eye to their beauty and magnificence; Parker viewed them with a mind containing acquisitive ideas and a strong desire of temporary ownership—possession long enough to realize their value and live the rest of his life in luxury. Although Eleanor communicated her thoughts to him he wisely did not reciprocate. And it was later in the evening at dinner that he again kept certain thoughts to himself. They had chosen an inexpensive restaurant and among the topics that came under discussion was the fact that Parker had never married and lived alone.

"You should have someone to look after you, Bert. It is not good to live alone."

"Well, yer told me that you live alone."

"That's different, Bert. I have been married and lost my husband eighteen months ago. I still have memories of him and when you lose a partner you really care for it takes time to adjust."

"Well, I've managed pretty well so far."

"Yeah, I suppose you have, but you really ought to have a nice woman to look after you."

"I can look arter meself, Eleanor," Parker had replied with feeling. Although he liked Eleanor, enjoyed her company and was flattered that any woman would seriously take an interest in him, he did not relish his life being shared with the possibility of it again being dominated by a woman. He shuddered inwardly at the thought but made a point of not sharing it with Eleanor. Instead he said, "Nice of yer ter fink o' me welfare, but I really kin take care o' meself," and promptly changed the subject by discussing when they would meet the following day. They decided he would come to the hotel as before at eight in the morning having caught the tube train.

They rode back to her hotel on the top of a double-decker bus.

Eleanor enjoyed that experience and, to Parker's surprise, when he asked her if she had ridden on one before replied, "Yes."

"I fort yer nevver bin in England before."

"No, this is my first visit."

"But yer don't 'ave double-decker buses in Yankeeland."

"You are quite right," Eleanor replied, laughing at his term for the USA. "There are double-decker buses in Victoria, on Vancouver Island in Canada. It is just across the Juan da Fuca Straight north of Washington, which is the state next to Oregon. I have been on one of these buses there. You know in Victoria they are more British than the British."

"Oh, yus. Do they speak Cockney?"

"No, the diction is Canadian, but it is nearer to the English in dialect than the American one hears in Oregon."

"Well, if they don't speak Cockney then they ain't British."

Parker escorted Eleanor to the hotel and again felt pleased when she gave him a hug on saying good-bye. He felt he was walking on air as he made his way to the underground to get a train and connection back to his apartment. As the train clattered its way through the tunnel he reviewed the day he had spent with Eleanor and it reminded him of when he had first met her in Yorkshire. She certainly made him feel good and he knew he had not enjoyed a day so much since he had won a large bet at the race track. But her remark about having a woman to look after him suddenly intruded into his pleasant pensiveness and made him feel uncomfortable.

Sod it, I don't need a woman ter look arter me, he told himself. And the following day was to unexpectedly verify this statement to both of them.

■ ❑ ■ ❑ ■

Eve hummed to herself as she prepared for bed. She was once again at the zenith of bliss. She had once read that Eden was another name for happiness and laughed out loud when she realized how aptly her surname fitted her present mood. It had been a wonderful evening; there had been interesting conversation, an excellent meal which she had helped to prepare, joyful music and Sean had shaken off his depression. It was not surprising that she felt so buoyant and that the world seemed a wonderful place in which to live.

She glanced in the mirror as she dried her hair, having just emerged from a refreshing shower. She did not have eyes for her flawless beauty, but for the radiance that seemed to shine from her very being. She knew that before getting into bed she would pray to the Virgin Mary and thank her for the wonderful revelation that had finally removed any doubts that her mind had harbored.

Of course she had heard some disturbing ideas, inadvertently put forward by Richard to Rachel, who had agreed with them. How had that conversation arisen she wondered? And then recalled its origin. There had been news that more Palestinians had been killed by Israeli soldiers and there had been another bombing of a Jewish Embassy. These events had resulted from the massacre of over forty Muslims in a Mosque by a deranged American Zionist.

There was no doubt there were fanatics on both sides who were determined to upset the peace process started by Yasser Arafat and the Israeli Prime Minister Yitzhak Rabin. The subject had been innocently raised by the Indian friend Pankash who had been listening to the radio en route to Bracken. Someone had asked why people with different religions could not live in peace and this had started Richard off. That thought made Eve smile.

She remembered being introduced to Nurse Mona who, during the course of conversation had said, "The trouble with Richard is that if you ask him a question you are liable to get a lecture instead of a straight simple answer." And Eve had discovered that for herself. But in her present euphoric mood she made allowances for this defect in his character. She knew it did not arise from a desire to show off his knowledge, substantial though it was, but because part of his job was to lecture and teach. All his staff and students benefited considerably from his desire to impart as much knowledge in their various fields as possible.

Over and above his normal routine, despite its demands, he held special classes for the ophthalmologists, optometrists, housemen, nurses, orthoptists and dispensing opticians in his department. This resulted in good team spirit, enthusiasm and very efficient service to the patients. Unfortunately it also resulted in his lecturing at home which, coupled with Dawn being a teacher, resulted in the children having considerable knowledge beyond their years. Unfortunately another outcome was that unless one was interested in the subject he could be a crashing bore. There were also occasions when he imparted information and opinions that listeners did not want to hear.

On the topic of the problem between Israel and Palestine being brought up, Rachel had said that if the Israelis and Arabs had only accepted partition when the British had offered it to them in 1937 the present troubles would not exist. Richard did not agree, pointing out that after the holocaust in Germany and the tradition of the "Promised Land," the Jewish refugees would invade Palestine anyway as they were sick of the pogroms in Europe.

"And have you ever thought of why these pogroms occurred throughout history, Richard?" Richard had but Dawn was looking at him and he decided to put the ball in Rachel's court.

"You tell me," he had said, knowing that, although a Jewess, Rachel was not orthodox and had similar views to his on religion.

"If strangers enter a foreign country and conform to the rules of the country and adopt the customs of the country then they become accepted."

"Providing there is available space," Richard interjected.

Rachel nodded. "Yes, the space makes all the difference, and that is why various different religious and ethnic groups can live in the USA in relative harmony. But put the different ethnic and religious groups close together and trouble is bound to occur."

Gerard joined in the conversation at this point saying, "Of course—the Territorial Imperative."

"What's that?" asked Pankash.

"It is a theory by Richard Ardrey that many living organisms on this planet are territorial in that they need a certain amount of space in which to live and acquire food. Organisms will fight for their own space or territory if they think it is threatened. What is more, in many animals the instinct is so great that even if an intruder is physically stronger they will often be driven out by a weaker defender."

"How do nomads fit in there, Grandpa?" asked Jean who had been taking the conversation all in. Gerard smiled, proud of the fact that there was always sufficient evidence that his grandchildren were bright.

"A very good question, Jean. Actually, nomadic tribes follow the pastures as the seasons change, and so use a fixed territory although it is very large. They cannot tolerate other tribes using their territory if the grazing lands become overcropped, so the Territorial Imperative still applies."

"You can't squeeze quarts into pint pots, Jean," added Dawn.

"Quite right," Rachel once again entered the conversation. "There is not enough room for all the Jewish immigrants in Israel and that is why they keep developing new settlements. That is what the Palestinian Arabs don't like. The trouble is that the Zionist idea that Israel must offer room for any Jewish immigrant who wants to go there is impracticable."

"You tell that to the Zionists, Rachel." Dawn looked sharply at Richard, guessing what was coming, but he had been looking in Rachel's direction and did not catch her warning glance.

"You know I think it is very funny. The main terrorists in the West are bound up with religion. The Catholic Irish fight the Protestants, both incidentally Christians; the Muslims fight the Jews, both believers in the same God."

"I am not so sure that they do have the same God," Rachel interrupted. "The Jewish God is Jahweh, the tribal God of the Hebrew Tribes. The Muslim God, Allah, was originally the God of the Arab Tribes. And the Christian God is a Trinity which also embodies Jahweh."

"Well, they all claim that they have the same God and that He is on their side. And, what is more, they all claim that He revealed himself to them despite the fact that revelation is more easily and accurately accounted for by chemical changes in the brain. I think all the prophets and even Christ underwent what is technically known as a psychological fugue and unwittingly deluded themselves and others."

"Would anyone like coffee before we go into the music room?" asked Dawn who did not like the way the conversation was going. Gerard had immediately said yes, realizing that the topic was not likely to be of any comfort to Eve nor to Sean, and Richard took the hint.

Eve and Sean, for that matter, had not paid much attention the trend in the conversation—they were enjoying too much holding each other's hands under the table. Apart from that, Eve's "revelation" had given her the feeling that anything adverse or contradictory to her religion despite its logic, was not important. What was important was her belief, her love for Sean and the prospect of her being fully admitted into the Church and marrying him.

She and Sean had also sat together holding hands in the music room and Eve had particularly enjoyed that. With Rachel playing the violin, Dawn the piano and Gerard the cello they had listened to a superb performance of Mendelssohn's first piano trio. The cheerful melodies and rhythms interspersed with some lyrically beautiful passages had been a delight to all. Eve's happiness was enhanced by her good fortune in having been introduced to good music in contrast to the drivel that emanated from the so-called "Pop" music world. She realized that Pop listeners were being cheated and conned by music promoters who took full advantage of the human weakness for simplistic rhythm, and anti-social and sexual connotations.

It was not surprising that the young were the target for Pop propaganda.

Holding Sean's hand still made her body tingle, and she felt especially thrilled when a beautiful melodic passage occurred and he gave her hand an extra squeeze. She had been worried about him when he returned from Ireland. Things had not gone well and only one of his stepbrothers had shown remorse and apparently not much at that. Sean had been more upset by the fact that Sinn Fein and the IRA had turned down the peace initiative. Fortunately their negative decision received such a bad reception from all the political parties including the other republicans, that they had reversed their decision. The populace at the grassroots were sick of the unnecessary bloodshed and it was realized that change had to come about. This news cheered Sean immensely and Eve rejoiced in his release from his depression.

Eve knelt beside her bed and prayed in gratitude for her happiness and felt that this must feel what it is like to be in heaven.

■ ❏ ■ ❏ ■

It was later during the second day of escorting Eleanor around London that Parker revealed to her that he was capable of looking after himself. They had taken a river bus to Hampton Court in the morning and Eleanor enjoyed the majesty of the palace and grounds although they did not stay long as they had to get back to attend the theatre. She also enjoyed the musical *Miss Saigon* and realized that it was an updated version of *Madame Butterfly* but in somewhat poor taste as far as she was concerned. Rightly or wrongly she felt that it implied that all young men in the services sought after prostitutes and this she felt could not possibly be true. Parker sat through it out of consideration for Eleanor. He knew what prostitution really involved and he felt cynical about it being glamorized on stage. He knew that most prostitutes lived on a knife edge and were subject to abuse and danger, both physical and mental. If anything, the musical brought feelings of disquiet about his occupation and he began to wonder how much longer he would be serving Boss.

They had left the theatre and after dinner, walked into a side street in order to take a shortcut when a black man and a white woman in their early twenties came running towards them. Eleanor was not immediately aware of danger until the woman ran straight towards her and made a grab for her handbag. Parker guessed what was coming and waited until the man was close with a raised fist aimed at Parker's face. As the blow fell Parker nimbly stepped to one side, grabbed the man's extended arm by the wrist and simultaneously stuck his right foot out tripping him up. The assailant hit the ground and was on his way to getting up when Parker kicked him hard in the crotch from behind then leapt into the air and jumped down with all his possible force on the attacker's head, knocking him unconscious.

Parker then turned his attention to the woman who was pulling on Eleanor's handbag. He did not hesitate but punched her in the solar plexus and, as she doubled forward, struck her on the nose, breaking it with a loud crunch which made Eleanor wince. The woman screamed, fell to her knees and loosened her hold on the bag, enabling Eleanor to retrieve it.

"Not supposed ter 'it a lidy, but you ain't no lidy," Parker remarked, and, taking Eleanor by the arm said, "Come on, luv, time ter go. Let 'em stew in their own juice." And at that they had both left the scene of the intended crime and Parker sought out a cafe to give Eleanor a cup of tea to recover from the shock. She had certainly been shaken but soon recovered in the comparative safety and relaxed atmosphere of the cafe. Her first reaction was to ask Bert if they should call the police.

"Nah. Not much point. We'd bofe 'ave a lot o' trouble an' they would probably be put on probation. Wot's more," he added, warming up to the subject, "They would find some crooked lawyer or do-gooder ter sue me fer assault in usin' more force than woz necessary and probably racial discrimination at the same time."

Eleanor smiled at that remark but knowing how that was often a real legal scenario in the USA did not dispute it. Her main feeling which intruded strongly into her thoughts was that of gratitude to Parker. She looked at him in a new light and that included amazement and wonder at his skill in handling the situation. "I don't know how to thank you, Bert. You saved me from being harmed and robbed and I'll never be able to repay you for that." Eleanor felt at a loss for words and then gave him a look that made him feel ten feet tall.

"I'd no idea you could fight like that. The man was so much bigger and heavier than you, and you were so quick he was not a match for you. I think you are wonderful." Then she leaned forward and kissed him.

His face lit up into a broad smile increasing the wrinkles around his eyes. "Quick, did yer say. Well, me friends call me Twinkle Toes."

Eleanor grasped his right hand in both of hers, looking at him in admiration. "I don't know what to say, Bert." He folded his other hand over hers and said with a chuckle, "Well, yer don't 'ave ter tell me I need a woman ter look arter me. As yer kin see, I kin look arter meself."

Bert began to feel that the relationship was getting dangerously intimate. Eleanor made him feel good but his old fears of a close relationship with a member of the opposite sex were too deep to be dismissed lightly. He decided to change the subject and voice other concerns at the same time.

"You told me yer got nearly anuvver week in England before yer go back across the Pond?"

Eleanor nodded. "Yes, I planned to visit Windsor Castle, Oxford, Stratford-on-Avon, Cambridge and Bath. Now I am wondering if I should. Is there any chance of you coming with me?"

Bert shook his head. "Nah, I've 'ad me time orf. Wot yer must do is ter go wiv coach parties. There's a travel agency near yer 'otel and yer kin see em first fing in the mornin." Then he added, "As fer goin' ter Barf, use the intercity train an' use taxis in London. The chances of gittin' mugged agin ain't 'igh. There ain't no really safe cities these days."

Eleanor reflected on the advice and felt reassured. She had been to New York and Los Angeles several times and knew that they were crime-ridden cities. What made her feel better was that in Britain people were not legally allowed to carry firearms or any implement that could be used as a weapon. She was unaware that Parker had a cut-throat razor carefully concealed on his person but it only made an appearance as a last resort.

Bert settled the bill and escorted Eleanor back to her hotel. At the desk Eleanor collected her room key from the receptionist on duty, who raised her eyebrows when she saw them both enter the lift. Bert looked back and caught her expression just as the doors closed. That look brought back memories of early rejection by a woman he had deeply cared for, and they lingered with him as they left the lift and walked along the corridor to her room. Eleanor opened the door and, once inside, placed her handbag on the dressing table, turned to Parker and flinging her arms around him kissed him on the lips.

"Oh, Bert," she said, "How can I thank you?"

He felt a surge of panic as his fears of deep involvement came to the fore.

How can I get out of this? he thought to himself.

He kissed her in return and then stepped back. "You've orlready fanked me by givin' me a wonderful couple o' days. I shan't fergit it, luv." He paused and, squeezing both of her hands, said, "An' nah I gotter go. Give me a ring before yer go back. I want ter make sure yer are safe."

He walked towards the door and opened it quickly before Eleanor could say more. "Enjoy the rest of yer 'oliday—an' take care." And at that he closed the door quietly behind him. After descending in the lift he passed the receptionist at the desk who looked surprised to see him so soon, and looking her straight in the eye remarked, "G'night, toffee-nose. Evil ter those who evil fink." Her face reddened as she realized he had read her mind.

■ ◻ ■ ◻ ■

Parker whistled as he waited for the kettle to boil. He was in good spirits; seldom had he enjoyed a day more. Back in his apartment he had picked up a copy of the *Sporting News* and wondered what fixtures would show promise. Poring over the items he was surprised to hear the front doorbell ring. He looked up at the clock on the mantelshelf and noted the time, a quarter to eleven.

"I wonder 'oo the devil that is at this time o' night." The bell rang again sounding a degree of urgency.

He walked towards his apartment door and picked up a loaded stick and then opened his door and went into the hall. Walking across the hallway he ensured that the security chain was in position. The bell rang again as he opened the front door the small amount permitted by the security chain. The figure of a big man stood there. Parker looked at him and his jaw dropped in surprise as he recognized him. "Wot the 'ell!" he exclaimed.

chapter twenty-three

Boss was feeling annoyed. It was two weeks since the IRA and Sinn Fein had turned down the Peace Initiative, but now there had been a complete reversal of the decision. This was just what he and the two other members of his cell did not want. He had angrily phoned the HQ and was told that all operations were now to be suspended indefinitely. The leaders felt that the aims of the Sinn Fein could now be achieved politically and no more bloodshed was necessary. He was seriously considering joining the so-called "National Liberation Army," a group of Irish terrorists more fanatical and to the left of the IRA. This group had not agreed to the Peace Initiative, and the Eirean or Southern Irish Government was seeking members out. There were two other members of his cell who benefited from the activities of the Londinium Club who shared his views, and he also wondered if Rory and Bernadette had learned of the change of plan. They too enjoyed the perks of the Club and were not likely to throw them away in a hurry; or were they? On further reflection they were not the sort to disobey the leaders and that could prove difficult.

He had planned for them to get rid of Eve just after they landed. He considered going after her himself prior to the landing of the two terrorists, but any activity in Essex might jeopardize the success of the *Erinyes* delivering the next shipment of drugs and explosives as arranged. It was too late to make other arrangements. Although they had a code word for cancellation, replanning also involved the distribution side and everything there was set up.

There were a few days before *Erinyes* arrived and this would give him time to go to Ireland to see if he could persuade the leaders to recommence terrorist activities. Alternatively there were other extremist contacts there who might consider doing so for an inducement.

■ □ ■ □ ■

To Bounce's credit, he always obeyed orders as far as he could comprehend them. He had received definite instructions to follow Caria's car and avoid being seen en route. That he succeeded was due mainly to his having accompanied Parker on such expeditions and learning from a master the art of shadowing. That he managed to follow her all the way to the public house in Cogglesham bordered on the miraculous, for the chances of him doing anything relatively complex by himself were as slim as winning the British and American lotteries simultaneously. Unfortunately, two miracles seldom occur in succession, for had he shown some discretion he might have seen the person Caria met without being detected. It was that part of his assignment that required a degree of skill which he did not possess. He had shown some initiative by waiting a few minutes before entering the pub and this turned out to be his undoing.

On entering, Caria had been greeted by Barney and then, after an embrace, they sat at a table at which he had been waiting. In the interim he had been chatting with a middle-aged couple at an adjacent table. Barney introduced Caria to the couple and she sat down and chatted with them while Barney went to the bar to order drinks.

When he made his way through the door Bounce saw Caria talking to the middle-aged man and immediately assumed he was the person she was meeting. He recalled his instructions to find out who she met and felt the moment had arrived, so he made his way to her table and said, "Who's this bloke?"

Caria was startled to see Bounce but quickly recovered and gave him a venomous look. "Who the 'ell d'yer fink yer are followin' me?"

Bounce ignored her question and, grabbing her by the wrist, repeated his question.

At that point Barney looked up in their direction, holding a pint of best bitter in one hand and a gin and tonic in the other. The sight of a tough-looking man grabbing Caria by the wrist did not please him, to put it mildly. He promptly returned the drinks to the bar counter saying to the barman, "Hold those for me, Tom," and went over to Caria who had managed to pull her wrist away from Bounce and was rubbing it. She had a few tears in her eyes, not from pain or fear but sheer anger at a member of the Club having found out her trysting place.

Without hesitation Barney walked over and, grabbing Bounce by the wrist said, "Did 'e 'urt 'ee Caria?" She nodded.

Bounce looked round to see who was interfering with his amateur detective work. "Piddle orf, mate," he said, addressing Barney.

"No, you," was Barney's reply, hoping to avoid a fight in public. However, Bounce was not in the habit of having anyone tell him to desist in obeying his orders as he interpreted them, and he swung a blow at Barney. What had always given Bounce the edge on anyone he mixed it with was his incredible strength and stamina. Unfortunately, Barney possessed two factors which weighed in his favor: his superb physical fitness and his being a black belt in both judo and karate. He caught Bounce by the wrist with his right hand and with his left pushed Bounce's elbow up, then deftly twisted Bounce's arm behind his back.

Bounce made the mistake of opening his hand and Barney immediately corrected his handhold and with thumb and fingers so twisted Bounce's wrist that he could not get out of the handlock. Effectively keeping his hold with his right hand, Barney grabbed Bounce by the seat of his trousers and, pulling tight, gave Bounce an exquisite pain in the gonads which temporarily deprived him of his strength. With that posture achieved, Barney frog-marched Bounce out of the pub to the delight and astonishment of onlookers. Technically the action is known as "the bum's rush" and it did not meet with Bounce's approval, especially as he was unceremoniously thrown into the gutter by his tormentor.

Had Bounce possessed more intelligence than he did, he would have recognized a master of the martial arts and suppressed his desire for revenge. Unfortunately, the necessary gray cells were lacking and he immediately rose to his feet and again swung a blow at Barney who was standing at the ready anticipating something of the sort. By this time a few sightseers had gathered, anticipating an entertaining scrap. And in this they were not disappointed.

At first Barney boxed Bounce very skillfully, landing blow after blow on Bounce's face and body. He soon realized that after several good punches in Bounce's solar plexus his opponent possessed a rare degree of stamina. It was his speed and footwork in keeping out of the way of all Bounce's swings that enabled him to avoid damage to himself. While sparring he decided the only way to defeat Bounce, short of giving him an illegal karate kick on a knee or to break one of his legs, was to knock him silly with blows on the head, but this might take up too much time with fist-fighting and anyway, Barney did not want to damage his fists unnecessarily.

So his strategy was to give Bounce a number of blows on his eyes in order to render his vision unreliable and then he again resorted to judo and used Bounce's own weight and momentum to hit the ground with his head. The onlookers cheered when Bounce first went flying over Barney's shoulders, but their cheering countenances changed to pained winces when they heard the sickening thud of Bounce biting the dust. It took four such demonstrations of the art of judo before Bounce was knocked out, unable to rise and effectively dead to the world.

By that time the entire human content of the pub, including the landlord plus all passersby, had witnessed the fight of a lifetime and when Bounce failed to rise they gave Barney a cheer which, to his credit, he did not relish. He was more concerned that the damage done to Bounce was not fatal and his immediate reaction to Bounce's immobility was to check his pulse. Relieved that Bounce had not shuffled off his mortal coil, his next action was to return to the pub and ask the landlord to phone for an ambulance.

It said much in favor of the National Health Service that within twenty minutes of sending the request, an ambulance arrived and Bounce was gently placed on a stretcher and soon whisked away to the casualty ward of the local hospital. The tenderness with which he was handled contrasted somewhat markedly with the handling by Barney, and it was late in the evening before he had recovered enough to leave and find his way back to his car. Completely shattered by his defeat he drove back in the direction of the Club and his only thought was to see Parker and explain his failed mission to him. And so Parker found himself looking at the bandaged and battered visage of Bounce as the time approached midnight.

"Wot the devil," said Parker, on seeing the sorry sight of Bounce when he opened the front door of his apartment.

"I bin beat," Bounce managed to splutter out to Parker through swollen lips. He repeated it several times as if he could not comprehend what had previously been an impossible situation.

"Well, yer 'ad better come in," said Parker on grasping what had occurred. They both sat at a table in the living room where Bounce regaled Parker on his misfortunes, while Parker regaled Bounce with a pint of beer.

Parker listened to Bounce's description of his excursion and defeat with mixed feelings. He was sorry that Bounce had been given such a good hiding and yet amused that he had at last received his comeuppance. On the other hand he was annoyed that Bounce had acted stupidly, for had he bided his time he might have found out who Caria was meeting. Obviously he should have watched and waited; he had acted foolishly but he could hardly have been expected to do otherwise. By trying to show initiative he had foiled the objective of the enterprise. And that was the opinion of de Vere-Smythe when Bounce and Parker sat before him in his office at nine o'clock the following morning.

De Vere-Smythe questioned Bounce on the appearance of the people to whom Caria had spoken and surmised that they were probably harmless, but he had a different opinion of the man who had given Bounce such a pasting. Was Caria in league with the strong man of another gang, he had wondered? He had a dossier on the few gangs that existed in and around London. Later when he consulted it no one fitted the description of Bounce's assailant. De

Vere-Smythe blamed himself for having chosen Bounce for a job that would have been better left to Parker's superior skill, but Boss had given orders and one did not disobey orders from Boss. He recalled a phrase he had once heard in a radio play: "Orders must be obeyed without question at all times"—and that reminded him.

He looked at Bounce, who made a sorry figure with his head in a bandage and sticking plaster on his nose, and contemplated the order he must give. He had noticed that although Bounce had walked into his office a little stiffly, his enormous physical strength and stamina had enabled him to recover quickly where others would have been out of action for days. He decided Bounce was fit enough to carry on his duties.

There was little point in reprimanding Bounce, de Vere-Smythe concluded. Instead he commiserated with him expressing his sympathy and then gave him his orders: "Go and get your gear ready. The cruiser *Erinyes* will be here at the dock at one o'clock this afternoon and you will report on board."

Parker who had been sitting next to Bounce spoke as Bounce rose from his chair, "Wot abaht me?"

De Vere-Smythe shook his head. "Not you, Mr. Parker. Stay here," and addressing Bounce added, "Off you go, Bounce. Be at the dockside at one o'clock."

He watched Bounce walk stiffly to the door and after it had closed Parker looked inquiringly at him. The Londinium Club manager did not delay in satisfying his inquisitiveness.

"Mr. Parker, I imagine you are now fully fit?"

"Yus, Mr. de Vere-Smyve."

"Good. *Erinyes* will be bringing some goods the day after tomorrow. She will be at Fambridge at 8:30 P.M. You are to take your car and collect some goods which you will then convey directly to Charlie B." Parker understood: "Charlie B." was a code name for the agent in London who accepted parcels and packages that Parker delivered. In return he took back small packages which he handed directly to Boss. As mentioned, Parker never knew what any package contained; he was not interested as long as he got paid—and he was paid well.

Parker's active mind reflected on the task he was given. It would take three to four hours to get to Fambridge. To arrive there at the precise time would mean leaving in the rush hour. From 4:30 P.M. onwards the roads would be congested with vehicles leaving the city and there could be long delays.

"Guess I'd better leave at free firty," to which de Vere-Smythe nodded, interpreting it as three-thirty. "Good," and then added,

"Boss will be there to collect two guests. He will be back in the country that day."

Parker just nodded. Boss's comings and goings were none of his business.

"That it, Mr. de Vere-Smythe?"

"No. Have you seen Caria?"

"Nah. I looked in her apartment last night an' she wasn't there."

"Did you notice anything unusual?"

"Yus. 'Er bed ain't bin slept in an' all 'er cloves an' toilet fings 'ad gorn."

"Tut, tut. Foolish young lady."

So Eve and now Caria had fled, de Vere-Smythe thought. So far he had not been made aware by either Boss or Parker that Eve had been traced. Boss had kept the information to himself and had warned Parker not to divulge it to anyone. As far as the manager knew there were two girls who had decided to leave without permission. He was surprised at Caria for she had been with the Club six years and owned her own apartment. She was hardly likely to have surrendered all that without good reason. He was shaken out of his ruminations by Parker.

"Is that all, Mr. de Vere-Smythe?"

"Yes, Mr. Parker. Glad to see you back," and with that remark the manager rose and showed Parker to the door. Although accustomed to de Vere-Smythe's politeness, Parker knew never to take advantage or show familiarity. He had made the mistake of the latter once, but once was enough and he had learned his lesson.

He left the office and went on his way leaving his superior to puzzle about Caria's sudden departure. Neither he nor Parker were aware that once having met Barney, Caria had schemed how to get away from her sordid employment without losing everything. For some years she had been very good at getting extra "tips" for special services rendered to the clientele of the club. After her first year she started saving hard. She had opened an account in a tax-haven in the Isle of Man and was stashing money there. She was also astute in making some inroads in her mortgage. This gave her the idea of taking out a second mortgage on her apartment and salting that away.

Should she have to leave in a hurry then the mortgage company could repossess the property. That the mortgage company might have difficulty in selling the property and regaining their loan, did not trouble Caria's conscience. She had known Barney for several months now and they had decided to get married. She had moved several items to a house that Barney owned for temporary storage.

Unfortunately, thanks to her being followed, things had come to a head more quickly than anticipated.

Caria had her mind made up for her when she saw the condition Bounce was in after Barney had finished with him. When he was taken away in an ambulance she reckoned she would have time to get to her apartment and retrieve all she could into her car.

Barney was naturally curious and wanted to know who Bounce was and why he had grabbed her wrist. She explained that he was employed by the Club where she worked and she had had an argument with the manager about a raise in salary. She told Barney that she had threatened to leave if she did not get a raise and the manager was so annoyed that he had sent Bounce to bring her back. Barney was so head over heels in love with Caria that he accepted her story unquestioningly. He had even offered to go and see the manager, but she was able to persuade him against such action. He was agreeable to her staying with her friend in Walton while they both made arrangements for their forthcoming wedding.

■ ❑ ■ ❑ ■

"You may have a slight mitral insufficiency, Mr. Cooley."

"What is that in lay terms?"

The patient fastened his shirt buttons after examination by Sean who had sounded his heart. He had consulted Sean complaining of occasional shortness of breath and fatigue.

"The mitral valve in your heart is a bit floppy and therefore not at its most efficient. Actually it is nothing to worry about. Many people have the same condition but are not troubled by it and lead quite normal and active lives."

"Will it shorten my life?"

"Good heavens, no. Sometimes one needs to take medicine for it, but in your case all is well and treatment is hardly necessary. However, I am going to give you some digitalis to see if it stops your symptoms. There is a new brand which I would like you to try but I will need to check the dosage."

Sean looked on his desk for the up-to-date copy of the Monthly Index of Medical Supplies and, not finding it, realized that he had left it behind in his apartment.

Addressing his patient he remarked, "I must have left my copy at home. Wait a moment and I'll borrow Dr. McMurrough's."

Sean rose and left his surgery and walked across the corridor to Dr. McMurrough's and entered. The senior doctor was away in Ireland and would not return until later in that day. Actually both he,

Dr. Fitzgerald and the chemist, Mr. Slioghan, were absent; both Sean and Dr. Bannu Sind were extremely busy.

On entering the room, Sean glanced at Dr. McMurrough's desk but did not expect to find the book there. He knew of his senior's tidiness and then looked up at a bookshelf. Scanning it rapidly he spotted the index and, reaching forward, extracted it with a little difficulty from between other books. As he withdrew it a photograph fell, fluttered downwards and landed at his feet. He picked it up and glanced at it before putting it back in the Index. He saw a smiling Dr. McMurrough standing between a man and a woman. The picture had been taken in front of what appeared to be an Arab tent; sand dunes were visible behind it and the sky was a brilliant blue.

Must have been a holiday snap, Sean thought to himself. He was about to replace it in the book when he noticed that the faces of the two companions of Dermot McMurrough looked familiar. He felt he had seen them both before but could not immediately place them. Not wanting to waste time he found the drug he was looking for, memorized the dosage and then replaced the photograph in the book. He realized it may have been used as a bookmark but had not seen the pages from where it had been dislodged. Returning the Index to the shelf, he retraced his steps to his room and, sitting at his desk, wrote out the prescription.

Addressing Mr. Cooley, he said, "This drug is the one I want you to take daily. The instructions will be written on the bottle. In addition, I am prescribing some antibiotics which I want you to keep in reserve. With mitral insufficiency there is a slight risk of infection when undergoing surgery or dental treatment—as a precaution you should take antibiotic drugs before doing so. I will give you a prescription for Amoxyllin and you should take a capsule an hour before dental treatment. There will be a note on your case history should you ever need surgery." He handed the prescription to the patient who thanked him and left the room.

Sean pressed the intercom button and one of the reception staff answered. "Is that the lot?" he queried, and on receiving an affirmative reply, he looked at his domiciliary list. One of the patients he was scheduled to visit was a Mrs. Sataphan who had a kidney complaint. He knew she would need fresh drugs and, as she was bedridden and had to rely on outside help he always took medicines from the surgery to her. He looked up her case history in his computer, found the drug she would require, rose from his desk and went to the pharmacy room.

Mr. Slioghan, the resident pharmacist, was away for a few days, and a locum pharmacist was engaged in making up a prescription for Dr. Bannu's last patient when Sean entered the room. He greeted the woman pharmacist, whom he had met before, and went to the appropriate shelf to locate the tablets he required.

There he found the bottle, discovered it almost empty and realized there were not enough tablets for his requirements. "Do we have many more of these tablets, Helen?" he inquired, showing her the bottle. Helen paused in her work and, noting the name on the label, pointed to a cupboard. "There may be some in there."

Sean went to open the door and, finding it locked, asked Helen for the key. She reached out to a group of hooks on each of which a key was suspended, removed one and handed it to Sean. Thanking her, he opened the door and looked inside. There were four tiered shelves, the upper three were recessed but the bottom shelf was empty. Scanning the bottles and packets neatly displayed he found the bottle he was looking for and went to take hold of it when Helen asked, "Any luck?"

Sean turned to speak to her and in doing so displaced a large bottle which fell and landed with a thump on the bottom shelf. He instinctively reached out to grab it as it landed and in doing so displaced the bottom shelf, which moved several inches and the bottle fell in the gap between the shelf and he wall. "Stupid of me," he said out loud and lifted the shelf to retrieve the bottle which he found resting on numerous transparent plastic packets of white powder. Retrieving the bottle he then lifted a packet to see if the contents were labeled and was surprised to note they were not. Helen looked at him, having finished her morning's work.

"Do you know what is in these packets?" he asked.

Helen shook her head, querying, "Are they not marked?"

"No."

"That's odd."

He then inspected several other packets and found no labeling. "I would like to know what is in these, Helen."

Sean handed one of the sealed containers to her. She took it, slit it open and placed a small amount on a glass tray. She sniffed it, then tasted a fraction of the powder. Then rinsing her mouth with water she spat it out into the sink. She looked at Sean. "It's cocaine, Sean."

Sean counted the number of packets of cocaine in the cupboard and then went to the drug inventory. The amount he found considerably exceeded the amount noted in the inventory.

"I'll sort this out when Mr. Slioghan returns," he said to Helen, then replaced the drugs and shelf, took the tablets he required, entered the amount in the record book and they both left the pharmacy, locking the door behind them.

Back in his office, Sean switched on his computer and checked the list of addicts seen by the practice. Clearly there was far more cocaine stored in the pharmacy than should be in the practice for the number of patients. "That's odd," he reflected. "I wonder if our friend Eion Slioghan is up to no good?"

He tidied his desk and left his consulting room to commence his domiciliary visits. Approaching the door to the street, Helen suddenly burst in and bumped into him.

"Whoops. Oh, I am sorry, Sean. I left my bag in the pharmacy." He laughed good-naturedly and moved to one side to let her pass. In doing so, he suddenly recalled where he had seen the two people in the photograph. They were the two people who had been in a hurry and collided with him in the Piccadilly underground station when the terrorist bomb had gone off several months ago. The more he thought about it the more he was convinced. He remembered, too, that they had spoken with Irish accents. What were they doing with Dermot, he wondered, as he drove off to see his first patient.

Sean got through his three visits in less than an hour and, still puzzling over the photograph and the cocaine, called in at the local police station and asked to see Inspector Blanchard.

The inspector welcomed him affably as he entered his office, rising from his desk and extending a hand in greeting. "Come in, Sean, long time no see. What can I do for you?"

Sean explained his discoveries and Rodney Blanchard listened attentively. When he had finished, the inspector picked up one of the phones on his desk and ordered a file from the records office. He sat drumming his fingers on the desk before speaking and Sean waited for him to break the silence.

"I think you are in for a surprise, Sean." He paused and was about to speak when there was a knock on the door.

"Come in," Blanchard said loudly and a policewoman entered carrying what looked like a photograph album. She placed it on the table in front of the inspector, who thanked her, then turned the book round and slid it across to Sean. "Take a look at these and take your time. Tell me if you recognize any of the faces."

Sean looked carefully at each photograph as he slowly turned the pages. At first he had no success, then on the fifth page he pointed at an image displayed. "This is the man I saw." He looked again and read the name printed below the photograph: "Rory O'Higgins. Who is he?"

"I'll tell you in a moment. Please carry on looking." Sean continued and found the woman's photograph two pages further along. He read the name aloud, "Bernadette Malone," and glanced up at the inspector with an inquiring look on his face. Blanchard looked steadily at Sean as if to note his reaction.

"They are both members of the IRA and are wanted for terrorist activity. I suspect they were involved in the Piccadilly bombing."

"What have they to do with Dr. McMurrough?"

The inspector did not answer but put a question instead: "Where is Dr. McMurrough now?"

"I am not sure, but he is expected back in the practice later this afternoon—why?"

"I cannot answer that question yet, Sean. I must see that photograph you found. Would you mind going back to the surgery now?"

Sean shook his head. "Not at all. Can I give you a lift?"

"No, I'll follow in my car."

Sean drove to the practice and was entering the waiting room door when Inspector Blanchard arrived. The surgery was closed but one receptionist was on duty to answer phone calls and arrange appointments. She looked up in surprise when Sean walked in followed by the inspector. Sean smiled at her and asked, "Has Dr. McMurrough returned yet?"

"No, Dr. O'Neill, I don't expect him until later. Actually he is not expected in the surgery until tomorrow morning."

Sean nodded and he and the police officer entered McMurrough's room. Sean walked straight to the bookshelf and took out the copy of MIMS. Extracting the photograph, he handed it to Blanchard who asked, "Do you know where this was taken?"

"No."

"In Libya. It is a piece of evidence that will come in very handy. I shall keep it and advise you to say nothing about it to anyone." He put the photograph in his wallet and placed it in his pocket. "Incidentally, when will you see Eve Eden again?"

"Tonight. Why?"

"It may not be necessary but as a precautionary measure, I shall send along a couple of police officers to keep the house under observation. I cannot say much more than that but it might be as well if Eve and the family stay indoors."

■ ◻ ■ ◻ ■

Boss returned from Ireland feeling somewhat frustrated. He had seen some of the members of the IRA and had little success in persuading them to break the truce, although one member had participated in a post office robbery and the killing of a post office employee. There had also been a bomb scare. British soldiers had defused the bomb but whether it had been planted by dissident IRA, UDF or UFF he did not know. Obviously, there was a hard core on both sides that wanted to disrupt the peace process for various reasons, but he had been unable to make direct contact while there. One member had plans to blackmail a VIP for a large sum of money but had been trapped and caught. He had been told that it suited Sinn Fein to pursue the peaceful path as they felt the British Prime Minister, John Major, would give away so much through connections with the European community, that Northern Ireland would be virtually ruled from Eire. It was a delicate situation but as the vast majority of Irish were sick of the terrorism it paid to encourage the peace process.

He sat in his apartment thinking over the situation and then realized it was time to drive to Fambridge to meet the cruiser *Erinyes*. He smiled to himself as he drove off. He would get Bernadette to finish off Eve that evening.

■ ❑ ■ ❑ ■

It was about the same time Boss set off that Parker prepared to depart for the same destination. He had drunk a final cup of tea and had just placed the cup in the bowl when there was a knock on the door.

I wonder 'oo the 'ell that can be? he said to himself as he opened his door and walked across the hall to the street door. He received quite a surprise when he saw two uniformed police officers standing there. It had been intimated to him earlier that the charge of breaking and entering for his occupation of the caravan had been dropped, for he had compensated the owner for the repairs and use of the propane gas.

"Mr. Bert Parker?" one of the policemen inquired. Parker nodded and had a sinking feeling in his stomach which was not associated with the tea he had just drunk.

chapter twenty-four

Gerard Rutherford drove along the motorway with mixed feelings. He had said good-bye to Dawn, Richard and their children and felt a little sad leaving them. He had enjoyed himself as always and only wished that his late wife had also been present. However, he accepted the reality of existence and in any case was still recovering from his bereavement. It was always a lot of fun to play with the children and he delighted teasing, and in turn, being teased by Jennifer. He also derived great enjoyment from the intellectual stimulus he always experienced when with the Rutherford family. This time there had been an added bonus, for he had made a friend of Father Patrick Brendan, and obtained considerable pleasure from the conversations he experienced with that highly intelligent and well-educated priest. The last conversation they had together came back to his mind.

"Whatever you say, Gerard, no matter the accuracy of the facts you mention and how clever and persuasive your logic, you will not sway Eve from her faith. She has experienced a revelation such as that only known to saints such as Saint Theresa of Lisieux and Saint Bernadette."

Gerard clearly remembered that morning when he called at the church. He had earlier promised to discuss his agnostic views in front of Eve. Patrick Brendan, having been aware of Eve's revelation, was confident that her faith could not now be shaken. And the priest was right.

The question of revelation had cropped up, it being the cornerstone of many faiths. All faiths claimed that their revelation or revelations were the truth. He had stated that so many people claim divine revelation and so many claims are contradictory that none can possibly have any credence.

Mormons claim that divine revelation is an ongoing thing. There is a grain of truth in that he felt, insofar as many people make the claim that their god, saint or spirit reveals itself to them.

Like many other scientists he knew of a more plausible and satisfying explanation for the emotional feeling associated with revelation. It could be brought about by the use of drugs such as LSD, mescaline, and so on, and this indicates that the associated religious experience is nothing more than physiological cerebral activity.

Unfortunately, the claimants of revelation get followers who often become fanatics. Not only were there examples of this in the

USA where such zealots had brought about the deaths of their acolytes, but history is full of religious wars and the sufferings of countless people through religious intolerance.

Father Brendan had stated that the Bible and especially the gospels, were living evidence of the truth of Christ's teaching and that the Roman Catholic religion is a permanent truth. He added that scientists appeared to know all the answers. Gerard recalled countering the statement. It was the position of all believers in any faith that their religion depicted the truth and all others and science were wrong. Scientists and those who used the scientific and logical approach knew that they did not know all the answers about the nature of the universe. What they did know was that their method of not accepting anything as true until it was experimentally verifiable, or until they had adequate evidence, was the only honest approach. And even then they knew that their views might have to change with an increase in knowledge or new evidence.

One thing they did not count on was divine intervention—all scientists have to go on is the universe itself. If there is such a thing as the so-called "paranormal," then only as it is supposed to affect one's senses can it be scientifically investigated.

Father Brendan had also stated that mankind is a special creation. This Gerard had disputed saying that all living things on this planet have evolved from lower forms. Not only are *Homo sapiens* not a special creation but the building blocks of living matter, such as the amino acids, the essential ingredients of protein molecules and all five of the organic bases used in the genetic code, had been identified in meteorites. It was clear that organic molecules formed naturally from inorganic matter and it is probable that where suitable environments exist life will evolve.

The evidence so far indicates that this universe was not created for mankind alone. Furthermore, the recent research on genetic material of the eye of the fruit fly, drosophila melanogaster, and the discovery that one with this gene could grow an eye on other parts of the fruit fly's anatomy and also, with the same gene a mouse eye on a mouse, meant that all living organisms are related. It is scientific proof that the claim that mankind is a special creation is a fallacy.

The question arose on the nature of God and the probability that the nature forever remained hidden from man. Man created God in his own image and always made of God what he wanted to be himself. Father Brendan had said, "It does no harm to recognize that there is a greater Power in this universe than oneself."

Gerard had replied, "I quite agree, but it frequently does harm if one pretends, assumes or believes that one is the Power's mouthpiece."

But even the significance of that remark had been lost on Eve. There was no doubt that she had experienced a fugue and her faith was now unshakable. And in a way Gerard was glad.

It had occurred to him more than once that the fundamental basis of religions was not really so important. What counted was the way the believers lived. If their religion tolerated the beliefs of others and the adherents were good law-abiding citizens, worked and contributed towards society and played their part in the community, then such religion was harmless—indeed, it could be a cementing force in society. However, as Richard had pointed out, he did not need religion to make him a good husband, parent and good citizen.

Another real problem was the fact that there are too many people on the planet and the demand for food and living space resulted in starvation, crime, constant wars and needless suffering. The leaders of the two dominant religions, Islam and Roman Catholicism, failed to understand the situation and by encouraging their faithful to have large families added to the sum of human misery and the spoilation of the planet.

Gerard Rutherford smiled to himself at the pointlessness of the conversation. The Principle of Insecurity he and his son believed in was certainly vindicated. Any facts or logical argument against a person's belief or faith made such a person feel insecure and would be rejected on emotional grounds. He had been unwise to present his views after Eve had experienced her "revelation" or fugue. Not that he had wanted to shake her faith. He knew she needed the security and peace of mind that it gave her. He only hoped that later she would not become disillusioned.

Dawn had told him of a conversation she had with Eve regarding having a family. Eve had expressed hopes of continuing her education, retaking her entrance examination and attending university. She was not too keen on starting a family too soon and had been disturbed when she had learned that the Pope was against family-planning and contraception. She knew that the so-called natural rhythm technique advocated by the church did not work. Gerard reflected that even before marriage the seeds of doubt were being sown. But enough of that. He turned his thoughts to going to his home and the sailing voyage he was to undertake in a few days.

He looked forward to spending a week on the sail training vessel, *Lord Nelson*. Possessing a sailing master's certificate he qualified to become a watch leader on the three-masted barque which had been designed to give handicapped persons a chance to sail. For many it was the experience of a lifetime and he was glad that he would have the opportunity to put his skills to some practical use where others would benefit. There were four watches on the square-rigger and he would be in charge of ten personnel, five of whom would be handicapped. It was extraordinary that the one hundred and eighty foot vessel had been designed around an invalid wheel chair. He had promised to show his grandchildren a video of his voyage when he next saw them and that was something else to look forward to. He smiled at these thoughts and drove contentedly along the busy road reflecting that the world was very kind to him.

■ ❏ ■ ❏ ■

Rory O'Higgins checked the carabiner on his harness and nodded to the officer who signaled to the seaman at the donkey engine. He felt the wire rope tighten and then was lifted from the firm deck of the *El Arabayana*. The container vessel was moving at the slowest speed which was just enough to give her steerage way and Rory was swung out until he was poised over the *Erinyes* which was bobbing in the sea as close to the larger vessel as was compatible with safety. He saw the cruiser getting larger as he was carefully lowered to her deck.

The familiar figure of Bounce was waiting for him to assist his landing on the lurching vessel and it was not until his feet touched the deck that he noticed that Bounce had bandages under his woolen seaman's cap. He felt one of Bounce's powerful hands grab him and steady his descent. With both feet on the deck Rory immediately unclipped the carabiner, waved to the officer on the *El Arabayana*, who in turn signaled to the seaman, and the wire rope was quickly hoisted aboard the container vessel.

Rory thanked Bounce, walked to the wheelhouse of the *Erinyes*, ascended the ladder to the upper station and was there greeted by Eoin Slioghan and Liam Fitzgerald. While he and Eoin watched Bernadette being hoisted towards the cruiser, Liam skillfully kept her on course. The same procedure for Rory brought Bernadette safely aboard and her arrival was followed by three further loads, the first their personal baggage, then one of drugs and the other of explosives and remote control detonating devices. With the loading completed, the officer on the larger vessel and the crew of the *Erinyes* waved good-bye and both vessels gathered speed, the *El Arabayana* heading for the English Channel and the cruiser towards the River Crouch.

Liam Fitzgerald felt quite pleased with himself, for after a trip to Ostend, he had cleared customs the night before at Harwich. He had informed the officers he would cruise to the River Crouch the following day and then proceed to London. The obtaining of customs clearance meant he could land the two terrorists and all they had brought aboard at Fambridge where they had the rendezvous with Boss. Leaving Bounce on watch and steering temporarily, with Rory he descended from the upper steering station to the wheelhouse. There he tapped in the coordinates for the next waypoint on the Sat-Nav, set the autohelm, phoned up to Bounce to stop steering and then greeted Bernadette. With celebratory drinks of Irish whiskey, he and Eoin were regaled with information on the training the two terrorists had received in Sicily. The listeners were particularly interested in the attack on the villa and the wiping out of an entire Mafia family.

"It was too easy, thanks to brilliant planning on the part of Luigi Furari. It is hardly surprising that he is now the leading godfather in Sicily. We learned a great deal." And at that, Bernadette nodded in assent, saying, "Maybe we can put it into good use soon."

Liam shook his head. "We have had orders from headquarters to stop fighting but Boss does not think it is a good idea; we all stand to lose too much."

"How so?" asked Rory.

"All the funds from the USA will probably dry up and all the loss of life so far will be seen by everyone to be pointless. It won't do our image much good."

At this remark from Liam, Bernadette and Rory looked at each other. Due to the time spent in their training and the lack of opportunity to listen to overseas broadcasts, they had not had the opportunity to follow the peace negotiations between the British and Irish prime ministers. They had heard of the possibility of a cease-fire but not of its confirmation. On questioning Liam and Slioghan, they learned that they were to hide their weaponry and explosives in caches and not use them unless the negotiations broke down. Training and recruitment were to continue. Should any agreement be made to hand over their armaments they were to surrender only part; the rest was to be retained in case the hard-liners did not agree to the peace terms or the Protestant gunmen started trouble again.

Neither Rory nor Bernadette were happy with the thought of a political agreement being reached unless it entailed complete surrender of Northern Ireland and full submission to rule by Eire. Furthermore, they also wanted the opportunity to wipe out all the Protestant gunmen and several of the Protestant members of Parliament. They considered that any Irishman who still wanted independence from southern Irish rule was a traitor to the Irish cause. However, as the orders had come directly from the headquarters then they would comply for the moment. Whether they would recommence their terrorist campaign would depend on the peace terms agreed between the British and Irish governments.

Their discussion with Eoin and Liam was interrupted by a call from Bounce at his station, "I can see the Whittaker Beacon!"

Liam picked up his binoculars and trained them ahead of the vessel. "You're right, Bounce—that's it. I'm switching off the auto-helm so take over the steering until I come up."

"OK," Bounce replied, glad to be responsible for steering even if only for a short time.

Liam advised Rory and Bernadette to go below into the saloon and keep out of sight in case a customs vessel came near the cruiser. Although he had received customs clearance the previous day the two terrorists had not been on board and he did not want any complications. Picking up his binoculars from their slot, he ascended the ladder to the upper station and, using the handholds, made his way forward across the lively deck to stand beside Bounce.

Sensing him there, Bounce pointed ahead and Liam nodded, shading his eyes against the glare of the sun which, through partial cloud, shone directly ahead and being some thirty degrees above the horizon had two hours to set. He could now clearly see the thin vertical metal beacon with its two balls on the top marking the edge of the Foulness Sands and beyond that he could discern several tall radio masts. He looked at the sea in all directions to ascertain if any other vessels were close and then issued an order to Bounce, "Steer to the right side of the beacon, Bounce. Keep it about fifty yards to your left; the deep water channel is there."

Bounce nodded and under the watchful eye of Liam brought the cruiser fifteen degrees to the starboard of her original course.

"You see that red can buoy ahead, Bounce?"

"Yus."

"Steer towards that and keep it to the port side, that is, your left hand side."

Bounce did as he was ordered and within ten minutes the *Erinyes* entered the fairway leading to the River Crouch. Here the vessel rode more smoothly, the swell from the North Sea being tempered by the protecting sandbanks.

Raising the binoculars to his eyes, Liam brought into view the green conical Buxey buoy and then the sunken Buxey buoy which marked the safe channel. He noticed several vessels in the fairway, a number of yachts and what looked like two motor cruisers. The size and shape of one roused his curiosity and, as they drew nearer, he could make out the shape of the customs vessel that had intercepted them the previous day. It was obvious that the *Erinyes* had been seen for one of the crew gave him a wave as the cruiser sailed past. However, it was apparent that the customs officials were not interested in the *Erinyes*—there were three yachts and a cruiser ahead that were displaying a yellow "Q" flag, and Liam watched with satisfaction when he saw the customs vessel make for the nearest one and intercept her.

Liam hummed happily to himself; his calculations had been correct. The time was a quarter to seven and with the tide and allowance for reducing speed once they were in the River Crouch, the cruiser should arrive at Fambridge at exactly seven-thirty as planned. Boss and Parker would be meeting them there and the "goods" on board would be unloaded and Rory and Bernadette would land to be transported to their destination by Boss. With that job done he would take the cruiser back to Burnham where they would spend the night at the marina and have a good meal and some liquid refreshment in a local restaurant he knew. Life could be very pleasant at times and this was one of them.

He looked back at the customs vessel and, aided by his binoculars, noted that the vessel had dropped off an officer onto a yacht and was proceeding to another which also displayed the yellow square flag.

Erinyes made its way past the Outer Crouch buoy, then the Inner Crouch buoy; the dominant building of the Corinthian Yacht Club came into view on the northern side of the river, followed by the picturesque waterfront of Burnham. Liam slowed to a speed of eight knots and kept the vessel in the fairway between the left bank and the lines of buoys to almost all of which a pleasure craft was moored. Here were rows of sailing yachts ranging from seventeen feet to over one hundred. Sloops predominated, and then the odd ketch and old "gaffer" with its protruding boom, to the occasional schooner. A Thames barge was riding at one buoy, her seventy-foot length and tall mainmast with its characteristic spritsail rig dwarfing some adjacent pocket cruisers.

Riding majestically at her buoy was an old-fashioned steam yacht, reminiscent of the halcyon days of Edwardian Britain—an expensive piece of real estate seldom used in these days of economic recession.

The rows of vessels marshaled by the tide into all pointing downstream, stretched upriver for the distance of a mile and a half before petering out at Cliff Reach, a height of ground on the north bank flatteringly named, for it hardly exceeded twenty-five feet above the mean water level.

Rounding a bend in the river, the cruiser gradually overtook two large sloops slowly motoring upstream. The crews of each gave them a wave as they went by and Bounce and Liam returned the normal nautical courtesy. Liam noticed that one was still flying the "Q" flag which could involve the presence of the customs vessel coming upstream. He did not like the idea of the vessel being present when they unloaded their contraband cargo; he would have to be careful and "play it by ear."

The sun was noticeably lower and the low thin cloud to the west presaged a glorious sunset. The flat green fields and marshy wasteland of the Crouch Valley stretched for several miles on each side of the river. Here and there a farmhouse building stood out from the even terrain, which was relieved of its monotony by several small copse-covered knolls, by the wooded hill at Canewdon to the south and the high ground towards Latchingdon to the north. The inhabitants of the bird sanctuary at Bridgemarsh Island chorused their presence as the vessel motored by, its speed in the water assisted a further two knots by the flowing tide.

They passed a group of yachts at moorings, masts nodding in the wake of *Erinyes* and entered the final stretch to their destination. Eion came up to the upper steering station carrying a cup of coffee for the two at the helm and, as they slowly drank it, the masts of the cluster of yachts at Fambridge came into view and Liam spoke through the intercom to Rory and Bernadette informing them that they would soon be arriving.

The riverside jetty at Fambridge is situated on the northern bank of the River Crouch and is used mainly for vessels loading and unloading. The marina proper is reached by sailing further upstream and is only accessible for a few hours around high tide. It was to the riverside jetty that Liam piloted the *Erinyes* and he noted that three yachts were berthed alongside which left little room. Two were close together but there was a large gap between them and the third yacht and that was big enough for the cruiser.

Liam glanced back to see that a yacht he had overtaken was far enough away for it not to interfere with his intended maneuver. He then scanned upstream squinting against the setting sun to note that a cruiser was stemming the tide, but it was making for the lane between the first and second rows of moored vessels and was therefore clear of him. There were four lanes of moored vessels in the river off the jetty, but adequate room for him to turn his vessel in the fairway between the first line of moored vessels and the jetty. The tide was still swiftly pushing the cruiser upstream and as he came opposite the space beside the jetty, with good judgment Liam reversed engines, stopping her progress upstream. Skillfully he swung the vessel one hundred and eighty degrees to point downstream and with enough way on her to counterbalance the flow, eased her sideways into the dockside. As he did so, he ordered Eion and Bounce to get the mooring lines, get ashore at the appropriate moment and tie her up.

Liam's skillful handling did not go unnoticed. As the gap lessened between the cruiser and the two adjacent yachts so members of their crews became active. On the yacht downstream a woman in the cockpit called a man from below and he came on deck, picked up a boat hook and walked to the bow of his vessel, standing there as a precautionary measure in case the cruiser got too close. The cockpit of the other adjacent yacht was close to the cruiser and in it there were four occupants, two men and two women apparently enjoying a drink after the exertions of loading or unloading. While the women, one with a boat hook stood at the stern to watch the cruiser, the two men jumped ashore and moved forward offering to take the mooring lines. However, both Bounce and Eion were ready amidships and both stepped ashore simultaneously and walked their lines to the dockside cleats; there they made fast and Liam stopped the engines on a signal from each.

Liam scanned the jetty for signs of Boss and Parker but they were nowhere to be seen. The sun was setting and he knew that there were only about twenty-five or so minutes of daylight left. Several vehicles were parked near the buildings and he could see some people there. Two men were carrying a dinghy along the jetty and they put it down near the yacht where the man had stood with the boat hook. They were engaging Eion in conversation. He noticed, too, that the two men who had apparently gone to assist with the lines were talking to Bounce. He looked back to the car park and then noticed two vehicles approaching along the narrow roadway with its tall hedgerows. He was unable to identify them, but assumed they were being driven by Boss and Parker. Feeling more reassured, he spoke on the intercom to Rory and as he descended to the main deck so Rory and Bernadette came up from below.

"Looks like Boss and Parker are just arriving," he commented to the two terrorists. "Better get your gear up."

Both Rory and Bernadette went below and Liam looked towards Bounce and called out, "Come back on board—it's time to get the gear ashore!" To Liam's surprise, Bounce did not move and with a feeling that something was wrong Liam looked quickly towards Eion and saw that the two men who had been carrying the dinghy were standing beside him. Just as he noticed Eion's hands were behind his back he felt a slight bump and saw the following sailing vessel draw alongside. He glanced around quickly and his gaze took in the two women in the cockpit of the moored yacht astern; they were both holding pistols pointing at him.

At the bows of the other yacht the man who had held the boat hook a few moments ago was also pointing a gun in his direction. With a sinking feeling in his stomach he looked at the sailing vessel now attached by lines to the *Erinyes* and saw four policemen, each carrying a gun, step onto the cruiser. One officer addressed him, "You had better come quietly, Liam Fitzgerald. You are completely surrounded."

As he spoke, Rory and Bernadette came up on deck encumbered by handgrips. The other officers stepped forward and one ordered the two terrorists to drop their gear and raise their hands. Bernadette slowly complied but Rory, stooping to put down his handgrip, flung it at the officer, ducked and, springing across the deck, dived into the river. As he sprung overboard, an officer raised his gun and squeezed the trigger but the sergeant standing by knocked up his arm and, with a loud report, the bullet sped harmlessly into the air.

"We are to take them alive, Dick. Catch this," and he threw his gun to his colleague and dived in after him.

Rory was a good swimmer and struck out for the lines of vessels in midstream with the intention of using them as shields against pistol fire while he made for the opposite bank. When he surfaced from his initial dive he had expected to hear further shots and was surprised when he heard nothing. Nevertheless, he took in a lung full of air and dived again, swimming under water for several yards before surfacing. He was closer to the line of yachts now and felt that the descending dusk would give him a good chance of making his escape. He surfaced for a third time between two moored vessels and was surprised when a hand grabbed his hair.

Unknown to him, the police sergeant who had dived in after him was a champion swimmer and regularly represented his station in swimming competitions. He had no difficulty in catching up with Rory and hadn't the slightest intention of letting the terrorist go. Bigger than Rory and physically very powerful, he grabbed Rory by the hair with his left hand and with his right grabbed him by the neck, quickly feeling with his fingers for a nerve and applying pressure there. Simultaneously, he pushed Rory under the water, not giving him time to take a deep breath. Rory felt himself go under and reached for his gun in his shoulder holster. He took hold of his gun and, choking, started to withdraw it when his arm became paralyzed and he lost consciousness. The police sergeant had found the pressure point and effectively put Rory out of action. As he and Rory were swept upstream, he swam to an adjacent buoy and awaited the arrival of an inflatable which had been quickly launched after his diving into the river.

Within a quarter of an hour Rory was lying on the jetty, his arms pinioned behind his back and wearing handcuffs. He had been given artificial respiration on the dinghy and started to regain consciousness. As he opened his eyes he saw Bounce, Bernadette, Eion and Liam all handcuffed and lying on the jetty—it was clear the officers were taking no further chances in risking the escape of any of them.

Liam had anticipated the arrival of Boss and Parker in their respective vehicles but he soon learned that he had been over hasty in his surmise. The cars he had seen both carried police, including Inspector Blanchard, and a member of MI5 who had cooperated in the plan to catch the cell of criminals and terrorists red-handed. Both were feeling pleased at the apparent success of the operation and Blanchard walked up to each of the captives, looking at their faces. He said nothing until he had seen the last and then, turning swiftly to the sergeant in charge, stated: "There should be seven. Where are McMurrough and Parker?"

"I've already queried that, sir. Neither came down the road to Fambridge. I have had a patrol car go up and down there since early this afternoon and we would not have missed them."

Blanchard considered the message and said, "Get this lot in the cars and don't let any get away. You have orders to take them alive, but don't hesitate to shoot if any try to escape." Then he turned to the driver of his car, "Get back to headquarters and find out if Parker and McMurrough are there—and hurry."

The driver dashed off, and Blanchard ordered the sergeant in charge to caution each one of the prisoners and then get them in the cars. Meantime, the customs vessel had drawn up and moored beside one of the yachts and the officers were taking dogs aboard the *Erinyes* to thoroughly search the vessel for drugs.

While the prisoners, all looking sullen, were being taken away, the driver returned to the inspector: "They have Parker only in custody, sir."

"Oh, where did they arrest him?"

"At his house just before he was due to leave."

"What! Get through again—I want to speak to the station sergeant."

"Yes, sir."

Blanchard followed him to the car and spoke to sergeant Hillary. "What's this I hear about Parker being arrested at his home?"

"It was an error, sir. We had a message from Essex about the possibility of Parker being involved with a stolen car and brought him in for questioning. The officers involved did not know that you had organized a raid."

"Alright, dammit. Where is he now?"

"He was allowed to go home as there was nothing to pin on him."

"Bring him back in. See if he knows where Dr. McMurrough is and this time hang on to him. Send an armed squad to McMurrough's apartment and surgery without delay and if he is found arrest him. Contact me immediately if you ascertain he is in either place or not—and hurry."

The inspector turned to the MI5 officer. "You had better notify all ports and airports." Blanchard was feeling annoyed; it had taken a lot of time, patience and planning to set the trap and he had hoped to catch McMurrough red-handed and involve him in smuggling drugs and weapons. His frustration, however, did not prevent him thinking of other possibilities on his whereabouts.

Suddenly a thought struck him. "Oh, my God!" he said out loud. Grabbing the telephone he got through to his office at the police station and his secretary answered the phone. "Hilda, give me the phone number of Bracken—and hurry!" Within a minute he had the information and immediately phoned the Rutherford residence.

It was Richard who answered the telephone and he did not like what he heard. "Richard Rutherford, I am Inspector Blanchard and there is a possibility that an IRA terrorist is on his way to your home to attack Eve and your cousin Sean. I have notified police to intercept him, but in the interests of your family's safety I suggest you all get away from Bracken immediately. Tell Sean that Dr. McMurrough is the terrorist. I am coming myself immediately. Don't waste any time."

■ ❏ ■ ❏ ■

It was earlier in the afternoon that Dr. Dermot McMurrough, alias Boss, drove rapidly towards Fambridge. He had been delayed at the early stages of the journey by visiting his surgery and then by rush-hour traffic. He not only felt balked by delays but also somewhat puzzled. When in the surgery he had noticed the Monthly Medical Index had been put back in the wrong place on the shelf. Being very methodical in his habits he had replaced it in its normal position, unconsciously flicking through the pages when he had removed it from the shelf. He had asked the receptionist on duty if either Dr. Bannu Sind or Dr. O'Neill had gone into his room.

"It was Dr. O'Neill," the receptionist had stated, and as the telephone had rung and interrupted, failed to add that a police inspector had accompanied him. Not expecting further information, he had left hurriedly.

It was getting on for seven-thirty when he arrived at the roundabout from which the road ran to Fambridge. As he entered the road he noticed a police car with two officers inside parked a short distance along another road leading into the roundabout. Their presence gave him a feeling of unease. Not wanting to arouse their suspicions, he did not immediately turn back but drove along the winding road with its high stone walls and hedgerows for a quarter of a mile. Stopping at a field gate, he leapt out of his car, opened the gate and returning to the vehicle drove into the field where he knew he would be protected from being seen by the tall stone wall and hedge. Driving the car into the field, he backed it behind the wall. Parking it he again leapt out of the car and closed the gate, positioning himself so that he could observe any vehicles passing along the road without being seen.

He had not long to wait. Within three minutes two cars each containing two police officers drove past the gate in the direction of Fambridge. Suspecting a trap, his immediate reaction was to get back onto the road and drive back in the direction from whence he had come. It was on reaching the roundabout that his suspicions were confirmed; he heard the sound of a gun shot and realized that despite all precautions the police had caught up with his game at last.

Dr. McMurrough to his patients and Boss to the members of his cell and minions, had a contingency plan for the possibility of being found out and realized now that it would have to be put into operation. He would drive to Liverpool where he knew there were expatriates with whom he could hide for as long as necessary. He would then have the choice of getting back to Eire or flying to the USA. A false passport would be made available without any problem. He would have to drive through Essex and make for the motorway.

As he drove his mind worked furiously, puzzling on how the police had got onto the trail. Something nagged at the back of his mind and he recalled thumbing through the copy of MIMS. Of course! The photograph he used as a bookmark was missing. So Sean was a police informer. This he found difficult to believe, for he was not privy to the activities of the cell or the Club. Another thing occurred to McMurrough. Sean had been the last doctor to see Eve and he always drove in the direction of Essex every weekend he was off duty. Was it possible that he and Eve were in love? Another recollection seemed to fit the line of reasoning: Parker had found the identity of the owner of Bracken, the house where Eve was hiding. He was an ophthalmologist and McMurrough recalled that during his initial interview Sean had mentioned he had a cousin in the medical profession who lived in Essex.

As he drove, McMurrough noticed that he was close to the village where Bracken was situated. It was possible that Sean had made his way there for he was now off duty for the weekend. This made McMurrough decide to go immediately to Bracken and kill both Eve and Sean, if he were there—and anyone else who got in the way. He would then go on to Liverpool. Parker had provided him with details of the position of the house, for all the houses were named, none being numbered. As he drove into the road leading into the village, he noticed a police car with two officers inside being driven in the opposite direction. He slowed before turning into the road on which Bracken was situated, but the police continued on to turn into the main road which he just left.

He knew he did not have much time and drove along the road, turning his vehicle at the end of the cul-de-sac to face in the opposite direction to give him the best opportunity to escape. Parking his car in the roadway outside the house near one of the two entrances to the driveway, he screwed a silencer onto his gun and, leaving the engine running, opened the large iron gate. Dusk was falling and as he ran along the drive, which was longer than he had expected, twin garage doors at the opposite end of the house started to open. He heard two cars being started and prepared to shoot the drivers as they left the garage. At this point he saw a vehicle enter the driveway opposite the garage. It was another police car which appeared to have come from nowhere, but unknown to him had been stationed out of sight beside a house in the cul-de-sac.

McMurrough did not hesitate but fired three shots at the driver. The officer saw the gun raised and ducked and stopped the car near the garage. The second officer was getting out of the car and McMurrough fired two more shots, hitting him in the shoulder and then in the head. He fell out of the open car door onto the driveway. By then the driver had got his door open and, raising his gun, fired twice, hitting McMurrough in his left thigh. He felt the blow and severe pain of a broken bone and collapsed onto the driveway as his leg gave way beneath him. Raising his gun again he fired and hit the policeman in the chest who immediately collapsed and dropped his gun.

McMurrough tried to get up but the pain of his shattered thigh was too severe. He looked up and saw a dog run out of the open garage door, barking as it ran towards him. Then he heard a child's voice scream, "Poppet!" The dog ran towards him as if to attack and he shot it. It howled in agony as the bullet ripped through its body.

In the gathering dusk and with the shouts and the scream of a woman yelling "Jennifer," he saw a small figure run out of the garage after the dog. He brought it down with another shot. The figure was followed by two taller men, one of whom bent to pick up the fallen girl. He aimed at him and heard the click of his gun, the magazine now being empty. He felt faint with the pain from his shattered thigh, but made up his mind that as he now had little chance to escape, he would kill everyone in Bracken.

It was Richard and Sean who ran out of the garage after Jennifer and, on seeing her hit, Richard went to scoop her up quickly from the ground. They both heard the click of McMurrough's gun and realized that it was out of ammunition. Simultaneously, they saw the police officer's gun on the driveway and went to retrieve it, but Sean said, "He's mine—you get Jennifer."

Sean picked up the pistol and ran towards McMurrough who had managed to discard the empty magazine from his gun and was feeling inside a coat pocket for a spare he carried. Recognizing Sean, he swore, "You bloody Irish traitor, Sean," and struggled to retrieve the full magazine.

Sean pointed the police gun at McMurrough. "No, you're the traitor, Dermot. You are a traitor to your profession and you and others like you are traitors to the Irish cause. Even a half-wit can see that unification can never be achieved by the murder of innocent people."

He stood over his partner, covering him with the gun and intending to keep him there until Blanchard arrived. He heard the sound of vehicles approaching rapidly down the road and wondered if he would have the courage to shoot McMurrough should the need arise. He was soon to find out.

In the half-light McMurrough had managed to retrieve the magazine and, partly obscured by his bent good leg, slipped it into the gun. Sean, however, heard the click and as McMurrough brought his gun up, Sean shot him straight through the heart. McMurrough jerked reflexively, squeezed the trigger of his weapon and fired, sending a bullet plowing up Sean's left arm. He just felt a sting and was then bathed in the headlights of Inspector Blanchard's car. The inspector alighted and ran towards Sean and the now-twitching body of McMurrough. Sean handed the gun to him and the inspector noticed blood dripping from Sean's arm.

"We had better get you to hospital, Sean. Anyone else . . . " He did not finish the sentence on seeing the police officer lying in the driveway, illuminated by the headlamps of Richard's car.

The floodlights of the house were suddenly switched on and the whole driveway was illuminated. Driven by Richard, his car left the garage and Sean saw Dawn holding the unconscious Jennifer with a pad bandage held to her head and realized that they were taking her to hospital. He felt sick as they drove past, both looking white-faced.

"Oh, God, Jennifer. Oh my God," was all he could say as Blanchard started to issue orders and another police vehicle arrived.

chapter twenty-five

Boss or Dr. McMurrough, to use his real name, had no qualms when he callously shot Jennifer. Like all terrorists, no matter what race or creed, he had no respect for human rights or the sanctity of human life. The driving force behind his thinking was that the achievement of political ends by any means, no matter what suffering, anguish, maiming and loss of life resulted, was perfectly justified. Those that got hurt did not count; they should not have got in the way. All that mattered was the end result, even if individuals and minorities had to suffer. He had heard that one of the victims of an IRA terrorist attack was now a quadriplegic—a young mother who was confined to a wheelchair for the rest of her life. She could only achieve movement of her chair by blowing into a tube because the bomb had left her paralyzed from the neck downwards. The suffering she experienced was also shared by her family and all those near and dear to her. Like all terrorists his reaction had been one of callous indifference. All that mattered was that his actions force the British to abandon their loyal subjects the Northern Irish, and enable him and his like to subordinate the Protestants and make them grovel.

When he felt the blow and excruciating pain of the shot through his heart his mind had been on killing Sean. In the few seconds he had consciousness, he had the satisfaction of seeing Sean's left arm jerk as he squeezed the trigger of his own weapon. For him, from that moment for eternity it was oblivion.

Eve had phoned for an ambulance as soon as Richard, Dawn and Jennifer left. The police officer accompanying Inspector Blanchard gave first aid to the wounded officer and the inspector, with Eve's assistance, stopped the bleeding on Sean's arm. He in turn went to help the prostrate officer in the driveway, but all efforts to resuscitate him were of no avail. As they worked, an ambulance and another police squad car arrived.

"Get these two officers in the ambulance," Blanchard had ordered the paramedics. "I'll bring Dr. O'Neill." They had quickly put the two police victims of the shooting in the ambulance, and while one gave oxygen to the wounded man, the other drove rapidly to the local hospital with the siren blaring.

Supporting Sean, Inspector Blanchard sat in the back seat of his car while his driver raced to the hospital. The inspector's mind was in a turmoil. He had succeeded in his main aim of capturing a dangerous nest of terrorists and the ringleader had been killed. He felt it ironic that McMurrough had been shot by one of his own countrymen, his colleague and a Catholic to boot. He glanced at Sean and saw his pale face. Obviously he was now feeling the pain and no doubt was also in shock. He spoke to his driver, "Make it as quick as you can, Bill." But the driver needed no prompting. He was making as much speed as safety would permit and the blaring siren was clearing the roadway ahead.

Although satisfied at the outcome of the trap to capture the terrorists, Blanchard was not happy. He had learned that Jennifer had been hit; how badly he did not know. One of his officers had been killed and he now had to explain it all to the officer's wife and two children—he was not looking forward to that. The officer's parents were both old and frail and the news that their only son had been killed would be a terrible burden for them to bear. The only consolation, if any, he reflected, was that they would have their daughter-in-law and grandchildren to comfort them. The wounded officer was engaged to a policewoman at the station and she would now be worried until he recovered. In turn, his parents would be very upset. No man is an island he reflected, putting another meaning on the aphorism.

His thoughts were interrupted by a phone call from the officer left at the *Erinyes*. "Blanchard here."

"Sir, the customs and excise people have found drugs, explosives and some very sophisticated detonating devices on the cruiser."

"Good. Is Sir Alan Smith of MI5 still there?"

"Yes, sir."

"Tell him McMurrough has been killed and unfortunately we have had casualties. I am off to the local hospital with one and will get in touch with him later."

"Yes, sir."

As the inspector rang off, the car swung into the driveway of the hospital and stopped opposite the casualty department. Blanchard quickly helped Sean to the waiting room and then used his official position to get the staff to attend to him without formalities. On learning that Sean was a doctor, the houseman needed no second bidding, and organized a porter to bring him immediately to a cubicle where he examined him and got his nurse to organize an intravenous drip. Although in pain, Sean was more concerned and anxious to find out about Jennifer, and expressed his fears to Blanchard.

"Don't worry, Sean, I want to see how my wounded officer is as well. I'll get back to you before I leave." He was directed by the nurse to the intensive care unit; she recalled that Jennifer had been admitted only a quarter of an hour before. He made his way to the unit, introduced himself and inquired about his police officer and Jennifer. The nurse supervising the department informed him that both patients were under intensive care and two senior specialist surgeons had been informed and were on their way to operate; she could give no idea of the prognosis in either case.

"Are Mr. Rutherford and his wife still here, sister?"

"Yes, sir. They are both sitting with Jennifer. Did you wish to see Mr. Rutherford?"

The inspector paused before answering. He realized that he was partly to blame for the child having been shot. If he had not agreed to Eve going there for safe hiding and if he had got his officers there more quickly, Jennifer would not be in the intensive care unit. It was not a good time to see her father who would obviously be desperately worried about his daughter, but he felt he had to apologize to him for what had occurred. He looked at the nursing sister and made his decision.

"Yes, please, nurse."

"I'll go and tell him you are here."

"Thank you."

The nurse left and shortly returned with a pale-faced Richard. Blanchard walked over to him and extended his right hand, "I'm Rodney Blanchard and want to tell you how terribly sorry I am that your daughter has been hurt."

Richard shook the officer's hand almost automatically but could not speak for a moment. He had heard that the inspector was initially involved in Eve staying at his house, and at first had feelings of anger, but his mind was too rational for it to last long. He realized that Sean and he himself, also shared responsibility for Eve having been sheltered there; even Dawn had been involved in the decision. His thoughts were interrupted by Rodney Blanchard speaking.

"I know it is not much of a consolation, but Dermot McMurrough, the man who wounded your daughter, is dead." Richard looked at him inquiringly. "Your cousin Sean shot him through the heart." He paused and added, "It was in self-defense, of course."

"Where is Sean now?"

"In the casualty department. He was hit in the left arm and has lost a lot of blood. I understand he will need surgery."

"Thank you for letting me know. I shall go and see him shortly."

That good intention was not, however, fulfilled. The nurse came into the room and addressed Richard, "I'm sorry to disturb you, Mr. Rutherford. Mr. Karl Sherring, the neurologist, is with Jennifer and she is to be prepared for an operation immediately. One other thing:

the registrar told me that the police officer has some foreign bodies in his left eye, and would you come and see him."

Richard nodded. He knew he could do nothing for Jennifer and that her life was in the hands of his colleague. He heard Rodney Blanchard speaking again.

"For yours and for Mrs. Rutherford's peace of mind, with the arrest of the terrorist and drug-running cell, your family and Eve Eden are no longer in danger. I left orders for a police woman to stay tonight to assist in any way possible. I wish I could do more for you."

Richard nodded. "Thank you. I appreciate your having seen me. One thing before you go: do you know how McMurrough discovered that Eve was at Bracken?"

Blanchard shook his head. "No, but I intend to find out and will inform you as soon as I do."

They shook hands and Blanchard went to see Sean before leaving the hospital. He found him partly sedated to relieve the pain and told him that Jennifer was undergoing surgery. On his way out he thought of his own daughter and the heartache he and his wife had experienced when she had been attacked by a drug-crazed man. She had been unconscious for five days and he appreciated the hell Richard Rutherford and his wife were experiencing.

On leaving Inspector Blanchard, Richard had gone to see Dawn and found her with two nurses who were preparing Jennifer for the operating theatre. Karl Sherring had informed her that there were some splinters of bone lodged in Jennifer's brain and he intended to get them out. Dawn knew Karl Sherring socially and not just as a colleague of Richard's.

"Karl has gone to the theatre, if you want to see him. He suggested I stay the night."

"I think you should, Dawn. I have just seen Inspector Blanchard and he has a policewoman staying at Bracken with Eve and the children. Eve is no longer in danger. I am afraid Sean was hit and perhaps you would see him in Casualty while Jennifer is in the theatre. The officer who was wounded also has an eye injury and so my services are required." He held both of her hands and squeezed them. "It looks as if we're both in for a long night."

He left her and made his way to the adjacent theatre before going to his patient. He found Karl scrubbing in preparation. Karl, a middle-aged man of medium height, looked up at Richard who caught his eye.

"Hello, Richard. No doubt you have guessed there are a number of lesions in the left temporal lobe. I have to get some bone fragments out."

"What's the prognosis, Karl?"

"I'll do my best, Richard." Richard nodded; there was nothing more to be said. He left to see the wounded police officer.

■ ❑ ■ ❑ ■

Parker sat in his living room and sipped at a mug of tea. Occasionally he shook his head in disbelief. The events of the past two days were such that he realized how lucky he was to be sitting there; he went hot and cold each time he thought of what had occurred.

He felt his stomach churning when he recalled sitting in front of the desk in the office of Inspector Blanchard's room. He had spent the night in a cell having been arrested the previous afternoon. An interrogation prior to his latest arrest about the car he had stolen in Essex had left him feeling confident. He had soon discovered that the police had no concrete evidence and the circumstantial evidence was too little to warrant his being held. After several hours of questioning the police had given up and let him go. His second arrest had occurred within minutes of his having arrived back at his apartment. He had not had time to raise Boss on his car phone before the police were again knocking on his door and once again he was on his way to the local police station.

"Ain't you blokes got anyfink better ter do than ter go abaht arrestin' innercent citizens?" he had protested. And when he arrived at the station he continued to complain. "Wot the 'ell d'yer want wiv me this time?" he had asked the station sergeant.

"The inspector wants to see you, Mr. Parker. He is not here, so you will be a guest of Her Majesty until he arrives." And at that, Parker was shown to a cell and advised to make the most of the situation. He had sat on a bunk bed and had been left there to ponder on the reason for his arrest. To his annoyance, he had all night to cogitate, and it was not until ten the following morning that he was brought before Inspector Blanchard.

The inspector had seen the police officer's report on the earlier questioning of Parker and realized that he had nothing legal with which to incriminate him. His original plan to catch Parker redhanded as he had caught the others, had been foiled by lack of liaison in his own police station. That had annoyed him immensely, but it was no use crying over spilt milk. The problem he had to solve was how to get Parker to supply him with information which would enable him to pursue his intention of putting the drug gangs and pushers behind bars.

All he had to go on was that he knew Parker worked for McMurrough at the Londinium Club; he was probably involved in drug distribution and possibly petty recidivism but he had no real evidence to substantiate his suspicions. He also suspected that Parker knew many members of gangland and if he could make him talk, his knowledge would be of inestimable value to Blanchard. Another thing was that he reckoned Parker might know how Boss had found out the whereabouts of Eve. Before ordering Parker to be brought before him he had worked out a strategy which, although distasteful to him, he felt warranted.

"Ah, Mr. Parker, I understand you spent the night as a guest of ours."

"Guest! I don't fink much of your 'orspitality or room service."

"Well, Mr. Parker, I am sorry you were inconvenienced, but it looks as if you will be a guest of her Majesty's for some fifteen years."

"Waddaya mean fifteen years? You ain't got nuffink on me!"

"Unfortunately for you we have. Our detectives found traces of crack in your car. You worked for Dr. McMurrough who, among other things, was running a drug and arms racket. You are known to have aided and abetted your boss in his illegal activities. You even accompanied him on his motor cruiser several times to bring drugs and arms into this country and attempted to evade the customs and excise in the course of their duties. That is not all. You received financial emoluments from the illegal sales of drugs and evaded your commitments to the Inland Revenue. You were also involved in the procurement of young women for the purposes of prostitution—pimping, Mr. Parker, pimping."

Parker sat dumbfounded at the list of charges that the inspector had unfolded. For once he resisted his normal facetious type of response and sat tongue-tied. The inspector let him think for a few minutes in silence and then added, "Come to think of it, I may well be wrong about fifteen years. It could easily he twenty. Your Boss committed a murder yesterday and we know that he and you were involved in the killing of a man and a girl who worked at the Londinium Club. Twenty years or even a life sentence at your age means you won't get out until you are getting on for seventy."

Parker looked hard at Blanchard but read nothing in his face. Then he heard himself being addressed again, "Of course, it would go in your favor if you assist us in our inquiries . . . "

"If yer fink yer kin make me grass, nuffink doing, mate. I ain't a copper's nark."

"Any information you give us will be kept confidential. You don't want to spend the rest of your useful life behind bars do you, Mr. Parker?"

Runt Parker astutely avoided the question and decided to reverse the tables and become the interrogator. "Whaddaya mean Dr. McMurrough committed murder yesterday?"

"He killed a police officer and badly wounded another—a Dr. O'Neill whom you know. He also shot a little girl aged six years who is now critically ill."

Blanchard let that piece of information sink in and then added, "Your Boss was a member of the IRA and it is probable that you are implicated in his terrorist activities."

That additional piece of intelligence sent Parker's active mind working overtime. He had not known that McMurrough was a member of the IRA. He knew that he had probably arranged for the "disappearance" of two former employees of the Club and that he was involved in several rackets but terrorism was new to him. He himself had not participated in anything except delivering and collecting parcels. It was true he had undertaken several voyages on the cruiser and dropped bulky packets into the North Sea, but in no case had the customs and excise officers arrested them.

He thought carefully about of what the inspector had accused him. He doubted that traces of drugs had been found in his car. He had always been very careful. He had known when he had been followed and also had a very good nose for the situations when police observers were present. No, he decided, the inspector must be bluffing. There was only one thing they could pin on him and that was when he tricked Eve into prostitution. Only Boss knew about Parker's petty criminal activities which he had given up, finding them unnecessary once he worked full time for the Club.

He looked Inspector Blanchard squarely in the face and said. "I fink you're 'avin' me on. You ain't got no evidence against me."

Blanchard realized that his bluff had been called, but decided to play a trump card.

"Evidence can be arranged, Mr. Parker. The presence of traces of drugs in your car and even on your property would need a lot of explaining to a judge, especially when the judge knew that you have been involved with a criminal gang and an IRA cell."

Parker looked at him furiously. "You'd be breaking the law you pretend ter up'old, inspector. Yer wouldn't dare."

"Do you wish to try me, Mr. Parker?"

Parker felt he needed more time to think and asked, "'Ave yer got Dr. McMurrough?"

"Very much so. He is dead and Dr. O'Neill killed him in self defense."

"Did you say 'e is dead?"

The look of relief on Parker's face made Blanchard wonder if it would not have been better to keep that piece of intelligence to himself, but it was too late. He studied Parker's face and just said, "Well?"

"The only fing yer kin pin on me is tricking Eve ter join the Club n' even that is dahtful. All the rest is a load of bull. 'Owever, I know yer kin frame me and wouldn't put it past yer. I knew nuffink abaht Boss bein' a member of the IRA an' 'ave nuffink ter do wiv 'is uvver activities. I 'ave a legitimate job at the Club an' it's all legal. I'll tell yer wot. Quit the frame-up an' any uvver charges an' I'll 'elp yer. I don't 'ave nuffink ter do wiv terrorism or murder. It ain't my line. Do yer agree?"

Blanchard realized that in the circumstances it was the best deal he could get, and in any case, he did not intend to frame Parker, tempting though it was. "I agree. You've got yourself a deal, Mr. Parker."

"OK. Waddayer want ter know?"

"First, how did McMurrough find Eve?"

"'E didn't. I did, but it was by accident." And he explained how she had been seen during the voyage of the *Erinyes*. The next hour had been spent in providing the inspector with names of certain gangland members and their activities.

When he thought about those members, Parker smiled to himself. The naming of them and where they could be found was not in itself evidence for arrest. He knew that they would now have to be under police surveillance and caught in the act for his information to have any real value. And that had given him an idea. He had later phoned one of the gang bosses and explained that his own Boss's organization was now finished and made a deal with him to supply him with his late Boss's list of drug contacts. Parker found it hard to believe his luck; not only had he escaped arrest but he had made a tidy sum on the top of it.

Parker had phoned Mr. de Vere-Smythe to learn that the police had raided the Club. He chuckled to himself when he recalled how the manager handled the police raid. They had brought drug sniffer dogs but found nothing. Two computer experts had gone through the Club computer files and found nothing incriminating. Parker was not surprised. De Vere-Smythe left nothing to chance and, although he had two computer discs containing information the police would only be too happy to have got their hands on, he always kept them safely hidden in a place the whereabouts of which he alone knew.

The police had questioned Ma Donna Ke Babe and also Taika Vozrekin and Jenny but they produced legitimate employee papers as secretary and hostesses respectively, and the evidence required to prove that the premises were used for prostitution and other illegal activities was lacking. Scott was not there when the raid was on and as his services were not frequent he was not included in Ma's file; his services were paid for directly by his clients. The only substantial evidence the police had to go on was the information given by Eve, but as Parker had struck a deal with Inspector Blanchard he was not unduly bothered.

Parker rose from his comfortable armchair and poured himself another cup of tea. While drinking another mouthful he thought about his own future. If the Club stayed open, he would still be employed there. His registered occupation was that of handyman. If the Club was closed then he had a choice: either he could start fiddling for a living again or take a chance in the USA. Eleanor had invited him to visit her and, although the outcome of such a visit was uncertain, it might prove both interesting and lucrative. It would be nice to see Eleanor again and he smiled at the thought. He'd see what happened in the next week or so and then decide.

■ ❑ ■ ❑ ■

Dawn sat holding Jennifer's free hand. The other had a drip needle inserted into a vein. Jennifer had survived the operation. Several pieces of bone and bullet splinters had been successfully removed from her brain but the damage had been extensive. It was now eight days since the operation and Jennifer had not recovered consciousness; she was still on the life-support apparatus.

Dawn looked at the pallid little face dominated by her bandage-swathed head and noted her shallow breathing. A bed had been brought into the room and she slept there when not keeping vigil, only being relieved by the nurse on duty. Richard had been in every day and she had gone home only twice to see the other two children. There she had found them being well taken care of. Eve had looked pale and tearful the first time she had gone home. She had suffered agonies of conscience about staying at the home and inadvertently being the cause of Jennifer's condition.

Like Richard, Dawn had found it difficult to speak to her, and although there were no more threats against Eve and the family, her presence was a reminder that their happiness as a family had been shattered. All three adults knew that Eve would have to leave as soon as the emergency was over, or as soon as other assistance in the home was obtained.

The noise of the door of the sickroom being gently opened made Dawn look up to see Gerard Rutherford enter. She rose as he moved forward and tears rose in their eyes as they hugged each other. He looked down at Jennifer and whispered, "How is she?"

Dawn shook her head and a lump rose in her throat. "She doesn't respond to anything. Once I thought she squeezed my hand, but I must have been mistaken." She looked at her father-in-law's face; his tan showed the signs of a week at sea but he looked tired. He had raced back to Bracken as soon as he returned from his voyage, for Richard had left a recorded message on his answerphone.

The last three days afloat had been rough and he had been kept very busy as over half of his watch had been seasick. He had phoned Bracken and spoken to Eve and learned of Jennifer being on the danger list. Despite his fatigue, he did not waste time but had driven that night for five hours as fast as he could. Arriving at Bracken in the early hours of the morning, he had rested for a short time and then, after a quick meal, driven to the hospital.

Gerard leaned over and held Jennifer's free hand and gently squeezed but felt no response. He spoke quietly to her but the pathetic little body showed no sign of reaction. A few tears ran down his cheeks as the realization of the hopelessness of her condition came home to him. He surreptitiously wiped away his tears, hoping that Dawn had not seen, but she had. She moved forward and put an arm round his shoulders in an instinctive motherly way and he responded with a similar action. They both stood looking down at Jennifer who was now a shadow of her former self. The door quietly opened and Richard and Karl Sherring entered.

Richard went straight over to his father and they shook hands.

"Thanks for coming, Dad," was all he could say, for there was a lump in his throat. His father just nodded. Richard turned to Karl and introduced him as the neurologist who had operated on Jennifer.

"Dr. Rutherford and Dawn, Richard and I have been discussing Jennifer and have both come to the same conclusion."

Dawn looked at Karl apprehensively, and Gerard, who had surmised what was coming, said nothing.

Karl continued, "Perhaps you would both like to come to my office and we can discuss the prognosis there." On that remark, Dawn nodded and they all left the sickroom and walked along the corridor to enter Karl's office. Once inside he motioned them to chairs and sat at his desk. Gerard Rutherford looked around the room interestedly as he entered. He noticed several book shelves well stocked with medical works and journals. Beside them was an x-ray viewing screen. A computer rested on a table to the right of the desk on which lay a number of patient files.

Karl looked down at Jennifer's file, situated in the center of the desk, and picked up two x-ray photographs. He put them on the viewer and switched on the light. Dawn glanced at Richard and he responded by taking one of her hands in his. Having placed the photographs in position, Karl went back to his desk and picked up a print from a brain scanner. He glanced at Richard and then addressed Dawn and Gerard.

"As you know, it has been eight days since I removed the foreign bodies from Jennifer's brain and she has not regained consciousness. I am afraid she won't. The shock wave from the bullet caused such extensive damage that a large area of the brain has been irretrievably damaged."

He paused and then pointed out the areas on the brain scan and x-rays.

Dawn glanced at Richard as tears welled up in her eyes. He squeezed her hand and bit his lip. With Karl he had examined the x-rays and brain scan and also a printout of the brain wave machine. He knew that there was no hope of Jennifer's recovery but felt it better for Karl to inform both Dawn and his father.

They heard Karl continue: "Jennifer is only being kept alive, if that is the correct term, by the life-support apparatus. Only certain motor areas of the brain are functioning and she virtually died when the bullet struck her. I regret that nothing can bring her back to consciousness. I am also afraid we have no choice but to either keep her as she is or stop the life-support."

Tears ran down Dawn's face as she spoke, "Are you sure there is nothing you can do? Is there really no hope, Karl?"

"I am afraid not, Dawn. Damage is so extensive that the part of the brain associated with memory and consciousness is dead."

Both Dawn and Gerard looked at Richard who knew that he would have to acquaint them both with the decision he had already made. He felt it better not to go into details although the term "living vegetable" entered his mind. He looked at Dawn and then at his father, sighed, and then spoke.

"The best thing we can do for Jennifer is to let her have the dignity of release from the state she is in. Were it myself, then I would rather have the life-support switched off than continue what can hardly be called an existence. It is wrong for us to let her endure just existing as a living shell of her former self. I am in favor of stopping the support. How do you feel about it, Dad?"

Gerard paused for a few moments before replying, then, with a hopeless shrug of his shoulders, nodded and said, "I am afraid I must agree with you, Richard. Jennifer is really no longer with us. I, too, would not want the indignity of being artificially kept alive with no awareness or mind of any sort."

All three men then looked at Dawn who dabbed her eyes with a tissue, swallowed hard and, with an intake of breath, nodded in agreement. "I suppose you are right. As there is no hope of recovery, we have no other choice."

Dawn released her hand from Richard's and rose from her chair. "I'll go and say good-bye to Jennifer," and walked from the room as the three men stood up, saying nothing, each busy with his own thoughts.

■ ❏ ■ ❏ ■

Eve knelt in front of a picture of the Virgin Mary in her bedroom and prayed that Jennifer would make a full recovery. She also prayed for the Virgin to comfort Dawn, the children and Richard in their distress. She knew that she would have to leave the Rutherford home in view of the tragedy for which she felt responsible, but had stayed on to help with managing the children while both Richard and Dawn were at the hospital with Jennifer. Now that Gerard had arrived, she knew that he would look after Jean and John until a new au pair was engaged. Sean was still recovering from his wound and as there had been bone damage, he had experienced major surgery on it. The arm was in plaster and some months would elapse for healing followed by physiotherapy, before he had full use of it again.

The door of Eve's bedroom was slightly ajar as Dawn walked along the corridor. Followed by Gerard in his own car, she and Richard had driven to Bracken in silence, save for Dawn asking Richard how they would break the news to Jean and John. Richard had replied that he would do so and had no choice but to be honest. He added that dodging the issue with religious fairy tales would only alienate the children when later they discovered that they had been lied to.

While Dawn mounted the stairs, Richard and Gerard had taken Jean and John into the living room. Dawn intended to tidy her face before they all assembled to break the news to the children. Walking past Eve's room, she stopped when she saw Eve praying. Eve crossed herself and, looking up from her devotions, saw Dawn. Noticing Dawn's tear-stained face, Eve felt her heart sink within her. She quickly rose to her feet, and slightly trembling, walked towards Dawn.

"Oh, Dawn. What is it? Is Jennifer . . . ?" Dawn just nodded and tears ran down her face.

Eve suddenly felt the sting of tears and she felt faint. "Oh, no. Oh God. Oh no."

The enormity of the part she had played in the death of Jennifer suddenly hit her and left her feeling responsible and shocked. "Oh Dawn. It is all my fault. I should never have come here." Dawn moved forward and put her arms around Eve.

"Please don't feel guilty. Several of us made the decision and none of us are guilty of our losing her. It was that murdering Irish doctor." She suddenly realized what she had said and bit her tongue, recalling the fact that Sean was also an Irish doctor. Yet he had loved Jennifer and had been shattered by her being wounded. She knew that the news that Jennifer was dead was going to hit him very hard as well. She looked across at the picture of the Virgin Mary in front of which Eve had been praying.

I wonder if God has punished Richard and me for our disbelief? she thought to herself. Suddenly, she found herself saying, "Let us both say a prayer for Jennifer, Eve."

Downstairs in the living room, Gerard sat alone. Richard had gone to bring in Jean and John from the playroom. He had wept when driving back from the hospital, but now had wiped away his tears and restored his composure. Like Richard, his character was that of the traditional Englishman, to keep a stiff upper lip in the face of adversity. He looked up from where he was sitting to see Jean and John enter the room followed by Richard. Jean walked straight over to him and kissed him.

"Hallo, Grandpa." Then in her grave way she said, almost without emotion, "Jennifer is dead isn't she, Grandpa."

He looked up at Richard with a questioning look on his face but Richard just shook his head and looked puzzled. He put his arm round Jean and sat her on his knees. "What made you say that, Jean dear?"

A single tear ran down Jean's face and she quietly said, "I found Jennifer's favorite mouse, Castor, dead. I think he wanted to be with her."

John suddenly burst out crying as the realization of the loss of Jennifer came home to him.

■ ❏ ■ ❏ ■

Eve lay in bed in a troubled sleep. She had wept and prayed but found it difficult to concentrate. She found the question of why God had allowed innocent Jennifer to be cruelly shot and then die, to keep intruding into her prayers. It seemed so wrong and unfair. She tried to concentrate on praying for comfort for the Rutherford family and for Jennifer's soul, but the same question, "Why did God let it happen?" again came to the forefront of her mind. Eventually she fell asleep, but her sleep did not go undisturbed. A vision of Jennifer appeared before her. Jennifer stood before Eve with an accusing look on her face. The child's head was covered with a white bandage and Jennifer slowly raised her right hand in Eve's direction. Eve looked at the hand which slowly turned over and opened to reveal her dead pet mouse.

As Eve watched, Jennifer's white bandage slowly reddened with blood which began to spurt from her head in an increasing stream. Then the mouse suddenly came to life and jumped towards her and seemed to fly across the intervening space between her and Jennifer. As it flew it became bigger and developed horns and became transformed into a bull with a long forked tail. In her bed Eve twisted and turned as she tried to escape the onrushing animal, but to no avail.

Then it was on top of her and her old nightmare returned. The forked tail was again cutting into her entrails and the heavy weight of a man was on top of her. "Lie still you bitch—I've paid good money for you!" The voice was loud in her ears and the red panting face was smothering her with slobbering lips. The forehead with the port-wine stain in the shape of devils' horns jerked up and down in front of her eyes.

In her sleep, Eve sensed that her old nightmare had returned, then she awoke. Panting and perspiring freely, she shuddered at the recollection of her nightmare. "Oh, God," she found herself saying out loud, "Please make it go away."

chapter twenty-six

A short sharp shower spattered raindrops on the windows of the vessel and bounced dancing droplets on the surface of the River Thames. Inspector Rodney Blanchard sat in the prancing police patrol launch bound for Tilbury. He had boarded the vessel at Charing Cross Pier and was on his way to participate in a meeting with the Port of London Authority to discuss security arrangements. His mind was engaged in running over points on the agenda when the rain cleared and spring sunshine sparkled upon the ebbing waters of the river.

As they rounded a bend he looked up and on the port side saw the elegant building of the Londinium Club bathed in sunlight. It was just after high tide and, it being a spring tide, the water level was high enough to give him a good view of the pleasant garden and the fine three-storied building beyond. The brilliant light showed the dignified stonework to advantage and the balconies of the bedrooms and the guest rooms were clearly defined.

His gaze came back to the jetty, now riding high in the flood, and he gave a low snorting laugh as he recalled his efforts to get the Club closed. His two visits with his police experts had resulted in nothing. They had found no sign of drugs, no weaponry or explosives and no incriminating documents. It was clear that Mr. de Vere-Smythe was a very astute man who daily covered all tracks involving past criminal activities. In any case he knew the Club was not engaged now in any undertaking that could be described as illegal. The exception could be prostitution, but even the hostesses had not been helpful, that is, except Eve.

Taika Vozrekin, Jenny Thalia and Caria Crompetta were all registered as hostesses and refused to give evidence to the contrary. He had found Caria more by chance than design. Eve Eden had met Caria again and informed her that Boss was dead and his gang no longer in circulation. With this information, Caria had gone back to her apartment to take various items. On the off chance of her returning, Blanchard had instructed his officers to keep her apartment under observation and so he had been able to interview her.

Unfortunately she had not been helpful and refused to testify. She was going to get married and wanted her past to be buried behind her. She knew that if she went to court, the press and news media would have a field day and wreck any chance of her marrying Barney. He understood her logic and in his heart of hearts he sympathized with her. He had seen too many lives wrecked by reporters who callously probed into the privacy of innocent and harmless individuals, pilloried them in the press and made their lives a living hell in order to sell their stories.

The only evidence he had to go on to close the Club was supplied by Eve's testimony and the fact that the owner of the Club had been McMurrough. That it had been used for purposes other than legitimate Club activities could not be substantiated. He had sent a report of Eve's testimony and his suspicions to higher authorities and was specifically ordered not to proceed. Later, news trickled through the grapevine and he had learned that the property and Club had been sold. Mr. de Vere-Smythe, a member of Parliament, a diplomat and an Arab had purchased it. His orders not to proceed had been quite clear and when he had asked why, he was informed that it was not his concern. This had made him wonder if there was a fear of scandal by the new owners or whether membership involved matters of national importance and interest; he could but guess.

He did know that the charming de Vere-Smythe still managed the establishment. He did learn that Caria no longer lived at her apartment but still owned it. She obviously had an eye for business, for she had rented it to the Russian hostess, Taika Vozrekin, who still happily worked at the Club. Much later he was to learn that the German hostess, Jenny Thalia, had paid the price of her sexual activities by contracting AIDS. It had taken a somewhat virulent course, her body became shattered and she had died in agony.

His mind turned to Eve and he suddenly recalled the date. Eve was to be married tomorrow and he and his wife had received an invitation to the wedding. In view of the fact that she and Dr. Sean O'Neill had put themselves out to help him, he had accepted the invitation. He had learned that the Rutherford family and the grandfather, Gerard Rutherford, would also be among the guests.

Initially, this had surprised him, for the loss of their daughter Jennifer was painfully associated with Eve, Sean and himself. However, on second thought, it was just the sort of thing that the family would do. He had discovered that they accepted the reality of life and had enough compassion and caring for the feelings of Eve and Sean, to forgive. They obviously did not bear malice despite their tremendous loss. Yes, he and his wife would go to the wedding and reception. Notwithstanding the tragedy of several months ago, it would be good to meet them all again.

■ ❏ ■ ❏ ■

It was a pleasant May morning when Eve awoke. The sun shone warmly through her open bedroom window and she could hear the sound of meadowlarks in the field nearby. In the distance, the call of a cuckoo echoed in the woodland and the occasional bleating of lambs reminded her that the year was well on its way.

There was a knocking on her bedroom door and she heard the voice of Mrs. Millard, the owner of the house, calling her. "Are you awake, Eve? It's half past nine, dear, and you have to be at the church at twelve o'clock."

Eve sat up suddenly and looked at the clock. She had overslept—and on her wedding day, too! "Thanks, Mrs. Millard. I'll get up straight away."

"All right, dear," Eve heard in reply. "I'll get some breakfast ready for you."

As she washed, Eve realized why she had overslept. Despite having gone to bed early, she had spent half the night with memories of the past few months invading her consciousness. It was now many months since Jennifer had died and in the meantime so much had happened.

She had left the Rutherford household as soon as another au pair had been found. Fortunately, she had obtained employment as a housekeeper and companion to a wealthy elderly lady in a nearby village. Mrs. Millard by name, she had been widowed for five years. Her only daughter had married an Australian and gone to live in his homeland. She had welcomed Eve who was like a surrogate daughter to her and Eve's staying at her home had been beneficial to them both. Mrs. Millard still owned a car, a somewhat antiquated Rolls Royce, and she was only too happy for Eve to drive it and also drive her round the countryside. As Richard was to remark later, the relationship was a living example of symbiosis. It was also convenient for Eve to use the car to visit Caria, to go shopping, to go to church and to visit Sean.

Sean had recovered slowly from his wound. There had been complications due to the humerus being shattered, but skillful surgery and physiotherapy had enabled him to regain full use of his arm. However, the scars he bore would forever be a reminder of the insanity of a fanatic countryman. He had resigned from the practice in Docklands and left Bannu Sind to take on three other practitioners, one a Pakistani relative, one an Indian Hindu and the other a Caucasian. Between them they comfortably catered to the changing population in the area.

Bannu Sind had been questioned by Inspector Blanchard but the inspector concluded that he was not involved in the drug smuggling despite his frequent visits to Pakistan. The Inspector had been intrigued by the fact that Bannu Sind was always accompanied by his wife and daughter on their frequent visits abroad. He could only guess, but he had a shrewd idea of why the family traveled together despite the cost of air fare. Apparently, the ladies traveled on their outward journeys wearing cheap brass jewelry. This they left behind in Pakistan and returned wearing pure gold jewelry in considerable quantities. As what they wore was not subject to customs charges they made an excellent profit on each journey.

Sean had joined a practice in Essex in order to be near Eve and he got on well with his partners. He had found a thatched roofed cottage in the country which was very picturesque and moved in there himself prior to Eve joining him after they were married. What had pleased him and Eve the most was the day when she was converted to the Catholic faith. Father Brendan had officiated her conversion and this had brought all three considerable happiness. No longer a catechumen, Eve felt pure at last in the sight of God. For her it had been a long road and a tragic one but she thanked God and the Virgin Mary for having arrived at her goal and daily included Jennifer's soul in her prayers.

Eve remained friendly with Caria, now Mrs. Barney Buntingford. She was pleased to note that Caria had become a model housewife. Neither she nor Eve ever referred to their previous occupation, nor did they discuss sex. Both believed that sexual relationships were private matters between consenting couples, preferably husband and wife. Eve was even interested to see that Caria did not hold with the modern ideas of political correctness. In her own mind, Caria regarded the feminist movement and advocates of using Ms. as being mainly lesbians. She herself was very happy with the differences in the sexes and made sure that she provided her adoring husband with a sex life that would have been the envy of all his married friends had they been privy to it. Both were fortunate in possessing a good business sense and so the Buntingford marriage flourished and later was to be blessed with children.

Relationships with the Rutherford family had been difficult for some time after the death of Jennifer, but Eve was to learn that despite their tremendous loss the family was not wanting vengeance and, as Inspector Blanchard discovered, were ready to forgive and allow time to heal. She recalled Richard once remarking that there was enough unhappiness in this world without adding to it.

Sean had asked his mother to the wedding and, despite her frailty, she made the effort to come. She was accompanied by her husband who somewhat grudgingly accepted the invitation only because Eve had been converted to Roman Catholicism. Sean and Eve had driven to Stanstead Airport to meet them and although his mother greeted them warmly they both sensed some coldness from Sean's stepfather. Sean put them up in his cottage for the duration of the visit in order to look after his mother.

Sean's sister Morag and her husband Gordon, who had been married in a Registry Office, were invited by Mrs. Millard to stay at her house. It being a large house with six bedrooms, she had also invited Eve's brother to stay there. He arrived in London a week before the wedding and visited friends in the city, and there recovered from his jet lag. Mrs. Millard was particularly pleased to have Sean's relatives at her home, for she was gregarious by nature and their presence reminded her of earlier halcyon days when her daughter had her friends come to stay. Morag would have liked to stay with Sean, especially as she loved her mother and wanted to spend time with her. However, the presence of her stepfather whose sons had so mindlessly beaten up Gordon brought back too many painful memories.

■ ☐ ■ ☐ ■

Having quickly showered, Eve donned some casual clothes and went downstairs to the breakfast room. She was greeted there by Mrs. Millard and Morag who were both lingering over breakfast drinking tea and discussing the forthcoming wedding.

"There is some porridge in the porringer and warm toast here, Eve. Would you like a fried egg, bacon, mushroom and tomato, dear?"

The thought of a large English breakfast did not appeal to Eve. She smiled at Mrs. Millard's motherliness and instinctively went to her at the table and kissed her on the cheek. Eve felt like saying, "My own mother could not have been kinder to me," but refrained as she felt she might feel embarrassed in Morag's presence. Instead she said, "I don't think I can eat too much this morning."

"I know, dear, it is the excitement. I was just like that on my wedding day. But you must keep up your strength." She paused and then added, "I'll get you some porridge anyway. Now you stay there and visit with Morag," and she left them both and went to the kitchen. Eve kissed Morag on the cheek before sitting down. When they first met they immediately liked each other and this had pleased Sean immensely. Both the girls felt completely at ease in each other's company and were never at a loss to find topics for conversation. They were thus deeply engaged when Mrs. Millard returned with a plate of porridge. She placed it in front of Eve and poured herself another cup of tea as an excuse to sit with the girls at the table.

"Where are David and Gordon?" Eve asked.

"They went for a walk across the fields after breakfast and should be back soon," Morag replied.

Eve ate slowly while Morag and Mrs. Millard discussed the wedding arrangements. Gordon agreed to drive Mrs. Millard and Morag to the church and then return for Eve and David. Morag had arranged for buttonhole flowers, a bouquet for Caria and the bridal bouquet to be delivered to the house by eleven o'clock. Caria had agreed to be the maid of honor and Barney was to bring her over to ride to the church with Eve and David.

While she was finishing her breakfast, there was a knock at the front door and Mrs. Millard bustled off to see who it was. She returned with the news that the marquee had arrived and the workmen were about to erect it in the garden. She had often supervised such arrangements before and insisted that the reception and wedding breakfast be held in her spacious grounds. She had already instructed her gardener and odd job man to show the workmen where to erect the marquee, and it was ready just as Gordon and David returned from their walk.

With her breakfast completed, Eve joined in the conversation regarding the wedding arrangements. It was shortly after that Barney arrived with Caria. Eve introduced them both to her brother. They had already met Morag and Gordon. From then on, with the help of Morag, Eve and Caria retired to Eve's bedroom to dress for the wedding. The men went to their respective rooms and within half an hour were waiting downstairs in the living room. It was then that the telephone rang and, as Mrs. Millard was engaged with her dressing, David took the message.

It was Mrs. Millard who first descended the stairs and entered the room. Both men immediately rose to their feet and congratulated her on her appearance. She responded to their compliments graciously and then went out to the marquee to ensure that the seating had been correctly arranged. She had organized the wedding breakfast with a local catering firm and they would have everything in position by one o'clock.

Satisfied that everything was going to schedule, she returned to the house to find Caria looking stunning in her gown, making the most of the admiring glances and compliments of David and Gordon. It was then Morag's turn to display her dress and bask in the masculine compliments. Gordon smiled at her in his loving way and suggested that as she looked so lovely they should get married all over again. However, he now had his duty to do and looking at the clock on the mantelpiece suggested that he drive Mrs. Millard and Morag to the church. David and he escorted them to the Rolls Royce and David waved them good-bye as he returned to wait for Eve.

He was in the hallway when Eve descended the winding staircase. He gasped at her beauty which was enhanced by her wedding dress of white satin and lace. "Wow, Eve, You look fabulous," he said out loud, revealing that some of his American environment had rubbed off on him. "Sean is certainly a lucky guy."

Eve smiled and thanked him as she entered the living room and picked up her bouquet from the table. She felt very happy wearing white, for her conversion and redemption made her feel pure and virginal once more. She and Caria both exchanged compliments on their appearances and the telephone rang again. David answered and suddenly recalled that he had received a message for Eve earlier.

"Oh, Eve. I had a message for you from Father Brendan. He is very sorry but he has contracted a bad chest infection and is not fit enough to conduct the wedding service. His housekeeper just phoned again; he has had to go to bed and has pharyngitis and cannot speak very well. He is very sorry and disappointed. A priest from another parish is coming in Father Brendan's place."

At this information Eve looked crestfallen, for she had looked forward to Father Brendan conducting the wedding. She felt he would be completing his job with her for it was he who had started and guided her on her road to happiness. She sighed and then realized that she was being very selfish. He was ill, and instead of feeling sorry for herself, she should feel sorry for him. As she genuinely did, she closed her eyes and prayed to God to grant Father Brendan a speedy recovery and to be free of pain and discomfort. While she was praying, both David and Caria discreetly moved across the room to the window and observed the marquee in the garden.

They were quietly talking when they heard Gordon return with the Rolls Royce. He entered the living room and announced, "Matron and Better Half safely delivered to the church. The carriage awaits, your chauffeur is here but whether he will have anything to show for it is another matter." Eve, Caria and David all groaned loudly and David said, "It is a good thing you are sitting in the front, Gordon. We'll close the interconnecting window." And with that banter they escorted Eve and Caria to the car.

Eve sat between David and Caria on the spacious and comfortable back seat. She had to admit she was feeling nervous and, holding her bouquet in her left arm, took her brother's hand in hers. He looked at her fondly and smiled "Oh, by the way, the substitute priest is called Father Caddell. Do you know him?"

Eve shook her head. "No, I have never met nor heard his name mentioned. Perhaps he is new to Essex."

They went silent as Caria commented on some lambs gamboling in a field as they passed by. "They are full of the joys of spring," she remarked, not realizing that she had made a pun. Gordon had heard her, for the sliding window between passengers and chauffeur had been left open.

"That was worse than one of my jokes, Caria," he remarked, and Caria responded with a giggle both at her sudden comprehension and partly through nervousness, which resulted from empathy with Eve. But her nervousness did not last long. Within ten minutes they had driven the short distance through the town to the church and there Gordon stopped and opened the car door for Caria. With an exaggerated display of subservience he took her hand and helped her out. As Eve alighted, he repeated the somewhat foppish performance and she brightened up at his playfulness. As David descended out of the same door, Gordon turned and again held out his hand. David slapped it hard and said, "Get lost." And at that they all laughed and a small crowd that had collected at the entrance joined in appreciating the banter.

As Eve and Caria were escorted into the vestibule by David, they heard many gasps and comments of admiration from the onlookers. While waiting in the porch for Gordon, who was parking the Rolls Royce, Caria and Eve checked each other's dresses and bouquets to ensure that all was well. Caria adjusted Eve's veil, stood back, nodded and said, "You look beautiful, Eve."

David peered into the body of the church and noticed that all the invited guests were there: the Rutherford family including Richard, Dawn, Jean and John; Barney Buntingford; Mrs. Millard; Morag; Sean's mother and stepfather; Inspector Rodney and his wife. He could see Sean with Dr. Hamish Cameron, who was the best man, sitting beside him. He could also see the priest who was facing the altar and kneeling to pray. With the organ quietly playing and the sun sending streams of light through the stained glass windows, the atmosphere was one of tranquil anticipation.

As Gordon, somewhat breathless, entered and immediately made for his seat beside Morag, the verger approached David and asked if they were ready. David nodded and, standing on the left of Eve, had her place her left arm in his right. Then with Caria behind her, they slowly proceeded down the aisle to the strains of Wagner's wedding march. On hearing the music change from its previous gentle piano to the marching mezzoforte, many heads turned to admire Eve. Richard surreptitiously recorded her progress with a video camcorder. Through her veil Eve saw the smiling and admiring faces and smiled back at each one as she passed. Her heart felt so full of happiness that a few tears came to her eyes and she was only too glad that the veil was there to hide them. The last few steps to Sean seemed an eternity.

Reaching Sean's side she looked at him, they exchanged amorous smiles and he took her hand. Until then Eve had not noticed the priest who, while she had been walking up the aisle, had been praying. He rose as Eve was exchanging loving looks with Sean. The priest rose to his feet and with his hands still clasped and his head slightly bowed turned to face Eve. She raised her veil and dabbed her eyes which hitherto had been misty, and looked at the priest with a smile. He looked at her in benevolent response.

As her vision cleared, both the priest's and her body stiffened in recognition. She saw the head of white hair, the florid face that reddened as he looked at her and then her gaze fell upon the port-wine stain in the shape of devils' horns on his forehead. Then she remembered that terrible day a year ago when his harsh voice had said, "Lie still, you bitch, I've paid good money for you," and the terrible pain when he deflowered her.

She had walked into the church feeling pure and wholesome in the sight of God. Now all the pain, the degradation and humiliation she had experienced returned to her in a flood of obscene memory. With a rapidly beating heart she looked at the priest. This is a servant of God; a man of the Church; a follower of Christ's disciples; a representative of the Christ, the Son of God; a man blessed with the Holy Spirit by the laying on of hands by the Holy Father, the Pope himself or one of his bishops.

She stepped back and took her hand from Sean's, then she raised her right arm towards the priest. To the consternation of all, she pointed her index finger at him and, in a quivering voice, said, "You whorehound. You hypocrite."

Then she turned on her heel, walked past Caria, and left the church.

*Si Dieu nous a fait à son image,
nous le lui avons bien rendu.*

—Voltaire, *Le Sottisier*, xxxii

(If God made us in His image,
we certainly have returned the compliment.)